The Butterfly Summer

Harriet Evans grew up in London. As a child she loved reading and making up stories. She then progressed on to teenage geekdom and agonised Sylvia Plath-style poetry it's probably best not to dwell on. The career in musical theatre she'd always dreamed of never materialised for whatever reason, and so she ended up at Bristol University where she read Classical Studies. In her twenties she was lucky enough to get a job as a secretary at a publishers and instantly realised working with books was what she'd always wanted to do. She was a fiction editor for ten happy years but left in 2009 to write full-time, making up stories all day.

Harriet still lives in London with her family. She likes old films, property websites, sloe gin cocktails, feminism and Bombay Mix, not in that order. *The Butterfly Summer* is her ninth novel.

She'd love to hear from you – please contact her on Twitter at @HarrietEvans, Facebook at facebook.com/harrietevansbooks or via her website, www.harriet-evans.com.

The Butterfly Summer

Harriet Evans

headline
review

First published in Great Britain in 2016 by
HEADLINE REVIEW
An imprint of HEADLINE PUBLISHING GROUP

Cataloguing in Publication Data is available from the British Library

ISBN 978 1 4722 2133 9 (Trade paperback)

Typeset in Garamond MT by Palimpsest Book Production Ltd,
Falkirk, Stirlingshire

Printed and bound in Great Britain by Clays Ltd, St Ives plc

Headline's policy is to use papers that are natural, renewable and recyclable
products and made from wood grown in sustainable forests. The logging and
manufacturing processes are expected to conform to the environmental
regulations of the country of origin.

HEADLINE PUBLISHING GROUP
An Hachette UK Company
Carmelite House
50 Victoria Embankment
London EC4Y 0DZ

www.headline.co.uk
www.hachette.co.uk

It must not be supposed that every caterpillar which hatches thus attains to perfection. From the egg onwards relentless and watchful enemies are ever on the lookout for its destruction.

H. Eltringham, Butterfly Lore

Mary Poppins stared from him to Jane in silence. Then she sniffed. 'I'll stay till the wind changes,' she said shortly, and she blew out her candle and got into bed.

P. L. Travers, Mary Poppins

Nina Parr, locked herself in, Charlotte the Bastard,
    daughter of a king,
Nina Two, mother of Rupert the Vandal, Nina the
    Painter, mother of a scandal.
Mad Nina that was, then Frederick the Vicar, then
    Lonely Anne, then Alexandra the Fly-catcher,
Then Charlotte the Sad, and then comes me,
Little old Teddy, the last girl you see.
All of them butterflies, and then only me.
All of them butterflies, and then only me.

Part One

Chapter One

The kind of books I like usually begin by telling you about the family you're going to meet. 'The Fossil sisters lived in the Cromwell Road.' 'They were not railway children to begin with.' They have each other, that's what the author wants you to know.

I like stories about families. They're like fairy tales to me: I never knew my father and Mum is . . . not really like mothers in books. The people who really looked after me, who did the boring things necessary to sustain a child (teeth, zebra crossings, shoes that fit), are Malc, my stepfather, and Mrs Poll, the old lady upstairs – and I was wrong about them. Oh, I was wrong about all of it! And it's still such a muddle, the story of what happened, that summer everything changed. It jumps in and out of years and months like Max in *Where the Wild Things Are*: we never really escape our childhoods, do we?

But if you want a beginning, I suppose that day in April is where it began to unravel, and it was a tiny thing which started it all off: the zip on a new pair of boots.

Malc, my stepfather, says there are no coincidences, that everything happens for a reason. I would always have met her, he says; I went to the library most lunchtimes. But I still believe something else was at work that day. Some kind of old magic, the sort that's still at work when you need it, lurking just out of sight, hidden along dark corridors, up tall towers, and in long-forgotten corners of dusty old houses.

The reason I know the exact date is because 15th April was a dreaded day for me, marking two years since I had started at Gorings and two years since my divorce was finalised. It's strange, being twenty-five and able to say that: 'My divorce.' ('Ooh. That's one to chalk up on the experience board,' one of my new colleagues said admiringly, as though I'd done it to be able to show off about having made a disastrous teenage marriage.)

The 15th of April 2011 was one of those spring days where even though the daffodils are bobbing bravely about, it might still be winter because it's so bitingly cold. My daily lunchtime walk from the office on Hanover Street to the London Library was eleven minutes, long enough to work out whether a pair of new boots is comfortable or not. I'd bought them the day before, at lunchtime, to cheer myself up. I put them on when 1 p.m. arrived, a sort of act of defiance against the date. *'Hey! I've got new boots on! You can't say my life's rubbish!'*

And yet, less than a minute after I'd left Gorings and was striding towards Piccadilly, I realised these boots had a zip at the back which ran from the base of the heel up to the calf and which rubbed, little teeth nipping at that tender skin above the heel bone. By the time I reached the library, my socks were worn through, each soaked in blood. This was a determined zip: the Achilles-heel-locator of zips. The London Library is definitely not the kind of place where one peels off one's bloodstained socks in the lobby and I hurried upstairs as fast as I could, hiding myself away so I could examine my gory feet in relative privacy.

There are over a million books in dark metal shelves known as the Stacks that rise up for four storeys in this unassuming corner of St James's. The library smells of things I love: mildewy dust, old leather and polish. I come here to be alone, away from ringing phones and typing and people calling out for a cup of coffee, away from chatter about husbands or the relative merits of different IKEA kitchen units. I hide amongst books all waiting to be picked, some unopened for forty, fifty years. There are shelf-marks with labels like:

Human Sacrifice
Nubian Philology
Papier Mâché
Snuffboxes

My father bought me life membership to the London Library before he went away. Mum doesn't like me coming here every day; I think she believes it makes me wonder about him.

When I was little, Mrs Poll and I would play a game where we'd pretend my father had come back. She'd move her kitchen table against the wall, set the two orange-covered dining chairs upside down upon it and fetch the tablecloth, under which I would crawl, feeling my way through the humid, tangled, grasping undergrowth of the Amazon where he was last seen, and I'd pretend to be escaping from a tiger who wanted to eat me, shouting:

'No! I will serve you these ten years now as your slave, if only you will not eat me, for I must return to my wife and child in London, a great city far across the sea!' – brushing leaves and other jungle detritus from my shoulders and backing away, as Mrs Poll roared convincingly, eyes huge, mouth bared in a terrifying rictus grin, and then she'd stop and hold out a paw for me to take.

Then we'd pretend I was home again. 'Delilah, my darling,' I'd say, quickly – because Mrs Poll always hurried through this part – 'I have returned. Where is my dear child, Nina? Here are some emeralds to match your beautiful eyes, now bring me an egg and ham sandwich, for I have not eaten anything but leaves and marmalade these last ten years past.'

'That's enough now, Nina,' Mrs Poll would say, gently, and the world I'd conjured up would recede, like cardboard figures on a toy stage sliding away, and it'd be me and her again, in the warm little kitchen. 'Time to go back downstairs. Your mum'll be waiting for you.'

That was a bigger lie than the rest of it: Mum was never waiting, we both knew that. Mum was often barely there at all, or she'd be lying under a blanket weeping, or shouting at someone down the phone – usually the Council. But I couldn't stay with Mrs Poll all the time, much as I'd have liked to, so I'd trundle down the stairs, feet scratching on the splintered wood that stuck up through the worn carpet, back to our flat.

Later, I realised Mrs Poll was trying to make me understand you couldn't keep hacking away at the same make-believe game and one day expect things to change. When I was about twelve, and a know-it-all, I was ashamed of having played that game with her, mainly because there are no tigers in rainforests. But a little part of me still wondered about him.

I'm twenty-five now. Don't worry, I'm not stupid – I know he's not coming back.

After I'd stuffed as much lavatory paper as I could into my boots, I collected the book I'd set aside on the Saved Books Shelf and limped to a desk. I began to read, but the words meant nothing, and I stared out of the window, trying to buck myself up a bit and quell the rising tide of thoughts that seemed, at that time, to crash over me out of nowhere, leaving me limp, bedraggled, struggling to see anything clearly.

At that very moment someone tapped me on the shoulder. I screamed, jerking back in my seat.

'Lunch break's over. Get back to work,' the voice behind me whispered.

I turned around, slowly.

'Sebastian? Oh my God. You gave me a fright.'

Sebastian crouched down beside me and kissed my cheek.

'Sorry. The British Library didn't have what I wanted. I should have texted you to let you know I was coming. We could have had a sandwich.'

Sebastian is a teaching fellow in English Literature at UCL – it's where we met, seven years ago. He looked down at the book I was reading.

'*Children's Literature and British Identity* – wow, Nins, don't you just sometimes want to have a sandwich and look at rubbish on your phone? Like normal people?'

'I'm not like normal people. You know that.' There was a short, tense pause. I said, sort of jokingly, 'Anyway, my phone—'

He looked sadly down at my cracked, ancient, barely-smartphone. 'She's like a museum piece, ladies and gentlemen . . .'

He raised his voice and the old lady at the table next to mine, some two metres away, looked up crossly at us and then stared, open-mouthed, as though horrified at what she saw.

'. . . Yes, Nina Parr. Roll up, roll up. It wasn't until after we were married I discovered she had twelve copies of *The Secret Garden* in her childhood bedroom. Yes, twelve copies, m'lud.'

Sebastian's voice carried and I flushed. 'Shh,' I said. 'Don't be funny about it. Not today, especially.'

'Today?'

'Our divorce.'

'What about it?'

I looked at his smiling face. He didn't remember. I wondered why I did, why I hadn't just allowed myself to forget about it too. 'Two years ago today. The decree absolute, I mean.'

'Oh.' He looked down at me, contrite, as I shifted in my chair, the atmosphere deteriorating still further. 'I didn't remember. I'm sorry.'

The trouble with being friends with your ex-husband – whom you married, to the horror of your respective families, aged nineteen and 'out of hand', as they say in Georgette Heyer novels – is that you can often forget you were ever married, and that's a fatal mistake. You can be ever such good mates, like us: we liked each other enough to marry one another, after all. And it's all lovely until one remembers how awful it became. The rows, the heartbreak, the final showdown, the division of mess . . .

We should never have married in the first place, that's the trouble. We were a year-long university relationship, a first-love thing, and we should have burned out by finals time, instead of creating this storm of drama. I think other people were more wound up about it than we were – his parents, especially. It was ugly, and perhaps it was a terrible mistake, but the strange thing to both of us is we got through it. We're friends, close friends. His parents don't like that much, either.

Attempting to sound more jovial, I said, 'All is forgiven. And listen, on *The Secret Garden*, can I just say for the umpteenth time it's my favourite book? And it's not weird to own a few copies of your favourite book.'

'Not weird!' He gave a cheery laugh, and ran his hands through his scruffy hair. 'Nothing you do is weird, Nina. One man's psycho-intensity is another man's charming idiosyncrasy.'

'Oh, you patronising git,' I said, pushing him gently, but we were smiling.

'Agreed. Let's move on. Shake on it—'

And then, from the table next to us, came a harsh whisper:

'Would you, both of you, *please* keep the noise down!'

The old woman along the way was still glaring at us, and her huge eyes were dark with fury. I released my hand from Sebastian's and, turning to her, I said hurriedly, 'I'm so sorry.'

She stared at me. 'You—!' she hissed.

'Yes,' I said, pushing at Sebastian's bulky form and hoping he'd sort of melt away – he is, for such a thoughtful person, utterly blind to other people's moods. I, an only child, have spent most of my life studying people, watching carefully to see the impact of what they say. 'I'll call you later,' I hissed at him, almost desperately, because he showed no signs of seeing the old lady was probably going to explode.

'When, Nins?'

More to get rid of him than anything else, I said, 'Don't know. Let's have a drink sometime, shall we?'

'*Drinks?*' said Sebastian, faux-serious. 'Just you and me?'

'Why not?'

As soon as the words were out of my mouth we glanced at each other, nervously, smiling at what we both knew to be true: we didn't do drinks. We spoke on the phone, we had lunch every other week, he dropped over to our house all the time – Mum and Malc still adored him. We texted about silly things, but we didn't plan things, nor set aside time to meet in the evening. No, we didn't have drinks, just the two of us.

'Well, that'd be lovely, Nins.'

'Would you *please keep your voice down*!' The woman next to us actually waggled a finger at Sebastian.

Hastily, I said, 'Well, or with some of the others . . . Elizabeth . . . or when Leah's back from Mexico . . . you know. Just go, I'll call you later.'

'OK. Or, just you and me. Be nice. All right, I'm going, ma'am,' he said, to the old woman. 'She dies, you know,' he said, gesturing at her copy of *Wuthering Heights*. 'They both do. Rubbish book, if you want my opinion.'

The old woman was shaking with a kind of stupefied rage, her bobbed hair shuddering around her head.

'Do I know you too?' she said, glaring at him. 'I think I know you.'

'Um—' Sebastian looked slightly apprehensive then, because his family knows absolutely everyone. 'No, I don't think so. Sorry.'

'Hmm.' She looked at him again, beadily. 'Well, listen, whoever you are, I don't want your opinion. If you don't leave immediately—'

'OK, OK,' Sebastian said, admitting defeat. 'Goodbye, Nina.' He waved at me. 'I'm . . . it was . . . it was nice to see you. Really nice.' And he was gone.

'Sorry again,' I said, softly. I half nodded and gave a smile-grimace to my furious neighbour, which I hoped encompassed contrition and a distancing of myself from Sebastian. I knew I'd have to head back to the office in a moment too: as office manager, I was supposed to reopen the phone lines promptly at 2 p.m. But some kind of pride made me sit there, reclaiming my own ground. I started scribbling messily in my notebook, imitating someone glad to get back to the very important work she'd been doing. I wrote:

I don't want to go back after lunch.

I don't care about Becky's kitchen extension or Sue's Easter egg hunt.

I hate making tea ten times a day. I hate being called 'Hey, you!'.

I shouldn't be having a drink with Sebastian. I should be going on exciting dates with people I've been set up with, or met on the internet, or something.

I don't want to do this any more. I don't want to feel like this any more.

I was writing so furiously I didn't hear the old woman come up behind me, and when she jabbed my arm with her pencil, I really did jump, properly scared out of my wits.

'I think you owe me a little more than that, my dear,' she said.

It was then I felt the atmosphere change. She was staring at me in fascinated horror, almost panic: I'd never seen an expression like that before.

'I've said I'm sorry – and I really am, if we disturbed you.'

'Are you? Are you?' She shook her head. 'Yes. Look at you.'

She was dressed almost entirely in black. The only note of colour was her tomato-red tights. Close up, I could see her face was lined, criss-crossed with age, her shingled hair white. Her eyes were entirely black and on her sack-like dress she wore a big jet brooch. The stones winked lazily in the hazy dusk of the Stacks.

'There isn't anything else I can do, other than apologise again,' I said, watching her curiously. 'He's very loud—'

'You could stop lying and tell me the truth.'

I thought she was a bit crackers. Slightly coldly, I said, 'You know, the Reading Room downstairs might be a better place for you in future, if you want peace and quiet.'

She stared at me in complete silence, scanning my face. Then she laughed, throatily, with a wild kind of freedom.

'Oh, that's good. That's very good. My dear Miss Parr.'

I stiffened, then I glanced down and saw *Nina Parr* scrawled on my notebook, and relaxed, but only a little.

She followed my gaze. 'Then I'm right,' she said softly. 'I'm right.' She rubbed her eyes. 'Oh, goodness!'

I didn't know what else to do so I sat back down. I heard a rustle as she pushed my bag aside with her foot, and grunted. I stared at my notebook again, pretending she wasn't there. I could hear her breathing – sharp, shallow – and then after almost a minute of silence she said:

'You really are just like your father, you know, Nina.'

I felt my scalp tighten, my skin prickle again: half anger, half fear. I didn't know how to respond.

'Did you hear me? You are very like him.'

As a stray beam of sunshine caught her I looked down at her glinting brooch and saw it was in the shape of a butterfly. And I was scared then. Because butterflies are what killed him, and I sort of hate them.

'Look, Miss — I don't know your name. I'm sorry, but my father's dead.' Then, because she wasn't saying anything, I added, 'I don't remember anything about him. He died when I was six months old. All right?'

She barely spoke above a whisper:

'So that's what they told you, is it? Of course they did.'

I had twisted around to look at her, and I could see now that she was upset. Her face sort of crumpled and the dark, beady eyes were shining with tears. She brushed her hand away.

'They didn't tell me anything,' I said, sure she must be able to hear my heart, thumping in my chest. 'I don't know what you mean. My father's *dead*.'

'What about Keepsake? Is she still there?'

I shook my head. *Keepsake*. For a second, I thought I knew that name. 'What's Keepsake? Who's still there?' She didn't reply. '*Who's still there?*' I said, angrily.

'Perhaps it's not you.' She blinked, as though she was suddenly confused. 'I was so sure. You're like her, too. You're very like her.'

'I don't understand what you mean,' I said, but she was backing away. 'My father's dead,' I said again, in case she needed confirmation. 'Miss— ?'

'Travers,' she said, staring at the floor. 'My name's Travers. I have to leave now. She's coming. I have to leave.' And she turned, and disappeared.

'Miss Travers!' I called out after her, louder than before, and my voice echoed, bouncing off the metal shelves and into the gloom. 'What do you mean? *How do you know my father?*'

But she'd gone. And though, after a few seconds, I stood up and followed her into the labyrinthine darkness of the Stacks, I could find no trace of her. She'd vanished.

Chapter Two

'Doing anything tonight, Sue?'

'I'm going to try and finish the scarf. Then I'll start on some nice socks.'

'Gosh, Sue. No rest for the wicked!'

'Tell me about it! How about you, Becky?'

'Thought I'd go to Westfield to look for a present for Sean, it's his birthday next week. He likes aftershave. I want to get him the new Gucci one.'

'Oh, very nice, Becky. I love a trip to Westfield. That Waitrose is marvellous. It's massive.'

'Isn't it . . .?' There was a slight pause. Becky said, 'How about you, Nina? Got any plans?'

I pushed aside the pile of invoices I was working on and sat up straight. 'Oh. Not really. The usual.'

'Right.' Becky gave me a friendly smile. 'I'm starting to miss *Downton Abbey*, aren't you? I can't wait for the second series.'

'It was good, wasn't it?' Sue swivelled her chair around, eyes alight with eagerness, as though they'd literally never discussed *Downton Abbey* until this moment. 'I did love it. Lady Mary! And that Turkish gentleman!' She chortled.

'Sue, you are naughty!' said Becky. 'How about you, Nina?'

'I didn't really see much of it,' I said, quelling my inner desire to scream: *If you two start talking about* Downton Abbey *again, I will actually condemn myself to death by a thousand papercuts using only these invoices!*

'Didn't you?' said Sue. 'Really? Oh. Well, it's awfully good. What I like about it is seeing the servants' world, not just the lords and ladies upstairs. Carson's my favourite! I hope he and Mrs Hughes—'

No! I wanted to shout. *Stop it. Stop going on about bloody* Downton Abbey. *Every day since October.* But they were well away. I scribbled *SEND HELP* on a Post-it note and briefly considered holding it up to the window, which made me feel a little better, if nothing else.

'You'd really have enjoyed it, Nina,' said Becky, eventually, taking out her hairbrush and vigorously brushing her long, thin hair. I looked at the clock on the wall: 4.48 p.m. 'It's right up your street, you loving history and old stories and everything. Trust me.'

'I watched some of it,' I said. 'But all those rich people and their stupid non-existent problems were silly. I just didn't believe it. Plus the servants were like cartoon characters. Something like *The Shooting Party*'s much better. Or *Gosford Park* at the very least.'

I'm getting better at knowing when I'm about to say something 'Nina-ish'. Sebastian used to slap his face with his hands and groan when I'd do it. To my credit, I recognised immediately that this was pretty Nina-ish. Becky shrank back into her chair and I cursed my sharp tongue. Normally I don't mind Becky and Sue, they're nice people. Sue was kind to me when I first joined Gorings and she found me crying in the loo about something silly. She made me a cup of tea and gave me a ginger nut. No, it's my fault, not theirs. It's just that they want to chat and be friendly, and it's always about nothing important – stupid, whiling-away-time chat – and I'm no good at that. I never was.

Becky tried another tack.

'Did you see *Hello!* this week? About the secrets of Kate's dress? Apparently, it's definitely going to be designed by Armani.'

'They'd never go Armani. It has to be a British designer, Becky,' said Sue, authoritatively. 'That reminds me,' she added, as an afterthought. 'I must order the ribs tonight.'

'Ribs?'

'For the street party. I'm making a hundred sweet and sour ribs. What are you doing for yours?'

'Bunting,' said Becky, succinctly. 'Fifty metres of it, can you believe it? What am I like! What about you, Nina?'

I took a deep breath. *Come on, Nina.* 'We're not having a street party. But I am going to watch it. My stepfather's making Coronation Chicken and he's calling it Royal Wedding Chicken instead.'

Sue and Becky smiled, happily, and we chatted for a while. Or rather they did, and I nodded and pretended to listen while period-ically my eyes stole to the clock on the wall (fake teak and brass, ordered by me at Bryan's request to match the fixtures and fittings in the rest of the office): 4.53 p.m. 4.55 p.m.

For the hundredth time since lunch I wondered, with a thrill of fear and panic, about the woman in the red tights. Was she still at the library? Would she be there tomorrow when I went back, at the same place? Was she mad? Was *I*?

She had to be mad. *I've seen the newspaper reports of his death*: I wished I'd said that instead. *Ask my mother, left with no money and a six-month-old baby. He's dead, trust me.*

Sue had segued from the situation with the ribs to the latest rumours in today's *Daily Mail* about Carole Middleton's hat when Bryan Robson (my boss and one of the partners – 'not the foot-baller!' as he introduced himself to everyone) appeared with a dictation tape.

'Hey, Nina, can you type these up before you go home?'

'Sure. How many?'

'Five, but one's a little bit complicated. Is that OK, my dear?'

'Of course,' I said, gratefully, grabbing the tape and sliding it into the Dictaphone, putting in my earpieces, mouthing apologies to Sue.

I liked Bryan because he loved talking about books – he was a big fan of Dickens – but mostly because he was a nice man. He'd handled my divorce, and I'd applied for the job here after he mentioned it to me during our first meeting. Six months after I'd joined Gorings and realised it was a terrible mistake but that I couldn't leave without somewhere to go (and I had nowhere to go, no job prospects at all, nothing except an abandoned PhD), Bryan had found me crying at my curved reception desk, which stood at the front of the second-floor offices. I think this was around the time Sue found me crying in the loo. I suppose I cried a bit after the divorce.

Bryan hadn't said anything – he didn't need to talk all the bloody time, unlike some people. He had patted my shoulder and handed me a large cotton handkerchief.

'What's up?' he'd said, conversationally.

'Everything,' I'd said, melodramatically. And then, after wiping my eyes and blowing my nose heartily on his handkerchief I'd half handed it back to him, and we'd both laughed. 'I'll wash this. I'll bring it back tomorrow.'

'Like Mrs Tiggy-Winkle. Don't you worry. I must say, I've no idea why a girl like you is working here,' he'd said enigmatically, patting my shoulder again. 'But I'm very glad, anyway.'

A girl like you – it didn't sound like a compliment, that's the trouble. Bryan had three children and lived in Alperton and was a cricket umpire at the Ealing Cricket Club on the weekends. Sue lived in Ealing, next to the Chinese school, helped out at her family's restaurant specialising in Hunan cuisine in Ealing Common in the evenings, and was a grandmother of five, all of whom lived nearby. Even Becky, who was only a year older than me, was married and pregnant and had just moved to Acton from Hanwell where she'd grown up. They each loved their West London lives, hurrying out of the city back to quiet, straight, leafy streets. Becky had told me she couldn't wait to move further out and have a proper garden.

'Who wants to live in London?' she'd said. 'All that noise. All those people. Wouldn't it be lovely to feel like you're in the English countryside?'

But I knew nothing about the English countryside, except what I'd gleaned from books. I'd never really been anywhere outside London – apart from holidays to various beaches when I was little, which were invariably a disaster, as my East Coast American mother didn't really understand British holidays, along with many other things about life in this country. We'd sit on a mingy towel smuggled out from our B&B, in the freezing cold, on a thin strip of damp sand, watching families play ball, put up windbreaks, eat complicated picnics, listen to the *Radio 1 Roadshow*, a cacophony of noise and fun all around, and then us, huddled together like shipwreck survivors. I couldn't wait to get back to London.

I had always loved the city, how it kept its best side secret, how the more you examined it the more it rewarded you. I loved the little alleyways through Soho, the old enamel signs on long-established hardware shops, the adverts for relief of pox painted on the side of Bloomsbury houses. The vast, beautiful caryatids holding up the apse of the St Pancras New Church on the Euston Road, the wooden tortoise and frog on the stairs in Liberty, the ancient Westbourne river flowing in a boxed-in, man-made tunnel over Sloane Square tube platform. The secret lanes and town houses rippling out of Clerkenwell Green like ribbons from a maypole, the chunks missing from the Victoria and Albert Museum, bombed during the war . . . I felt safe here, amidst the drama and bustle and excitement of life. In a city this big you're not that important. Your problems are minuscule. London reminds you of that daily.

At five thirty, Becky, Sue and I switched off our computers and put on our coats. Business at Gorings finished promptly for us, while the others – the actual solicitors – stayed later. I said bye to Becky and Sue as chirpily as I could. They scurried off happily together, calling goodnight. Left alone in the warm, cramped reception I walked slowly around, checking the switches, my head singing with tiredness. On my way out, I dropped the letters I'd typed off at Bryan's office for him to sign.

'Thank you,' he said, looking them over. 'Um . . . right, then. Yup. Yup . . . oh dear. Oh . . . oh. No. No.' He handed the letters back to me. 'Nina, you've spelled "client" as "clinet". Three times. And there are two "there"'s instead of "their". And you haven't put the address on this one.'

I tried to say sorry but my throat had closed up, for some idiotic reason. I took the letters back, wordlessly, hanging my head.

'Do them tomorrow. They're not urgent. Um . . . everything all right today, Nina?' Bryan said, watching me, his hands resting lightly on the desk, fingertips touching.

'Sure,' I said.

'Fine, then. Just one more. You've put "Dear Miss Bags". Her name's Bahr. Miss Bahr. I mean, that's really quite different, Nina—'

'Mr Robson,' I said, suddenly, swallowing hard. 'Can I ask you something?'

He nodded. 'Of course, my dear.'

I wasn't even sure how to frame the question. 'If you thought someone who was supposed to be dead actually wasn't, could you find out if they weren't?'

Bryan Robson didn't flinch, to his eternal credit. 'If you'd previously been told they were dead?'

'Yes.'

He put his fingers together. 'Regarding the death itself. When and where are we talking?'

'Oh. Um . . . the Amazon jungle,' I said. I knew I must sound completely mad. 'March, 1986.'

'I see. Well, that makes it a little harder, but I'm sure one could . . .' He looked at me carefully. 'Look, Nina—'

I interrupted. 'I mean maybe there's a register you can check, if someone was from here and died abroad?'

'Not really. The death certificate, if one was issued – do you know?'

I shook my head.

'Was there a death notice?'

'Sort of. A newspaper article. In *The Times*.'

'Well, *The Times* isn't usually wrong, Nina.' He gave a small laugh. 'Didn't use to be, anyway.'

'Yep.' I stood on one foot, then the other, and realised he was waiting to go home. 'Look, never mind. It's probably not important.'

'Anything I can help you with?'

Good, kind Mr Robson. He'd bought himself a putter for his eighteenth birthday, and when he first moved from Jamaica to Bristol, the local golf club hadn't let him in, because of the colour of his skin, so he'd taken the putter back and bought some books instead. He didn't know anyone then, so he just stayed at home most evenings, reading. Then eventually he reasoned if he was going to stay in, he might as well be learning something. So he did a law degree through the Open University. He was twenty-two.

I thought of the old lady's dark flashing eyes, the utter intensity with which she'd stared at me. '*You* . . .'

'I think I'm going crazy,' I said. 'Forget it. It's nothing.'

'Doesn't sound like nothing,' he said, quietly. His voice was so kind, it sort of felled me a bit.

17

'Thanks.' I muttered something about being late for my mum – there's a phrase that's the sign of a well-adjusted adult, if ever there was one – and made my escape down the worn linoleum stairs, tears stinging my eyes.

It wasn't supposed to be like this, you see, that's why Bryan Robson is sad about me. He's seen my CV. He thinks I should be a professor by now, or be given a grant to go and study at Yale. I have the curse of the Clever People.

I was offered a place to read English at Brasenose, where my father went. But I chose University College London instead because I could stay at home – isn't that pathetic? I was going to be a teacher. At least, that's what I wanted to be. An English teacher. But everyone else around me had other ideas. 'Yes, of course,' my headmistress had said. 'One should have a *plan in place*. But in your case, my dear, one should also *vigorously* aim as high as one can.'

Oh, how disappointed in me she must be. I got my first in English Literature. I did an MA in Children's Literature. I was going to do a PhD: I'd been given a grant by a foundation and I was all set. Still keen to ensure I didn't take my big brain off to Oxbridge or, worse still, America, UCL had assured me I was doctorate material; I even had my mentor, Professor Angell, take me to one side and tell me that, if I liked, I could apply for the D'Souza Fellowship: only awarded once every five years to exceptional students, but in this case, etc. But my marriage was falling apart by then, and the whole mess of it all meant . . . well . . . anyway, I didn't do the PhD.

Though I was the one who left him, Sebastian seemed to emerge from the breakdown of our marriage more energetic than ever. He just shook it off and went on to great things – his own doctorate on Conrad (I mean, good grief), co-authoring a book, lecturing around the world. And I haven't done anything, really, other than this job. I missed the chance to apply for teacher training college two years in a row, and then I applied and didn't get in. So I'm really lucky Gorings took me on. But my job could be done (and done better) by almost anyone: someone who remembers to order new pens and fixes the printer when labels get jammed. Becky's a trainee solicitor, for all that she spends her whole life booking nail appointments and flicking through Mothercare catalogues. Sue is a qualified bookkeeper – she does the books for her restaurant in the evenings. These people have qualifications – vocations, even – and then they go back west and have whole other lives, too.

I'm glad to have this job, though. And I should be grateful for this quiet, small life. But I'm not. I hate it. I like studying. I like reading. I'm happiest when I'm imagining some world other than the real one, and that's why it's hard to explain to people like Bryan Robson, or my teachers at school, or the special counsellor I was given at fifteen – the ones who help 'gifted children' not to turn into crazy psychopathic loners – that I'm not that clever. Because *I* know I'm not. I'm just unusually intense. If I'm interested in something – funerary architecture, or Tutankhamun, or children's literature, or that brief summer I spent being obsessed with musicals, after Jonas, my best friend from school, got his first role at seventeen in a touring production of *Calamity Jane* – I'm *really* interested. I suck the lifeblood out of it, a mosquito draining all facts and interest out of it, then I move on.

Mum once said I get it from my father. She never talks about him, so I remember this as with every nugget of information about him: like sieving for gold. I had been reprimanded at school for correcting a teacher and she'd been called in to talk about me. I'd overheard her telling Mrs Poll what they'd said that evening.

'She just told Mrs Cousins she was wrong, that it was Austen, not Brontë. Turns out she was right, of course, but . . . oh dear, the way she went about it – I'm afraid she's even more intense than her father.'

I had been coming down the stairs, and the two of them were having this conversation in the kitchen over a glass of sherry. I'd stood behind the door and watched through the gap. Mrs Poll was sitting at our kitchen table, and I saw her, glancing over, making sure I wasn't there. 'How do you mean "intense", darling?' she asked, in her comfortable voice.

'I'm trying to think of how best to describe him,' Mum said. 'He was something of a misfit, her father. Oh, hugely charming, such a big brain. But absolutely crazy to deal with. Yes. A misfit.'

'A misfit?' Mrs Poll had appeared to take this information and muse over it. 'I see. Such a satisfying word, don't you think?'

Which meant, I knew: *that explains a lot.*

Limping in my boots towards the tube, the evenings newly light, I looked up at the faintly blue sky, veiled with white drifts of wispy cloud. It was getting colder, and I shivered: two years since the divorce, six months since I'd moved home again. These last few months, usually, at this point in the afternoon, I'd feel some sense of achievement. Another day nearly over, one more to mark off on the calendar. The thing is, though, I had no idea why I was marking days off, or what I was counting down towards.

Chapter Three

'Evening, Mum! This woman I met says my father's not dead.'
'Funny story, are you ready? Dad's alive!'

Our house is thin and tall, with black railings at the front and long, draught-loving windows. My parents first moved into the basement flat before I was born, and now, after three decades, two deaths, one stroke of good fortune and the passing of the years, we own the whole house, though it's been a long journey to the top floor. We've crept up there, like ivy.

The irony is, most of our time is still spent in the basement. The kitchen is there and it's where we tend to gather, whoever's around. In the early days, it was the Islington Women's Collective, bringing Mum soup and 'Out Maggie Out!' posters, haranguing each other around the tiny rickety kitchen table with competitive stories of the evil patriarchy. Later it was me, Mum, my stepfather Malc, and our liberal kaftan-wearing neighbours, the sort who used to live in Islington before the bankers moved in. Then it was us and Sebastian, my unexpected husband, the two of us happier here amidst the gentle chaos than at his family home, a vast Arts and Crafts villa on the edge of Hampstead Heath where a constant stream of important people always seemed to be dropping by for drinks or dinner or Sunday lunch. Mum may be unpredictable, but at least you know she's not going to have laid on dinner for twenty – including the Director General of the BBC – when you want to sprawl on the sofa and watch TV.

Our kitchen is warm. It is dark, and covered in cork tiles – they are on the floor and on the doors of the units. There are French windows that lead out to the tiny garden, backing on to the canal. The bookshelf next to the windows is filled with cracked and food-spattered paperbacks: Elizabeth David, Claudia Roden. The posters are de rigueur: Elizabeth Blackadder prints, Babe Rainbow – even that Steinberg *New Yorker* cover, bought by my father for my mother so she wouldn't miss home.

There are always *things* in Noel Road: magazines and books on the stairs, odd cable leads or keys in jars, postcards of Crete, Sicily, Granada from holidaying friends propped precariously on radiators, odd clean socks in small lonely balls, looking for pairs. We're all rather disorganised. Well, Mum is. I am now, though I didn't use to be. Poor Malc isn't, at all. Mum's mess rules us. Yet my university friends, transplanted to London, would come here and swoon at the messy Bohemianism of it all. 'Nina, your mother is *so cool.*' 'I want a kitchen like this one day.'

Funnily enough, I never liked being down in the kitchen. I was always trying to get out of the basement, up to the top of the house, back to Mrs Poll.

That evening, I kicked off my treacherous boots and thudded downstairs. You have to make noise, otherwise Mum won't hear you and she'll jump and scream.

'Ow,' I said loudly, as I reached the bottom step and collided with something, stubbing my toe. 'Who left a mug there?'

Mum was tapping away on her laptop at the kitchen table, but she looked up when I appeared.

'Hi, honey! How are you?'

'Hi, Mum . . . Good, good.' I hesitated, I'm a terrible actress. 'How've you been getting on today?'

'Not bad.' Mum pulled at her fluffy, honey-coloured hair, so that it stuck out at the back, rather like a duckling, and peered at the screen over her huge tortoiseshell specs that she wore to write. 'Give me a couple of minutes, would you? Why don't you put the kettle on.'

'Sure.' I watched her for a moment, wondering how to find the right way to say what I had to. Mum works best from four in the afternoon till eight, which is not great if you have a young child, as I well remember from years of trying to get her to be interested in my A+ in English, my feud with Katie Ellis, the torn button on the school shirt I needed help with to sew back on.

She lives off the royalties of her most famous book, *The Birds Are Mooing*: she's written two more books but since the last one, around ten years ago, she hasn't published anything. She goes to festivals and visits schools and libraries all the time, but otherwise she's here, sitting in that spot all afternoon, and supposedly writing. She says she's nearly finished a new book, but she's been saying that for years: since before I married Sebastian.

I made the tea, as slowly as possible. Still she went on typing. I looked at my phone, but I don't have anything interesting on it, only texts. I'm a dinosaur.

What did the eighty-year-old pirate say on his birthday?
  'Aye matey.'

That was from Sebastian, last week.

So I gazed out of the window a bit and then, eventually, put a cup of tea down firmly next to her. As ever at this point in the day, the same thought thrummed in my head.

You don't have to write in the kitchen. There's a study on the top floor you never use. I wouldn't be disturbing you then.

'Mum? Tea's ready.'

'Just one more second, honey.'

We could have just kept Matty's room up there the way it was. Why did we rip out Mrs Poll's cupboards with the floral gold beading from MFI that she was so proud of and pull up the carpets and put in that desk and those shelves if you weren't ever going to go in there?

Normally I'd just let it go. You have to with Mum. But I couldn't today, so after another minute, I took a deep breath.

'I had a strange day today,' I said, loudly.

'Did you, honey?' The keyboard shook with the force of her clattered typing. 'Uh-huh. Just give me a moment.'

'I saw Sebastian. He sent his love.'

She looked up and smiled. 'Ah, you give it right back to him. How is he?'

'Fine. He's always fine. Listen, Mum—' Her eyes had slid back towards the screen and so I put my hand on the desk and bellowed, '*Mum!*' She looked up then, shocked, with that old, dangerous look on her face, but I ignored it.

'You gave me a fright! What's up?'

'While I was talking to Sebastian . . . um, well, this woman saw us. She said she knew my father. She said he wasn't dead.'

There are some things Mum and I didn't talk about. Her breakdown, my childhood, the early years here, oh, loads of things. But these days we never, *ever* talked about my father.

Slowly, Mum closed her laptop. 'That *is* a strange day,' she said, after a minute's pause. 'Oh, honey. Who on earth was she?'

'I don't know. Her surname was Travers, I think.' I scanned her face, looking for some reaction. 'She knew who *I* was. At least—' I remembered the notebook, her eyes flitting over and around me. 'I think she did. I'm not really sure.'

'What did she say to you, then?'

I related the whole encounter to her and she didn't interrupt, just listened, her hazel-green eyes fixed on the worn tabletop.

'It's the "So that's what they told you, is it?"' I said at the end. 'That's the bit that freaked me out. Like there's some . . . um . . . something I don't know,' I finished.

Mum got up and went to the fridge. She peered inside for so long that I wondered if she'd forgotten where she was. Then she took out some tomatoes and onions, got a chopping board and started slicing them up.

I waited.

Eventually, she said, 'That's pretty crazy, honey. I'm sorry this lady put a crimp in your day, but I don't know what to tell you. Except that your father wasn't organised enough to remember my birthday, you know. I highly doubt he'd have been able to pull off an international conspiracy about his own death.'

'Really?'

'Oh, yes. He was hopelessly vague about everything.' She put down the knife and smiled, closed her eyes briefly. 'And oh, he could charm the birds out of the trees. Butterflies, too. I wish—' She stopped, and shook her head, fingering the thick glass beads of her necklace. 'Never mind.'

'What?'

'Oh, I was going to say I wish things were different sometimes. But then – that's how it is. That was how it was.' She plucked at some thyme in a pot. 'Oh, honey. I'm so sorry this upset you, especially today.'

'What do you mean?'

'Well, two years since the divorce, and the job starting, isn't it?' She looked surprised. 'Don't you remember?'

'Of course. I just didn't think you would.'

'I try to keep track, Nina darling.' She sounded hurt. 'I am your mum. I know I'm a pretty terrible mum, but I do try.'

She says 'mum', but it always sounds mangled with 'mom', which is what she wants to say, so it always comes out as 'mwuom'. 'I'm your mwuom,' she'd say, in one of our many fights during my moody teenage years. 'Do what I say.'

'I think this old lady was slightly unhinged,' I said, trying to turn the subject back. 'But I did believe her. Don't know why.'

'Nina.' Mum almost glared at me, and I saw the film of tears in her eyes. 'I wish I knew what to tell you, honey.' She shook her head. 'I wish you remembered him, that's all. Because of how it happened . . .'

There was no funeral, because of how it happened. He had no family, and she was alone in the UK, and but for a newspaper cutting the whole thing might have been a dream. I might have been born without a father, no sense of where I come from or who he was at all.

I had details about him, like his big feet and his passion for beetroot, his love of the English countryside in the face of my mother's total indifference, his romantic gestures – like the gift of the Steinberg *New Yorker* cover – and the photo of them outside the Bodleian that summer they met. But they were all such tiny nuggets of information, like the worn pieces of glass and stone I used to collect at the beach on those miserable holidays and keep in a bag as though they were jewels. And gradually, what few traces there were of my father's existence had gone. I still had the stones, but the facts about his life had been erased, like he'd never been here at all.

Now Mum and I stared at each other, and where the conversation might have gone next I don't know, but then the front door slammed and the steady tread of my stepfather Graham Malcolm, known to all as Malc, thundered down the stairs.

'Evening, all,' he said, dropping a pile of post on to the counter. 'Here's your post, gentle womenfolk of the house. Brought to you by your friendly butler. Been lying on the floor all day waiting for your friendly butler to pick it up and bring it to you. Some might say one of you could pick it up and not leave it every day for me. Some might say that.' He blew a kiss at my mother. 'Hello, my love. Hello, Nins.'

'Evening, Malc,' I said, giving him a kiss, glancing over my shoulder at my mother, who was now absorbed in chopping something else. 'How was your day?'

'Excellent,' he said. 'I had a nice drink with Brian Condomine. He's just finishing a book on popular methods of murder in Victorian London. It's marvellous! Really fascinating.'

'Ooh, sounds lovely,' I said, heavily sarcastic.

'Aye,' said Malc, dreamily. 'It was. Went to the Pride of Spitalfields. Very interesting old boozer in Heneage Street. They *say*,' he rocked on his feet, in pleasure, 'James Hardiman drank there before he murdered Annie Chapman. Now, I've done a lot of research, and it could be true, but in fact it's more likely . . .'

I fetched another mug, trying to listen attentively: when Malc gets going on Jack the Ripper it can be hard to stop him. I handed him a cup of tea, and so that he could sit down I moved my bag from the stool next to me. It was slumped on its side with the zip open and when I put it on the floor the contents fell out.

'Mess, mess,' said Malc, instantly arrested in the middle of a description of the main arteries of the throat. 'I sometimes think you both get home before me solely so you can run around the house knocking over things for me to clean up.'

I was scrabbling about on the floor, gathering up my book, my headphones, my purse. Malc crouched down and picked up a small cream envelope from amongst the pile. My name was written on the front, in a faint, spidery hand.

'More post,' said Malc, handing it to me. 'Did I miss this one?'

'There's no address,' I said, curiously. 'It must have been in my bag.'

'What is it?' Mum said.

It's the silliest thing, but my hands were shaking as I opened the envelope. Inside was a photo. A small figure in the middle distance: a slim girl with a black bob and a strange, brooding expression. She held a long oar in her hands, like a punt pole, and she was standing up in a small wooden boat, in the middle of a river, trees on either side, her posture one of defiance. It might have been taken yesterday: though it was black and white, you could see the movement on the water, the sparkles, the breeze in the thick, ruffled branches of the woodland on the banks.

I felt that curious, aching itch in my scalp again, as I stared at the scene, at the sky and the water. I turned the photograph over. In faded black ink, a strong, tightly scrawled hand had written:

Teddy at Keepsake, 1936

You look *just like her*,
You should know about
KEEPSAKE by now.

That lunchtime, after she'd vanished, I had searched fruitlessly for her then gone to the Ladies before gathering my things up and hurrying

27

back to work. Now I glanced at my bag; the pocket at the front was open. She must have been watching me, waiting for her moment.

'I don't understand,' I said, staring at the words. I looked at Mum. 'Your mother's not called Teddy, is she?'

But I knew Mum's parents. Only vaguely, but I knew who they were, at least: Jack and Betty, Upper West Side professors of literature, Betty dead, Jack growing old and ever more senile in a home in upstate New York.

Mum was shaking her head, blankly. She said slowly, 'That's not my mum. I don't know what your father's mother was called. I didn't know—' She put down the chopping knife again. 'Isn't . . . isn't Teddy a boy's name, anyway?'

'Girl's too. Theodora. Thea,' Malc took the photo. 'But what's Keepsake? And why should you have the photo?' He rubbed his hands, unconsciously, on the scent of a new case. 'How strange.'

Mum turned to Malc. 'This woman came up to Nina in the library today and said she knew her, and that her family was lying to her about her father being dead. And that there was some conspiracy. And Nina's never seen her before.'

'Ah,' Malc said. I saw them glance at each other. 'Anything else?' he asked me.

I shook myself. There seemed to be something dark, cold, swirling around the kitchen, blocking out the spring sunlight. I pushed the photo out of the way, wishing it wasn't here. 'Oh, well, yes. I'm having a drink with Sebastian,' I said. I didn't know what else to say, how to keep them on the subject.

'You see him more now you're divorced than you did when you were married,' said Malc, riffling through his pockets and, one by one, methodically removing to the kitchen countertop all the cash, receipts and sweet wrappers. He did this every evening; a sort of winding-down ritual. 'How are either of you going to meet anyone, that's what I want to know . . .' He trailed off, as though speaking to himself, then looked up and laughed, nervously. The atmosphere was heightened, as though we were all aware of the parts we were playing. We'd been playing them for years, of course.

But this was different. My chin sank on to my hand and I stared into the middle distance, frowning. In the background I was aware of Mum stirring a pan, methodically.

After a moment's pause, Malc said, 'Listen. Don't dwell on it, you two. I had a neighbour in my bedsit in Archway who was convinced I was this Scottish footballer who was wanted for tax fraud, and that it was her duty to dob me in. She wrote letters to the police, everything. You couldn't persuade her, no matter what you did. Yet if you met her on the street, you'd think she was perfectly sane. There are more people like that out there than you'd think.'

'She was rather like that.' I thought of her wild, crazy eyes, the intense way she'd spoken to me. *You really are just like your father, you know.* And yet – and yet I had believed her.

Malc came around to Mum's side of the kitchen, put his arm around her protectively. 'Mystery solved, don't you think? We have a childlike need to believe in the bogeyman, when the reality is often just that people get addresses wrong, or are forgetful, or angry about something you have no idea of.' Mum started stirring with renewed vigour, and Malc swung out his arms, breathing deeply. 'Now, the real mystery is what we do for my birthday.'

'In June, a mere seven weeks away?' I said, gently mocking. 'That birthday?'

'I've booked the day off. Brian wants to take me to meet this retired copper who knows where the Krays hid two dead bodies but can't say for fear of reprisals. Would that interfere with any plans you had in that direction, may I ask?' There was a slight pause. 'Dill?'

My mother, to whom Christmas comes as a total surprise every single year, looked slightly amazed. 'It's your birthday *again?*'

'Yes, Delilah. So strange. You could almost set your watch by it.'

I stared at the photo, slid it into my Hercule Poirot novel, and leaned on the kitchen counter, to join in with the fine art of winding poor Malc up. Sweet, fuggy steam rose up from the tomato and onion sauce in the pan. I ignored the voices that swirled around my head. That's the problem with having an overactive imagination. It gets you into all sorts of trouble.

Chapter Four

The second photograph arrived thirteen days later. I was in the office stationery cupboard, supposedly doing a stocktake but actually partly doing that and partly sometimes taking a break from the stocktake to eat toffees and read *4.50 from Paddington*, which I'd found at the library that lunchtime. At university, and at Sebastian's, I'd been as organised as anything. Even when, post-divorce, I'd lived with Leah and Elizabeth in our single girls' fun-times flat, I'd been the one who wiped down surfaces and did most of the washing. Now, both at work and living back at Mum's, I was in a constant state of chaos; I couldn't find matching socks and repeatedly lost my Oyster card, not to mention buttons, shoes and hair ties. Books, too. I'd get off the tube and just leave them behind. I kept forgetting things at work, ordering items from the stationery catalogue we didn't need – two extra hole punches, the wrong printer cartridges. Most of my time in the office was spent on the phone to the stationery company arranging postal refunds. As I kneeled on the ground, one hand holding the Agatha Christie, the other stacking staples into satisfyingly smooth beetle-grey lengths, Sue opened the door and I jumped.

'There's a phone call for you, Nina.'

I shuffled around on my knees, quietly dropping the book on the floor.

'Oh, thanks, Sue. Can you tell them I'll call them back? I'm a bit busy.' I looked at her face. 'Who is it?'

'It's Sebastian. He said it's important. He sounded very nice, Nina. Very chatty.' Sue was always trying to find a way to ask me about my love life, or lack thereof.

'He's—' I tried not to sigh. 'Yes. Can you tell him I'll call him back?'

'He was very clear that it was important,' said Sue, eyes resolutely fixed on me and not on the mess of the stationery cupboard. 'Urgent, in fact.'

'Right.' I sat up, scattering staples over the floor. 'Oh, damn.'

'I'll do it,' said Sue. 'You go and speak to him.'

'Thanks, Sue,' I said, getting up. 'Toffee?'

'Oh, how kind! Yes, please. Now hurry!' she beamed, like a match-making mother. 'He's waiting for you!'

I didn't have the heart to say, 'He's my ex-husband Sue, and he slept with my new flatmate two weeks after we split up.' So I picked up my book, casually, as though it was fine to be reading mysteries and eating toffees at three thirty in the afternoon.

'Hi,' I said, a minute later, sweeping a stray staple off my skirt. 'You all right?'

'I'm fine. Nina, can you talk?'

'Sure. Is everything OK?'

'I wanted to speak to you about something sort of . . .' He trailed off.

There was another staple, on my tights. I plucked it out too fast and it laddered the wool. I said, trying not to sound impatient, 'I'm at work, Sebastian, what is it?'

'Don't put the phone down. My mother wants to see you.'

'Zinnia . . . wants to see *me*?'

'Absolutely.'

'I don't want to sound rude, Sebastian, but . . . um . . . why?'

'Well, *we're* still friends, aren't we, Sally?' We'd had a period of calling ourselves Harry and Sally, one of many phases of giving ourselves little labels to explain our strange situation.

'Yes, of course we are. But your mother doesn't see it like that, does she?'

'I still maintain you shouldn't have thrown that vase at her.'

'I didn't *break the bloody vase*—' I stopped. 'Look. I'm at work. Don't wind me up.'

'But it's so easy with you, Nins.' He was laughing; I said nothing. 'No. Honestly. Don't know what it's about, actually, she's just said she'd like to see you. Says she's got something she needs to tell you.'

Zinnia did actually ask me round to High Mead Gardens for tea, six months before the end of our marriage. We sat in the long, low sitting room with the worn parquet flooring, walls covered in photographs of the happy Fairley family at work and at play over the years. Zinnia had had a photo of me and Sebastian on our wedding day framed, to be fair – but she never hung it, just propped it up on a sideboard. Not worth damaging the plaster with a nail for it. She was right, of course.

She served cucumber sandwiches and those biscuits with the hard pink and chocolate icing – the ones that promise so much and deliver so little. She told me he was 'struggling to cope with it all'. That I had 'ruined his life' and was 'making him utterly miserable'. That if I loved him, I'd leave and never contact him again.

The irony is, I actually ended up doing what she advised. Not because I agreed with her, but because we'd both worked it out for ourselves by then. It's funny to remember how much it hurt, at the time. That Nina seems like a different person to the one I am now: she was a risk-taking girl, impetuous and heedless. Zinnia was part of that life too, my old, drama-filled life, when it was routine to scream and sob in public, and stay up all night having sex, when London was full of possibility, the days endless, and I believed for a short while that I was this person – this girl who lived – not the blank, always-watching-never-doing Nina on the sidelines who I'd been before I met him and now continued to be.

I wouldn't even know what to say to Zinnia if I met her now. I swallowed, and changed the phone over to my other hand.

'You still there?' Sebastian said, softly.

'I am. Sorry, Sebastian. Just say you couldn't get hold of me. I'm fairly busy at the moment, anyway, and . . .' I trailed off. 'Is that OK?'

'Of course,' Sebastian said and I wished that just once he'd call me out, challenge me. 'You should come over to my parents' for lunch sometime, though. They'd love to see you again, I know they would. I just mean in general. It's been ages.'

'Sure,' I said, weakly.

'And we haven't made a date for a drink yet.'

'Yes,' I began, about to just front up and say I didn't think it was a good idea, when suddenly Becky appeared and waved a biscuit selection under my nose: we were having a tea party that afternoon to celebrate the Royal Wedding the following day.

We rang off, having made a vague promise to meet up the following week: usually one of us texted the other if we happened to be at a loose end and fancied a coffee or lunch, someone to kill time with. I chewed my finger, thoughtfully, staring at the ladder in my tights. Apart from Zinnia, I liked Sebastian's family: I loved his brother and sister, whom I rarely saw, and his fearsome Aunt Judy who lived with them. But we were divorced. We were *divorced*, and had been for more than two years now.

'How are either of you going to meet anyone, that's what I want to know . . .' Unbidden into my mind came Malc's remarks of a couple of weeks ago, that night in the kitchen. I shrugged, irritably. Zinnia brought out the worst in me: I always felt she knew me and my worst habits in a way no one else did. That she saw straight through the person I was pretending to be. What was she up to?

I stood up, meaning to hurriedly finish the stationery before our tea, be a good co-worker and colleague and enter fully into discussions about Uncle Gary, Kate's hairdresser and who the bridesmaids were. I picked up *4.50 from Paddington* to put it back in my bag. Something fell out from between the yellowing pages. I jumped, looked down, and then drew in my breath with a sharp cry.

'Goodness!' Becky said, dropping her stack of Union Jack flags. 'What on earth's wrong?'

I picked up the card that lay on the chair and pressed it to my thumping heart. 'Nothing. Thought I saw a spider but it's just a shadow. I'm sorry, Becks.'

'Come and have some cake,' she said, smiling. 'We're all excited, I know!'

I didn't want to look. I wondered, perhaps, should I just throw it away, unseen? Pretend it had never got to me?

It was another photograph, black and white. I have it next to me as I write this, three years later, and I can still recall that first glimpse of it. A grey corner of a grand-looking house. A large downstairs window and a mullioned row of casements above it. The details of the building are old, covered in lichen and climbing roses. Flowers crowd in at every corner. A familiar, grave-faced little girl of ten or so, hair in ringlets, dressed in a velvet pinafore-type dress over a cream silk shirt. She is looking up at the camera with a half-frown. Standing next to her, slim and elegant, is a woman in a long skirt and dark blouse. There's a lace parasol, fallen on the floor, listing and slightly blurred beside the woman. The little girl is holding a small wooden box in her arms; the woman holds a long, drooping white-grey object – at first I thought it was a silly costume, a ghost, and then I realised it was a large net. Above them, a fleck in the cloudless sky. I looked at it closely, heart thumping. It was a butterfly.

I turned the photograph over.

> Butterfly Hunting.
> Mother, and me. Keepsake, 1926.
> (Taken by Grandmother before
> she disappeared.)
>
> That is your family Nina Parr.
> You don't know them/don't know
> what they did. Write to me at the
> enclosed address. L.

But there was no address, nothing, no envelope, just this photo-graph. I tried to remember where I'd been in the library that lunch hour, how I could have missed her again. She was looking for me, watching out for me, a scuttling spider in her corner. I shivered again.

I sat very still and I stared at the girl in the photo, unblinking, until my eyes ached. Did I look her? Is that why I thought I'd seen her before?

34

'Nina?' Bryan Robson was standing beside me and I glared up at him, blinking rapidly. 'Aren't you coming for some tea? We're opening the sweepstake on the colour of the Queen's dress now!'

Sliding the photograph and book into my bag again, I stood up. 'Of course. Just coming!' I put my bag under the desk, almost kicking it out of the way. *I'll deal with this at home*, I told myself – *this is all fine. I'm coping with this. It's fine.*

Yet the rest of the afternoon, I couldn't concentrate. A tight headache squeezed itself around my skull, and I kept making mistakes – even more than usual. I wasn't good enough to be able to screw up as much as I had been doing lately. I left the office as soon as I could, and on the way out caught Bryan Robson.

'Everything all right with you today, Nina?' he said, holding his umbrella.

I stared straight ahead at the brushed-metal wall of the lift. 'Yes, Bryan. Why?'

'I'm worried about you. You're very pale lately.'

'Don't be!' I said, though I could feel the book, with that photograph, pulsing in my bag, like an alien life force in *Doctor Who*.

That is your family, Nina Parr.

You don't know them.

I stumbled out of the lift, smiling and waving farewell, pretending I was catching the bus, but I walked, through Fitzrovia, through the thronging, happy streets of a spring Thursday evening in Central London, workers scattered over the pavements clutching plastic cups. It was chilly, but there was a sense of excitement in the air, about the Royal Wedding, from cheesy appropriation (the trendy bars that had ironic signs chalked up outside: *Tomorrow 11 a.m. – Waity Katy vs Bald Slick Willy, Super Heavyweight Bout! Watch here! Free ceviche with a pitcher of caipirinhas*) to the more traditional London pubs festooned with Union Jack bunting and tea towels, floral baskets and special plastic signs: Congratulations to the Happy Couple.

It felt like everyone was out, excited about the next day. I looked at the girls like me, laughing over drinks in floral dresses and flats, hair pulled up into messy buns, wearing bright lipstick, with cheery cheap and bright sunglasses. I felt like an alien myself.

Maybe it was because I hadn't thought about Matty for so long, or maybe it was the phone call from Sebastian. Or the Royal Wedding: how excited everyone was and how little I cared.

Probably it was the second photograph, and how the many questions I had that were unanswered seemed to be shouting louder than ever since I'd met Miss Travers. Probably it was that I knew the little girl in the photos, that I had always known something was missing – not just my father, but something else, some central component that made me whole, made me understand myself and my mother and why we were the way we were.

Because when I got back home it began. I shut the front door and called out, 'Hello!' for Mum's benefit, but no sound came from my mouth. Then there was a roaring noise in my head, and suddenly I found myself pressed against the wall, as though something huge was pushing into my chest, stopping me moving. I couldn't see. There were waves of blurry colour, fizzing in front of my eyes. My throat closed up, and I couldn't breathe.

There's something in there, trying to get out. That's what Mrs Poll used to say, when I'd have a really bad dream. When we invented Matty. *No good comes of bottling it up, darling. Trust me.* But in the intervening years, I'd not listened to her.

You see, I'd known this since that first day in the library, that I knew the name already. Knew the face of the girl, knew about butterflies, recognised something about it all. I just needed to get to the memory, let it in. It was outside, dancing and screaming to be let in, and I couldn't see it, couldn't find the door—

'Honey? That you?' Mum called from the kitchen, and I jumped, guiltily.

'Yep, Mum!' I croaked, trying to sound bright, thankful my voice worked. 'Hi, how're you?'

'Good. I'm just finishing up.'

'Take your time,' I said, leaning against the wall. 'I'll . . . I'm going to get changed.'

36

'OK,' she said, and there was silence.

And I knew then that I couldn't simply go downstairs and tell my mother I'd found another photo, that this woman was real, that she knew me. And the fact I knew somehow that it had to be secret scared me more than I can say. We had an unspoken pact to pretend we'd come through it unscathed, she and I, but we both knew it hadn't been like that.

I closed my eyes and that was when I saw it, the image I was searching for. A sketch, a picture of something: I was running towards it but it was always, *always* just out of reach. *You're looking in the wrong place* – that's what Mrs Poll used to say, when I got annoyed I couldn't remember a fact or a name. *Don't look there.*

In the glass panels above the front door Mrs Poll had helped me hang pictures I'd drawn, for my dad. Pictures of him, Mum and me. They faced out, looking up to the sky so he could see them in heaven. I wanted him to be able to see which house was ours in case he wanted to pay us a visit, see if we were OK. Mum had taken them down. The Moaning Lawsons had complained, she said.

And suddenly I was eight again, and I knew Mrs Poll was there, only a few metres away, and I saw it. I saw the picture, it was in her flat, it was a book we used to read together, her and me, when I knew I could go upstairs to find her and everything would be OK.

So I began climbing the stairs and I whispered the old, well-worn phrase I used to call out every afternoon.

'Mrs Poll? Are you there? Can I come up?'

That voice: warm, wry, cracking just a little with age. 'Now, who's that, making all this racket? Is it a herd of elephants, climbing up the stairs?'

Only that last flight up to her flat remaining, and I'd be home.

'It's not elephants, Mrs Poll. It's me, Nina.'

And Mrs Poll's voice again, calling me back. 'Well, of course it's you. How very nice. I've been waiting all day for you to come and keep me company. Shut the door, poppet.'

Nina and the Butterflies. I jumped, as I reached the first-floor landing. A funny story. A list of butterflies. A girl called Teddy.

I reached the top of the stairs at the second floor, where fear and chaos abated and order and warmth ruled. And I could see the book, now. A square hardback, its edges worn. Someone called Matty. *Matty.* Two figures, chasing across a field, running after butterflies. I'd read it countless times as a child. She was gone – her bright, light kitchen was gone – but that book was here, I knew it, and it must have something to do with it all. My mother. Me. My father and what happened.

Chapter Five

I suppose here is probably the best place for a little biographical interlude. In February 1986, when I was nearly six months old, my father went on an expedition to the Venezuelan rainforest to search for the Glasswinged butterfly and he never came back. At the age of about twelve – it was after Mrs Poll died, I know that – I made it my mission to know all I could about Glasswinged butterflies. The local library soon ran out of books to help me and I think my poor mother might have remembered the London Library membership then; I borrowed every book I could on the subject and read them all, understanding very little. I hated butterflies, really: like any self-respecting London child I was rightly wary of bright, fluttering insects that flew into your face. I knew they'd lured my father away, yet somehow it was soothing to learn about them: it made me feel in control.

He'd also been studying Batesian mimicry – I knew this from the news report too. On the off chance you're not fully conversant with Batesian mimicry, it is the syndrome where butterflies who are particularly vulnerable to attack in the jungle learn to evolve so they resemble a totally different species of butterfly, one not attractive to enemies. My father was, apparently, doing important work in this field. He was seen as a forward thinker in the matter of butterfly evolutionary theory – he and Nabokov, would you believe it?

I don't think he wanted to go on the trip. My mother once told me it was terribly difficult for him, leaving his wife and baby daughter behind. Mum knew virtually no one in London: several years earlier, you see, she had been like one of those heroines in a novel, who gives up everything for love.

When she was nineteen, in 1979, Mum had come to Oxford on a Fulbright Scholarship. She met my father at the Bodleian Library when her book fell off her desk on to the floor; George Parr happened to be walking past and picked it up. (I'd always imagined this book to be *Anna Karenina* or *The Last of the Mohicans*, something sweeping, torrid, worthy of their love, and was disappointed when, one of the last times we talked about my father, Mum revealed that the book in question was a study on the exodus of Cornish tin miners to California during the Gold Rush.)

My mother's fingers closed over my father's as he handed the book back to her and, at that touch, their eyes met. It was the same for both of them: they knew instantly.

There is a photo of them from their first summer together. They're standing in front of the Bodleian. My father is blond and square-jawed. He has his arms around my mother, as if showing her off to the camera, and she, in return, has one arm locked around his torso. Her hair is a halo of frizzy curls around her freckled, apple-cheeked face, her nipples like hard little beads in her thin spaghetti-strapped vest, and the arm that is free is outspread wide, and she's smiling, head tilting up to the sun, and my father is grinning at her, as though he cannot believe he's with this exotic, sensual goddess, because that's what she is.

(I don't look like either of these golden, beautiful people, I'm sad to say. I'm dark, lanky and cross-looking – 'Bitchy Resting Face', Jonas says it's called, though I'm not doing it on purpose. People used to come up to my mother and peer into my 1950s-era sprung pram, one of many donations from the Islington Women's Collective. 'What a lovely bab—' they'd begin, and the words would freeze on their lips as I'd glare at them furiously, lips pursed in an angry asterisk.)

After her perfect year at Oxford Mum had torn herself away from my father, both of them sobbing so uncontrollably at their parting by the airport gate that the TWA air stewardess had asked them to remove themselves as they were upsetting the other passengers. They had broken their favourite Vashti Bunyan album in two and each taken half – oh, young love! When I was a child this part used to make me wide-eyed with admiration of such hooliganism, then as a teenager moony-eyed at the romance of it all. Now I roll my eyes when I think of it: what a waste of a perfectly good LP.

Mum went back to New York to finish college but then, to the eternal disapproval of her parents, abandoned her degree and, selling the pearl necklace that she'd been given for her sixteenth birthday, flew back to London, dramatically turning up at my father's door in Oxford. She moved in then and there. They kept the empty necklace case above the front door, a symbol of their love.

One day, a year or so later, they decided to get married. The way she always told it, it was something of a lark. They'd gone to the registry office with a neighbour and a couple of old friends as witnesses, then had lunch in a pub out towards Headington afterwards. No family. My father's upbringing was eerily similar to Mum's: only child of elderly parents, in his case both dead by his mid-teens. He had stayed with friends in the holidays from boarding school during the last couple of years before he went up to Oxford. He had one second cousin called Albert, in Birmingham, whom he'd seen only once or twice in his life and Mum had never met. So it was just six of them that cold November day. My mother wore a white lace dress she bought from an antique shop – it was slightly too small and you can see, in the wedding photo, one of the buttons from the seam at the back flapping over her shoulder as she stands with my father, oddly formal, facing the camera.

She was twenty-two when she married, he twenty-three. Who took that photo? Who took the photo of them outside the Bodleian, the one that was always on her mantelpiece? I remember her talking about them buying the basement flat in Noel Road, marvelling at how cheap it was. The day they moved in, my father carried her over the threshold and they fell down the slippery steps: he injured his back and had to lie on the floor for a week.

When Mum used to talk about him, she always told these stories with a smile. I filed it all away, in my neat little brain. I had perfect recall of everything she told me about my dad.

'We thought we'd invented being in love,' she said to me once.

She'd tell me about the happy times they had in Islington, how I was born, the walk at midnight through Bloomsbury to the hospital, but she became vague on details after my birth: she doesn't like

41

remembering that period. Because then my father went away and didn't come back.

Up in Matty's room was where I kept important things: my favourite books, my best dresses for Matty to wear to appease her, and my Father File. This was a box file Mrs Poll had given me, containing carefully written-out lists of known facts I had about my father – a few coaxed out of my mother, the rest just acquired, somehow.

My Father George Parr

1. George William Parr was his full Christian Name.

2. Grew up in a house with lots of butterflies.

3. Knew lots about butterflies, was very kind to them and their friend.

4. Had blond hare. In photograph is tall and handsome. Like Doctor Kill Dare. (Mum says this.)

5. Died in the jungle. They buried him there because of disease and heat. That is why we don't have a place to leave flowers for him like in Grave Yards like Jonasess Granny Violet.

Each point written in a different coloured pen, the border decorated with butterflies. It was stuck up on Mrs Poll's fridge for years,
until the Sellotape turned brittle and dry in the sun. Besides, it
seemed babyish, that and the other things of his I kept around. At
some point, I don't know when, I must have put it in the file, along
with various other silly little items, like his old broken watch strap,
his favourite book, *Nina and the Butterflies*, and this cutting, long
learned by heart:

Noted Young Lepidopterist George Parr
Dead in Venezuela

REUTERS Caracas, March 1986: The Oxford Museum
of Natural History confirmed yesterday night the death
from a suspected heart attack of the youngest member
of its expedition to the tropical Andes. George Parr,
27, was a noted young entomologist recognised as one
of the most brilliant of his generation whose work in
the field of Batesian and Müllerian mimicry, and the
varying mutations of lepidoptery, was rapidly gaining
attention in the wider scientific community. He leaves
behind a wife and six-month-old daughter. The museum
has yet to respond to questions surrounding the circumstances of his death.

In my more attention-seeking phase, and especially after Mrs Poll
died, I was very proud of that cutting: people at school didn't have
fathers whose deaths had been in the papers.

I don't know when but, gradually, we stopped talking about him.
The house changed again, things were moved around, and the box
file was put on a shelf in my mother's study. The list and the photographs and the book were all, slowly, forgotten.

For years that photo of my parents outside the Bodleian Library was in Mum's bedroom: I saw it every day because she and I shared the front room of the dark, damp, rat-infested basement – Mrs Poll was on the top two floors. The Lawsons lived below her, and Captain Wellum below that, above us:

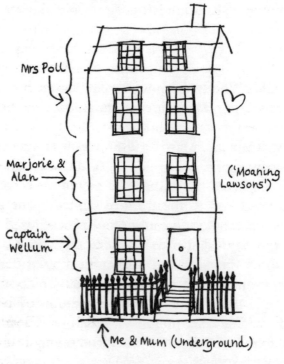

123 Noel Road

Most of my earliest memories are of the kitchen of our flat, and the Islington Women's Collective. I have two very clear snapshot pictures of them and this time. Firstly, the evening Tanya, de facto head of the Islington Women's Collective, brought Mum a coat one of their members, Elsa, had been wearing when she'd been knocked down by the number 19 bus the previous week. Mum actually took it and cried, and more and more of them turned up and they all sat around the kitchen table hugging each other and drinking elder-flower wine. She wore that coat – a dark pink fluffy thing, gradually coloured yellowing-grey by London pollution – until last year, when the moths finally polished off the last bits upon which they hadn't already feasted. They meant well (the Collective, not the moths, who were a bloody pain in the neck for years until Malc sorted them out), but they tended to take up a lot of space and time – time I wanted with my mum, by myself, instead. I wanted to show her she didn't need anyone else, she didn't need to be sad, because I could look after her.

They cried a lot, the Collective. When Tanya appeared at the front door, I knew to scarper upstairs, past the laundry, avoiding the naughty nail in the hallway where the carpet had worn bare, under the sheets Mrs Lawson used to hang over the bannisters to dry, up, up to the top of the house, to Mrs Poll's. I never much liked any of them. I think it's because they were almost comically uninterested in me except as a future oppressed minority. 'Can't your kid cook for herself?' Allison asked Mum once, wearily, when Mum broke off from a Collective meeting to fix me some tuna-out-of-a-can-on-toast – our favourite meal. I was five.

I wasn't ever scared Mum would hurt me. But I was often frightened of her. When the gas was turned off, or when the damp was really bad, or when the Moaning Lawsons had a go at her about something – and when, I suppose, the toughness of her situation made her feel even more trapped than usual – she'd get angry and start slamming the kitchen doors. Then something really would go wrong – a broken cup, a leaking tap, I'd make a mess by dropping some food – and all hell would break loose. I knew she didn't mean it. I understood that, even then, but I was still scared of the mercurial nature of her moods.

The second memory is that, when I was five or so, Tanya sent the manuscript of Mum's book, *The Birds Are Mooing*, to a book editor she knew. Mum had been working on it, in secret, for years, on and off: I was often aware of her, sitting up in bed with me half asleep next to her as she furiously typed on her old mushy-pea-green electric typewriter. She'd agreed to let Tanya see it, because Tanya had nagged and cajoled for weeks. Then one night, out of the blue, Tanya turned up on the doorstep and announced she'd posted the manuscript to her friend that morning. Expecting Mum to be pleased.

My mother's rage was like nothing else I'd seen before. She saw it as a betrayal of trust, of everything the Collective stood for. She was so cross, yelling and throwing things, that I hid under the table. I didn't want to move, because I was terrified, and so I wet myself. Eventually Mr Lawson came downstairs and banged on our door and told her to shut up, but Mum ignored him. Eventually, after Mum and Tanya had been screaming at each other for about twenty minutes—

Delilah, I think it's really sad you don't want to help yourself, and help us validate you.

For Christ's sake, you had no right to do it, Tanya! How dare you interfere in my life, I don't need any help and I can't stand people sticking their noses in! We're doing fine! We don't need anyone!

—even Mrs Poll appeared in the doorway, to suggest they keep it down a bit, and took me back up with her. I remember kicking at the door, wanting to stay down there for once, not wanting to leave Mum. But Mrs Poll was surprisingly firm, and hauled me upstairs for a bath and pyjamas, then cheese on toast with chips. She let me watch *Hi-de-Hi!*.

For a few days afterwards Mum constantly said Tanya had stabbed her in the back. I think she was simply terrified. And Tanya was right, because the editor loved it and made Mum an offer to publish it, and though Mum was dead against the idea at first, she came round, though I don't think her friendship with Tanya was ever quite the same.

The book is dedicated to me. 'For little Nina: I hope this makes things better.' I think that's such a sad inscription.

The Birds Are Mooing is about a young girl called Cora who wakes up one morning and finds everything is different. The sky is made of cake sponge, the flowers smell of gravy, the birds are mooing, and her mum and dad are tiny creatures she puts on the mantelpiece whose voices are so small she can't hear what they're saying. The little girl has to work out why it's happened and whether she can turn everything back the way it was.

She never read it to me, that's the funny thing. I read it – I read all her books, of course. Teachers at school used to say I was the luckiest girl in the world, having a mum who wrote books especially for me. 'Are they about you? I bet they are!'

I couldn't ever say what I'd worked out at about seven or eight: 'No, they're about Mum.'

She writes books about the little lost girl she was and still is, but I don't think she's realised that's what they're about. The truth, which I'll say once and then never again, as it makes me feel crummy, is: I've never got on with Mum's books, I don't know why. I just don't quite believe them. And that makes me, in my way, the worst, most ungrateful daughter imaginable. *The Birds Are Mooing* sold, and sold – it's in every library in the country. I should love it, because it saved our bacon: just before it came out, my head teacher had called in Social Services about my shoes and clothes being too small, again, but this time there was a social worker circling. Mrs Poll had to lend Mum money to buy me some proper warm shoes (not those canvas ones with the rubber soles, which had long ago split and were too small) and a coat (not last year's, which the moths had enjoyed all summer and whose arms only reached my elbows).

Once *The Birds Are Mooing* had been a success and we had some money, we bought Captain Wellum's ground-floor flat after he died, and I kept the basement bedroom – by now damp-proofed and papered with rose wallpaper from Laura Ashley, along with matching rose duvet and pillow set. I thought I'd died and gone to heaven.

And that photograph of my parents outside the Bodleian went into Mum's new bedroom on the ground floor. It was always there, for years, on the mantelpiece next to her brass tree she'd bought at the antiques stall in Camden Passage. She started buying necklaces, after the book deal, when she had a bit more money: just junk things, coloured plastic or glass, or shells. She hung them everywhere; sometimes they'd knock together like wind chimes if the windows rattled in a storm, or when someone slammed the front door. So Mum bought necklaces, and we started having holidays – not very successful ones, but time away nonetheless – and when I was seven, she gave up waitressing at the Italian down the road. I think she was afraid of not having money again, so she kept on with it longer

47

than necessary. I went to Mrs Poll's, on those evenings – which I preferred, anyway. Poor Mum.

Then the Moaning Lawsons moved into a home, and we bought their first-floor flat off the Council. Mrs Poll used to look down at us from her landing. 'You're creeping up, like ivy,' she'd say. 'You'll have the whole place off me while I'm sleeping, I bet.'

When she died, Mum was contacted by Mrs Poll's extremely serious and grand solicitors. Convinced she'd been landed with a bill for something, Mum was instead flabbergasted to learn Mrs Poll had left us a bequest of £50,000, to be shared between Mum and me, and that she had also left us her flat: 'So that Delilah and Nina have a house of their own and can be a family.'

We hadn't felt like a family up till then, she was completely right. So that's how we came to own the whole of this tall, higgledy house by the canal. Bad luck, then grit and hard work, then good fortune: as I say, it has been quite a journey, to that top floor. And at some point, Mum must have put the photo of her and my father away, because though its image, their smiles, their postures are burned into my memory, it never reappeared.

You hear people say it all the time these days: 'I'm a bad mother.' 'She's not a very good mother.' 'Oh, I'm an awful mother.' As though it's something you can call judgement on, either way. That person there: bad mother. Three along to the right: good mother. I have never thought of Mum in those terms. She's the only mum I've had, so how would I know any different? I always knew she loved me, even if sometimes I didn't have a bath for a week or never went to birthday parties because we couldn't buy presents. She was always trying to make things better.

Besides, I was lucky. I had someone else looking out for me.

Chapter Six

Mrs Poll arrived, like Mary Poppins, out of the blue when I was about six months old. I was almost eleven when she died suddenly at the beginning of her holiday in Lyme Regis, so we had her for just over ten years. At the time I considered it especially unfair she'd died there, as she'd always wanted to visit Lyme. She never went on holiday, preferring day trips instead: she had a friend in Bath and a remote relative in Cambridge and occasionally she'd take herself off for the day or night, but rarely. I still look up out of habit as I walk down Noel Road, hoping to see the lights on in her flat. She was always in. Similarly, I wish I could picture her more clearly, but my memory of her face is hazy. I don't have any photos of her. She was just always there.

For years Mum waitressed at an old-school Italian restaurant on Upper Street. Three days a week, when I was little, Mrs Poll used to pick me up from school and give me tea while Mum was working. But most days I'd go up there, anyway. I came to dread weekends: no excuse to go and see her. Sometimes I'd find reasons: *I think I can smell smoke, Mrs Poll. Come and look at this ladybird in the garden, Mrs Poll. Mum has been gone for hours and I'm lonely, Mrs Poll.* She left her door on the latch, but I always knocked. Mum had drilled it into me that I mustn't assume it was my home, that I must give her her own space. But I didn't believe her. I was convinced, with the arrogance of youth, that she loved having me there.

The kitchen was stylish, for its time. So was she, but she'd worn much better. It was decked out in violently orange kitchen units and a brown freestanding cooker; there was a bench on one side of the yellow pine table, upon which I used to kneel and look out over the canal our house backed on to, and the City of London behind. Now, monolithic offices and empty millionaires' flats have wiped out that view. But then, you could see the edge of the great Smithfield meat market, the open space of the ancient Charterhouse, the dome of St Paul's Cathedral, the patchwork of streets sewn together with new estates and offices built in the spaces left by bombs.

'How was school today, my little Nina?'

'Good, thank you. Mrs Poll, it's Friday.'

'Well, so it is. Would you like some cinnamon toast, perhaps?'

'Yes, please.'

The beringed hand, beckoning me to come and give her a kiss, then smoothing my hair, then turning to the cooker and switching the grill on, the buttered bread sprinkled with sugar and cinnamon that she'd let me mix together, the smell of caramelising, nutty, spicy toast – do you have that smell, that one smell that takes you back? That is mine. And it is so wonderful to recall, to feel her again, that I often make it when I am by myself just to capture the essence of her again.

I knew her better than anyone, but I wish I had asked more about her life before me. I was a child when I knew her, and children are selfish, and though my mother pressed her for more details she, too, was afterwards always vague on Mrs Poll's background: her Americanness sometimes meant she missed nuances of speech, anyway, and didn't understand things, like Kent being a county. But I knew Mrs Poll was a widow who, having spent her married life in Bromley, or thereabouts, had decided to move back to London after her husband died. She wanted to live in the city again before she was too old to enjoy it: 'Before my mind goes, or my body – whichever's first.' And I remember this terrifying me – the idea that Mrs Poll, the centre of our world, might not be here one day.

I think she was Jewish, I don't know why. She had grown up in the East End and she'd talk about the kosher butchers and the old weavers' houses and the Bethnal Green Boys' Club organising dances the girls would attend. They had day trips to Kent every summer to pick strawberries, and if I'm right her family were dockers, had been for generations. She had a young brother who'd died of the measles when he was two. Little April had held him as he died, and then wrapped up his body so her mother wouldn't have to see it. She was a proud woman, proud of herself for growing up there and for getting out of it, and proud of this new life of hers.

She was exactly the same, every day – and to me, coming from the basement flat where papers and clothes lay scattered on the floor and open tins of baked beans rusted on the kitchen counter, where I knew I was loved but often wasn't sure where my knickers and vest and socks might be, or where I was sleeping, I can't tell you how comforting this was. She smelled lovely, was always immaculately turned out, her solid but elegant silhouette decked out in neatly pressed tweed skirts and silk shirts, with court shoes in a variety of browns and blacks, some with tiny, dashing, decorative buckles. She wore a watch on a chain around her neck, rose-gold earrings and a matching bracelet. She had a thick, black woollen coat with huge velvet collar and cuffs, lined with sky-blue silk – it was a beautiful thing, and she wore it every winter I knew her. She didn't have much money. I knew this because she constantly told me how poor she was. She economised religiously – I knew this also because she hammered home to me the cost of everything in her cupboard, taking me shopping for food, making sure I knew what was in the basket and how much it would be. To this day, I can calculate exactly the shopping in my basket and I'm sure one of the reasons Sebastian and I couldn't stay together was his total disregard for budgeting. Mrs Poll would have fainted clean away at his cavalier adding of Ibérico ham at £15.99 a packet to our paltry food basket. I used to wonder what she'd make of my husband, what she'd say if she could see so many things today. I miss her.

She liked music – she'd get tickets for the slips at Covent Garden to see the ballet and the opera, although she preferred the former. She said opera made her feel too sad and she couldn't watch *Tosca* again. She loved exhibitions, and was often to be found in the café at the Royal Academy or the Tate – if you wonder who those smartly dressed older ladies you see having tea and cake alone are, they're a version of Mrs Poll. She organised jumble sales for the local community centre, sorting out clothes and keeping some back for me and Mum, which she paid a good price for. She liked travelling on buses, knew London like the back of her hand, albeit a version of London several decades out of date. She, like me, loved the city, its nooks and secrets, its passageways and adventures. But mostly she liked her cosy flat, with her books and her radio and her small plastic TV with the neat white handle on it that she'd carry from the kitchen into her bedroom if we watched a film together. She was a homebody, she'd tell me, as we snuggled together in bed. 'I don't like to go too far from London. I've got everything I need here, haven't I?'

Her husband, whom she'd met during the war, was a Russian refugee, Mikhail Polianskaya, and I think she rather liked the exoticism of her married surname. I wish, too, that I'd asked her to tell me more about him and their life together before she came to Noel Road. I ran upstairs once on a sunny day to ask her if she wanted to come with me along the canal, and when she didn't answer I crept into the kitchen, and found her holding a photograph of a short, dark-haired boy with a wide, grinning smile.

She was sniffing into a tissue, and when she saw me she wiped her eyes. 'There, now. Hello, darling. Don't mind me, just having a cry.'

'Is that your husband?' I asked, curiously.

'Yes, poppet. Just before – just before we were married.' She stood up and put the photo carefully away, in her bureau drawer in the hallway.

I followed her. 'Are you sad?'

'I am, when I think about him. He was a good man.'

I never knew her maiden name: it was Mum who christened her Mrs Poll, all those years ago, the first time they met. Mum told me about that moment over and over again; it was my favourite story, growing up. My father had been confirmed dead a few weeks before. Mum was still waiting for the Oxford Museum of Natural History to give her more information – what had happened, would they bring the body back home? Not least so she could work out what to do next – she had no money, and actually hadn't eaten that day. Her parents were sending a cheque, almost begrudgingly; she'd had to reverse the charges to call them. Jack and Betty Griffiths had almost seemed to welcome the news of her misfortune, inasmuch as it proved them right in their dire imprecations not to throw over her promising future for this 'butterfly hunter', as her father referred to him. Her child benefit hadn't come through, because of some problem with proving that she, an American, was married to a Briton. It was another bitterly cold April – spring refusing to arrive, frost every morning – and the damp in the flat was blooming, forming its own terrain. The few friends she possessed had long since melted away, and she was utterly alone. This was, as she used to tell me when I asked about Mrs Poll, her Lowest Point.

We were in the hallway, Mum and I, on our way out for a walk, with me crying in the home-made sling my enterprising mother had made out of a torn-up sheet (we had not been donated the pram yet) bundled up in a padded all-in-one Mum had been sent by a girlfriend in the States, which she used to put me in most days – especially to sleep in, because it was warm, and we were always cold. Mum was wild-eyed with lack of sleep, and grief. As she attempted to soothe me, she saw a woman coming down the stairs, and knew it must be the new neighbour from the top floor who had moved in swiftly, neatly, the day before. 'A very classy lady,' Mr Lawson had told Mum pointedly, that morning. 'We like her kind.'

So Mum had flattened herself against the corridor wall, hoping to avoid an encounter: she said she really couldn't face people much, in those days, and often Mr Lawson or Captain Wellum, before he went deaf, would complain about my crying. I would not be soothed though, I carried on crying.

'Hello, there,' came a voice, and Mrs Poll reached the last step and smiled at Mum. 'What a beautiful baby.'

It was the first kind voice Mum had heard for days, and she looked at Mrs Poll like a drowning woman seeing a life raft. Mrs Poll was in the soft, sleek woollen-and-velvet coat, her shining black hair shot with grey and neatly pinned up, her sparkling eyes smiling. She had a basket over her arm, and a neatly written list clutched between her gloved fingers.

'April Polilan— Poli— Oh!' she'd said, holding out her hand to Mum. 'Polianskaya. I'm sorry, I'm a little tired and my name is something of a mouthful. My husband was . . . Russian.'

Mum thought she was a little nervous. 'Let's just say Mrs Poll,' she said to her.

'Oh yes, let's,' this strange, kind woman agreed, and she smiled at me. 'So we must be neighbours. And who's this?'

Mum told her, 'This is Nina. She has a tooth coming through and she's very grumpy and her mummy is a little tired, too.'

Mrs Poll apparently took me, holding me so that I was facing her, and I stared at her, bright red with rage, nose running, eyes bulging with anger. She blew softly on my face, then gave me a gentle kiss. 'Oh, you're lovely,' she said. 'But what a cross little person you are!' She looked at Mum, and Mum said she knew something then, that this woman was a good woman. 'Why don't I take you for a quick walk and your mummy can have a cup of tea and close her eyes for five minutes. How does that sound?'

'Oh. Thanks, but . . .' My mother began to give reasons as to why this wouldn't work. '. . . don't worry. You don't want to do that.'

And Mrs Poll said, 'I was a nurse, I'm used to babies. I miss them dreadfully, in fact. Please, dear, go back downstairs and have a rest. She'll be fine with me.'

You may think my mother was crazy to agree to this, but if you had met Mrs Poll you wouldn't find it strange.

She was rather grand, in her way, that's what strikes me now: she liked things just so, was punctilious about manners and timings, and yet never put herself forward. She always said it was her East London upbringing. She was taught to respect others, to do good. She was from a different generation, of course, and sometimes she and Mum clashed, as she tried, I think, to buck my mother up. But she and Mum loved each other. Mum called her a 'trench friend' – someone you needed next to you in the trench when times were rough. And how we needed her.

Over tea one afternoon, Mum asked her why she did it, helped us, made us her project. Mrs Poll smoothed down her skirt and was silent for longer than Mum had ever known.

'I'd sit there every day, waiting at the bus stop for the little hopper bus to come and take me into Bromley,' she said eventually. 'I'd walk around the shops, go to the library. Sometimes I'd end up in the park with a sandwich, sitting on the bench, watching everyone else's lives, and I'd be screaming inside, wanting to stroke a little girl's hair, or chat to a father, or help a mum with her baby's buggy. And I couldn't. The man three doors down from me, he died, and no one knew for a month. I realised then, you see, I was totally alone, in the place I'd lived for thirty years. You don't know what that's like.'

'I can guess,' my mother said.

'Of course. Well, I knew I'd go mad if I didn't do something about it. My husband's dead, my sister's dead, my nieces are in Canada. I needed new things to look at, places to go, ways to be helpful. So don't ever thank me. I should thank you. I'm very lucky to . . . to have found you.'

On my ninth birthday, Mum gave me a card and a present and a harried McDonald's expedition with four uninterested friends. As she and I walked home, holding hands, she said, 'Well, that's over, what a relief!' and we went upstairs, as Mrs Poll had said to come up for tea.

Mrs Poll had always cut out recipe ideas from *Woman's Own* or *Good Housekeeping*. She was waiting for us, and as we got to the second floor she called out, 'Happy Birthday!' She had made me a castle cake, replete with battlements, portcullis and moat, and she had found in Chapel Market a massive candle that played a kazoo-like 'Happy Birthday'. And she'd got me a CD Discman, which I'd wanted for years but never dared hope for. And a Take That CD. I played that CD for years and years, until the outer casing of the disc itself actually cracked and it came apart.

It wasn't the CD player, though. It was the cinnamon toast, the trips to the library, the three little china dogs on the mantelpiece I was allowed to name, the bath-time egg whisk and the Matey bubble bath she used to make the frothiest foam, as well as the castle cakes, because they all made me understand that someone cared about me, someone was looking after me, that someone loved me. That's all children need, really. It's very simple.

That year Mum's third book was published and she was away a lot, visiting libraries and reading to children in schools, and for one blissful week I stayed with Mrs Poll. On the third night in a row that I woke up screaming from a nightmare, having wet the bed again, Mrs Poll ran me a bath and made me some cocoa and then we climbed into her bed together. The clock in the kitchen said 2.13 a.m. I'd never been up this late: the previous two nights, she'd bundled me straight back into bed again.

'Do you want to tell me what's so terrible it makes you scream in your sleep like you're being torn apart by a pack of hungry wolves?' she asked me eventually, in her nicest voice.

I giggled, nervously, because I didn't want to go over it all. 'Just stuff.'

'Just stuff. Hmm.' She drank some more of her cocoa and I nestled against her, feeling the heavy eiderdown pressing on my toes; I wasn't at all tired. 'Nina, if something's bothering you, you can't just lock it away. Otherwise it gets stuck.' She tapped her head. 'Up here. What's the dream about?'

'Nothing.'

'Stuff and nothing,' said Mrs Poll. 'Do you know what I was doing, when you woke me up? I was writing in my diary.'

'You keep a diary?' It seemed such an un-Mrs-Poll-ish thing to do.

'Yes, I do, young lady. For my eyes only, so don't go getting any ideas.'

'Don't worry. I don't see the point of diaries,' I said, loftily.

'I didn't use to. But I like keeping mine. It's only for me. I put everything in there that's worried or upset me that day. I write all the little mistakes I made, how I could have done things better. And then I do a list, of what made me smile, what I'm grateful for that day and then I read it all through, and remember how lucky I am, and then I turn the page and I don't look at it again.'

'What were you grateful for today?' I said, curiously, because she never talked about herself.

She was silent for a moment. 'Well, Nina. I'm grateful the bus came when it started to rain. And I'm grateful my friend Ann and I met today and had a bite to eat at the British Museum.'

'Oh, what did you see? Did you see the Egyptians—'

Ignoring this, for she had long ago tired of my all-consuming Egyptology obsession, Mrs Poll carried on, 'And I'm grateful that you went to school, and even though you got a four out of ten in your maths test I'm grateful you gave it a go. And I can tell your mother that, when she asks me, because the teachers keep saying you're not concentrating enough, but I know that's not true.'

I didn't say anything, just rubbed my toes against her soft feet, and took another sip of my drink.

She said, 'Oh yes . . . well, I'm grateful for you, and your mum. That's all.'

'Me?'

'Yes, you.'

I huddled closer to her.

'I've told you what I'm grateful for,' she said. 'Do you want to tell me about that dream, then?'

I bit my lip. 'There's this girl,' I said, rubbing my eyes. 'She's mean. She comes and talks to me when I'm asleep. She looks like me but she's got yellow-blonde hair. And she has a party dress on, lace, like she's from olden times. She tells me all the bad things I've done. She puts her hands on my head so I can't see and moves my head around so fast and then . . . all the time she's laughing, telling me I'm weird, I'm weird, I'm weird.' My voice broke. 'And I'm afraid she'll keep me there and I'll never get out of the dream.'

I hadn't told anyone this, though it had been going on for months, because I was terrified they'd take me away to a madhouse, like some Victorian child. But now I'd started I couldn't stop. 'She comes to me when I'm asleep and she sits in my head . . . I can't concentrate at school lately because she yells at me, and when I'm reading now she's always there whispering to me. I hate her.'

Mrs Poll's cool hand smoothed my hair, but she didn't immediately reply. 'She doesn't sound very nice,' she said eventually.

'Of course she's not,' I said, annoyed she hadn't fully grasped it. 'She's horrible, Mrs Poll.'

'I think she sounds lonely.' Mrs Poll clambered briskly out of bed, and tied her dressing gown around her. 'Tell you what, let's give her a name.'

'A name?'

'Yes. And she can have the room next door. And some clothes to hang in there.'

I kneeled up in bed, my legs crackling in Mrs Poll's spare nylon nightie, and stared at her in amazement. 'I don't want her in the room next door,' I said. 'Don't you understand? She's scary. I hate her!'

Mrs Poll grabbed my hands in one of hers, large and strong. She came up close to me. I could see the lines around her eyes, the grey flecks in her brows, smell the rosewater scent that always clung to her. She said, almost furiously, 'Listen to me, Nina Parr. You have to face your fears. You can't let them control you. I turn the page every day. *Every day.* Do you understand me? You have to do the same, darling. Look. Come with me.'

I'd never seen her like this. She pulled me out of bed, and we went into the room next door, the room I usually slept in. She opened the built-in cupboard doors, pulled open the little drawers of the teak dressing table, drew back the curtains.

'Here!' she said, loudly. 'Here you are, young lady. This is your room.' She looked around her. 'Can you hear me?'

'Are you OK, Mrs Poll?' I said. I thought she must have lost it, like Jonas's Granny Violet when she started giving her things away to the neighbours on the estate.

'Shh. This girl who's giving you all this bother, what shall we call her? Let's give her a name.'

'Call her?' I said, horrified. 'I don't want to give her a name! Mrs Poll, stop it.'

'How about Matty?' she said.

'No! I'm not—'

She crouched down in front of me, smoothing the hair out of my eyes. She was beautiful, in the darkness, her own hair falling in front of her face. 'For me, darling. Just try it. Give it a week. All right?'

Along with *Face your fears*, the exhortation to *Give it a week* was a big feature of Mrs Poll's bargaining tactics. It was how she changed my mind about going to school, about my plan to run away when I was six – and, every year, about going on holiday with Mum.

I stood in the doorway, hugging myself, my chin resting on my chest, and I suddenly felt tired. 'OK, then. Matty's a good name.'

'Right.' She picked up *Nina and the Butterflies*, which was our favourite book, because there was a girl in it called, yes, Nina – and because my father had loved it as a child, I knew, and because it had always been in Noel Road, it was one of the few things he'd left behind. At some point, it must have migrated up to Mrs Poll's flat. 'Matty, this is your room, as well as Nina's,' Mrs Poll said. 'Come in, make yourself at home.'

'Who are you talking to?'

She ignored me, and spread her arms wide, smiling up at the ceiling. In her blue velvet dressing gown, her hair loose around her shoulders, she looked like a witch – a good one, of course. 'Listen to me, Matty. We'll put some clothes in the wardrobe for you. You can play with Nina's toys when she's at school. You can read this book, there's a little girl called Matty in here, too. Just don't bother us when we're asleep. Otherwise we'll open the window and send you tumbling down into the canal.' She looked over at me. 'Nina? Anything you want to add?'

I stood in the centre of the room, looking at my small, single bed, the orange varnished bookcase, the lamp, swinging slightly from the ceiling. I looked over at Mrs Poll, magnificent in royal blue, and she smiled at me.

I spread my arms wide. 'Yes, Matty. Listen to me now. We can play together when I'm up here when I say so. And I will bring you marvellous silks and cloaks from ancient lands, and oils and jewels from distant kings. Otherwise don't bother me. Or Mrs Poll.'

'That's it.' Mrs Poll clasped her hands together and bowed her head, then looked up, and around the empty room. 'Come back to my room. I videoed *Coronation Street* and I'm about to watch it, and as a very, very special treat you can, too.' I followed her out of the room but in the doorway she turned and glanced up at the still swinging ceiling lamp. 'Right. I don't think we'll have any more trouble with *her*.'

* * *

She was right, of course. Gradually, the room became known as Matty's room. I kept my best clothes and toys and books in there. Matty mutated from a tormentor to an imaginary friend – a sort of alternate me, the best version of me. We'd play together. She was ideal company, of course. She came up with the most imaginative ideas, had the most friends, knew what to say to grown-ups, never made *her* mother cross. When I slept up at Mrs Poll's it was in Matty's room, and I no longer had nightmares, because I felt Matty there, a benign presence now.

For years after Mrs Poll died, and before it was made into Mum's study, Matty's room wasn't used, but the idea of her stayed with me. I'd talk to her sometimes, run through ideas, leave books in her room she might want to read. When we took over the empty flat I chose Mrs Poll's room as my new bedroom. Matty's room was recarpeted and painted, but it stood half-empty, cleared of Mrs Poll's possessions, a repository for our papers and boxes.

And that was where the box file about my father ended up. In Matty's room. I'd put it all away when I married Sebastian, hadn't looked at it for years. Until the day the second photograph arrived and I climbed upstairs, and felt Mrs Poll's presence again, went into Matty's room, lifted the old, strange book out of its box-file hibernation.

Holding it again was as rich and potent as the smell of cinnamon toast. I sat on the floor of the bare office that evening, cross-legged, and when I opened the first page I froze. The pictures unchanged, the words I knew so well, and there – yes, there it was. This place again. *Keepsake.*

That is your family, the old woman had written on that photograph. *You don't know them / don't know what they did.*

As I began to read it again I realised something. I could probably have recited the story to you off by heart. I'd locked it away in my memory, forgotten about it, and it had been in this house all along, waiting to be found.

Nina And The Butterflies
Alexandra Parr

*

For Theodora, Whom I Call Thea

Lady Nina was the only child born to a great lord. His sorrow was great for he had no sons. When he died, he left her Keepsake, the house fashioned by the greatest craftsmen of its day and now hidden away on a green and silent creek, invisible to the casual traveller by road and from the water.

'Be modest, and good, and kind,' her father had told her as he lay dying. 'You bring me great sadness for you are not a son. Do you endeavour to give a great man sons that our name might endure through the ages to the glory of God. This house is the greatest built by the hand of Man. It will hide him and it will save him.'

But during the great Civil War which rent our fair Land in two, Nina lost also her mother and her betrothed, Francis, from a great family across the river. And so she was left utterly alone at Keepsake.

But Nina was not lonely, for she had butterflies in her garden, clouds of them rising up into the fragrant rich air in summer. Now, Children, in this time, butterflies were more plentiful than flies, and filled the air. They had not been caught and killed in vast numbers, or exposed to man's destruction of the green Earth.

Each winter, Nina watched the eggs they had laid, and cared for those that hibernated in the chapel, waiting for the sun to shine and the cruel winds that raged over the estuary to drop. In spring, she saw the caterpillars, eating their way through her garden, neatly slicing their curved lace patterns through the leaves. And in summer, she watched as they broke out of their pupae, as they gently, tremulously unfurled their wings that they might dry out in the breeze, fill with blood and become sturdy for that first journey.

She knew them all, from the smallest and humblest Meadow Brown to the Purple Emperor, whose great beauty and size has driven men to insanity. They knew her too. For butterflies are our friends. They show man the Earth at its finest. When we hurt the Earth we hurt them. Where there are no butterflies there is no good growing in the Earth thereabouts.

The house might have slumbered on, drowsing in the sunshine and playing host to its winged guests, but that was not its destiny, as forewarned by Nina's father. For one night under cover of darkness His Majesty King Charles II arrived by boat, accompanied only by his most trusted companion, Colonel Wilmot.

The King came seeking shelter from the evil Roundheads, who wrought so much damage to our peaceful land. He had been routed from Worcester, and he had hidden in oak trees, disguised himself as a stable hand, worn too-small shoes that bent and cut his sore feet. This gentle King had aped the manners of the stable boy, the farm hand and the humble country gentleman to avoid detection. He had skittered across the country, searching for a place to hide, and it was to Keepsake that he eventually came.

He remained there for two long weeks. At first, he was quiet, hidden in the tiny chapel at the back of the house, where Nina and her mother had long prayed for peace to come, where the butterflies sought shelter inside the cool walls. Then he grew more confident, and walked in the garden with Nina in the shade of the evening, where she offered him sweetmeats, and sliced pineapple grown in the special pits laid for that purpose in the garden. Side by side they watched the butterflies, a mist of colour and movement above them.

'You have made a beautiful world here,' the King told Nina.

The servants would hear them, laughing together. One afternoon, as they sat together, and Nina sang to the King, hooves were heard in the distance, and a terrible sound – the sound of the horn, heralding the arrival of the Roundheads.

Charles hid in the chamber, and though Cromwell's men searched the house, they did not find the chapel, hidden as it was behind the staircase, with windows thin as slits for light. And Nina stood under the arch of her house, and bade them leave.

'This is my home,' she told them. 'I will die here, rather than give it to someone else.'

At that time she understood at last that Keepsake belonged to her.

When the King left her, Nina was distraught. She spoke only of him. He wept as he left her. Months passed and there was no word from him. In time, Nina gave birth to a child, whom she named Charlotte, for her father.

She gave the servants holiday leave, and left the child with a nursemaid, her most trusted servant and friend who was called Matty. And then she went into the tiny chapel where the King had hidden himself, and she took her own life, in a manner not suitable for a child's ears.

After her death, the servants returned to the house with the child, and found a note that had arrived in their absence from the King, leaving Keepsake to his child, and to every daughter born there. And he sent a diamond brooch, shaped like a butterfly, which Charlotte his daughter wore when she was older, and which she gave to her own daughter before she died. Upon the thorax of the butterfly are engraved the words:

What's Loved Is Never Lost.

I myself think Nina was very brave. She died because she did not want to live any more without him. She knew what the King said was true. What's Loved Is Never Lost. She knew that though he was far away, attempting to win back his crown under threat of death, and though later he would sit upon the throne and rule over us all, and his life be made public, his body and personage be for us all, that there were two weeks, long ago one September, at the edge of summer, that were his and hers and theirs alone.

What's Loved Is Never Lost.

The house slumbers on, guarded by Nina's descendants, who keep her secrets. Perhaps one day, Children, you will find it. Along the river, down the creek – you cannot reach it by road, or using a map. You will know when you arrive. Only a clear, pure heart can find its way there.

*

The End

Chapter Seven

When I was nearly ten, Mum started seeing Malc. He used to come into the Italian restaurant where she worked to have a big bowl of pasta before going off on a story, and they'd chat. She used to talk about him – how funny he was, how he'd tell her these awful stories about the cases he was reporting on: usually stabbings in pubs or headless bodies in the canal. I remembered her saying she pitied his girlfriend or wife, having to listen to that every night, it was so gruesome. The fact was he had neither, and was trying to pluck up the courage to ask Mum out. When she gave up the waitressing, they lost contact.

A year or so afterwards, soon after Mum had begun decorating the Moaning Lawsons' flat, which we'd bought the previous year, she happened to be looking at raffia matting outside the carpet shop on the Essex Road when Malc walked past. True to form, he spent ten minutes pretending he was interested in whipped edging for some carpets for his staircase – and nearly ordered some, so nervous was he at seeing her again. He lived in a ground-floor flat, too; afterwards, we mocked him about it. 'You couldn't just pretend you wanted a new carpet for your sitting room?'

'I wasn't thinking straight. I was knocked for six,' he'd say, defiantly, as Mum and I rolled our eyes.

Eventually, after Mum had paid for her raffia matting, she turned to Malc and said, 'I'm going for a drink over there.' She pointed at the New Rose pub, opposite. 'What the hell – do you want to come with me or not?'

'Yes,' Malc said. 'Just let me—' and he'd looked down at the carpet samples.

'Are you going to buy any of those?' she'd asked him.

And Malc shook his head, smiling. 'I don't need carpets. I don't need any at all! I'm coming for a drink with you!'

He moved in a year later, and on that day we had a party for him, the three of us and Mrs Poll, in the garden, with some bunting. I was even allowed a minuscule glass of champagne. Mum bought quiches from Marks & Spencer, to denote it was a blue-chip kind of do. She also bought a new necklace and all evening she smiled, properly smiled, where she showed her teeth. She didn't touch him once – she is not demonstrative. But she could barely stop smiling at him.

And then, a couple of months after Malc moved in, Mrs Poll went away to Lyme, for her much-anticipated holiday. She and I had been shopping, she'd even bought herself a new dress – a denim shirtwaister, very sensible – and some cork-soled wedge heels. She had an old schoolfriend in the area with whom she was going to stay. I had to be dragged out to say goodbye to her, but Mum, Malc and I waved her off in her taxi, wondering what it'd be like to be just the three of us in the house, alone. To be honest, though I tried to pretend I was grown-up and didn't need Mrs Poll so much any more, I was already looking forward to her coming back.

But she didn't come back.

It took us a long time to get over Mrs Poll's death. Still, she'd as good as told us to carry on as normal without her in her will. 'Be a family.' She'd said so. And it was easier than I thought, getting used to the three of us: me, Mum and my stepfather. Because there is no joy like the joy of two people finding each other and making each other happy, then and now. Mum and Malc are glorious together – how she adores him, venerates him, looks up to him – my prickly, passive, absent mother! She learned to cook for him: who knew, after all these years of crisps and fish fingers, that she'd turn out to be a great cook? She even went fishing in Scotland with him. And how he worships the very ground she walks on – the look in his eyes when they rest on her golden head, when she takes the piss out of him, the way he hums and talks happily to himself as he folds the laundry, loads the dishwasher, does all the mundane tasks that make a household run so she doesn't have to, so she can write and cook. She makes mess; he clears it up.

I screwed up my marriage because I thought passion, like my mother and father had, was what mattered. I was wrong. It's adoration, and it was right under my nose these last ten years or so. They adore each other. They can't believe they found each other. He made her happy: finally.

Only once did we think it might all be over. On my fourteenth birthday, when the recent history was beginning to recede into the past – Mrs Poll's death, us living in one whole and large house, the newness of Malc – my mother had another setback. We refer to it, if we mention it at all, which is rare, as her nervous breakdown. But I'm not sure it was. I don't know what it was, but something changed that day.

We were on our way out to the Pizza Express near the British Museum. We were to look at the Egyptian necropolis artefacts first, in fact, and then have a pizza. This was my idea of a perfect birthday, you understand: no bitchy girls, no annoying boys, no stupid questions; just me, Mum and Malc and several Ptolemies. They'd given me a bike, and Malc had made pancakes, and Mum had written me a poem, which she recited over breakfast, about a girl called Nina.

> Nina the teen-a, lived in a marina,
> She had long black hair, and was in love with a hyena.
> Nina the teen-a received a subpoena,
> To return the hyena right back to Argentina!

I didn't say it was a good poem. ('And,' as Malc pointed out, under his breath after Mum had gone to buy more milk, 'a subpoena isn't the right legal document. To return a hyena to Argentina would require a court order from a judge. I'm just telling you. While she's out of the room.')

I'd forgotten my new handbag which Jonas had bought me – a beautiful purple baguette thing from Accessorize with a thin, detachable strap – and had run back inside to fetch it. Malc was teasing me as we left the house, Mum waiting impatiently for us on the pavement. 'When I was fourteen, missy, do you know what I did for *my* birthday? Aye, I went out with my best pal and we drank a bottle of my mother's sherry and we threw up in my neighbour's front yard and she beat me around the face with the *Daily Record*. Now *that's* a birthday, Dill, wouldn't you— Dill, love?' Then, sharply, '*Delilah?*'

I turned, at the tone in his voice. Mum was looking across the road, face grey-white, utterly immobile.

'No,' she said, eyes fixed on the middle distance. 'Not again.'

We followed her gaze, but there was nothing. A man unchaining his bike from the lamp post. Some takeaway wrappers impotently fluttering on the rain-sodden road. The cat who lived opposite, running down the street.

'Dill, love?' said Malc, pushing past me towards her. 'What's wrong?'

It was quiet in the road and the man opposite glanced up at her, curiously, as she stood rigidly still, just staring at nothing, unblinking. As though she was frozen. A van or something large rumbled past, I remember, because it was like a magic trick: when it had gone Balthazar the cat had vanished, and the man too, cycling away alongside it. A piece of white wrapping, loosened in the breeze, fluttered after them towards the canal.

'Mum?' I said. 'Mum, are you OK?'

'I knew it,' she said, staring at nothing. 'I knew I was right.'

I stood next to her, trying to understand what it was she could see. But she turned, almost pushing me out of the way, and went inside. 'Go without me,' was all she said, and as we stood there, in shock, the front door slammed in our faces.

For two weeks she didn't get out of bed. Malc repeatedly called the doctor, who refused to come on a house visit. If she wasn't physically ill she could come into the surgery and be examined. But though we knew there was nothing 'physically' wrong with her, and kept explaining this, still they wouldn't come. I hope things would be different now.

At night I was sure I heard her crying, but by day she just lay there with the curtains drawn, only getting up to use the loo. I was so scared. She'd stroke my hair when I went in to visit her, she'd ask how my day was – but she wasn't listening, and sometimes she'd turn her head away and start crying, weeping brokenly into the pillow. It was like being very small again, only this time I didn't have Mrs Poll to run upstairs to.

We didn't know what to do. We felt completely alone. I think it was the first time I realised Malc was my father, in effect. It's one of the many reasons why, when I refer to 'my parents', I mean Mum and Malc. He did the washing, he and I cooked together, he sat on the end of my bed and chatted to me before I went to sleep. He started working at home in the afternoons so he was there when I came back from school.

One Sunday, two weeks and one day later, he and I returned from one of our walks on Hampstead Heath, a golden but hellish afternoon where we had both pretended we were enjoying ourselves, and Mum was in the kitchen, dressed and with her hair washed, deftly feeding dough into the pasta machine as though nothing had happened.

'I'm sorry,' she said, as we watched her, warily, across the warm dark room. 'I'm so very, very sorry.' She came towards me, gave me a big hug, folding me into her, and I noticed I was almost as tall as her. 'It won't happen again.'

'What was it, Mum?' I said, trying to hide the dizzying relief I felt.

She looked over at Malc, who was watching her with his arms tightly folded, her eyes brimming with tears. 'Oh, something was wrong, but it's OK now,' she said. I saw the lines around her eyes, a tautness in her expression.

I didn't know it then but I came to realise, a long time afterwards, that whatever happened to her that day altered her. Something now hung over her. It is hard to describe, but it was a kind of dully alert wariness. As though she knew something was waiting to catch her, and she had no choice but to walk towards it. I'd think through what we'd seen: the man with the bike? But he'd been doing nothing, and then he'd cycled away, nor had he even looked our way. The cat? How could Balthazar mean something? The flapping pieces of rubbish? The grey day? I came to believe it was none of those things, just that *something* had occurred to her, some thought in her fizzing, wild brain.

It's OK now. And it seemed that way for a long time, though I don't think it really was. But we had to believe it, of course, and life carried on somewhat unremarkably – which means, I suppose, contentedly. I studied, and studied, and now Mum was called into school by teachers to advise her not on where to buy second-hand clothes but on how to take care of me during my exams as I was 'highly strung' and 'exceptionally bright'. I wasn't: I just liked studying. Picking away at a problem and finding a solution. Control, control, when so much of the world was obtuse and didn't make sense.

Ironically, I think I gave them more trouble than I would have done had I been out all hours, God knows where, in Camden or Soho or wherever. They could have punished me if I'd been smoking and drinking and stealing and bringing home unsuitable boys. I didn't. Instead, I stayed in my room: writing, reading, thinking. Thinking too much.

So to the final part of this little biographical backstory, which is that when I was eighteen, I was accepted into UCL. I remember my old headmistress saying to me, as I opened my A level results, 'Your life lies ahead of you, Nina. I can't wait to see what you do with it.'

Perhaps I'm more like my mother than I realise, perhaps not. Either way it's a shame I didn't get my rebellious streak out of the way a little earlier. I'd always been a perfectly good girl on the outside, as I say. No trouble. And then I went and fell in love.

Chapter Eight

'But it's a beautiful day! Come on, Nina. Isn't she looking pale?'
Malc appealed to my mother, who was reading the paper. 'Don't
you think she ought to get out?'

'She's twenty-five, Malc,' said Mum, but she looked outside and
then over at me. 'It is a lovely day, honey. You might want to go
for a walk or meet some friends.'

'They're all away,' I said.

'*All* of them?'

'The ones I want to see are. I don't mind staying in, you know.'

'Sure. I know. It's just . . . you've hardly been out of your room
all weekend.'

'Reading,' I said. 'I just wanted to read. And sleep.'

It was a lie. Lately I couldn't sleep. I'd start thinking about it all:
*Where's Keepsake? Where is Miss Travers? What does she think happened
to my dad? What does Mum know?* And the silence would overwhelm
me, and my heart would beat faster and faster, trying to piece it all
together yet, like a dog chasing its tail, never seeming to get anywhere.

Something skittered past outside, in the light spot in the tiny
garden, and I gazed out of the window. Suddenly, unexpectedly, the
thought of staying inside all day was unbearable. I stood up.

'OK, I'll come,' I said. 'But you know perfectly well why I don't
like the Heath on Sundays. If we bump into them, I'm . . . I'm . . .'

'Gee willickers, Katie Morag,' said Malc, rubbing his hands in
glee. 'We won't. It's a beautiful day for a walk.'

'Gee willickers,' I muttered. I glanced at Mum. 'You be all right
on your own?'

'Me? Of course! I'll do some work,' Mum said. 'Wonderful!'

'Wonderful,' I echoed, and drank the rest of my tea. 'Come on,
Malc.' I looked at my watch. 'If we go now we'll miss the crowds.'

* * *

'What shall I do for my birthday?' Malc said. We were walking past turreted Victorian flats on the edge of the Heath that when I was little I used to imagine was a row of fairy-tale castles. The sun was warm on our newly bare arms, the trees bursting with fresh green, and I felt almost drunk on it all, exhilarated with spring.

'Let me think. You've booked the day off, haven't you?'

'Oh yes. Barty and I are seeing the ex-copper who found the dead dog in the Louis Vuitton suitcase, and that pair of hands, for lunch at the Grapes. Be really lovely to meet him at last.'

'You're having lunch with a pair of hands?'

'Ha-ha, Nina. Some of us *like* birthdays. Some of us, unlike you and your mother, actually *enjoy* marking the day of our birth.'

'Yes,' I said. I remembered with a pang of guilt that last year he'd had to buy his own cake: I was still living in Palmers Green and Mum was useless. 'Listen,' I said, knowing I'd regret it as soon as the words were out of my mouth, 'why don't we get some people round in the evening? Just a few neighbours and friends. Barty, Brian Condomine, your old reporter muckers, Lorelei and Roger from down the road, etcetera.'

'Banners? Balloons, shall I get some balloons?'

'No. You know Mum's allergic to them.' This was a blatant lie which Malc chose not to challenge every year.

'Fair enough.' He gave a huge, pleased grin. 'Hey, we could order pizzas. And taste some different ales.'

'Um . . . sure. If you want.'

'Definitely I want.' He rubbed his hands. 'This'll be fun, you wait. How about we ask Sebastian?'

'Well, again, if you want to, Malc.'

But Malc waved a hand. 'No, it's stupid of me to suggest it. Not fair to you. I just keep expecting we'll bump into him because we're on the Heath. Him and Lady Muck.' His eyes twinkled as I made a face. 'Forget it.'

'It's all right, Malc. He was a good man. Is.'

'Ah, lassie. He is. He is.' He patted my shoulder and gave a sigh. I felt he was about to Say Something, so I changed the subject.

'Malc, may I ask you a question?'

'Sure.'

'That photograph . . .'

He looked blank.

'. . . the one of the girl on the creek.'

'I've been wondering about that.' Malc put his hands behind his back. 'Did you hear anything more from that woman?'

I sidestepped. 'I can't stop thinking about it. I don't know what to do next.'

'It is rather strange, isn't it?'

We were both silent. We knew that if we were to start discussing it now, just the two of us, we'd be going behind Mum's back, though I couldn't have told you why.

'Malc, do you think Mum knows something?'

He shook his head. 'Your mother's never heard of her, or seen her. I know that much.' We were climbing uphill now, over towards Kenwood, and he sounded short of breath. 'What is it you think she wants to tell you?'

'No idea!' I threw my hands up in the air. 'Keepsake? What's that?'

'Google it.'

'I did. I looked it up. Got absolutely nothing.'

'What do you mean?'

'Well, I googled Keepsake. And Keepsake and House or Place. Oh, and a hundred other combinations of those two. Teddy, boat, river, butterflies, families, dead father, and nothing comes up. Well, it does, if you're interested in teddy bears as a keepsake or keepsakes in general. Nothing else at all.'

'Google isn't the answer to everything, I know that from bitter experience,' said Malc. 'But ye-es. That's strange.'

'But that book Mrs Poll and I used to read, the one my dad left me . . . she's called Nina. And the house is called Keepsake.' Malc nodded, though I hadn't told him this before. 'First the photos, then finding the book again . . . all these messages,' I said, the words tumbling out. 'I sort of think everything I *do* know is a lie, or there's all this stuff I don't know.'

'*Messages?* You really believe that?' Malc was incredulous. I stopped, and looked at him, and blinked. Did I really believe Malc, of all people, was lying to me? What did I actually think was being hidden from me? And yet again, doubting voices jabbed into my conscious. *Don't be ridiculous, Nina.*

'I'm not imagining it all,' I said, firmly, as much to myself as to Malc. 'I can't be. And you'd think . . .' I shrugged. '*Something'd* be on the internet. But there's nothing. I don't know what to do next.'

I suppose I was hoping he'd tell me what to do. But Malc just said, after a moment's pause, 'You have to wait for her to get in contact with you again, I suppose. Try going to the same place in the library.'

'I have. I've been going there every day since. And after work. I'm there all the damn time.'

'And?'

'She gave me another photo, ten days ago,' I said, in a rush. 'I haven't told Mum, Malc.'

'Oho.' Malc raised his eyebrows. 'Who's the photo of?'

I told him, describing the photo, the young girl and her grand-mother, the edge of the house, Miss Travers's message. *That is your family Nina Parr.* A pulse ticked slowly in Malc's cheek, as he listened. 'The thing is,' I finished, 'how on earth can I solve this damn mystery when I'm not sure what any of it's even *about?*'

'Well . . .' Malc said eventually. 'Obviously this woman knows something about your father's family.'

'But isn't it a bit of a coincidence, her bumping into me at the library like that?'

He shook his head and put his hand on my arm. 'Nina. What am I always telling you? There are no coincidences. Trust me. Everything happens for a reason.'

I squirmed away from him; he's always saying this and I don't like it, as if we have no choice in our lives. 'Well, whatever it is, I can't ask Mum. She's completely shut up like a clam about it.'

Then I looked at him directly, challenging him to disagree with me.

'I don't think that's true.'

'The older I get, the more I want to find out about my dad. This

74

woman knows something, and Mum doesn't seem that interested, like – she hasn't asked me about it again. But I'm *sure* she wants to.' I looked at him, sideways, as if willing him to agree with me. But he said nothing. 'He was my dad, Malc. I don't know anything about him at all.'

We were walking through a wooded canopy of beech trees. 'Listen to me, Nina,' said Malc, after a few moments. '*I'll* tell you one thing, and then we'll not discuss it again, OK? Your father was not all your mother makes him out to be.'

'What do you mean?' I stopped, my feet crunching heavily on the ever-present dry-dead leaves that carpeted the woodland floor.

Malc's brow puckered. 'Things I've worked out. Things she's told me.' He stopped. 'You know I don't like talking about her behind her back.'

'I'm not, I'm just asking—'

'I don't want to be rude about your father, or make him sound less of a man than he was. I didn't know him, right? I'm just saying, I don't think things were perfect when he left. Something she once said to me when we first met.'

'What was that?'

I had to nudge him before he'd answer. 'OK, OK. When I first met her in that Italian restaurant, and we used to just talk – this is long before we were going out – I remember asking about her late husband once, and she said she'd have divorced him if he hadn't died.'

'What?'

'No idea to this day if she meant it. And when I asked her about it again, after I'd moved in, she denied it. Said things had been difficult, but that was all. She was really cross with me, actually.' He looked ruffled. 'All I mean by it is, relationships aren't just black and white. You should know that, more than most people.'

I sank my chin almost to my chest as we walked on, silent for a while, though my mind was racing. As we emerged out of the other side of the wood I looked up and saw we were just below Kenwood House, glowing cream-white in the spring sunshine. On the path on the other side of the house were silhouetted figures pushing buggies, children riding scooters. A small girl in a red coat was tangling herself up with a kite, and her brother and mother rushed over to help. I could hear them all laughing, voices carrying on the breeze.

I feel self-conscious with families, especially large ones – I suppose because I still don't really understand them. They always seem so overconfident, far too loud, determined to tell you as soon as possible how huge their clan is, as though being out alone in the world and separated from the pack would diminish them. Mum and I were not so much mother and daughter as a unit of one, awkward in public. We didn't know how to explain ourselves. Outings with Mrs Poll were even trickier: 'No, she's not my grandmother. She lives upstairs. No, I don't have any brothers and sisters. Who? My dad's dead.'

'Let's go and get a cup of tea,' said Malc, pointing at Kenwood and breathing heavily. 'I'm out of puff.'

'OK.' I put my hand on his arm, protectively. 'And . . . hey, thanks for talking to me about it, Malc. I know she's funny about my dad.' I swallowed. I wasn't sure where to start. 'Mum's very lucky.' I smiled at him, and he suddenly stepped forward and hugged me, crushing me into his be-zipped and multi-pocketed waterproof. I hugged him back, tightly, then we stood back, embarrassed.

'Bless you, Nina. And you know, all this business, I think it'll blow over. Sure, there are no coincidences, but it's all explained if you think this old woman got the wrong person, or she's just plain crazy. I honestly believe that.' I watched him, and knew he was telling the truth. He turned back and looked at the house and then he said, quietly, 'I know I'll never be him, you know.'

'Who?'

'The handsome explorer with the mysterious past who didn't return. It's fine. Your father's that person. The one she always remembers.'

'Oh, Malc. Do you really think that?'

'I do. But I only mean that sometimes we're better off leaving things as they are.'

'She's still in love with him, the idea of him?' I gazed at him. 'That's what you think? Malc, *you're* crazy—'

76

Then, suddenly, a voice behind us said, 'Nina? Malc? Hello! You two back on the Sunday walks, then?'

Someone touched me lightly on the shoulder, and I turned to see Sebastian.

They do this walk every Sunday, the Fairleys out in force, and they always end up at Kenwood, and Sebastian's Aunt Judy always stops off to look at the plants.

I'd hoped we might have missed them.

I don't know why I thought they'd have changed their routine: the Fairleys were, and are, set in stone, every act a little ritual of Fairley affirmation.

'Is that *Nina?*' said a voice I knew so well, behind us.

'Mama!' Sebastian called. 'Nina's here! With Malc!' I gazed at him helplessly, as he gave Malc a huge hug, then turned to me. 'Hello, Sally,' he said softly. 'I'm sorry about this.'

'*Gee willikers*,' whispered Malc, when he'd been released.

'*Gee willikers*, and this is *your* fault,' I hissed back at him. We stood there, immobile, watching the rest of the clan stride towards us, like the cast of a costume drama clad in Brora and Boden.

I was right, at any rate. And this was the reason I avoided the Heath.

Chapter Nine

'Nins!' Sebastian's sweet teenage sister, Charlotte, exclaimed, rushing forward and giving me a hug. 'Hello! It's been so long.' She brushed her long hair out of her face and stepped back, self-consciously, as her little brother, Mark, kissed my ear and mumbled awkwardly:
''Lo, Nina.'

'Hello, you two,' I said. 'Hi, Judy.' Judy was their father's sister, who lived with them, and who swam every day in the Hampstead Ponds.

Judy gripped my arm with a firm grasp. 'Jolly good to see you, Nina. And you, Malc.'

'You too, Judy.' Malc kissed her, then turned to Sebastian's mother, hovering behind the group. 'Well, Zinnia. What a surprise this is.'

'Yes!' I said brightly. 'What a surprise!'

'Nina. Darling, what a joy to see you.' Zinnia pulled me into a hug which comprised, as always, soft embroidered shawl, smooth powdered cheekbone and Givenchy Amarige. 'How extraordinary,' she said, in her thrilling low voice, 'when I've been thinking about you so much lately. Sebastian told me your flatmates left you rather high and dry so you've had to move back in with Delilah and Graham.'

'Well, it's only temporary,' I said, childishly keen to clarify. 'Elizabeth's sister bought a flat and asked her to share, and Leah got an amazing job working on a dig in Mexico, around the same time. We were all so sad to split the flat up.'

'Mmm,' said Zinnia, obviously not listening. She put her head on one side, periwinkle-blue eyes holding mine in her steady gaze. 'Wonderful.'

'Anyway, it's going well so far, isn't it, Malc? We haven't murdered each other . . . not yet,' I added, nerves making me giggle as Malc made strangling noises and rolled his eyes in mock disagreement.

'Ah,' Zinnia looked puzzled. 'Well, we *must* have you over, Nina. Why don't we ever see you?'

'You remember, Mama? The marriage? The divorce? The whole ex-wife shebang? The time you ordered her out of the house and called her a bitch?' Sebastian nudged me, jokily, but too hard, and I sort of lurched sideways into Malc's chest.

'Sebastian!' breathed young Charlotte in awe, eyes like saucers, looking from her mother to me.

There was a short, tense silence. Zinnia, rather magnificently, brushed this aside with one dismissive gesture of her white hand. She clutched my arm.

'Water under the bridge, darling, Nina knows that. Now, I met a marvellous children's author last week whom I'm sure you'd love—'

I waited for the invitation to lunch, wondering how I'd get out of it when it came. Some people collect Lalique, some people collect *Star Trek* figurines: Zinnia was a collector of people. Her weekend lunches at the Fairleys' house on the edge of the Heath were legendary. In my first year at UCL, already firm friends with Sebastian, I'd been invited to High Mead Gardens one Sunday. Everyone had known my name.

'Nina! Wonderful to have you here!' Sebastian's white-haired, stooping father, David, had cried, throwing open the front door and enveloping me in a great hug. (The Fairleys were very keen on enveloping hugs.) 'Come through! We're so pleased you could be here, Sebastian talks about you all the time. Would you like a gin and tonic? Don't mind the noise, we've just had the piano tuned and Claudio is trying it out.'

At that first lunch there had been an MP, a classical pianist, three other people who distinguished themselves by being quite posh-sounding, and two writers. I wasn't that impressed by the writers: Mum was a writer, after all. But I soon became aware they weren't writers like her. They were Writers: one was a novelist who'd been shortlisted for the Orange Prize and had a daughter called Goneril; the other wrote military history and kept dropping into Italian. Mum, for all her faults, never referred to anyone as '*simpatico*' and besides, she and I were united in our belief that King Lear was a terrible old man who deserved what he got.

As for the rest of it – the quail braised in red wine, the tennis court, the old mahogany furniture and the conversation at lunch, to which everyone, even ten-year-old Mark, was expected to contribute, and then listened to – the sheer exoticism of the whole thing was a revelation to me. I honestly didn't think people lived like that, not outside of books. Revelatory, too, was the idea that they were glad I was there. That Sebastian had talked about me. I really couldn't understand (and still don't, seven years on) why he'd singled me out, why we were already so close. I only knew that, for the first time, I felt like myself, not someone hiding in Mum's, or Mrs Poll's, or Jonas's shadow, the drab moth in a classroom full of butterflies.

I had sex with Sebastian for the first time, my first time ever, that day. In his room, walls lined with posters of books and black-and-white, brooding heroes: Brando, Hemingway, a poster from *The Graduate*. At teatime, dusky outside, almost dark, with the family all downstairs, the children noisily thumping out Beatles tunes on the piano. He made a cocoon of his duvet cover, and that first time, he came all over me, far too soon, and somehow that made everything all right, the sweet blush on his cheekbones, his vulnerability and humility when we were both under the sheets together, nervous, naked, full of grown-up wine and youthful, intense attraction. It made him human, and me the one who could help him. We stayed up there until eleven, laughing, doing it again and again, until he passed out, a sleeping lion, his fuzzy chest rising and falling as I stared at him in wonder. I felt as though I'd been sleepwalking, and now I was awake, alive to the world, everything making sense.

The following morning we crept out of the house together, me silently praying Zinnia and David wouldn't see me – I thought they wouldn't mind, but it was I who didn't want to answer questions, who didn't want the magical spell of the previous night to be broken.

We were married five months later, at the end of our first year at UCL. I was nineteen, he was twenty; we went to Islington Town Hall. I wore a white broderie anglaise cotton dress bought the previous day in H&M, £13.99. I still have it, but it's in Matty's room, hanging limply on a wire hanger at the back of the wardrobe.

It was just the two of us, and two witnesses: Sebastian bribed some guys in the Red Lion down the street. One of them had that hardened drinker aroma, of something rotten mixed with something sweet and fermenting, and to this day the smell of tramps, hungover colleagues, hot pubs all recall me instantly to our wedding day, my white cotton dress, his suit, his sweet blue polka-dotted tie, our hands white at the knuckles from clasping on to each other tightly during the ceremony. Though it was only the two of us, we really did take it seriously. It wasn't an ironic, Vegas-style wedding. We were absolutely sure. I thought of my parents, who were also young; they'd been sure, too. As I write this almost ten years later, I can still feel it, our certainty that it was the right thing. I have not and I think will never be in love like that again, you see.

Afterwards, the two of us shook hands with the witnesses, formally, and then hopped in a cab. We went to a tiny French restaurant in Shepherd Market for lunch and had champagne, bloody steaks, Béarnaise, salad and frites and then Sebastian, flushed with champagne and matrimonial pride, revealed he had booked us into Claridge's for the night. It was such a surprise, such a beautiful thing to do, but we got there and I knew instantly that the guilt would hit me unless we told our parents. In the lobby of this beautiful hotel, a little drunk, me in my slightly grubby cheap white dress and him trying to be a grown-up man: we played it all wrong. He was huffy that I wasn't more pleased; I was wrung out with nerves, fatigue, worry.

Perhaps that was when the fork in our marriage first appeared, that very moment, and we took the wrong path. We rang my parents and told them what we'd done, giggling and being slightly stupid, I think on purpose, to hide what we both knew, what had been glaringly apparent the moment, three hours earlier, when the registrar had released our hands and left us, facing each other, staring at our futures.

As I say, it's about ten years since I first met Sebastian and so now it feels like a substantial period of my young life. It didn't, for so long, and I think one craves those big chunks of time, as proof of stability and success. 'We've been married for three years *but* we'd been together for five years before that,' friends of mine say, when asked, as if only by demonstrating time do they convince the listener of their relationship's validity. By the time Sebastian and I had known each other for a year we'd been married three months. It makes me smile, to think of it, how back to front we got it, knowing as I do now what happened to us, later that summer.

Now, as Zinnia annexed Malc to ask him a question about some journalist she knew, Charlotte pulled at Sebastian's arm. 'Let's get some tea. Mark and I will bags a table.'

Sebastian glanced at me. 'Will you two come with us?'

'Perhaps not,' I said, looking at my watch. 'We told Mum we'd be back—'

'Fine . . .' Sebastian paused. 'Charlotte, why don't you run on ahead and get the table?'

'Sure. Bye, Nina.'

I blew her a kiss, and she dashed away.

Turning to me, Sebastian said, casually, 'Hey, I have to come by yours to collect a book I'm wanting to borrow off Malc. Do you fancy a drink next week? Thursday?'

'Oh,' I said, aware of Zinnia's eyes periodically flickering away from Malc and alighting on us. 'Well . . .'

I let myself really look at him for once, at his golden hair, the high cheekbones, flushed in the sun, those kind, toffee-coloured eyes, and the slightly too-large nose that made him human, knocked the perfection of the bone structure out a little, gave his handsome face a goofiness.

I remembered the first time I'd seen him, my second day at UCL. I was already late for my first class. I'd been staring with impotent panic at a map on a cork noticeboard in the Front Quad trying to work out where my Victorian Literature class was, frantically chewing a thumbnail.

He'd simply appeared beside me, and said, 'Hello! You're in my Fiction of the Indian Subcontinent seminar, aren't you? Are you Nina? Everything all right?'

I'd turned and looked at him and simply gazed, because he was –

ah, he was so beautiful. And so *nice*. I do not know how Sebastian came about, why he loved me. I only know I was lucky.

As we looked at each other now – we two, there in the sunshine and the blooming joy of spring, the unexpected reunion, the family around us – it didn't seem strange, being with him, or dangerous, exotic, or something to be consigned to the past, it seemed entirely natural, as it always had. In that moment I found myself thinking that I missed him: I missed everything about him.

'You keep changing the subject when I bring it up. I get the feeling you'd rather stay in for another night with your mum and Malc,' he said, half gentle, half serious. 'Look, I just wanted to say it's fine if you're not keen. It's just I miss you, Nins.'

I said, under my breath, 'Don't, Sebastian.'

'I do, though.' He said it lightly, and he was smiling, but his eyes were full of fear, like a little boy's. 'I . . . I know you once told me you'd rather have ringworm than a drink with me.'

'I never said that.'

'You did, and then you smashed the TV.'

'I didn't. You invited ten people for dinner when I had an exam the next day. I knocked the chair into the TV because you dodged. It's different.'

It was OK if I knew the rules. That we were doing this as banter, laughs, ha-ha, we're so mature. I was able to do that. But when he looked at me sometimes and when our eyes met, it was terrifying – like looking into a mirror of one's own deepest fears – and I couldn't (I still can't) stand to think about it, about how well he knew me, and how we still understood each other, because the ending had been so awful, so full of spite and blackness and hate.

It was my fault. I had always needed something to brood on, pick over, and a disintegrating marriage, a husband who's always out, who flirts and drinks with everyone, who couldn't save me in the way I afterwards realised I wanted him to, was perhaps my greatest subject. I aced it – I'd have got a first if I'd taken an exam.

'You want me to hate you!' he'd screamed at me, once, when he forgot my birthday and I stayed in bed all day. 'You're trying to make me fucking hate you, and I won't.'

Had I loved him? Yes, hugely. Painfully. Had he loved me? Yes, I know he did. So what went wrong? I don't think love's enough. I don't think we were ready. We thought it was our destiny, falling in love so young, marrying like that. I thought it was what I was born to do, the bookish, quiet girl who hadn't really lived – I believed this was my moment to fly. I was wrong: I thought he could save me, fill the gaps of everything else that was missing. You can't ask someone to save you like that. You have to do it together. I was the one who left, I was the one who slept with someone else – I was quite deliberate about it. I honestly thought it was the best thing to do, a pre-emptive strike to save myself from having my heart broken before he realised he could do so much better and went off and found someone else. Oh, it's so silly, written down like that, but that's how it felt.

It was painful to recall and yet when I looked at him, I could still remember the feeling of his skin on mine . . . his hands. His smile. How happy we were. How much he used to make me laugh; no one else has, before or since.

'Look,' I said eventually, 'we can have a drink on the Friday of Malc's birthday. But only if you come to the do afterwards. That's the deal. Then at least there'll be someone there I know to offset the ale-drinking crime reporters calling me dollface.'

'Sure,' he said and we smiled at each other, nodding together.

Zinnia broke in on us. 'Graham was just saying Delilah has several lectures next month, in Oxford. We must have him over for dinner. We can't have you starving on your own, Graham dear.'

'Oh, no!' Malc said, awkwardly.

'That'd be grand, Malc,' said Sebastian, giving him a light cuff on the arm. 'Hey, I loved that piece you wrote in *The Times* last week.'

'The house of horrors down the road from us? Oh, yes!' Malc nodded with pleasure and as they started to talk I shrugged, having a word with myself: *It's all fine! What a lovely day for a walk. How nice to see Sebastian, and to get on with him so well. And Judy, and Charlotte and Mark – even Zinnia; she's not so bad—*

And then Zinnia turned to me.

'Sebastian and I had such a strange encounter the other week, didn't he tell you about it?'

'No,' I said, smiling politely.

'Oh! How funny. I did want to talk to you about it.' Her eyes were fixed on me.

'Ah,' I said, unable to meet her eye. 'What did you want?'

'Well, it's more what you want, really, Nina, isn't it? We . . . yes, we met a very old friend of mine. Sebastian and I. We were walking through Flask Walk, because my lovely boy took me out to lunch for my birthday, and we were looking at a brooch I particularly wanted to buy, and suddenly Sebastian said . . .'

I'd almost stopped listening: Zinnia knows *everyone*, has been *everywhere*, and it can be quite hard to feign interest sometimes as she launches into a story about Prince Charles and Judi Dench at supper together. But then she cleared her throat and did an impression of Sebastian's relaxed growl.

'" . . . Mama, there's that strange woman from the Library. I saw her a couple of weeks ago, and it's been bothering me ever since, I'm sure we know her."'

She was watching for my reaction. I turned to Sebastian. He looked up, mid-conversation, as though he felt my eyes on him.

'You said you didn't know that woman,' I said.

'What woman?'

'The woman with the red tights in the library. The—'

'You mean Lise,' Zinnia said, easily. 'Lise Travers.'

Lise Travers. Her name is Lise. Not Teddy.

'Yep,' said Sebastian. 'I didn't recognise her. She looked totally different.'

'Well, darling, you hadn't seen her for ten years. I think that's fair enough.'

'Who's this?' Malc asked.

'Lise Travers,' Zinnia said again. 'She's an old friend of ours. How funny that she knows you, too!'

Malc looked blank.

'She doesn't know us,' I said. 'I don't know what she wants with . . . with me.' I swallowed. 'Did you talk to her?'

'Talk to her! She ran up to Sebastian and positively screamed at him that she'd known exactly who he was that day and how rude he'd been,' said Zinnia, rearranging her scarf. 'She's always been a little eccentric but I've never seen her like *that*. I don't know what you two said to her, Nina. She was terribly offended.'

'We weren't rude,' I said. 'We weren't . . . she said . . .' I swallowed, trying to gather my thoughts. 'Sorry, how do you know her, then?'

'We've known Lise for years,' said Zinnia, flatteningly. 'She worked with David on *Winds of the Raj*. She won the BAFTA . . .' She paused. *Winds of the Raj* was David's biggest film, the high-water mark of his career. The lead actress in it had won an Oscar. 'It's absolutely awful David didn't get anything. He *was* that film. For her to have won and not—'

I interrupted. 'She's an actress?'

'Oh, no,' Zinnia said, looking at me curiously. 'You really don't know who she is, then?'

'No, like I said, I've never seen her before. But she seems to know me.'

'Lise is a screenwriter. It's a shame, really. Rather a sad life. She never *quite* fulfilled her potential.'

In other circumstances, I would have smiled at the idea that a BAFTA-winning screenwriter didn't fulfil her potential. Zinnia looked over at Malc and smiled. 'Sorry about this, Malc. I'm afraid my son was very rude to an old friend of ours and she's taken it amiss.'

'No,' said Malc quietly, hands behind his back. 'Don't apologise to me.'

I said to Sebastian, 'Why didn't you tell me any of this?'

He looked confused. 'I was going to when we met for the drink. Sorry. Slipped my mind.'

And I remembered, I hadn't told him about the rest of it: the photographs, the book. I shrugged. 'Of course. No worries. Sure it's nothing.'

But Zinnia was still looking at me. There was a slight pause;

Sebastian turned back to Malc to finish their conversation, and she said, 'I wonder why she thinks she knows you.'

'I'm not sure. She knows something about my father. And my family. She's been trying to get in touch with me.' I threw caution to the winds. 'She says my father's not dead. I . . . I'm not sure if she's crazy or not. Do you, by any chance . . . do you have an address for her?'

'Oh, I'm sorry. No.'

'Nothing at all? Do you know where she lives?'

'Oh, in those flats on the other side of the Heath. The Pryors.'

The castle-like ones we'd walked past earlier. I rubbed my eyes.

Malc had stopped under a tree, and Sebastian was shaking his hand, making farewell gestures. In the distance, Charlotte had re-appeared and was calling out to him, something about tea. We were apart from them, at the edge of the slope.

'Zinnia, do you think you could get in touch with her for me? Find out if she wants to meet me again? I am getting rather desperate. It all seems so strange and—'

'Well, once again, no.'

'Sorry?' I said, not sure if I'd heard her correctly.

Zinnia leaned forward. Carefully, she pulled the embroidered wrap back over her shoulder. 'Dear Nina, don't take this amiss, but the fact is I simply don't want you in our lives.'

'What?'

'Please understand. I think it's best if we merely sail off in different directions.' She mimed pushing a toy boat off on a pond. 'This business of you two, having drinks, and so forth? These little extra connections, all of it, they're confusing, and upsetting. You mustn't waste his time. He was . . . you nearly broke him, I told you this at the time. You and he need clear blue water, to continue the meta-phor. A lot of clear blue water.'

I took a couple of steps back, as if she'd kicked me. 'But . . . you were the one who wanted to see *me*,' I said, rubbing the bridge of my nose, trying not to show how much this upset me. 'I don't understand—'

'Well,' she said evenly. I wanted to lay this all before you. Explain why it's for the best that you . . . you leave him alone, darling. It's difficult, I know. I really don't want to be unpleasant about it.'

I gave a short laugh.

'There, you see.' There was a tiny, glistening fleck of spit on her upper lip. After a pause she said softly, 'Nina, if you were my daughter-in-law I'd do everything in my power to support you. If you were the mother of his children I'd kill for you. But you're his ex-wife, it's been two years, and I think it's time for you to just . . . yes, push the boat on, sail away. That's why I don't want to help you. Do you understand, darling?'

I have come to admire Zinnia, over the years, and I admire her for this, strangely enough. It takes guts, or virtual insanity, to be so brazen.

'I understand,' I said. 'If you're determined not to help me . . . fine. Thank you for being honest, anyway.'

'Oh, not at all,' she said, as if we were chatting at a cocktail party. Her face relaxed. 'And really, darling, while we're on the subject, I think it's best if you forget about Lise, too. It's not fair to her. She's very confused about you, my dear.'

'Yes, I understand,' I said, trying to sound casual. 'What did she say to you?'

'Oh,' Zinnia said with a small laugh, 'well, for starters, darling, she kept referring to you as "Teddy".'

'Teddy? Really?' I said, as the others came up to us. 'How funny.' Then I shrugged, trying to hide the sudden anger that surged over me, wondering how best to deflect it. 'I'm sorry again if we embarrassed you. Oh, Sebastian.' I poked him gently.

'Oh, Nina.'

'I'll be in touch about next week. I'd love that drink.' I didn't look at Zinnia. I knew I was being childish – and yet, wasn't she? If I wanted to see him, what was the harm? Was I doing him harm? Was I the destructive force of nature she seemed to be implying I was?

But she was silent, as Sebastian nodded. 'Great,' he said.

And then suddenly Zinnia added, 'Yes, poor Lise. Oh, what was it she said to you, darling?' She turned to Sebastian.

He shrugged, looking at me curiously. 'Don't know.'

'I remember it. "Teddy did something bad." Kept saying it. "I read all about it. She did something really bad."' She was a good mimic, and the hairs on my skin and neck rose. I shivered in the sun.

'She does sound mad,' I said, carelessly. 'Well, I'm not Teddy, so it's all easily explained, isn't it? Say goodbye to Judy for me, it was lovely to see her again. And Mark and Charlotte.'

I had loved Charlotte, with her shy eyes and thick, long chocolate hair, and for a moment, I felt overcome – the realisation that I probably wouldn't see them again hitting me. 'Thank you, Zinnia.' I kissed her cold, perfumed cheek. 'Goodbye.'

She turned, sliding her arm through her son's.

As we walked off, Malc said, 'What did she want? Have you sold her one of your organs? Is she regenerating herself using some monkeys you're breeding for her?'

'Rehash the past,' I said, walking on so he didn't see my red face. 'Just some World of Zinnia nonsense. But she's right, and you're right. That poor old lady. I won't bother her, if I see her again.'

Malc caught up with me and slung his arm around my shoulder, as we turned south. 'Well, perhaps she's right. Pains me to say it. You know, I love Sebastian, but I'll never understand why you married into that family.'

Chapter Ten

She wasn't at the London Library on Monday, or any day the following week after our encounter with the Fairleys, though I went there every lunchtime, and every evening after work when it was open late. I'd stand still on the first and second floors, looking around for her, waiting in case she came to find me. But there was no sign of her. No record of her in the phone book, though I'd read all about her glittering screenwriting career (two BAFTAs, one Oscar nomination, umpteen awards). I rented *Winds of the Raj,* and *Mabel and Prudence,* and *By Hook or by Crook,* her three best-known films, watching them in my room on my laptop. Looking for messages, clues, signs that weren't there.

As May turned into June and Malc's birthday rolled around, I started to wonder if perhaps they were all right, all of them. But to give up on finding her was like giving up on some dream of another life for myself, a new version of me, someone who had more to her than twelve copies of the same book, scattered friends she never saw, an ex-husband, a stalled career. And so I didn't listen to the voices that told me I was wrong, laughed at me in my sleep, waiting in dark corners for others to disperse, and then fell upon me, mocking my own story-from-a-children's-book imagination. I kept on waiting in the library for her.

Several times, I went back to Hampstead and walked past the row of castle-flats, wondering which building was hers, praying she'd emerge, like Sleeping Beauty. I'd stand out there in the early evening, on the edge of the long grasses that waved and tickled my shins, watching Londoners purposefully striding back home from work: backpacks, trainers, sunglasses, everyone hurrying somewhere, the place they needed to be. And I'd wait until it began to get dark, leaning against a tree reading Agatha Christie and glancing up every thirty seconds, just to make sure she hadn't walked past. Nothing.

I knew it was strange. But no one asked me where I'd been. So not with a bang but a whimper, gradually the time came when it all seemed rather pointless, and slowly I stopped going to the Heath, to the London Library. One day, then two, then three went by and every day I'd be surprised at myself but I wouldn't go. I'd read at my desk, or chat to Sue, or traipse around the shops with Becky. Every evening I'd go home, pretending it was good I wasn't obsessing about her any more. I pushed the photographs, carefully placed in an envelope inside *Nina and the Butterflies*, further under my bed, where the book nestled against thick, plump balls of dust. I told myself it was sensible behaviour, that I'd feel better this way.

The first Friday in June was Malc's birthday and, by coincidence, Bryan Robson's too. That two such nice men should share a birthday pleased me; it seemed to disprove Malc's own theory and remind me once again that coincidences great and small are everywhere. That lunchtime I went to Tesco, to choose cupcakes for Bryan, whose birthday we were marking with a little tea party that afternoon, and something for Malc, to hide the fact I hadn't got around to buying him a present.

At around ten to two I cut through St James's Square, almost defiantly, carrying my haul of cakes. I glanced up at the windows of the library, but didn't stop.

The sound of a car horn from that corner made me look around again. A black cab had drawn up outside the library, and a young woman got out. She had thick, honey-blonde hair in a ponytail, and was dressed in sensible sports gear – trainers, a dazzling white top, wicking leggings. Her manner, as she opened the cab door, was one of brisk efficiency. I watched her, idly – some billionaire's nursemaid or secretary, back from a spending spree in New Bond Street – as she flicked away with a dismissive gesture a rude white van driver honking at them for holding him up, then with admiration as she helped someone out of the cab, still keeping her cool.

As the cab drove off, she and Lise Travers were left on the pavement together, and the younger woman said something to the older one, who seemed to nod, then turned and walked up the steps, hurriedly, though she moved slowly. The younger woman watched her for a moment, then turned away.

I stood still, rooted to the spot. I thought about approaching her, but after she'd walked past me, I ran towards the library entrance, as fast as I could.

Later that afternoon, when I'd return to the office, Sue would ask me, 'But where are Bryan's cakes, Nina?' and I'd shake my head, aghast, apologetic. I wonder to this day what I did with them, and with Malc's pirate cake. Possibly I dropped them on the ground in the park, where they were devoured by hungry office workers or pigeons. I don't know: I have no memory of it.

I know that I raced up the steps, swiping my card in a frenzy of impatience – *Please don't have vanished again, please* – and that I took the stairs to the second floor two at a time, dashing an old gent in a linen suit practically against the wall, frantic until I saw her, or rather the flash of red, disappearing into the Stacks again, the door banging shut behind her.

Carefully, silently now, I opened the door. I wanted to make sure it was her and I didn't know if she'd want to see me.

And then: 'Teddy? Teddy?' came a soft, sing-song whisper. '*Teddy! Are you there?*'

Feet padding slowly along the metal-grille floor, as I saw someone below, looking up through the slats at her, as she walked, pacing up and down, calling quietly. To herself? To me?

'*Teddy? Where are you, Teddy?*'

I cleared my throat, to let her know someone was here, and the shuffling footsteps stopped. I walked past the first passageway of shelves – nothing. I could feel her, sense her. The next – nothing.

I cleared my throat again, and said softly, 'Miss Travers? It's me. Nina.'

And I heard her, then, the next row along. She was crooning, half singing, half mumbling.

> . . . Little old Teddy, the last girl you see.
> All of them butterflies, and then only me.
> All of them butterflies, and then only me.

'Miss . . . Miss Travers?' I moved towards her, a foot or so, and she pivoted around towards me, like a cornered animal. She was tiny, and so much older than I'd realised. Her eyes seemed bigger than ever.

'You!' She pointed at me. 'You're back. I was looking for you . . .' She paused and glanced around. 'That dreadful woman, she's not with you, is she?'

'No,' I said, trying not to smile. I knew exactly who she meant. 'She's not.'

'Ach. I loathe her. You know her?' She peered at me.

'I was married to her son. I'm sorry we were so rude to you, Miss Travers.'

She held her hands out in a dismissive gesture, still leaning flat against the shelves. 'No matter. He was showing off. He's a nice boy. I remember him. Handsome. He has large ears.' She chuckled.

'May I ask you something?' I said, after a moment's pause.

She nodded. 'Of course you may.'

'I have your photographs. Why did you give them to me? Do you want to tell me something?'

'What photographs?'

I cursed my stupidity for not keeping them with me, at all times. 'The young girl, on the boat. And the girl and her mother, going butterfly hunting.'

She smiled, politely. 'I'm so sorry. I don't know of any photographs.' She looked around. 'That woman isn't with you, is she? Awful woman.'

It was like being on a roller coaster: my head spun. 'No, Miss Travers. She's not. The girl in the photographs – you said she was called Teddy.'

Lise Travers stopped. 'Teddy.' She shuffled towards me, so that we were inches apart and I curled my neck, looking down at her. 'Yes, I do know you. Poor Teddy. Will you tell her, will you tell her it's OK?'

'I . . . I don't know Teddy.'

'Yes, you do. I saw you with her.'

'No,' I said, unhappily. 'No, you didn't.'

'I saw you with her. In the park.'

I said, slowly, 'Miss Travers, I don't know who Teddy is. I'm trying to find out who she is, you see. If she's something to do with my family . . . my father. You said you knew my father. You said he wasn't dead, and then you wrote on the back of the photograph, "That is your family. You don't know them and what they did."' I was trying not to sound impatient, or desperate. 'It was you who wrote that, wasn't it? I'm sure it was you. What do you want to tell me?'

Her eyes were like molten metal, grey, black, steely, and she shook her head, still watching me, still peering up towards me. I heard footsteps, overhead.

'I did see you in the park with Teddy. You were playing hide and seek.'

'*I don't know Teddy*,' I hissed, and I thought I might howl then. 'Who is she?'

She blinked, and something seemed to change in her stormy expression. 'Oh . . . I don't know. Do you know Al? Did you remember Al? Teddy knew Al—' Then she shook her head and, with a frank, crooked, heartbreaking smile, she shrugged. 'I am sorry, then. If it wasn't you. In the park. I forget things, you see. Look.'

Fumbling in the pocket of her black skirt, she handed me a piece of laminated card.

> You are Alice Mary Travers.
> When watch beeps, turn it off.
> Pack everything away.
> Wait for Abby downstairs in the lobby.
>
> DON'T GO WITH ANYONE.
> DON'T GIVE ANYONE ANYTHING.

I reached out and took her hand, then stroked it. I said, 'Don't worry. It doesn't matter.'

'Yes, yes,' she said. 'It jolly well does. When I'm lucid, I'm furious about it.' She gave me the glimmer of a smile. 'Look, what did you want to tell me?' And I noticed she was softly tapping her foot on the metal floor.

'Please, please don't worry,' I said again. 'It's fine. It doesn't matter. I'll wait with you until your watch beeps. I'll wait for Abby.'

'No,' she said, suddenly agitated. 'She comes to pick me up. I look at the books and I walk around the Stacks and I count to thirty. I have my routes. You mustn't interrupt my routes. You must leave me alone. Abby comes to pick me up.'

I said, 'Of course. I'm so sorry—'

'You don't know Teddy, then? You don't know what she did? I wish you did. I wish you could tell me. She did something terrible. Terrible . . .' She looked down at her hands and then, almost ferociously, like a little rodent, nibbled at an old, horny hangnail. 'Goodbye. Goodbye, then. Please go. Oh, please go.'

'Nina,' I said. 'My name's Nina.'

She sang softly, '*Nina Parr, locked herself in.*'

I stiffened. 'What's that song?'

'What?'

'What's that song? You were singing? And at the beginning?'

It was like trying to catch a shadow; she just smiled at me again.

I scribbled a quick message on a Post-it note – *Dear Abby, if you have time, please call me on this number below. I know Miss Travers from the library and would very much like to discuss something with you – Thanks –* I didn't sign my name. I don't know why. I stuck it on the back of the laminated card, then slid it into her pocket. She was perfectly still, as though she was used to people handling her.

'Thank you, Miss Travers.'

'Sure, sure, very sure. Thank you for the cup of tea. That's what Mark said, after we got married. Thank you for the cup of tea. To the waitress. Thank you for the cup of tea.' She laughed. 'Thank you, too, I have to go to India. That awful woman will be there.'

I shook her hand and walked away, tears blinding me. Blinking them furiously away, I stood in the doorway in the shadows and watched her for a little while, wondering if she seemed familiar, if she could be my relative, what she knew that I could not unlock. I watched her too to make sure she was OK. I wondered how often she was left on her own like this, whether this was a good day or a bad day for her. I tried to make it all fit, to see some sense in any of it – and nothing stuck.

After a while I looked around me, realising I was standing back outside the entrance to the office with no recollection of how I'd got there and also, I registered with horror, no cakes. It was two thirty. I went back upstairs to the first-floor offices.

'But where are Bryan's cakes, Nina?' Sue said.

I sat down heavily in my chair. 'I'm sorry, Sue. I bought them but I left them . . .' I trailed off. 'I don't know. I'm sorry. Something happened at lunch today.' I was smiling – I couldn't explain it if I wanted to, without sounding mad – and I started to wonder if this was it, if I was just mad.

Sue came over to me, and put her arm around my shoulders. 'What's up with you lately, my love?' She stroked my hair. 'What is it? Don't you worry. Oh, don't cry now. I'll go and get some more. Don't be silly, sweetheart! It's only cake,' she said kindly, into my hair, giving me a comforting squeeze and I found myself hugging her back. 'Oh, love. You mustn't get so upset about things. Becky, sit with Nina for a bit, will you?'

Becky was standing in the doorway, consternation on her face. She waddled towards me, her huge belly right by my face, and patted me, reassuringly, as I wiped my eyes. 'Sure,' she said, as Sue put on her coat. 'Listen to Sue, Nina. It's only cake.'

'Thanks,' I said, sitting up straight. 'I'm sorry. Something a bit weird happened . . . I'll just check the messages. I'm fine, honestly.'

I felt, but didn't see, the looks Becky and Sue exchanged.

Chapter Eleven

'You're still on for coming back to Mum's tonight?' I said to Sebastian, that evening, as we sat in the Charles Lamb nursing our second drink of the night. 'I have to be there by eightish.'

He said nothing.

'Malc's birthday thing,' I reminded him.

'Oh. Yes, that's fine.'

I stared at him, at his almost comically gloomy face sunk heavily on to his hand. *He has large ears.* 'Hey. You've hardly said a word all evening. What's up?'

'Nothing much.' He sat up, and shook his head, waggling it around, rolling it back and forth like an athlete limbering up for the final stage of something. 'Just thinking.'

I knew it was my fault, actually. I was being too manic, talking incessantly, wanting to get the drink out of the way, then get to Malc's, then get to bed, so this day would be over. 'It'll be fun,' I said. 'You love parties. I love parties.'

'You don't go to parties any more,' he pointed out. 'You're Nina 2.0. Updated version.'

'How do you mean?'

He smiled at me, suddenly more alert. 'You don't remember the old you. Those grey Doc Martens and the poncho, with your legs in those cut-offs, and the long shaggy hair and the fringe. You were all angry about everything and so sure you were right, and your pupils used to dilate when you got worked up. It was incredibly sexy.'

'Oh, be quiet.' I knew he was joking, but I wished he wouldn't.

'It's true!' he said, earnestly.

'Well, I must have been insufferable,' I said, briskly. 'And now?'

Sebastian said vaguely, 'Well, you know. You live the life of a hermit. You're back to being teenage you, before you met me.'

'How arrogant! When I moved in with Elizabeth and Leah after you, I wasn't a hermit. I was pretty crazy I can tell you.'

'You went to the pub twice a week and you dated a man who had a pet rabbit he took with him to university. Sure. Kerrrrr-ay-zeee,' said Sebastian, sarcastically.

There was an edge to his voice, as ever when Tim – the extremely serious Beowulf obsessive who was the one I'd slept with when we were still married and then gone out with for a few months – came up. 'Oh, don't start on Tim,' I said easily. 'Where's Tim now?'

'Oh yeah.' He nodded, more cheerfully. It was true that Tim had been stripped of his PhD after allegations of plagiarism were proven and now worked in the Camden Nando's, where Sebastian occasionally liked to go and order a Wing Roulette off him if he needed cheering up. 'You're right. Let me get you another drink.'

I nodded. 'Definitely. Make it a double vodka, is that OK?'

'She's back!' he yelled. 'Watch out, North London! Lock up your *Secret Garden*-loving sons! Nina Parr's out on the lash!'

'Oh, shut up,' I said, shoving him towards the bar.

For the rest of the evening we avoided topics like Zinnia – and indeed families in general. We talked about Leah's job in Mexico (which made us sick with envy), his job, my job (less so, though he always dutifully asked), books we were reading, TV programmes we both enjoyed. Soliciting his opinion on things I liked was always interesting, because we often disagreed, violently, but on what, one could never quite predict. We had another drink, then another, and by then it was eight thirty and I said we should go, but the warm, softly lit pub was so cosy, and the rhythm of the evening was just right: Sebastian's body curved forward towards me, his long limbs sprawled around the tiny circular table, me leaning back against the wooden bench, laughing my head off with him.

The trouble with drinking vodka, lime and soda on an empty stomach after a long, odd day is that you don't ever start to feel drunk – not in a lurching, spinning way – you just get more and more relaxed and it was dusk, nearly dark, before I looked out of the window, realising with horror we were late.

So we stumbled out on to the pavement. It was a warm summer's night and out on the street someone was playing 'Moondance' by Van Morrison – the first time that year I'd heard music floating out of an open window. I felt warm, free, silly, the strangeness of the past few weeks receding. Everyone needs to go out and get a bit drunk now and then, chat to an old friend. I spread my arms wide.

'You've got a crisp on your shoulder,' said Sebastian, brushing it off.

I caught his hand in mine. 'Thanks,' I said, recklessly, squeezing his hand. 'Oh, Sebastian. Thanks.'

He stopped in the street and I stopped behind him. 'For what?' he asked.

'For . . . everything. I don't know what I'd do about you.'

'*About* me?' He laughed, and moved towards me. 'I thought you were going to say something nice, for once.'

'You know I can't do *that*,' I said, trying to sound flippant.

We were standing in the middle of the quiet road. 'You can't say anything nice about me?' Sebastian said. 'Not one single thing?'

I started walking. 'You know that's not what I meant.'

'What did you mean?'

'I meant we're old friends, and what would I do without you, because you understand me, I understand you . . .'

We'd reached the end of the road, where the canal ran ahead of us. A barge slid through the water, sleek and silent in the darkness. A bat, disturbed by its passage, fluttered out from the bridge up between us, and Sebastian gave an unexpected yelp.

'. . . I know you hate bats, for example,' I said, and he came towards me, and we were perfectly still, by the railings.

He put his hand on my shoulder and gently touched my collarbone with his thumb. Slowly, we looked at each other.

'Nina, can I ask you something? Do you still think we should be honest with each other?'

I blinked, foggily. 'What?'

'You and me. We promised we always would. Always tell the truth, always be honest. And I don't think we are sometimes. Do you agree?'

'Well, I . . . I don't know.' I saw his expression, and I was nineteen again, holding his fingers tightly and kneeling up in my bed at Mum's just after he'd asked me to marry him. 'Yes. You're right. We should be honest.'

'Good. Here goes.'

'Here goes what?'

Sebastian's face was half shadow, half light. 'I'm still in love with you.'

My heart started to thump insistently in my chest. 'Sebastian. Don't.'

He took my hands. 'I wanted to be s-sure that it wasn't regret, or hankering after the wrong thing. But I am, I can't help it. We're . . . we're just right for each other.'

'Sebastian, no, we're—'

Always be honest with me, that's what he'd said when he'd proposed. *Don't ever lie.*

'Let me finish this, will you?' he pleaded. 'Then I won't say it again. I know we're different. I know I'm posh and blond and bois-terous and make you want to crawl into a hole with embarrassment. But you need someone like that, Nina. You need someone who's the sunshine, who keeps you outside. Because you're the moon – oh, I'm *not* drunk, I know it sounds cheesy. But it's honestly how I see it. That's why we liked each other in the first place, wasn't it? Didn't it work, at first, us being so different? The first time I saw you, and you were curled over and chewing your cardigan sleeves and all bowed head and shyness and I just . . . You always looked so uneasy, like you thought you didn't belong and I knew, I knew I was the one who could make you feel all right, relaxed, at home.' His eyes were shining. 'I knew it right away.'

Here was the answer I'd sought for almost six years.

'And I don't want anyone else. I want you. Me and you, back together again. Don't you think about it, sometimes?'

How can I explain it, how it felt far more terrifying than the first time around? It had never been terrifying before. It was dramatic, funny, drunken, daring. This meant something else. Our lives, stretching out ahead of us. Him and me, walking towards the horizon, the great question of one's life answered.

My mouth was dry. 'I don't know. Maybe. It's not conscious, if I do. More, I . . . I always think you'll be there, that we'll be friends, you and me . . . not married, because it didn't . . . it didn't suit us . . .' I trailed off.

'Don't think about the things that didn't work. We were really young and we were really stupid. You know we should be together. You know it. We're . . . we fit.'

I wanted to believe it, so much. I *did* believe it. I leaned forward and touched my lips to his, there underneath the street lamp's light. I could feel my heart thumping, it seemed to be somewhere in my stomach. My arms hung limply by my sides. He pushed me against the railings and I nodded, a cry of something in my throat: I was aware of nothing else for a few moments, only the feeling of him against me, the taste of him in my mouth, the sensation of him all over again, like falling, falling into a bottomless pit where soft, plush pillows of goose feathers waited.

I heard, in the silence, the tiny clicks and calls of something and I looked up, to see three boys on tiny bicycles, the ones who rode around all day with seemingly nothing to do. Their hands were always free, texting, their hoods always up, and if you even glanced at them they stared at you with naked, brazen aggression. One of them, in a tatty green hoody, called in a low voice, 'Stuff her good, blud!'

We stood apart, awkwardly, and another one laughed.

I waved at him. 'Hi,' I said.

He looked discomfited; I think if I'd been sober I wouldn't have known what to do. They were always around and they liked the fact that, though they were about twelve, they seemed sinister. But I'd known him since he was a baby in a pink buggy, being pushed along the street by his mum. He had a badly corrected harelip, and thick brown hair. He'd be at the playground on Graham Street where my mum used to take me too, and where bigger children gather in the evenings, some up to no good: the police were always being called out because of them. They'd set fire to canal barges, mug people on the towpath. I hadn't seen his mum for a while, not since I'd moved back in. Mostly he was just alone, on a far-too-small bike.

One Halloween he'd come Trick or Treating to our house. He had a Tesco's bag in one hand. His hoody that night was orange, curiously seasonal, and filthy. He'd egged our door because we'd run out of treats, and when he asked for money instead Malc said no. We didn't wipe off the egg until it was too late, and so it warped the red paint, pieces of shell gripping the wood like a mini-mosaic.

I'd never spoken to him apart from that Halloween. Did he recognise me? We lived a hundred yards from each other, but he'd have no idea who I was, other than being someone who lived in one of those posh houses that backed on to the canal.

'Come on,' said Sebastian in my ear, pressing his hand around my waist, as the boys rode on, one of them upping his bike on to one wheel with a whirling motion, flicking something in the air. 'Let's go.'

'OK,' I said, clutching my hand to his waist too, and we crossed the bridge, in the sudden cool of the early summer. At the corner we joined hands, and walked slowly up the road. Figures moved around in their basement kitchens, lighted warmth pooling up to us on the street above. Someone cycled past behind us – I remember it all, very precisely, in fact.

'Should I come in?' Sebastian asked me, as we reached the front door.

'Of course you should,' I said. 'Mum will fall upon you like the prodigal son. Brian Condomine and Barty what's-his-name'll be there. The Websters from down the road, you like Lorelei, she's the one you used to flirt with—'

'Don't avoid the issue.' He grasped my hands. I loved him in that moment, his seriousness, how good he was. 'It's that if I come in, then it's your family and us. And we could slip into something again, and if it went wrong then it'd just be really shit.' He leaned forward, and whispered in my ear. 'Listen to me, stop mucking around. I'm still in love with you.'

'I know, Sebastian, but—'

'But you're not in love with me.'

'I don't know,' I said, bluntly. 'I don't know. I wish I was. Is that enough?'

'You wish you were?'

'Yes. And then I'm scared. Because we were horrible to each other. And the end of it . . .' I closed my eyes. 'I loved you so much, Sebastian. I don't know if I can do it again.'

'Oh.' There was an awkward silence and he gave a small, warm laugh. 'There's a man in your basement wearing a pirate hat.'

I looked down. Three people, possibly more, holding wine glasses, chatting in a rather desultory-looking fashion.

'Malc loves—'

'He loves pirates. I know. I've got him a book on Sir Francis Drake.' He pulled it out of his backpack.

I stared at the book. 'You are amazing. You—' I leaned forwards and kissed him again.

'So now you like me because you haven't got him a present and you want to pass mine off as yours.'

'No!' I said, smiling at him, as footsteps approached again. 'Oh, it's more than that, it's . . .' I grabbed his hands. 'Look. I need some time. Let me—'

The footsteps stopped, and we both turned around, angrily. A tall figure loomed in the darkness, peering at the front door. 'I'm so sorry,' he said softly. 'This is Delilah Parr's house, isn't it?'

'Yes?' said Sebastian, half interrogatively, still staring at me.

'Ah. Well, I'm a friend of . . . of theirs,' said the stranger, slightly taken aback. 'I've come to see—'

'Oh, are you Barty? I'm sorry. We're just going in,' I said, unlocking the door. Sebastian squeezed my hand. 'Are you coming in too?' I asked him, in a low voice.

'I'm not Barty,' said the strange man. 'Are you Nina?'

Footsteps sounded in the hallway, up from the kitchen. Mum flung the front door open. 'Darling! You're here. And is that Sebast—'

Then she stopped.

'No,' she said. 'No.'

Behind me, Sebastian said, 'Hello, Dill. Sorry to—'

But Mum was staring at the stranger. All the blood had drained instantly from her bone-white face. I have never seen anything like it, before or since, and I knew then.

The man said, 'You haven't changed, Delilah.'

'Mum, who is this?' I said.

Mum leaned forward, into the darkness. 'Why have you come back?' she whispered. 'Why now?'

'This is a shock, I know.' The man smiled, nervously. 'But I really wasn't sure how else to get hold of you, Dill. You didn't answer my letters . . .'

A heavy tread thundered on the stairs and Malc appeared behind Mum. 'Hello?' he said, pleasantly. 'Who's this?' He glanced at Mum, then me.

The stranger took this as a cue to move towards the doorstep. I backed into the house, able to see him more clearly in the light from the hall. He was tanned and ruddy, his hair bleached blond, his eyes a strangely incongruous dark brown.

'I'm George Parr,' he said. 'I'm . . . well, actually, I'm her husband, as a matter of fact. Who are you?'

I couldn't tear my gaze away from my father. All I could think was: *She wasn't lying to me. She was telling the truth.*

Mum was still staring at him. 'Why . . . why?' she said, under her breath. 'George, why?'

His smile faded and he looked around. 'Can't we go inside?'

Mum folded her arms; she was shaking. She said, in a tiny voice, 'No, George. You can't come in. What do you want?'

'I . . .' He gave a small laugh. 'Seems rather odd, saying it like this. Ah . . . I . . . I want a divorce.'

'You can have one. Just get out,' Mum said, more loudly.

He looked at me. 'I came back because of Nina, too. There's something I need to tell her.' He smiled at me. 'Nina. Hello, there.' He nodded at Sebastian, who folded his arms. 'Look, I am sorry about all this. Must be incredibly strange for you, me turning up on your doorstep.' He pointed down. 'Quite literally!' he said, almost jovially. 'Believe me, I didn't really plan to arrive like this. My plane was delayed, and I had trouble with the . . . I do see it is awfully late.' He cleared his throat, silenced by my mother's glare. 'The old house looks the same, I see.' I followed his gaze.

The front window had a little crack in the pane of glass where Mrs Poll and I used to stick up pictures about my day at school for my dad to see, face out, so that he could look down and see them from heaven. I'd cracked that pane one day being too firm with the Sellotape. The glass was original, and so we hadn't replaced it.

I shook my head. 'You knew he wasn't dead, Mum?' I said, very softly.

'Delilah, you told her I was dead?' said my father, swivelling around towards her.

'Of course I did! What else was I to do?'

'Tell her the truth?' His eyes flashed, then he turned back to me. 'You look like her,' said my father suddenly. 'Not at first, but yes — I see it. You really do.'

'Who?'

'Of course. I should explain. My mother. Teddy.'

Mum was twisting her fingers around and around. She drew in a great, heaving breath and then exhaled with a sob, as though she'd been holding her breath for years. 'Listen, George. I'll say this again. It's Malc's birthday. We've got guests downstairs. You can't come in.'

We've got guests downstairs — it does make me smile, in amidst the awfulness of it all. My hand sought out hers, and I slid my fingers into her open palm. She grasped hold of me so tightly I heard my bones crack.

But George Parr ignored her. He smiled at me and I smiled back, involuntarily, mesmerised by him. 'So, look. You really don't know any of it, then? About me, and Keepsake? And where you come from?'

'No,' I said.

'You don't know what happens to you, this summer?'

'George,' Mum stood up straight. 'For the last time—'

'Mum,' I broke her hand-grip. 'Let him finish. It's fine if you're really making him come back tomorrow. But for God's sake, please let him say what he wants to say, and then he can leave.' I nodded, looking back at him. 'Go on, then . . .' I trailed off. *George? Dad?*

'At the end of this summer you turn twenty-six. That's right, isn't it?'

I nodded, strangely pleased that he remembered it.

'She got it when she was twenty-six. They all did. The girls, that is. Only girls. The whole damn place is yours then.'

'What place?'

'Keepsake, all of it. It belongs to you. And it's time you knew about it.' He peered through the door, looking down at me. 'My dear girl, you're a Parr. That means something.'

The Butterfly Summer

by

Theodora Parr

For Al and for my son, George
In the hope that they understand it all a
little better afterwards

In the gallery at Keepsake, looking out towards the sea, there is a portrait of my ancestor Nina Parr. There are so many legends about Keepsake that it can be hard to separate fact from fiction but this – the most gruesome one of them all – happens to be true: in 1651, after the Civil War finally ended with his disastrous defeat at Worcester, Charles II sought sanctuary here. He came at dead of night, by horse and then boat, slicing silently along the Helford river and up the creek to our house. He would be safe in Cornwall. He knew we Cornish loved our King. Had we not fought with him at Lostwithiel? Had we not risen up only three years previously for him, not two miles from this very house?

Nina welcomed him though she was alone in the house, save the servants. Her parents had died, her mother of dropsy, her father killed in the wars that tore England apart. Her fiancé, a Grenville, was hanged at Plymouth. She had no one, until the King came here.

He stayed three weeks. We know nothing much of those weeks, though I have imagined her and him often; sometimes I think I hear them laughing together in forgotten, dusty, corners of this secretive house. Sometimes I hear them in the garden. I used to wonder where was the first place he took her. They fell in love, that we do know.

After the King left, Nina was distraught. Her maid told afterwards of how she would not eat. How he rode away with her kiss on his lips and a lock of her hair and a promise that Keepsake should be hers forever.

In the history of that terrible war, our role in it, however small, has been overlooked and what happens next is also known only to us: Nina was silent for many months and then gave birth to the King's child, a pregnancy she concealed from the household until her time was upon her. A few months after her daughter was born, and quite disordered in her mind, Nina dismissed all the servants save the nursemaid, and walked into the tiny family chapel, the place where the King himself had hidden when the Roundheads came looking for him. She had herself bricked in, the men weeping as they obeyed her. Then she slowly starved to death.

She gave her baby daughter's wet nurse Matty wax earplugs, so that the poor woman would not hear Nina, pleading to be released. But the nurse caught the sounds of her sometimes, poor girl. She said she took a long time to die. That she was delirious, and thought she saw the King again, and other things too: sea serpents and bright lights.

Matty was Nina's childhood friend and companion and they loved each other; she had lost a child and was glad to suckle her mistress's. But each time she went to her, Nina always called out, 'Leave me to die.'

Broken-hearted, Matty eventually left with the babe and moved outside to the old ice house, now our Butterfly House. When she returned after a week, there was silence.

Nina had written to the King begging him to return. She never saw the letter he wrote in reply, which we keep deep in the most secret part of the house. I have his signature next to me as I write this, his declarations of love, his explanation of the brilliant, beautiful diamond-and-gold butterfly brooch he sent her. *Read well the inscription, my lady.* By this we know that the King loved her. *What's loved is never lost,* it said.

It's a lie though. I do not have his brooch any more. That was lost. It was lost by me, when I lost everything.

This is the house I grew up in. When I was a child, my father had a staircase removed at the edge of the house, where long ago another ancestor of mine – Rupert the Vandal, Nina's great-great-grandson and much given to demolishing parts of the ancient house – had knocked down a medieval wing, the bones of which still remained in my early years.

My father wanted this last vestige of the ancient house tidied up: he hated disorder. My mother begged him not to, but he insisted.

By the time even of my childhood Keepsake had been crumbling for years; cracks had appeared in the crenellations that ran around the top of the house. The wall of the North Wing, exposed since Rupert's renovations, had a fissure an inch wide, where the ivy had got in. The house stands at the head of a creek, and is built on clay and sand – its foundations are not stable.

Though it was my mother's house, my father's will, as always, prevailed, but my grandmother, who was able to stand up to him, demanded she be the one to look inside. Behind the staircase they found the old chapel, long thought demolished or a fiction, no bigger than a small larder. When my grandmother wrenched the door open and finally entered she found a female skeleton there, kneeling in prayer, rosary in hand, and on the wall drawings of hundreds of butterflies, scratched in brick.

My father boarded up the chapel and we never spoke of it again. There is another entrance to the chapel, a wooden door under the great staircase of the house, but that has never been opened, not in my lifetime. At nights, listening to the wind in the trees, I'd think I heard her crying to be let out. Even now, sometimes. I think she's there, in the bricks, in the air.

When I was a girl I used to stare at the portrait of Nina Parr, at her flat, heart-shaped face, her grey dress, her sad black eyes. The painting is nearly three hundred and fifty years old, yet time does not diminish its impact: she is my blood and I am hers. And I know what happened in those weeks it took her to die for love, in that awful cell of death. The butterflies kept her company. They always do. I do not know how often in those long, lonely years I sat at my window, looking out over the meadow above the house, when a Peacock or a Comma has not surprised me. When I felt this house is not my birthright, my soul, but a prison in which, like Nina, I will come to die, I stare at the thick trees and the river that flows to the sea glinting at me through them, and there will always be some sign of life. There will come shortly, because there always does, a butterfly, flying out of the woods towards the sanctuary of Keepsake where we have made a special garden for them. And that is how I know that when Nina was there, the butterflies flew in. To tell her that, even in a world where one dies for love, where love sucks out every breath from one's body, there is still beauty amongst us, fleeting, golden, summery beauty. They are such foolish things, butterflies. They exist only to give pleasure. They live such a short time on this earth.

When I decided to write this story down, the story of my life, and how I met Al, you'd have wondered what I might want for. I had money, jewels, land, a husband and son, and I had Keepsake, rising up like lichen-covered stone out of the land that made me, worn through the years by the salty, sweet sea air and the wind that blows down the Helford river to the sea.

I write this for you, dearest Al, for the love we had and lost, to explain who I am and why I did what I did. And to my son, dear George, I am determined you will have a copy of this, too, when it is finished, so that you might understand what made your mother this way. Not to excuse: I cannot be forgiven. But so you can shrug your shoulders and then, perhaps, forget about me. I have done so much that is bad in my life. I have caused such pain and suffering to others. And how I have been punished, too, as you will discover.

The Parrs have been on this plot of land for a thousand years. The current house was built by the first Nina's great-grandfather, in the early days of Elizabeth I: Lionel Parr, the first Parr to be recorded. Legend has it we were mermaids who, hundreds of years before, swapped our tails for life on land, and whose beauty made us rich. Another more prosaic version says we were boatmen, who rose to become wealthy enough to buy land, and then charged for the privilege of crossing the creek: little more than bandits, in fact.

Lionel Parr was a great man at Elizabeth I's court. So convinced was he of his favour with the Queen that he began to dream of a house suitable for her royal personage should her Majesty deign to visit Cornwall. Of course, she never did, but she gave him a knighthood and a sum of money to help him build. So most of the sprawling medieval house was demolished, and Keepsake rose up in its place. They say Lionel brought men down from London and paid them double time to build as fast as they could, because he was sure the Queen was to make a royal progress down to Cornwall. Work was completed in less than two years. And that is why the locals never knew of the place, and still hardly do, even today. You do not visit Keepsake for a day trip. There's no welcoming sign off an A road; no car park, no converted stables serving cream teas. You will never, either in 1580 or in 1999, if I live that long, come across a lane shooting off any road that leads you to Keepsake. You have to be told how to find it. Even then, you see, my family was not the welcoming kind.

Lionel had not reckoned on one complication, however, and that was us. Daughters. He married an Italian noblewoman with hair like black velvet, whom he had met on his travels through Europe, and brought her back home with him. Her name was Nina. They say he was quite mad for her, that he dreamed only of her, wanted only to possess her, night and day. We know nothing of what she thought, naturally.

But Nina gave him daughters, and his daughters had daughters, and even though they all kept their name – Parr – Lionel died a disappointed man. His great-granddaughter was Nina Parr, who welcomed Charles II and bore his child and killed herself for love: little can Lionel have imagined how she would come to keep his name alive. As it was ever so: women thwart the plans of men simply by being born, and are punished for it for the rest of their lives.

Two things happen, when you are a Parr girl, that don't happen to other girls: when you are ten, you are told about your future role.

The second thing that a Parr girl at some point must learn is harder to tell of, and I cannot find the words to explain it to you – not yet. It is dark work indeed, the business of this house, hidden from the world.

You may drive your car, or ride along, seeing nothing but narrow lanes, high thickets, bramble tangled with wild honeysuckle, purple vetch, red campions, until the land falls away from you and the view is sparkling blue, glittering seductively in a midday sun, with tiny barques, like floating kites, sitting gently on the halcyon river-sea. Then the golden fields, and the green shadowy valleys, and the mulchy sweet earth – I used to think myself sometimes drunk on the sense and scent of it all. Inland, up the river from the sea, past Helford, until the trees get thicker and taller and closer together, and then, a little way down Manaccan Creek, and you are there.

There is the secret pathway, barely wide enough for a horse and carriage, through which we used to ride up to the fields, but nothing else. You can only come from the sea, then along the river, like the King did, three hundred and fifty years ago. You disembark, and you will climb up the stairway cut into the rock, like he did, and climb the short winding path through the thick trees until it curves round and you spy the lichen-covered stone gateway: two creatures, butting heads, but you can't quite make them out. There, hidden by trees, invisible to anyone from the road three hundred yards away, the centre of its own world, is:

KEEPSAKE

You pass through the arch with the fox and unicorn, Lionel's and the Queen's crests combined. The house is square, low. You walk under the long, imposing loggia of arches to the enormous wooden door – oak, long ago bleached white-grey. They say a baby elephant could fit through those doors – at least, that is what my grandmother used to tell me – but, like all her stories, one never quite knew if it was true or not. There is a statue of Lionel himself on the outer wall of the East Wing, in an alcove, hands on hips, beard pointed and bristling, as if to remind his guests of his importance. His head is missing. He has bombasted breeches, great stone rings on each finger, an intricately carved sword, but no head.

Our greatest treasure is not inside the house, however, but flanks it: the garden, a hidden paradise, laid out by my ancestors, cultivated and developed until it has become like nowhere else. Pineapple pits, the rarest blooms, the strangest trees, like alien creatures, a scent like perfume heady in the air. It is filled with our secrets, marvels that are too strange to relate here. The gardens slope up behind the house towards a meadow, and in front of the house they lead down towards the creek. Behind the head of the river and up to the harsher north coast of the country, in the moors, are the tin and copper mines, the source of our wealth for so many years and now long abandoned, sold or closed.

In summer the river and the sea are sometimes sluggish. The house is warm and dry, shaded by the trees which hug it close, the ivy and creepers that try to pull the house to the ground. In autumn the mists swirl around it and winds fly in through the windows and we shutter ourselves in, boarded up for winter. We are protected against the worst of the storms and the cold.

That is why the butterflies came.

For ten years, my world began and ended at Keepsake. I wasn't a prisoner there, I left the tangled headland that was ours many times; by the time I was eight I could row myself along the Helford estuary, to where the river meets the wide sea. I knew the tides better than my times tables, and I knew the sound of the birds in the woods, the owls and the blackbirds, before I knew the sound of most human voices.

My father wintered in town, dozing at the Club, doing whatever work it was he said he needed to do to justify his existence, that of enjoying my family's money. So it was that I was brought up by two women: my mother and my grandmother. Mother taught me to sail, to read, to listen out for the sound of the birds. She taught me how to plait my hair, and she sat with me at night when I was feverish and cried out from nightmares. Grandmother taught me about butterflies.

My grandmother, Alexandra Parr, was a celebrated lepidopterist, one of the great late-Victorian bluestockings. She was perhaps the most important person in my early years: I adored her. My father loathed her, but the money was hers, of course, and I suspect that is why he remained away so often – until she died, and his reign could begin.

Grandmother was formidable. Her mother, Lonely Anne, had died young and she was brought up by her grandfather, Frederick the Vicar, one of the few Parr men to inherit. He, a widower, had no knowledge of children and simply raised her as a boy. She had no fear; it pains me how signally her children and grandchild failed to inherit this trait. She believed she could do whatever boys did, and what she wanted to do was study butterflies. No one before (with the exception of Mad Nina, my most notorious ancestor) or afterwards (with the exception of my poor son, George) in our family understood, or examined them so minutely.

The desire to acquire knowledge was a kind of madness with her. She was the only female allowed access to the celebrated Darwin collection at the Natural History Museum. She was an Aurelian, one of a tiny handful of women to be so honoured in the Entomological Society's illustrious and varied history. Her speciality was the Fritillaries, the flickering orange-and-black butterflies that were once widespread over England and are now all variously threatened. It was my grandmother who taught me the difference between the Silver Washed, Pearl Bordered and Marsh Fritillaries, how to spot them, what they ate, where they rested.

My son has made a career out of his study of the glamorous butterflies of the rainforests: the Glasswinged butterfly, as translucent as day, the huge iridescent Morphos, or the Orange Oakleaf, which sits with its brown wings closed, looking so much like a leaf that it is often impossible to spot, before it opens itself out to reveal the most brilliant acid-orange and peacock-blue markings.

Grandmother would, I think, have smiled at this. I believe she made one trip abroad, to Portugal, in her youth, but preferred the native English butterflies. They are less glamorous, but more interesting. 'You could study Fritillaries for years, their habits, their flight patterns, their biology,' she'd say. 'They're remarkable little things. And what need have we to travel? We have them all to ourselves.'

In fact it was my grandmother who was remarkable. I miss her very much and wish she had not chosen the path she did. For years I held myself responsible for her end, thinking that I could have averted it had I been aware of her intentions.

When one comes from a family like this, one knows every member, their foibles and eccentricities. They live here, in the walls, in the air – they are in the house as much as the ivy. You might say one understands them better than many living people. I certainly understood the Parrs better than the scant outsiders I knew. Take, for example, the story of my most extraordinary relative, my great-great-great-grandmother, Mad Nina.

Mad Nina, the fifth of the line to inherit Keepsake, was born in 1790. She was the mother of the aforementioned Frederick the Vicar. She ran away one night, abandoning her son when he was still a small child, and not until he was in his late teens and fully expecting to inherit Keepsake did she return from the Orient, having quite lost her mind. Where had she been these fifteen years or more? Grandmama used to tell me that Frederick didn't recognise her. That she had been so changed by grief she looked entirely different.

She had always had a restless streak, the madness that haunts us all being strong in her and ill-suited to a hidden life. Poor, troubled Mad Nina. From childhood it chafed upon her, rubbing against her sanity. She dreamed butterflies were trapped inside her, that they flew into her mouth and other parts at night, that she would one day give birth to thousands of them. When she married and had a child it became worse. Later, I was the same way myself; in fact, you might say at times her ghost has kept me close company.

One night, when there was a full moon and the countryside around shone silver-bright in the dark, Mad Nina had saddled her horse and, making for Portsmouth, had run away to Persia – yes, Persia. Who knows why? She had always loved Scheherazade and tales of distant lands, and since she was a child had longed to leave Cornwall. Yet she only got as far as Turkey, taking passage on a boat bound for Constantinople and disguising herself as a boy. She was soon discovered by the ship's captain and subsequent grave indignities were suffered by her, culminating in her being dressed in women's clothing again and being taken to a slave trader; he knew this exotic, English lady with skin paler than milk and huge, blue veins that throbbed visibly on her forehead and neck was a rare prize.

So my ancestor was sold into the harem of the Sultan in the Topkapi Palace, where captured foreign women were the majority of the concubines in that lavish prison. Nina, greatly esteemed by Mahmud II for her refinement and race, was tended to by her fellow concubines. We do not know if she bore him children – and indeed know very little about her life there at all – but we know the concubines were not allowed to leave the palace, or see anyone else but their rivals: they could be killed at a moment's notice, or thrown out to die on the streets on a whim. But after fifteen years, and with the delicate intervention of the English ambassador in Constantinople, Nina was permitted to leave. I think perhaps, by then, she had begun to wholly lose her mind.

She arrived back at Keepsake when young Frederick was not expecting her. She had suffered greatly on the journey home: she was not escorted but made her own way across Europe, as swiftly as she could. She had to, as you shall see. When she arrived back she did not enter her home but went straight to the Butterfly House where she slept, waking only to tend to the butterfly garden. She died a year or so later, having spoken only once to her son, and that to say: *Look after them. Look after them for me.* And he did, for years, until he too died. My grandmother always said of him, 'He deserved better than her for a mother, poor man.' But I always felt sorry for Mad Nina.

By then the rumours had begun about what Mad Nina had concealed upon her return journey home, and they did not die for decades, rising to fever pitch when my own grandmother, as a young woman making her debut in London, would neither confirm nor deny the tales told to her of the extraordinary natural treasures to be found at her ancestral home. For there were rumours of the rarest of butterflies here, smuggled back from Anatolia, and able to survive only in Keepsake's hothouse environment. This was at a time when butterflies and their capture were akin to an obsession amongst a certain type of collector.

In my grandmother's youth we had Aurelians, and far less respectable collectors, creeping around looking for specimens – of course, they could not find their way to the house, much less into the garden itself. Boats were chartered to sail up the Helford, men creeping across the land on foot from Gweek or Helston. Some got close but none of them succeeded. Alexandra was quite impressed with, and eventually married, the one who managed to make it as far as the butterfly meadow above Keepsake. He learned the secrets of the house when he married her, though when he died – on a collecting expedition to India, leaving my grandmother with my mother and my Aunt Gwen, who was then but a baby – he was not greatly mourned by her. Grandmama had her butterflies and her daughters: she was content.

My grandmother often said that Mad Nina deserved a better legacy. I think often of her, of the poor, skeletal woman slumped in gratitude on the floor of the Butterfly House, not wanting to leave, only wanting to stay with them, home again after wanting to fly and be free, and after discovering what the outside world is really like.

From my earliest childhood, we three spent days in the meadow above the house, looking for butterflies: my mother, my grandmother and I, scuttling along behind them, short legs tangled in bloomers and skirts, crying out for them to wait for me. Over the fields and the meadows we would range, over our land and the common land, past walls hiding caterpillars and eggs, and hedgerows where friendly lemon-yellow-and-brown Speckled Woods flutter and rest. When I was quite small we had a pony and trap, and on long hot summer days Grandmother would drive us to Kynance Cove, almost the southernmost point of England, where the water is light turquoise and the sky is endless, and there we caught Clifden Blues that matched the sky itself. We ate crab sandwiches, which Pen, the scullery maid, prepared, and Mother and I removed our laced-up boots and ran in bare feet on the white sand while Grandmother, large hat on head, huge swooping net in hand, hunted for eggs and caterpillars amidst the chalky grassland on the cliffs above us.

When she caught a butterfly, with her long, looping, swooping action, she despatched it immediately with a pin, then took it home to be filed neatly away with the rest of her collection. It was understood that any serious study of diurnal Lepidoptera meant killing the object of your interest, but my grandmother was rare for her day in refusing to pin every butterfly she caught. She said, time and time again, that they were part of the air, as we were, and to kill each one was a grave mistake.

For me she wrote *Nina and the Butterflies*, so that I should understand my history, where I came from, why we were these people. So that I'd love these insects, as she did, she included a list of butterflies at the end, with descriptions that were interesting for a child. It was accepted by a publisher she knew in London, and proud indeed was the day we took possession of a copy.

Mother used to read this slim, modest volume to me over and over again, at my request. It is a strange book, there is no denying it – but then, our family's story is strange. She read to me every night for hours. Fairy stories and ghost stories, tales of pirates and Cornish giants. It is sixty years or more since she sat me on her knee and, tucking my hair behind my shoulder, whispering dear words into my ear, carried me into a world of imagination with her soft, sweet voice, telling me the story of our home, as set down by her mother, my grandmother Alexandra. But I remember it still, I remember the smell of her, the feeling of warmth on my back as I huddled against her. These two women, Alexandra and Charlotte, raised in the history of the house, proud and tall and clever and beautiful as women should be, were the twin pillars of my early life.

But in the autumn of 1926 everything changed, for ever. Mother and I went away to stay with my Aunt Gwen in London. I thought of this as an enormous treat: I was seven, and old enough to think myself a young lady. We were gone for a while, at least six weeks, possibly two months.

On our return Turl met us at Helford Passage with my mother's boat, her beloved *Red Admiral*. He admired my new brocaded coat with its fine epaulettes, my matching hat. 'You're quite grown up, Miss Parr,' he said. 'Those weeks in London, I should barely know ye.'

I was terribly pleased at this. He handed us in and took the other skiff back alone, slicing on ahead of us. I was First Mate, as was usual, helping to push us away from the shore before leaping into the boat at the last minute.

When we were away, Mother said, 'I have something to tell you, Thea, my dear.'

I remember it so clearly: it is the moment my happy life changed. I was crouched in the prow, looking out over the river, watching the sunlight flashing on the clear water.

'Grandmama is dead. She died several weeks ago. She was ill, and she didn't want us to know. She has been buried.'

I didn't really understand her. I remember the salt in the air, the gentle breeze, like sweet balm on my skin after weeks in smoggy London. I remember my mother's graceful, fluid movements, hand on the oar, looking upstream, towards the setting sun, face twisted away from me so all I saw was her soft hair curled high on her head.

I said, because I thought I hadn't heard her properly, 'Sorry, Mama, I don't understand. Who has died?'

'Grandmama, dear.'

I remember huddling into the prow, as though she had slapped me, pushed me away from her. I didn't understand why she wouldn't look at me, why her expression was so cold.

'Why?'

'Why? Because she died. Because we must all die, dearest one.'

'But couldn't we say goodbye to her, Mama?'

'It was not possible,' was all Mama said. 'This is how it had to be.'

'But I would have hugged her had I known,' I said. 'I would have hugged her especially hard.'

I could barely imagine her absence in the house. To never hear her booming, brisk voice, firm step, the way she owned every room. To never see her shining, cream-and-pink face, and those chocolate-brown eyes, the coil of cream-and-grey hair, the battered straw hat, the red-raw rough hands so unlike the rest of her, beautiful and dynamic. She was alive, every inch of her. How could she have been so ill she'd died, and we didn't know?

'I don't understand—' I began.

My mother interrupted, crisply. 'You'll understand one day, Thea, darling.'

She never called me Thea: that was my grandmother's name for me. I tried to think of a question to ask that would sum up the many I had. 'Are you sad?'

'Yes, I'm very sad,' my mother said. She grasped one oar in both hands, steering away from the path of a fishing boat making for the sea, raising her hand to them. 'I'm very, very sad.'

'Why aren't you seeming sad?'

'Because one doesn't. One must put a brave face on it. She is dead now, and gone. We must get used to it.' With that she steered a sharp left as we rounded the head of the creek, sliding quietly through the calm evening waters, along the creek, till we saw Jessie, the maid waiting for us with the rope. 'There. We're nearly home. One more thing. We mustn't discuss it with your father. We can talk about her, but only when we are alone. Do you understand?'

I nodded, wanting to cry, but knowing she didn't want me to. I barely knew my oft-absent father, except as a brusque, sharp-tempered man who barked orders and spat out his food when he didn't like it. I was to come to know him now.

There began my mother's decline, and indirectly mine.

I see now that she began to push herself away from me, that I stopped being allowed to comb her heavy hair like chocolate velvet, or play the piano with her, or listen to her read to me in the endless winter evenings, in her little parlour, my head resting on her soft, brushed-cotton knee. She was often away, or stayed in her room: Jessie dressed me and read to me. Turl took me out in the boat with him, gave me liquorice root to chew as a treat, and said I was to be his First Mate now. Children learn to adapt: I didn't understand at first, but gradually I realised my mother did not love me any more. Over time I believed those happy days of my early years, before my grandmother's death, were just a scene from a painting, not my own life.

In the meantime there were other distractions: Turl, and the *Red Admiral*, and Jessie and Pen, and Digby, my little dog, who came everywhere with me. And there was Keepsake to explore, a place where you knew you might walk into any room and see a scene from another time and place, where ghosts seemed to hover just around the corner, whispering while I slept or ate or read. I never tired of the place: the secret platforms that looked out to sea, the tiny chambers hung with heavy silk tapestries, the Victorian nursery we never used – complete with cot and baby, battered train set, wooden bricks made light and lacy with woodworm. There were portraits of my ancestors long forgotten in dusty stairwells, doors that were never opened, carved wooden chests filled with old dresses, not worn for centuries. Engravings hung on rusting curling wire, discarded in corners.

I had a doll's house, which waits patiently still in one of the rooms on the top floor, cast out of my sight as it reminds me so exquisitely of that painful time. For I played with it for hours, with the tiny dolls and their clothes, the heavy metal furniture. It had electric lighting and a garage for a car: our doll's house was more up to date than we were. I'd imagine the family who lived there, give them roles to play: the loving, intelligent wife who studied butterflies, the hard-working husband injured in the First World War, the sweet little boy who was the apple of their eye, and their elder daughter, a young me, who had soft chestnut hair I am sure was real and a painted china face which only ever seemed to express blank acceptance.

I wasn't lonely. I wasn't very happy, but I learned pragmatism. Then, when I was almost nine, I met Matty, and then I had her.

Down on the creek one day, with the *Red Admiral* moored up at the neck of the river, I was at the shoreline desultorily picking at the sand with a stick, skirts tucked up into my bloomers, boots caked in mud. I was trying to catch live whelks for Digby, and was debating whether to sail out a little further, or whether to walk up over the meadow. But when the tide was right and the wind and the sun were playing together, it was hard to be away from the water. Digby, next to me, was snuffling at a shell when we heard a cry.

'Hey! Get away, you're trespassing!'

I looked up to see a tanned, scruffy creature running down the slippery steps to the shore. 'Excuse me, this is my land,' I said, trying not to sound haughty. '*You're* trespassing.'

The figure passed a hand in front of its face, wiping mud off its nose and staring at me to reveal a pair of bright green eyes, which widened. It began to laugh. 'This is good! You're a girl, ain't you? I've got that clean wrong.'

Patting the old straw hat I had crammed on my hair, and looking down at my navy bloomers and thick boots, I stared up in annoyance. 'Yes, of course. How rude,' and then I laughed. 'Oh. Are you a girl, too?'

'I'm a girl all right,' she said, and held out her hand, gazing frankly at me. 'I'm Matty. I live in the gatehouse.' I knew the gatehouse of course, though I'd never been in. It had a neat curve of lemon-yellow roses that flowered around the front door each year and was the kind of house I dreamed of living in. Well-tended, pretty, compact. Two up, two down. I nodded recognition. 'Are you the little lady they talk about, the one who'll have that big house all t'herself one day?'

Her tone was mocking. I took her hand, and shrugged. 'Matty's the name of someone in a book. My – she was a servant here, a long time ago. Did you know that?'

She shrugged. 'My name's Matilda. We been here for centuries, just like you, you know. Plenty of Mattys in my family. My ma says we used to serve you, long afore your grandmother were born. My gran, she was a wet nurse to your gran.'

'Oh,' I said, slowly. I knew there must be a grain of truth to what she said and I liked the idea that the Matty who helped Nina nearly three hundred years ago had a descendant called Matty who was here now, on this beach with me. 'More like great-great-great-great-however-many-grandmother.'

She shrugged, obviously bored of this topic. 'Something like that. What you doing?'

'Looking for whelks. This is Digby.'

''Lo.' She nodded at the dog; Digby cocked his head on one side. 'There's plenty more over by the old Wyckhams' beach, if you want to sail round there. I was up there yesterday.'

'Right,' I said, and with the straightforwardness of youth we didn't ask each other any more questions. I turned the *Red Admiral* over, helped the strange girl in, and we cast off.

I remember that day still, the scent of saltwater burning on skin, the mackerel we caught and roasted, the smell of woodsmoke. Lying on the tiny secret beach, wet sand and silver shingle cold between our toes. I remember the conversation, as if it were yesterday.

'What do you do all day, then?' she asked me.

'Me? I catch butterflies and I play by myself and I study with my governess. What about you?'

'I do what I want,' she said, and I glanced at her, admiringly. She was leaning back on her elbows, face to the sun.

'Well, I can't do that. Someone would stop me.'

'Yes, you can.' She turned to me then, green eyes glinting, as though stray beams of sunlight had become trapped in them. Her skin was like caramel – in those days, still, it was rare to see someone deliberately tanned. Most of our lives were spent covering up from the sun's rays, for the shame of looking like a labourer. 'You can do anything you want, Teddy. Don't go thinking you can't.'

'Not me.' I laughed. 'It's Keepsake. I have to carry it on, no matter what.'

'Why? Because there's all that nonsense about your grandmother dying here and them over at Manaccan church refusing to bury her and all o'that?'

I put down the mackerel I was grilling. 'I . . . I hadn't heard that.'

'Oh.' Matty stood up, in front of me, blocking out the sun. 'Oh, right. Well, I'm sure you know better than me.'

'What do you mean, though? She was ill and she died—'

Matty raised one hand. 'Ain't none of my business. You forget it, yes? I'm right about one thing. There ain't nobody going to stop me doing what I want when I grow up, either. One day I'll just – I'll fly off, and I won't come back. If I fancy it.'

That morning Jessie had laid out my dress with the frilled, pin-tucked apron over the top, my black laced boots, polished so they gleamed, a new red ribbon for my hair. The idea I'd just do what I wanted was laughable. It was inconceivable.

I smiled at her. 'You'll have to show me.'

'You bet I will,' she said, fiercely.

We were friends from that day onwards. Probably I never had a better friend. Matty was two years older than me and could roam freely all day. She knew how to shoot an arrow, shoe a horse, light a fire, catch, bone and cook a fish, and after my grandmother died and my mother turned away from me she became the centre of my world. I had never had a friend my own age before, someone to explore with, to talk to, to share an apple with. Matty made everything better. I let her come hunting with me, and together we caught all manner of butterflies in my grandmother's laurel boxes and nets. I told her stories of the house, the sounds at night which terrified me. She made up ridiculous tales about goblins and circuses, invented wild jokes about Jessie and Turl and Talbot the agent and Reverend

Challis over at Manaccan church, which made us hysterical with laughter. She was naughty, I suppose; I'd never been that way and I loved it. We dared each other to greater acts of danger, balancing on cliff edges. We stayed out all day, coming back after dusk.

And then my tenth birthday arrived.

On the morning of my tenth birthday I woke up to find my smartest cream organdie frock laid out for me and Jessie hurrying me out of bed, so that she might twist my ragged hair into ringlets. I submitted, crossly, to this mauling, wondering why on earth such a fuss should be made. I came down to breakfast in the Great Dining Hall to find my parents in their usual positions when at Keepsake: isolated on opposite sides of the table, Mother absorbed in *The Times*, poking absent-mindedly at a boiled egg, Father grimacing and picking bones brusquely from a kipper.

My father had been abroad for the last month, in the South of France – taking the air, it was called, but of course he was doing no such thing. He had a heavy gambling habit already by then, and was reliant on my mother's money to fund him, having none of his own. He tended to come home when he needed more money, or when he thought it was time to impregnate her again: three times (that I knew of) she had been pregnant since she had me, but either they were born dead or lost early. I, young enough to know nothing of the travails of women, took a cold-blooded young child's interest in it, no more. After one such loss, I asked Jessie, who was snuffling into her apron, if I could see the dead baby, and was mystified at her response, which was to clip me around the ear and lock me in my room till morning for being a wicked, heartless child.

My father took no interest in my mother's well-being, beyond blaming her for her inability to carry his son full-term. He didn't want daughters, he wanted Farrars men, muscular gods to bestride the earth, till the soil, assault the scullery maids, shoot the deer and game.

'Good morning,' I said timidly, standing in the doorway of the large, oak-panelled hall.

They both looked over and my father stood up, and I suppose that was when I realised something must be different.

'Happy birthday, Teddy, dear,' said my mother, beckoning me towards her. I went and stood by her chair, and she took my hand and pressed it fiercely between hers. Then she jerked my chin, so I was looking into her dark eyes. 'Kiss me, little one,' she said, in a strange voice.

I kissed her dutifully on the cheek, and she glanced at my father, and then sat back, releasing my hand, ignoring me as though I had vanished.

'Theodora, now listen to me,' said my father, and I started, and turned towards him. 'We have to set before you certain facts about your future. Today is your tenth birthday and—'

'Arthur, please,' my mother interrupted, her voice low. 'Let her sit down first, have something to eat, and . . .'

I saw her hands, fluttering, and couldn't understand why she was nervous.

'. . . let her open her present first.'

My birthday present was a book: *When We Were Very Young*. I stared at the familiar brown paper cover, trying not to let my disappointment show. I had been reading this book with my mother, and latterly Jessie, since I was four. This was a book for babies, not for people who numbered their age in double digits. I had told Matty the day before that I wanted a new boat, or a sash for my blue grosgrain dress, or *Jane Eyre*, as mother had begun but never finished reading it to me and I could never seem to find it again on the shelves either of the vast Drawing Room or my father's study.

But I said, 'Thank you, Mother, thank you, Father,' and I kissed my mother again, and then walked around the table, footsteps echoing on the worn stone floor, to kiss him. He was still, as though I hadn't touched him.

'Sit down, Theodora,' said my father, and I scurried back to my chair, next to Mother, and faced him. He pulled out a parcel of papers. 'I am going to read a document to you, which was read to your mother on her tenth birthday, and her mother before that.'

'Grandmother Alexandra?' I said, instantly. 'Is it from her?'

He started, and stared at me, through gritted teeth. 'I would be obliged if you'd hear me out in silence. D'you understand?'

I nodded, welded to my seat, thighs sticking together, and my father glanced at my mother, and she nodded, and then he started reading, and at first what he was saying made no earthly sense to me at all. I have the letter here: I reproduce it in full.

Greetings, most trusty right and true,

Wheresofore as we are so highly sensible of the merits of the services performed to us by Lady Nina Parr and her brethren, and those at Keepseke in the county of brave Cornwall, in the year 1651, in a time when we could offer so little in assistance to our own defence, in a time when great and probable dangers were threatening our liberty, and our person. It hath pleased us greatly to reward thy loyalty and patience and to pursue thy prosperity and that of thy descendants. I hereby vouchsafe my protection and assistance to Lady Nina Parr and her issue from this day forwards and in sending by this trusty messenger a brooch which shall be in recognition of my time with her. Read well the inscription, my lady.

And I do forswear that, upon her tenth birthday, any female child born of the said Lady Nina Parr shall be apprised of this: that she shall inherit Keepseke, and all lands thereof, forthwith. I hereby vouchsafe my protection and assistance to Lady Nina Parr and her descendants from this day forwards and any man who takes her to wife shall be a Parr by name from that day hence, and their children Parrs, and that she who has pleased me so greatly with her gentle goodness, wisdom and strength shall found a line henceforth to continue upon the generations. That this pension due to them shall, when I am restored to the rightful throne, be rewarded to them as testimonie to her kindness to me. A pension of £1,000 each year, or however it shall be invested. And, upon her reaching her twenty-sixth birthday, I hereby declare that Keepseke be the sole property of Lady Nina Parr to be inherited by her female heirs upon attaining their twenty-sixth birthday also, as long as she hath been once or more within the boundaries of Keepseke before that day.

Godspeed my sweet and rightly so,
Charles II Rex

My father put down the paper, to silence. Both of them watched me.

After many more moments, trying not to be terrified, I tugged my mother's skirt. 'I'm sorry,' I whispered. 'I don't know . . . what it means.'

'It's yours,' she said, with what I know now was a note of joy, but I had forgotten what it sounded like on her lips, so used was I by now to her sharpness, her lack of interest. 'When you're twenty-six, this place and all the money becomes yours, my darling, and we your tenants, with a pension to be given at your discretion.'

'Thank you, but I'm not sure I want it,' I said, politely. I was ten: it seemed to make perfect sense to me then, as now. 'Excuse me, Mother, but what happens if I say no?'

My father stood up, walked down to where I sat next to my mother, and slapped me with the back of his hand. My head flew back; my eyes popped out, and I remember seeing his hairy knuckles, clenching into a fist as he strode back to his seat and sat down. My mother said nothing. I think that was the point at which I lost her entirely.

'You little fool,' my father said. 'You'll do what's expected of you, like the others before you, and I'll tell you what's yours to keep and what's yours to give away. Shut your damned mouth from now on. Do you understand?'

Without watching for a response from me he pushed his half-eaten kipper away, petulantly, then rang the bell and lit his pipe. My mother carried on eating, her head bent over the newspaper. Silence, broken only by the sound of rushing water and the wind in the trees, flowed over us.

1929

I was to learn to be a young lady now, not play in the fields all day: every morning, Jessie brushed my hair until it crackled and swelled in her hand. My ragged calico workdresses and smocked overalls were put away in the great wooden cupboards that lined the gallery outside my bedroom, small piles of brown and grey and white lost in the huge echoing space. I took to hiding in there when I heard my mother's step along the corridor, for I could not bear that she should see me and show her indifference. I can still recall the feeling of the cold wood against my back, the sound of her skirts, the dreamy, deathless way she would hum as she walked, and every time I longed to reach out, to open the door and touch her, call to her, but I dared not.

In the last year I had begun lessons with a governess, too, and for that I have to thank my father, the only good thing he ever did for me. My father was a brute but he was a canny brute: he didn't want an idiot managing the estates, if he was to continue to draw money from them. I must be educated, that I might understand how to make him money.

So a pale-faced, grave lady named Miss Browning was hired from Derby to teach me, and came to stay in a little house in Mawnan, across the river. She would arrive by boat every morning, clutching her furled umbrella, clearly terrified of her surroundings, of this house. Our lessons began promptly at ten and I enjoyed them and soon came to love Miss Browning: I was a bookish girl, for all my outdoors ambulation and Matty's scorn for those who wanted to learn. I liked learning – anything, from the course of the stars to the rule of Akbar – and quiet, scholarly Miss Browning was a wonderful teacher. She was particularly fascinated by Russia, and especially Tolstoy: she was horrified by the Revolution and the progression of Communism. Latterly, we read *Anna Karenina*, *War and Peace* and *The Death of Ivan Ilyich*. I do not think anyone had discussed world affairs with me: my parents read *The Times* at breakfast but we rarely listened to the wireless, and I never saw anyone else. Thank goodness for Miss Browning. I was lucky to have had her for the short time I did; I dread to think how stupid I would be without her.

So now Matty and I only had the weekends. She would wait for me, arriving early outside my window, throwing seeds or little stones if I wasn't awake. I'd creep out of the house and through the walled gardens, where friendly robins watched us curiously and rows of gently waving, deeply scented, velvet purple lavender were framed in backdrop by the ancient, lichen-coloured brick. In the mornings the sun cast the fox and unicorn above the gateway into a long, strange shadow so they loomed black and sinister on the side wall. Out through the crumbling arch, and we were off. Either along the tiny path that led up to the meadow, or down the track where the trees arched overhead and grew thicker, down to the stone steps and the tiny ancient jetty where for hundreds of years we had, all of us, disembarked or embarked.

They must have known we escaped like this, but no one stopped us. All day we spent outside, wheeling and rushing and twirling like the swifts above. Sometimes we went to Matty's tiny house at the edge of our estate, where her mother fed us bittersweet pippin apples and crumbling cheese; sometimes we sailed across the Helford and went exploring. We grew overconfident; we did not realise they could clip our wings whenever they wanted.

When I was eleven, calamity struck. I was brought back by my enemy Talbot to the house one damp March night, at the end of a long day of unparalleled excitement where Matty and I had sailed along to Falmouth and been turned back by a strong tide, a sudden storm and a capsized boat.

We had gone out early but with grander plans than usual – plans I still wonder whether we would have gone through with, had we been able. We had decided that was the day to make our escape from the creek. But though we knew the tides and the river, we had not taken into account the equinox, the spring tides, the full moon. After a frantic day of searching, Turl was called out of the Shipwright Arms and hurried across the Passage; his sister's cousin had seen us, bedraggled and struggling to shore. Matty had promised me we'd get far enough away that day, that we'd be in Falmouth by dusk; I had ten shillings, wealth enough for months, if not years, we'd thought. However, as it turned out, it was to be our undoing, the end of everything, not the beginning.

'You are to promise that you will not see that gypsy again, and she is never to come here. It is time you became aware of your expectations,' my father told me as I sat in my bedroom, shivering, Jessie fussing over me as she wrapped me up in Mother's paisley dressing gown.

'I was the one who—'

'No. No more interruptions.' Behind him, my mother stood, hands sunk deep into the pockets of her turquoise-blue night jacket, silent as usual. 'Give me your word, now.'

'Father—' I bit the tip of my tongue, and tasted blood.

'I said your word.'

I gazed at him then, stared full into his face. I was unused to looking at him, preferring to avoid his attention. His eyes were blazing white; pinpricks of black at their centre. Tiny circles of red burned on his already florid cheeks. His closely trimmed, ginger-grey beard trembled.

'No,' I said, trying not to show I was afraid. 'She is my best friend. My only friend.'

'Say it.'

'She says you keep me here like a prisoner.' I stared boldly at him.

He hit me again, an open-handed palm smacking my cheekbone with such force that my head jerked left and my skull banged sharply on the open door. I saw my mother wince, but stay still. She did not move towards me, or give me comfort. As tears stung my eyes, and I rubbed my scalp, I stared at my father, blinking to make him out, my vision blurry, my head spinning. I realised then that he hated me.

They left – my father first, my mother following him, her head bowed – and I was alone with Jessie. I stared up at her, rubbing my aching cheek.

Her eyes were brimming with tears; she shook her head at me. 'Oh, you gave us a scare,' she said, hugging herself, her breathing ragged with suppressed emotion. 'Come here, you naughty child,' and she threw her arms wide open. 'Come here, I've been so worried.'

Though all I wanted to do was run to her, feel her throw her plump arms around me, pull me against her so that I might sob on her chest, to know that someone cared about me, I stood still. I gritted my teeth, and turned away from her.

'Goodnight,' I said. 'Leave me now, please.'

I knew I was turning into them, turning to stone, but I didn't know what else to do, how else to survive.

From that day on Matty was banished to the village.

I walked the lands we owned with Talbot. He never shortened his stride and so I would stumble alongside him, legs stretching to keep up – I was tall for my age, but still only eleven – as he jerked his head and muttered, 'Land lies fallow there, the topsoil is bad. We'll seed again in a couple of years.' Or, at the mines north of the river, towards the north of the peninsula, 'Fella died last year in a fire. We have to make sure the exit carriage is oiled every week. You'll do well to remember that when you visit.'

When I was twelve, my mother took me to London again. We stayed with Aunt Gwen as before. I was taken to Harrods to be measured for clothes, and the London Zoo to see the elephants, and Piccadilly Circus to see the lights. But it was also arranged that I should visit the properties we held in London, in Bloomsbury and Kensington, with Talbot. And in addition I spent many hours kicking my heels in a waiting room in Harley Street while my mother visited her physician. My mother was not strong. She had lost another child, the previous summer, and Jessie had told me I must be gentle with her. 'Don't touch her, or hug her. She's not a toy.'

I wanted to laugh: I had not touched my mother beyond a peck on the cheek for years.

On the train home, Mother and I read in silence.

After we had crossed the Tamar Bridge, Talbot said, 'The boom is over. We'll sell the London property soon, I expect. Land's coming down. Don't want to be saddled with a lot of white elephants. We won't be going up there again.'

He might as well have spoken in Russian; I did not hear him. For I knew then that I'd go back to London, one way or another. I'd been several times before, but I was no longer a child on this trip, and London to me was – and still is – life, all of life in one glorious place.

I had always loved London but this time it had seemed to be a new heaven, worlds away from the one I knew. The noise, of traffic, horses, people calling, shouting out to you as you passed by! The ladies' gowns and bonnets, the beauty and grandeur of it all! The men outside hotels in top hats and with braid on their shoulders, who tipped their hat and opened doors for you, as though you were a princess! The gold work on all the buildings, the adverts painted on walls recommending products for pox and liver and gout, the buses with hard leather seats upon which you bounced furiously over uneven roads, holding on and holding your breath . . . and most of all the thrill of life and energy in the air, everywhere we went. One afternoon, walking through Mayfair back to Aunt Gwen's house from Green Park, Mother took a wrong turn and we ended up in Shepherd Market, where a woman in a silk negligee stood on a balcony, above a public house, smoking and leaning over, watching us. Wrapped around her was a cherry-coloured cardigan, with deep pockets and a trailing cord. Her lips and cheeks were red and her body looked as if at some point some part of it would fall out of the clothes she was wearing. I smiled at her shyly, heart beating, wondering why she should be there then, as Mother cupped my elbow and dragged me down an alleyway.

'Don't stare, Teddy. It's disgusting,' she said, staring herself, wrathfully, up at the red-cheeked, full-breasted goddess who gazed calmly down at us.

We clattered up steep old steps out on to the street. Soon, we were in the safety of Berkeley Square, and my mother could breathe again.

'Who was that woman?' I had asked her.

'Someone who sells herself to men, for sex,' she had replied. My mother rarely entered into any part of my life now with enthusiasm, but she never lied. At twelve, it was the first time I had heard the word 'sex', or had any notion of it.

When I was fifteen my governess, Miss Browning – by now very dear to me – left. She was called back home to Derbyshire by the illness of a parent and was not replaced. Of the many hours we spent in my father's library I remember so much still of what she taught me, yet I barely recall her face: I think she had pale ginger hair. I wonder what happened to her. She was kind to me and had a snuffling, small laugh, which reminded me of a dormouse. Once, I accompanied her to a recital of two Bach cantatas in Truro Cathedral, but my father found out and she was requested, I discovered later from Jessie, not to invite me on such expeditions again.

So my lessons stopped and I really was left to my own devices. What did I do then, how did I fill the long hours between waking and sleep? I read books. I went for walks – supervised by Pen or Jessie, who walked tremendously slowly through the lanes above Keepsake in their worn flat shoes, chattering inconsequentially about their sweethearts in Helford or their sister's troubles with her husband. I urged them to find strong boots so we might go across the fields, but no. They were afraid of my father. Everyone was.

I needed something to occupy my restless energy and so it was that, gradually, I began to study the butterflies – and with nothing else to divert me I found the obsession creep up on me, like my mother and her mother and all the others before me. On my doorstep was all I could wish for to feed that obsession. Now I watched them: I noted their different flight patterns, their behaviours, their mating habits. I knew that a lemon-curd-yellow Brimstone might be found as early as February, and a Silver Washed Fritillary only in July. My mother had given me my grandmother's old equipment: net, cotton and needle for mending the net, a matchbox filled with pins, a worn wooden collecting box, and the killing equipment (jar, poison, cork stopper). All in her old satchel. It gave me a thrill to handle these things, to be reminded of her again.

I roamed around the meadows and lanes less than before. I knew Talbot would report me to my father were he to see me outside the estate. Once or twice, the year after our friendship was terminated, I saw Matty, and we talked, but we were different people now – she of the wider world, I of this house, only this house.

'Keep your chin up,' she said, the last time I saw her. 'It can't last for ever, can it? I'm looking out for you, aren't I?'

'You?' I'd said, and it sounded more arrogant than I'd meant. 'What can you do?'

'Yes, me, you ungrateful little sod.' She'd turned on her heel, stalking off back down the lane, leaving me alone and flushed with regret at my loose tongue.

I am afraid I was less and less my grandmother's child. I spent hours with the killing jar and net in the walled garden hunting butterflies, and my pleasure in seeing their bright fragile wings flap uselessly against the silky hard glass for those few brief seconds before the cyanide overwhelmed them grew sharper with each new catch. Once, by climbing up a tree and lying in wait for hours with a plate smeared with Patum Peperium, I caught a glimmering Purple Emperor, his wings like raw silk, thick with indigo-purple-blue dust, almost indecently beautiful. I pinned him on to a piece of paper, and slid him into the unused drawer in Father's bureau along with the careful boards of Fritillaries and everyday Peacocks and Admirals I daily caught and killed.

One day, I was in the garden early, carefully watching a mating pair of Holly Blues. They settled down together on a twig, facing away from each other, and then slowly tipped their lower abdomens up so they touched and sperm passed from the blue male to the browner female. They remained perfectly still. I caught them in the jar and carried them inside to the study where I opened the drawer, unsure where I would put them after they were killed – it was almost full then, with butterflies of all kinds, collected by me in the year or so after Miss Browning's departure. The male, his post-intercourse stupor vanished, was now fluttering against the glass of the jar again.

Perhaps I should have set him free, and perhaps I would have done. I stared at them, at the female delicately lowering herself again so that she perched on a leaf I had placed at the bottom of the glass. How many eggs would she hatch, if she lived? I wondered. I wondered whether I would kill them.

But then the door burst open, and banged ferociously against the wooden panelling. I jumped, and turned to see Pen, clutching her dress, her red-rimmed eyes huge in her pale face.

'She's dying. Come quick, Miss,' she said, and that was all.

Up in the King's Room, Mother lay in her great wooden bed, dappled with the light from the long, mullioned windows that looked out over the fields towards the river. As I entered, I stopped, trying not to shrink back at the sight of her and the smell of the sickroom – starched sheets and antiseptic, and the cloying scent of chloroform. She was a sallow yellow, her lank grey hair hanging in a plait over her shoulder. She was so very thin.

I discovered afterwards that the previous month she had lost another child. She did not want any more. She had a girl to inherit the house. My father, though, wanted boys. So, though she begged to be let alone, he insisted he get more children on her, and every time, she lost them. Blood and more blood; sometimes they were later on, sometimes early. When I was older, Jessie told me of what she had heard, what Mother had told her. How he held her down when she turned away from him, and took her while she pleaded for him to stop.

Now she was losing blood, so much that her body, weakened after seventeen years of pregnancies and only one living child, was not strong enough this time. She was bleeding to death before my eyes.

I held her hand and sat down on the bed, but she winced, and dear Jessie slid a chair out for me to sit upon, and then tactfully withdrew.

I didn't know what to do; I'd forgotten how to be with my mother.

'Mama, may I fetch you anything?'

She shook her head firmly. 'Please, Thea. Promise me something?'

140

'Anything.'

'Get away from here. Far away until he's dead.'

Panic and adrenaline flooded through me at the blazing anger on her face. I clutched her hand more tightly. 'Yes. Yes, I will. Oh, Mama—' My lips pursed in and out with the effort of not crying.

'No,' she said, softly. 'You . . . don't be sad. I've tried to make it easy for you, you see. So it wouldn't hurt you, my going.'

'I . . . I don't understand.'

She gave a bitter, twisted smile. 'My darling girl. I have been a half-mother to you all these years for a reason. So you wouldn't feel pain at my end.' She seemed to summon every last piece of energy in her body. 'And the last blessing is that I'm going before you would have been called upon to do it. You won't have to do what I did.'

'Dearest Mama.' Now, my hot, childish tears dropped on to her waxy skin. 'What do you mean?' I was holding her fingers so tightly she cried out, and pulled away. 'I'm so sorry.' I kissed her fingers. 'I'm sorry.'

She beckoned me closer to her. In a whisper she said, 'I shut her in. Then we went away and left her. We left her.'

I moved a little away from her, at the stale heat of her breath. 'Grandmother?' My head spun; the thing was, I knew instantly. 'You . . . you shut her in? Where?'

She arched away from the bed, suddenly rigid, her teeth bared. Several were missing; I wondered when she had lost them. I wondered how much I didn't know about her, how much time we had wasted.

I turned for the door but she said, 'No. Don't fetch . . . anyone.' Her voice was no more than a soft breath of air. 'Only me and you, darling. You must listen to me. Do you know, when you were little . . .' She closed her eyes for a moment again. I waited. 'You kept two ladybirds in a tin. For two weeks? You were only four and you loved them. You won't recall any of these things, now she's gone and I'm . . . I'm gone, and I wish I'd told you . . .' Slowly, she licked her cracked lips. 'Yes. When you were born, you had one tiny perfect black curl on top of your head. Like a child in a painting. And you had a tiny red mark on your forehead that faded with time, and you had blue, blue eyes like the sea, before they turned brown . . .'

141

She trailed off, and was silent for many seconds, her eyes closed. Her pulse was so faint that eventually I got up again to call for Jessie, but she scratched at me, so weak now she couldn't reach out. Eventually, she pointed at me. 'Oh, I wish I . . . I was not leaving. You.'

I was still crying, my mouth twisted, my shoulders heaving with the pent-up love of ten years I had suppressed straining inside me to burst free. 'Don't, Mama. Don't go.'

'I thought it was right. That I was saving you. And I have wasted these years in pushing you away, my darling girl.'

I kissed her hands, trying not to sob.

'You have been so, so precious to me. My only child, the one who survived. I knew you, the moment they handed me to you, I understood who you were.'

'Mama—' I laid my head at her side, unable to look at her. I told myself I must stop sobbing, that I must help her.

'Yes, I did. I knew you were different. Strong, a tough little thing. And most importantly . . .' She paused. 'I knew you were mine, not his. All mine. I did it to save you, to stop you loving me, so that if you had to do it, had to leave me there, you would not hurt as I have hurt . . .'

We were both silent, my fingers stroking her warm, too warm hand.

'But I cannot be sad, now I know you are spared. So I will tell you.' She lay back on the pillow, staring up at the ceiling. 'All of us who have inherited it. Every woman since Nina, till me. And one day you. The final secret of our house.'

I raised my head, breathing as though I'd been running. 'Yes, Mama.'

Her hands scratched across my wet cheeks. Her nails were long, dirty. She spoke with a little restored energy, the last reserves of her strength. 'I would have told you when you were older. Before you were twenty-six, like Nina was. We're all here, darling. We all died here. We're all buried here. Here among the butterflies. I fought against it and then I gave up. She was so strong, your grandmother. It was what she wanted. Not like me. She . . . she loved this place. The house will get you in the end, you see.'

I nodded, trying to understand. 'The . . . the skeleton they found when I was young? Do you mean Nina, Mama, when they found her in the chapel? Grandmama saw her . . .'

She smiled, her sunken eyes fixed on me. 'Your grandmother told the men it was just her, just Nina down there. They believed her.'

'But they all saw her. When they entered the chapel, she was there . . . her skeleton, and the butterflies in chalk—'

'Yes, but they didn't look below. The others . . .'

'The others?'

'The others are in the tiny chamber under . . .' She swallowed, gathering more strength. 'Under the stairs. In the cellar. She knew, of course. She told me they were there.'

'You mean . . .?'

She hummed, quietly. *'Nina Parr, locked herself in, Charlotte the Bastard, daughter of a king, / Nina Two, mother of Rupert the Vandal, Nina the Painter, mother of a scandal. / Mad Nina that was, then Frederick the Vicar, then Lonely Anne, then Alexandra the Fly-catcher.'*

Her soft, steady, rasping voice was like a lullaby. She paused. 'I gave her the cyanide sticks before I locked her in – it is a quick death, compared to the alternative. When your time comes, my darling . . . take some sticks from the Butterfly House. I will be the only one they bury in a churchyard, you see . . . Oh, dear God, why do you—'

She arched away from the bed, rising up so that I thought something had possessed her, and her hand left claw marks on my skin. When she had recovered, her strength had gone, and I knew it would be soon.

'Do you know how it ends? I know how it ends. I have it now.' Very softly, she crooned, *'Then Charlotte the Sad, and then comes me, / My beautiful Teddy, the best girl you see. / All of them butterflies, and then only me. / . . . only . . . me.'*

'Mama . . . please, please, please don't go. Please try,' I said, my hand frantically clasping hers. I think I believed if I tried, just once, to chivvy her back into life it might work. 'Not like this. Let's talk about something else.'

But she smiled, and shook her head. 'You see, all this time and

I'd look at you and wonder about you . . . if you'd have to help me die.' She shook her head, very slowly. 'I'm so glad you won't. You are so clever. So beautiful. You are so good, Teddy, you are. My beautiful girl, full of spirit and intelligence and—' Another spasm twisted her and then she was still. Suddenly she opened her eyes, gazing at the ceiling. 'You must leave. The house is dying. Oh, my darling child, I can't be sad. I can't . . . be . . . sad, not now. You are here. You are here.'

She kissed my fingers. I felt a charge pass between the two of us and her hold on me slackened. I stared into her eyes, clear, softest brown. I felt the power of her love for me, more powerful than any love I have felt, before or since, and I have known great love. Then it was as though something slid over me, a cloak covering me, and when I looked again she was gone. In the distance, a sigh, a sob – those women, all watching her, with her, I believe that now.

Underneath the house. Of course. I remembered Matty, the first time I met her, saying they'd refused to bury Grandmother over at Manaccan church. She'd been wrong. They hadn't buried her there, because she was already dead, at Keepsake. There were no graves for my ancestors – save the men, who were in the family vault in the church. The others, the women, were all here.

I never entirely recovered from my mother's death, or our last conversation. She did what she thought was right but the tragedy is she was wrong: her assumed indifference had already altered me. I was changed, forever fixed as a quite different girl to the happy, excitable child I had once been, who had roamed carefree with my mother and grandmother through our own private world.

Her skin was still warm. I bowed my head, then looked up as the room faded into the normal grey light of day. A bird called outside and I knew I was alone now.

Nine months after my mother died, Father introduced me to my husband. William Klausner came to the house with his father, and we had tea on the terrace. It was autumn, nearly too cold to sit outside. As I hesitated in the great doorway, Father pinched my arm.

'He's not here to talk to you. He and his father are here to size you up, look you over. See if you're a suitable match. They want a good, sensible, healthy girl. Not a moony-eyed slut who spouts gibberish about what goes on in this house. You hear me?' His fingers dug into my tendons, my white flesh pink in his pincer grip. 'Take off that stupid pinafore and put a proper dress on.'

Get away from here, my mother had said. *The house is dying. You must leave.*

'Yes,' I said, sullenly, and I went upstairs to change. What else could I do? Since my mother's death I realised how much her presence, more ghostly then than now, had protected me. She had deliberately cultivated a vague, peremptory, cool air, and under this disguise had prevented some of my father's excesses. Now that she was gone, his mask of gentility was off. He was rude and brutish, crude and vulgar, drinking with Talbot the land agent long into the night, stalking the corridors looking for flaws by day. Pen, the sweet scullery maid, he dismissed on a whim because the starch in his collars wilted on a hot day.

My hair was too long and wild; I'd outgrown my dresses. I was eighteen now, and tall, but I wore what clothes I had been given the last few years, because I simply didn't care any more. I had no mother to silently supervise, and it wasn't until she'd gone that I saw how much she had carried on doing for me, even as she distanced herself. Things I hadn't known – the bunches of wild flowers in my bedroom, the new clothes that somehow appeared, the books I might want to read always within reach when I studied – she had loved me from afar, and now she was gone, buried in the church unlike her ancestors. I could not walk past the chapel at the back of the house. I had dreams that woke me, screaming in black terror. I understood now why people avoided my gaze, when I sailed into Helford or went out riding. I was unloved and unkempt, and I took great pleasure in pretending this pleased me.

So we made an awkward party, out on the flagstones, in the cool breeze of late September. Jessie hurried through the French windows with tiny sandwiches, pastries and tea. We were elegant still, as we always had been – even if I was not, sitting there in my lawn-cotton tea dress that was agonisingly tight under the armpits and stained with blackberry juice. My father and Aubrey Klausner made stilted conversation about the weather, the local Member for Cornwall, the latest news of Herr Hitler meeting Mussolini in Venice Lido. William Klausner and I sat in silence, I glancing over at the garden in the hope of spotting butterflies, he staring at the ground. He swallowed a lot, and each time rolled his eyes around from left to right, then pursed his wet lips, an unconscious action that was mesmerising. I wondered what it would be like to kiss him or to do what Matty had once told me I'd have to do with a man if I married him.

These thoughts kept me occupied, and I was a poor hostess. I could feel my father's furious, red-eyed glare on me but somehow couldn't stir myself to make a greater effort.

Eventually William said, 'I say, that's an interesting lichen. Is it *Caloplaca thallincola?*'

I followed his gaze to the spreading orange pattern flowering on our terrace. 'I'm afraid I don't know.'

Matty would have; she knew everything that grew here, but their country names, not dry Latin.

'I'm sure it is.' His eyes bulged. 'Have you been to London?'

'Yes,' I said, my heart leaping. 'Have you? I love it, don't you?'

He licked his lips. 'Don't know. Never been. What I meant was, there's no lichen in London. The air quality is so poor it cannot flourish there. It's an interesting indicator of levels of pollution. Awful place, I should imagine. And the lichen would agree.' He looked down at the flagstone again. 'This really is a remarkable specimen.'

I suddenly wanted to laugh. I bit my tongue, and looked down at the straining button on my dress. After a pause, I said, 'Would you like me to fetch a book? I believe we have a reference title on lichen in my father's . . . in the study.'

'No,' he said, leaning forward. 'No, it's not necessary. I believe I've identified it correctly, but it's unusual to see it in a domestic setting. I suppose you have a microclimate here, what with the garden and the walls being so jolly old.' I stared at him and he must have thought I was dull-witted. 'Oh, I'm sorry. You wouldn't know, would you? A microclimate, I should explain, is a special environment where flora and fauna flourish at odds with their immediate surroundings. Keepsake has a special microclimate. I've heard it . . .' He trailed off, and turned rather pink. 'Well, you'll find all kinds of interesting species that have been here for years and don't appear anywhere else, I expect, if you care to look.'

I tried not to smile. He had no idea what was here, and what had been here for centuries, and suddenly I felt calmer. This was *my* home, not my father's, and no one could take it away from me, whatever other indignities they might try to subject me to. 'My family has been on this piece of land for close to a thousand years,' I said. 'We're well aware of what's here, but thank you.'

He froze, bulging eyes fixed at the floor and deep red rising up his neck. I suppose he was kind-looking, until you discomfited him, and then he acquired the look of a rather alarmed fish.

My father turned to me, breaking off conversation with Mr Klausner. 'Go inside and ask Jessie for more hot water for the tea. Now.'

I stood up, stumbling on one of those very flagstones, for I knew he had heard my rudeness and that I would suffer for it later – a slap, a missed meal, a cruel speech. My father hit me fairly often these days: usually the open-palmed slam to the cheek, sometimes an arm, twisted up behind my back till I screamed for release. Afterwards I'd cry but I was, I suppose, drearily used to it.

Get away from here, she'd said.

Jessie would be upstairs making the rooms ready for the night, and it would be quicker for me to bring the water rather than bother her, so I turned the corner to cut through to the kitchen myself – and there was Matty.

She was the same as ever: slim, bronzed, that curiously boyish gait, gleaming eyes fixed on me with their thrilling intensity. It had been months since I'd seen her but it was as though we had last met that morning.

She leaned against the door and opened it for me, then said, 'Come on, then. Don't you want to go inside?'

'You shouldn't be here,' I said, pushing her and closing the door. 'If my father catches you he'll—'

'All right,' she said, and we walked swiftly through the empty house towards the kitchens, and when we were inside I reached for the pan of water but she pushed my hand away from it. 'No. Leave it. I had to see you. I want to know how you are. And you're all grown-up, aren't you?' She spoke like a lady, not a country girl.

'They want me to marry him,' I said, hotly. 'Matty, I can't. He's awful. He's like a fish. His hands are wet and his eyes water.'

She threw her head back and laughed.

'Please, be quiet,' I hissed. 'Honestly, Matty, Father is dangerous.'

Her clear eyes narrowed. 'Are you scared of him?'

'Yes,' I said. Then I said what I was afraid to say out loud. 'I don't know how to escape. I don't know what to do. I have to get away from here. There are things here, Matty—'

'What things?' she said.

'I . . . I can't say. Since Mother died I don't . . .' I shrugged. 'I don't have anyone.'

Footsteps, echoing through the house, down the long, low corridor which led to the kitchens.

'You have me,' she said. She leaned forward, and her lips gently touched my cheek, and she put her arms around me. She smelled of honey, of something sweet. 'I'll help you get away.'

'I can't ask you to do that.'

'I'd do it gladly, Teddy. If you want to go. Do you want to go?'

I didn't hesitate, but nodded. 'Very much.'

'Good. Do you have any money? I'll need money.'

'Yes, of course. Only . . .' My face fell. 'It's hardly anything. Two guineas. Wait there.'

She pressed herself against the wall and I left her, and flew upstairs to my bedroom, where I rummaged in my purse-book for the coins I owned. I never had much money to hand; it was, I was given to understand, 'all tied up'.

Returning as cautiously as I could to the side passage, I pressed the guineas and some florins into her palm. 'Here. It's all I have, I'm afraid.'

Matty grinned. 'It's masses. I must go. Wait to hear from me.'

She clasped my hand and then vanished, as quickly as she had come, through the back door, and as I put my hand to my breast-bone the kitchen door opened and Jessie appeared, huffing under the weight of a coal scuttle.

'There you are,' she said. 'What's the noise?' She looked around, suspiciously. 'Was someone here?'

'No one,' I lied.

Afterwards, in my room that night, feet drawn up under my chin, staring out over the fields, listening to the sound of the autumn wind picking up its refrain in the trees and the creek, I realised Matty was the first person to touch me – with affection, not with a slap, or a kick – since my mother died.

But days faded into weeks, then months, and autumn was winter, and Matty didn't come back.

Though it does sound odd, the truth is now I knew my grandmother was near I began to like it. I no longer had nightmares about what might be lurking below the house. It was my family, my history, my burden to bear, and it was something my father could not take away from me. He could strip me of my dignity, as he did when he ripped a ribbon from my hair at breakfast and called me a woman, not a silly girl. He could sell the last tin mine over in Penwith for below market price to pay off his debts. But he could not change the fact that Keepsake was mine. The women were here. The house would belong to me, no matter what he did.

For Christmas 1937, I dressed the great front door of the house alone with holly and bay, twisted around a wooden circle kept for just such a purpose in the stables, and used for decades. As I hung the glossy green-and-red foliage upon the door I thought about Christmases past, carriages rolling along the narrow lane bringing guests to dine in the great wood-panelled hall, years gone by when our neighbours would have offered us gifts and good wishes. This year, I wondered who would disturb the sullen silence of this house by knocking at Christmas? My answer came when I took the wreath down myself, twelve days later: no one.

My nineteenth birthday, in January 1938, came and went and I received a gold locket from my father and a bouquet of Lenten roses tied with the black grosgrain ribbon from her old hat from Jessie, which meant more to me than anything, because I knew she didn't have money for nice things and had been proud of her hat. My attorney, Mr Murbles, took me out to lunch, with Father, at a hotel in Truro, the Falstaff. Mr Murbles drank a little too much wine and was indiscreet about other clients, families we had known all our lives, their financial affairs, the suggestions of familial improprieties. My father greatly enjoyed this; I half listened, preferring instead to watch the other groups having luncheon. The elderly dowager, the young married couple, the impecunious, shabbily dressed woman. I regarded them all, as though they were specimens in my killing jar; I saw other people so rarely. I didn't know when I'd come to Truro again. Not for another six months at least. The thought of this strange incarceration, of time stretching ahead of me, began to send me into a depression.

Then it happened.

One dank, gloomy morning in late April the roaring of the swollen creek below us was louder than ever, enough to drive one slightly mad. I was in the long dining room, slowly eating my porridge and flicking through correspondence. A letter from my Aunt Letty, my father's impecunious sister in Plymouth who often required assistance, financial and otherwise. A request for aid from the lifeboat men. A woman who claimed to be a clairvoyant who had an urgent message for me from the dead—

A note. Folded in with the rest. It must have been left here. She had been here, and then gone.

Meet me in the Butterfly House tonight at sunset. Be ready. Bring all the money you have and otherwise only what you need. – M

You may ask, how could she have been so certain of me, that I would put my old life behind me and escape, knowing not at all what lay ahead? But if you ask that, then you do not understand how cold I had been trained to become. How the little girl who cried over a dead baby bird on the cliff-top path had become a young woman who killed butterflies for pleasure, who had no one alive she loved, or who loved her.

I hesitated, but only for a second.

At the other end of the long table, some ten feet away, my father looked up. 'Yes?'

I thought quickly. 'It's nothing, Father. An invitation from the Vyvyans.'

'I worry about your defective memory, Theodora. I've told you before. I don't like those people. Say no.'

Smiling, I bowed my head, because he had removed any doubt from my mind. 'Yes. Of course, Father.'

The nights were warmer than they had been, but there was still a sharp chill in the air that evening, as I let myself out through the secret door behind the kitchen and, picking out the soft mossy patches on the terrace, crept silently. I knew it well enough; I needed no light to guide me to the Butterfly House.

Over the last year or so I had moved my collecting to this place, with Father's permission. It was an old ice house, built with the hall to store the coldest items of the kitchen. It had a domed roof and thick stone slabs for shelves, and I found it invaluable for keeping my specimens, trays of dead butterflies stacked high, stuck with pins and neatly labelled – by me, by my mother, and by my grand-mother, the bulk of whose collection it was. Some of the most spectacular butterflies were hers. No one living, apart from me and occasionally Jessie, had seen the collection.

The Butterfly House was my only private place: too cold to sleep in, too small for Father to think it of any interest. He tolerated my interest in lepidoptery; I think because it kept me at home, and helped prevent me from meeting anyone else. William Klausner had visited once again before going up to Oxford. He had written to me, too: a letter clearly dictated by his father, as anxious for a share of the Parr name and stature as my own was for their money. It's funny to think, that evening, when I left, my father must have thought his plans were all in place.

The door to the Butterfly House opened smoothly, newly oiled, which was the first strange thing: it had always creaked before.

She was waiting in there, and at the sight of her my cold fingers clenched into fists. I moved forwards, to greet her, but she stepped back and said, 'My word. What on *earth* is that bag?'

I looked down at the rigid loaf-shaped Victorian bag into which I had flung everything I thought suitable for my new life in London – I would be able to purchase more when I arrived there – and on the top, nestling in the case my mother had had made for it when it was cleaned some years before, was the Charles II diamond butterfly brooch, which had been solemnly presented to me by Mr Murbles on the morning of my mother's funeral, in the Drawing Room, as the coffin lay in the courtyard, waiting to be transported to Manaccan church. 'It's a beautiful piece,' he'd said, holding it reverently in his hands. And indeed, the sight of it in his fingers and not on my mother's blouse or jacket or twinset was wholly heartbreaking and strange. 'There's an inscription on the thorax. See if you can read it, my dear.'

The forewings were diamond, the hindwings pale sapphire. The body was a rich, rose gold with twinkling, tiny diamonds at the tip of each feeler. I turned the sparkling, delicate creature over. '*What's Loved Is Never Lost*,' I had read aloud.

He had nodded. 'This might be one of the most extraordinary pieces of jewellery in a private collection, you know. See the King's arms below it, at the base?'

He tapped a short, ridged nail at the bottom of the slim, gold thorax. I squinted, and saw the royal coat of arms, no bigger than a flea, below the inscription.

'It's very romantic,' Mr Murbles had sighed. 'Whatever you think of the whole business, he must have loved her.'

I had pinned the brooch on to my black dress where it glinted, even in the gloom of the day. The romance of the story had never really struck me before. I suppose I had taken it for granted, and yet – to love so deeply you will die for him. To love so deeply and yet have to leave for the good of the country – to leave the woman you love, who is carrying the daughter you will never meet. He must have believed it, to have it written thus.

Now Matty had opened the bag and was riffling through my things. I snatched the case with the brooch in it out of her hands, sharply.

'It's an old hatmaker's. My mother had a hat delivered in it once, and we kept it. I think it's jolly fine. It's the only suitable bag I could find.'

'That's all you're taking with you?'

I felt a little irritated. 'Of course. Anything else and it'd have been noticed.' I reached out my hand to her. 'It's jolly good to see you, Matty – I have missed you.'

But she shrugged. 'You are strange, Teddy. One ungainly shaped bag with a few odds and ends in, and that's all you think you'll need?'

'I'll buy more things. I'll get a job. Something.' I was stamping my feet, to keep out the cold.

'You're certain you want to go to London?' Matty looked down, and I saw her chest, rising and falling with each breath that caught in her throat.

'Yes,' I said, watching her carefully.

'I don't think you should go that far, Teddy.' She swallowed. 'That's all. I'm not sure I should help you.'

'You write me notes and call me out here.' My nose was red with the cold, and I could feel it starting to drip – most unglamorous for a heroine running away to start her new life as a bohemian young woman in London. I glared at her. 'You make me risk everything and then you say you think it's a bad idea. You said I should go. I can't run off to Falmouth, or Exeter, can I? I thought you understood.'

'Of course I do, how dare you say that?' she hissed, and her pink mouth pursed with anger. I looked at her shirt, three buttons open, at the little dash of pink on her breastbone that would spread up her throat, the way it always did when she was cross. 'How dare you say I don't understand, when we understand each other more than anyone ever did? I had to lie to Ma tonight and tell her I was meeting a boy. I saved up all my money for months and the money you gave me to buy you this.'

She threw something on the ground and I picked it up.

'A scarf – it's beautiful.' I fingered the blue-and-green silk. 'Matty, I've . . . you shouldn't have spent all your money on this. I can't take it.'

'You damn well can,' she said, eyes blazing, stepping back from me, and I saw I had misjudged it, misjudged everything. 'Don't you dare tell me you're too good for my presents. Don't you know how much I missed you? How I wished I could kill your dad somedays, so we could be together again?'

'Me too,' I said, staring at her. 'I'm sorry. I wouldn't have spoken like that, only—'

'I'll never see you again, Teddy, you know that, don't you?'

I didn't really understand.

'You won't come back, you're not like me. David Challis wants to marry me, and I ain't got nothing else, and Dad won't have me here if I don't. I'll be someone's wife by Christmas and I'll have his children and be miserable the rest of my life.' She caught my wrists in her slim hands. 'Be something. Be something else.'

She put the scarf around me and we hugged, as we had done that day in the house. I smelled her sweet perfume, the wildness of her.

'Matty—' I began, and I stepped back and we stared at each other. Then Matty caught the back of my neck with her hand, pulled me towards her, and kissed me.

She tasted of fish, and honey – and something else, rich and pungent like truffles. She bit my lip, and wriggled against me, pushing her tight body on to mine. I did not have time to think, to wonder. I pressed myself against her, feeling her hips and belly square against mine, her small girlish breasts hard on my fuller ones, her lips wet, her tongue hot in my mouth.

I was mad for her then – quite mad, you see. I wanted all of her, though I knew it was wrong. I knew thinking about her in the way I sometimes did, that it was wrong, too. My father had once wandered into the library and caught me looking at a picture in the paper of Margaret Lockwood, my finger tracing her lips. He'd waited behind me, then hit my finger with a shoehorn, cracking my fingernail straight down the middle, so that it buckled, an inverted W.

What I was doing wasn't wrong then. I was looking. But he made me feel as though it was disgusting. I won't write more about how it made me feel, what it was like. I am already deep enough into lies and will tell many more before this story is finished, I expect. Forgive me.

This was my first kiss. Matty is long gone, a figment of my memory only. She was right. I never saw her again, for when I returned everything had changed. Sometimes, I wonder if I imagined her. I think of her now as a magic spirit, a sprite conjured up by the air to help me. I knew I must not think of her in any other way. Of what I wanted to do to her, how I wanted to touch her, as we clung to each other, panting, frantically fumbling in that cold, moonlit room.

It was she who broke away, holding my head between her hands, nostrils flared, eyes dark with it.

'I knew it,' she said, and she smiled her gap-toothed, enigmatic smile.

'Knew what?'

'That you were ready.'

'Ready?'

'For it. I've wanted to do it to you for years. I used to dream about you, when I was first having dirty dreams.'

I pressed my hands to my burning cheeks. 'No, Matty,' I said. 'It's wrong.'

'It's not wrong, Teddy!' She laughed. 'I used to do it with Patience Abney down at Abney Farm 'fore she was married and went off to Newquay – she was like a clam, wet, tight, she was fun, that girl – it's good, Teddy!' She shrugged her shoulders as I shook my head, horrified, wanting to show my revulsion. 'We have to marry men and put up with them and their dreary grunting and puffing and drinking and beating, why shouldn't we have some pleasure, too?'

'No.' I shook my head, frantically. 'Please, don't. We shouldn't have. Please – don't talk about it any more.'

'Well.' She shook her head, pinching my chin. 'You're a fool,' she said roughly. 'But I'll still help you. The sleeper leaves in an hour and a bit. Reservation's in your name.'

'But you said—'

'I was teasing. Or something. You always said you wanted to go to London. That's what I've been saving up for,' she said, smiling. 'David Challis gave me the scarf, I didn't pay anything for it. Didn't

I say he's sweet on me?' David Challis was the vicar's son. 'He lent me his car. I can drive you to Truro.'

I pulled her close to me, our foreheads touching. 'Thank you,' I whispered, and I allowed myself one more kiss off her – just once more, to feel that divine taste of her lips and mouth. 'Thank you for everything.'

'What do you mean?'

My throat thickened. 'Thank you for loving me.'

'I did,' she said, her voice cracking. 'And you me.'

We drove to Truro in near silence. I could not bear to say goodbye to her, and yet I knew that I must, not only to make this break with my life but because we could not repeat what had happened between us. I handed her the letter she had agreed to leave for my father, which I hoped would assure him I was not dead or eloping but going to London, as was entirely my right, and that I would be in touch.

Even at this late hour the dark bulk of the train was awash with activity; porters were loading goods and passengers. Matty had rashly purchased me a First Class ticket; had I known that in a few short weeks I would be weak with hunger and almost destitute, I would have quickly come to regret this. But now, this was the start of my adventure; I thought I knew London, that it would be only a matter of days before I was settled there.

We walked along the platform, arm in arm, to my cabin. Matty was gay, as though we were merely saying goodbye for a day or so. 'Would you like to go to the restaurant car, Madam? Or your cabin?'

'Cabin first, I think,' I said, looking at the train's metal embossed nameplate, worn and battered: *The Cornishman*. I felt a sudden mad desire to turn back and climb into David Challis's car again, to go home. I was a Cornishman – or woman – through and through. I wanted to wake up tomorrow and see the buds coming out on the trees and the first signs of bluebells and hear the woodpeckers and know that I was at home. 'Matty—'

But Matty pushed me firmly on to the train. 'Goodbye, dearest,' she said, and she climbed up with me. 'I am assisting this young lady, my cousin,' she said to the suspicious-looking porter. 'She is a very nervous traveller. Suffers *terribly* from dropsy.' She pushed her way past other passengers, who glared at her, until we found my cabin.

'Oh, it's darling,' I said. 'Look at the little cupboard and drawers. And the teeny basin!'

'Like a doll's house,' she agreed, flinging my bag up upon the soft grey blanket, and stroking it, then glancing at the printed card. 'Says here they'll bring you breakfast at six a.m., coffee and toast and jam.'

'Really?'

'Oh yes. You'll be all right.' Somehow her childish enthusiasm infected me again. She knocked on the wooden door. 'Nice and solid,' she said. 'You'll be comfy in here, Teddy.'

'I think I will be,' I said. I took out my folded banknotes, which I had been given by Mr Murbles some weeks previously, and handed some to her. 'Listen, thanks awfully. I don't know how I shall ever be able . . . how I'll ever . . .' I faltered, because simple grown-up thanks sounded insipid in my mouth, compared to what she had meant to me, what we had been to each other.

She nodded abruptly. 'I know.'

'I'll write to you,' I said, but she shook her head.

'No, you won't. And it's best you don't. They might find you.'

'If you're in trouble, or you need me, put a notice in *The Times* Personals column,' I said, suddenly remembering my grandmother had once said this is what one should do.

'And you too, Teddy. You will let me know if you're in trouble, won't you?' I nodded. 'I'll get David to look for me. He'll like that, he likes having something over me.' Her smile was weary.

'Oh, Matty.'

She said, almost furiously, 'I'm going to go now. Goodbye, Teddy. I hope you find it, whatever it is,' and she was gone, closing the door behind her with a sharp bang.

I was still for a moment, resisting the urge to open the carriage door, to shout after her. Then excitement flooded me. I was here.

It was happening. As I removed my hat I caught sight of myself in the mirror. My face was flushed, my lips bruised, my pupils huge. I looked different. The feel of Matty, the late scent of the garden at night as I left, the sounds of the train, snorting, preparing for departure; all seemed burned into my mind and experience. I climbed on to the uppermost bunk, lay down upon the blanket Matty had stroked, and stared at the opposite wall. And then, though I didn't mean to, I closed my eyes, and was sound asleep for the entire journey, fully clothed, until I awoke the next morning, utterly confused, to the knocking on my door and a polite, nervous voice:

'Miss . . . would you care for breakfast now? We're at the station, though we won't be asking you to disembark for quite some time.'

'Yes, please,' I said, sliding hurriedly under the covers to hide my clothes from the night before and trying to look as though I was a world-weary traveller.

A man appeared bearing a silver tray, upon which rested perfect triangles of buttered toast and great dollops of jam, a pot of tea and – oh, the magnificence of it – my own copy of *The Times*, folded neatly, newsprint unsmeared. I stared at it.

FRIDAY 15 APRIL 1938

I peered out of the grimy window, streaked with soot and rain. Through the feathered patterning I could make out a vast, curved ceiling, pillars, smoke, grit. A lone porter strode past, whistling, the sign he blocked clearing letter by letter:

L–O–N–D–O–N

I was here, I was here.

Only then did I start to wonder what I might have done. I thought of my last glimpse of Keepsake the previous night in the spring dusk, the ancient walls silver-grey, the light from the fire that burned in the Great Hall flickering shadows into the courtyard. But then, shivering with excitement, sipping my weak coffee, I pushed those thoughts away.

Later I folded my precious, still pristine copy of *The Times* up in the suitcase and climbed off the train, head aloft, certain I had made the right decision. At Keepsake Jessie would be whistling in the kitchen while she made the porridge. The long shadows which covered the house in the morning would be inching across the crenellated roofs.

You were in the city that day I arrived then, my darling. You must have awoken, combed your hair, pulled on your trousers, eaten your eggs. Both of us unaware that we were only days away from meeting, and our lives changing for ever. And I, free from my father, from Keepsake, sauntered down the train platform, swinging my bag, for all the world like a heroine in a film without a care in the world.

Thus began my butterfly summer.

Part Two

Chapter Twelve

It was Malc who invited my father in. If he hadn't, goodness knows how long we all might have remained stuck on the doorstep.

Having remained silent, he suddenly said, 'Listen, you can't stand here arguing on the street. Let's go inside, for God's sake. I expect we could all do with a drink.' And he gestured to George Parr, implicitly including him in the invitation.

As ever, when Malc took charge, my mother acquiesced, although with a sharp intake of breath. As we processed in single file down the corridor Mum pointed my father towards the sitting room.

'Are you coming too?' said Mum to Malc, looking up at him.

'Of course I am, baby,' replied Malc, and he went in after George Parr.

Sebastian looked over to the kitchen stairs, where the rest of the guests at the abandoned party were presumably making awkward small talk. 'I'll go down. Explain the situation,' he said. 'Might suggest they quietly melt away.'

'Oh, that's a good idea. You sure you'll be OK? You can take off if—' I began.

'I'll be fine,' he said, smiling reassuringly.

I watched him descend the stairs to the kitchen, wishing he were staying up here with me. A sure ally. Then I turned, shutting the door behind me.

We never use the sitting room. It's a long, thin space of two connecting parlours, lined with our hardbacks and nice old second-hand books, the CD player – and it has a cabinet of smart crystal glasses, and some paintings on the walls. It's the posh room. Perfect for a hushed funeral gathering or a light sherry party. Or, as it turns out, the first reunion of your family after your father's return from the dead.

The father in question was looking uncertainly around him, as if unsure what rabbit hole he'd fallen into. He picked up a china bowl that Malc had bought Mum from the Polish pottery shop on the Essex Road, because she loves their stuff, examined it and then put it back down, carelessly. 'So – you've taken over the ground floor, too?' he asked my mother. 'Old Wellum's place, am I right? RAF? Or was he navy?'

She was watching him, her arms folded, leaning against the shelves, and I thought she looked much younger in the dim light, her eyes huge. 'We have the whole house.'

'The whole house? Marvellous.' His gaze raked over her, then Malc. 'That's quite a feat. I suppose . . . gosh . . . that'll be a neat return on your investment.'

It was a curiously tone-deaf thing to say and I felt the three of us draw slightly closer together, in the face of this stranger's lack of knowledge. He *is* a stranger, I found myself thinking. This is the person I've dreamed of meeting since I was a child and I don't recognise anything about him. My mother has lied to me. My entire life, she's been lying, and not about something small. About *this*.

'You can have your share of the money on the flat, George. Is that why you're back? Look, what do you want?' said Mum, losing patience. 'You could have written to me and I'd have given you a divorce. You never said that's what you wanted in those meandering letters of yours. Why are you here?'

The shutters weren't closed and the dark from outside seemed to suck energy from the dimly lit room.

'I had some other business.' My father put his hands in his pockets, smiling easily. 'Something to do with Keepsake and I . . . I had to come back. I suppose, if I'm truthful, I wanted to look you both up, too. See how you were, see my daughter . . .' He trailed off, staring at me. 'I say, you do look like her. It's uncanny. Rather unsettling.'

I shifted uneasily under his gaze. I could see Malc raising his eyebrows: *that's* what's unsettling about this, the fact that Nina looks like her grandmother? *Really?*

'I suppose one sees what one wants to, doesn't one?' said

Mum, thinly. She cleared her throat. 'She looks like my mother to me.

'Of course. But really, she's very like Teddy. At Keepsake, there's a portrait—' He stopped. 'Sorry. Doesn't matter.'

There was a silence, heavy in the dim room.

'So, you thought since you had to come back anyway that now would be a good time to get back in touch?' Mum asked, as though genuinely curious.

I could see he didn't get the tone in her voice. He rocked slightly on the balls of his feet. 'Yes. Thought it was about time.'

'Ah,' she said. 'I see.'

Then Mum walked over to him, standing by the fireplace, and hit him. Not a slap but a hard, forceful punch in the ribs, to the side. He doubled over, with a gulping shriek, and she stood beside him, bent towards him and breathed hard. 'You dick,' she whispered, her voice low. 'You absolute fucking shit. You left me, you did everything in your power to ruin my life and your daughter's – for what reason I still don't quite understand – you broke my heart, you lied and lied and lied, and you walk back in here as though we're friends you met on holiday you thought you'd look up as you pass through town!' She punched him again, her mouth screwed up in a childish approximation of aggression that was comical and heartbreaking at the same time.

He gave a yelp, half anger, half pain.

'*That's* for Nina,' Mum said, and I looked at her, nostrils flaring, cheeks flushed, eyes glittering. 'The first one was for me.'

My father groaned, moving away down the mantelpiece, as Malc stepped forward, clutching Mum's arm and murmuring something.

'It's fine,' she told him. 'It's fine. I'm not going to do it again.'

'Do it again and I'll have you arrested, Delilah. I'll sue you,' said George Parr softly, and he smiled up at her, not with any warmth but with a nod of recognition. 'You haven't changed. Have you? Good to know. Jolly good to know I made the right decision. You . . . God,' he stood up, shaking himself, 'how squalid it all is, to rehash it all like this.'

'*Squalid?*' She gave a choking laugh. 'That's my life, George. That's what you left us with when you decided to play dead. Yes, it was squalid, let me tell you, buster.'

I made an involuntary sound in my throat, a kind of sob, and clamped my hand to my mouth. I wanted them to forget I was there.

He half looked around at me, but carried on staring at her, and she at him. And I realised then, they weren't aware of my presence or Malc's.

George straightened himself up, and said in a more normal voice, 'Here, I'm sorry. Let's not do this, shall we?'

'Do what?'

'Fall out. I've just come to—'

'*Fall out?*' Mum ran her hands through her hair with a despairing laugh. 'What did you expect? That I'd be all, "Hey, it's George! Come on in, buddy, pull up a chair! We're so glad you made it back after twenty-five years! Look what I've done to the place!"' She laughed, her accent more American than ever. 'You never even told me where you'd gone. You made me . . . you made me beg like a dog from them. The Royal Geographical people, those sneering men at the museum, they gave me nothing, nothing at all, just that notice in the paper! That's it!' She flung her hands out, fingers splayed. 'That's all! I don't understand how you could have treated us like that—'

Malc said gently, 'When did you find out he wasn't dead, my love?'

She swallowed. 'They reported it wrong, in *The Times*. They printed George's name instead of another George – another George who was on the same trip – some old guy with a—' She sank her head into her hands.

'That's – you see – that's how the misunderstanding arose,' my father said smoothly. 'We were a thousand miles from civilisation – by the time we got back to Caracas it was three weeks later, and the mistake had been printed. I . . . George Wilson was his name,' he said, suddenly. 'Had a heart attack on the way out. Lovely chap. Absolute tragedy.'

'Yes,' murmured Malc, his eyes never leaving my mother's face. 'I see.'

166

'You snake,' said Mum, softly. 'You slimy, lying, rat-faced snake.'

My father laughed. 'You wanted me to leave. Don't be ridiculous, Delilah. You told me never to come back.'

'*Your daughter!*' she shouted. '*You had a daughter! You told them she wasn't yours!*'

'Well . . .' He rubbed the back of his neck. 'Perhaps that was . . . yes . . . that was badly handled.'

Mum stared at him, in despair.

'Dill,' came Malc's voice, soft and steady behind them, 'you don't have to go into it all, not now. We can do it tomorrow. Or another time.'

'Oh, I do, sweetheart.' She pivoted swiftly, their eyes locking. 'I do. I want him gone, as quickly as possible. I never told you any of it, really, did I? Mrs Poll was the only one who knew. Did I tell you he left once before, when Nina was three months old? Went to Oxford. We had a terrible row. He couldn't cope with being a father, not to a baby who cried all the time. He was a child himself; I think it set something off, having his own child. Kept blaming his mother. He'd get these rages, then moods, he'd be utterly silent sometimes for the whole day.' She wasn't looking at George Parr as she said all this; he stood behind her, two fingers pressed to his lips. 'One evening he'd picked Nina up and shaken her because she wouldn't stop crying. I told him to leave – he went the next day, while we were both still asleep. Just upped and left. I had the police looking for him. I thought he'd . . . he'd done something stupid. He was very on edge.'

'You threatened me,' said George Parr. 'I was afraid you'd kill me.'

'I was afraid, too,' Mum said, flatly. 'I was afraid you'd hurt her.' She turned to Malc. 'They tracked him down to his old place in Oxford. And do you know what he told them? He said I was crazy. That I'd gone mad. That he was pretty sure Nina wasn't his, that I'd had an affair with an old colleague from the States. They never asked him for a name! It was enough that . . . enough to accuse me. And they just let him go. Those good ol' boys in the police force just accepted it at face value. Oh, she's a crazy hysterical bitch who

167

sleeps around, just ignore her. God, I miss the eighties. What a wonderful time of suppression it was.'

'Is that true?' I heard myself say, and my voice, so unexpected in that trio, abruptly halted the flow of conversation, and there was a deadly silence, as though my mother and father had forgotten my existence. 'Are you – is he not my father?'

'It's not true,' said George, coming towards me. 'I am your father, of course I am. Look, you have to understand – I was under a lot of pressure. Babies are hard work. You didn't sleep. Ever. We were both . . . the flat was hell, constant leaks, damp, so tired, and we had no money and no family around I . . . and I . . . and I . . .' He stuttered into silence, throwing my mother an imploring look. 'Delilah, I'm not saying I'm in the right. Some of the things I did were pretty shabby. But in the end I realised it was best that I leave.' He passed a hand over his brow. 'I had to go. Not just you. Everything. Get away to a clean start. Leave it all behind, all of it. And it – well, it worked, wouldn't you say?'

She gaped at him, open-mouthed, and then she threw her head back, and laughed, and it went on for too long.

'It's worked out wonderfully,' she said, eventually. 'You're right, George. It has. Now get out, and don't ever come here again.'

But my father ignored her, and placed his hand on my shoulder. 'Nina, I know this must all be a terrible shock. But I did want to see you. And I had to come back.' He glanced around the room. 'I'm with someone else now. She's not been well, and she wants to get married. And there's Keepsake. I had hoped not to involve you with it. That's what your mother wanted, anyway. But I see it's not possible. You have to know. You *ought* to know.'

I watched him, my gaze flicking between him and my mother, the impossibility of the idea that they were those golden young people in that photograph in front of the Bodleian, that they had made me with love. It seemed laughable. I shrank from their gaze, looking at Malc imploringly. 'I'm not sure—' I began.

'There's a reason he wants you involved in it all now, honey,' said Mum, slowly. 'It's a terrible thing to say, but it's true. Money, or something. He never told me anything about Keepsake. He never told me anything about his family, for God's sake. Why now, all of a sudden?'

'You don't understand,' he said, impatiently.

'Of course I don't! You told me your parents were dead and you'd grown up in a cottage in the West Country. So that's not really true, is it?'

'It's . . . true. They are both dead. But it's not a cottage. And I didn't tell you, Delilah, because – you won't believe me – but I didn't want you involved with any of it.'

'More lies.' Mum dashed her hand dismissively to her side.

I moved back, glad my moment in the spotlight was over.

'No. Because I wanted to start over,' George said. 'I was absolutely terrified you'd dump me if you knew how screwed up my family was. How screwed up *I* was. I was mad about you, Delilah . . .'

She turned to face him, eyes aglow. *Please don't still be in love with him.* I felt sick.

'. . . totally, utterly mad about you. I thought you were the one sent to save me, that we'd be all right if we were together, and I knew I had to keep you pure, unsullied by it all.' He shook his head. 'It sounds so strange. But you don't know what it's like in that house. What it was like, growing up there—' His voice thickened, and he broke off, swallowed, and then said in his warm, clipped tones, 'It was the right thing to do. Maybe one day I can make you understand. I don't expect you to forgive me, but . . . to understand.' He moved a little towards her, and I could see their reflection, in the big mirror above the fireplace. 'I need a divorce. I'm sure you'd like one, too. But we were . . . we were good, when it was good, weren't we, Dill?'

He touched her folded arms, gently, and their eyes met. I had to force myself to glance at Malc, wondering if he saw what I did, but his face was impassive.

Suddenly, I heard Mum say, 'I think you're kidding yourself, George. It was never good. It was a summer romance that went on too long, and the only reason I don't regret it is because of my daughter. Everything else was a mistake. I'd laugh myself sick at the idea you think some sob story about your childhood is going to make up for the damage you caused when you left, if it wasn't too hard to joke about. Do you realise the childhood Nina had because of you? Do you realise if we hadn't had Mrs Poll, and then—' Her voice cracked, and she whispered, 'If we hadn't had M-Malc, what it'd have been like?' She turned to me. 'Honey, I don't expect you to ever forgive me. I should have told you. I can't explain it.' She put her arms around me, but I couldn't return her embrace. 'I'm sorry. I'm so sorry. Hopefully, you'll understand one day.'

She released me and shot one last look at George Parr, standing alone in the middle of the room. 'Send the papers, George. Otherwise don't contact me again. I hope for all our sakes this is the last time I see you.'

'Delilah—'

'Now I really think you'd better leave,' she said.

I could tell he was taken aback, and I wondered how stupid he was. 'But I want to—'

'You don't get to choose anything, OK? Just leave.'

'Dill.' Malc caught her as she barrelled towards the door. 'Let him talk to his daughter.'

'If she wants,' said Mum, and she shrugged, and then went out, slamming the door behind her. I heard her heavy, slow tread on the stairs as though she were dragging herself up to her room.

'I suppose you've been told a lot about me that isn't necessarily true,' said my father. 'I'd love the chance to . . . explain it all to you. To catch up.'

'Catch up' – as if we were girlfriends arranging brunch in *Sex and the City*.

'Not tonight,' I said. 'It's late. I've had too much to drink. And besides—'

'Yes?'

'I'd like to think about it a bit.'

He looked me over again, musing. 'Of course. Look, here's my address.' He scribbled his email address on a page of a small notebook and tore it out, giving it to me. His writing was beautiful, calligraphic italics with flourishes. 'I'm staying at a hotel in Bloomsbury. I'm here till Wednesday. I have to go to Keepsake then.'

'What do you have to do there?'

'Your grandmother's ashes have been at the solicitors' for fifteen years. When she died she left me a package . . . oh, yes, quite a package.' He blinked. 'And she requested that I take the ashes back to Keepsake. Only me, no one else. Her last little yank of the chain – even in death, you see. She was quite something, my mother.' His smile didn't reach his eyes.

'So she didn't die there?'

He looked blank. 'No idea. Probably. We weren't in touch.'

'This house,' I said. 'Who lives there now?'

He hesitated. 'I . . . I don't know. That's the thing. You get it, don't you? It's yours. It should have come to you.'

I didn't really understand what he meant. 'Come to me? How come I don't . . .? It's mine, then?'

'It's complicated. Come and see me. I'll explain.' He clapped Malc on the shoulder. 'Look, thanks, old man, for putting up with all of this.'

'All of what?' asked Malc, politely.

George Parr waved one hand around. 'Oh, this . . . chaos. I hope it hasn't put you in a difficult position.'

'Not in the least. It's my usual position,' said Malc.

George squeezed his hand. 'Nina,' he said to me, and he looked at me curiously again, as if weighing something up, trying to decide. 'Do come to the hotel. Let's talk it all over.' He bent towards me to kiss me on the cheek.

I stepped away. 'I'll be in touch then,' I said. 'Bye bye.'

He looked at me again. 'Yes. Yes, do that.'

'Good night, then,' said Malc, shadowing him so that he was forced out into the corridor and towards the front door like a leaf caught in the slipstream.

I opened the door. This was my father, going off into the night. 'Bye,' I said, waving. I watched him wave confidently back, watched as he crossed the road and turned back to look up at the house. I think it was then I understood what Mum had seen the day of my fourteenth birthday.

He'd been there. Him. The man unlocking the bike. Of course.

'Malc,' I began, as I turned back to the house, 'do you know, I think I just realised something.'

Malc simply nodded and I saw he'd got it the moment George Parr had appeared and I wondered then if he'd known it for a while. 'I think we should go to bed,' he said. He rubbed his eyes, wearily.

I looked at my phone:

Guests all gone. Ate all the canapes and drank all the booze. Also have stolen anything that looked valuable. Have let myself out. Call me whenever you want to talk. Hope you're all OK. S

Not sure we are, I wanted to reply. I kissed Malc and walked upstairs, my step as heavy and tired as Mum's had been. Up to the top of the dark house I went, shoulders stooped. In my pocket was my father's email address. I could feel the heat of it, the damage it could cause. I understood only one thing then: nothing could be the same.

Chapter Thirteen

I didn't see Mum the next morning and, in fact, she didn't leave her room for the whole weekend. I went for a walk with Malc on the Heath (Saturday afternoons being a safe, Fairley-free time to go) and in the evening I went out with Jonas, who was back in town for a few days. It was strange, being with my oldest friend, and not able to talk to him about it all: I simply couldn't go into it, I found, not just yet. If only he'd been back two, three weeks later, when it wasn't so raw, and so very *bizarre*. All of it. Vignettes from the previous day: Lise Travers singing, losing the birthday cakes, kissing Sebastian, Roger Webster from down the road looming out at us from the basement kitchen window. My father, there on the doorstep, pleasant, polite, as though he hadn't really been away at all.

'So, what else is new with you?' Jonas had said at one point, stabbing the crushed ice in his drink with a flimsy straw. 'Really nothing you want to tell me?'

I'd stared at him. Jonas and I were friends from primary school. I'd known him since we were four; I knew he was gay before he did. We spent hours looking at each other's bits naked (at a young age, I should emphasise). One summer, we learned all the lyrics to *Annie*. I'd been able to tell him anything.

But distance is a killer. 'Really, nothing,' I'd said, smiling weakly, and though he smiled and patted my arm, in sympathy for the life he thought I was leading, I could sense Jonas's disappointment, his fixed smile, the gap between us widening.

So later on Saturday evening, I emailed my father:

Could I come and see you tomorrow morning?

Almost immediately he replied:

Dear Nina

I should love to see you. Please come to my hotel, if that suits. The Warrington Hotel, Bloomsbury.

Does 10 a.m. work? I'm out from 11 a.m. for the remainder of the day.

George

Mum hadn't emerged when I left on Sunday morning. Though it was not yet ten, the heat of the day and the traffic around King's Cross had already mingled to produce a smoggy mist as I marched past the Disney-like spires of St Pancras. I love St Pancras. I was so disappointed when Mrs Poll told me it was a railway station and a disused hotel, when I'd assumed – until the age of about eight – that it really was a fairy-tale castle. The towers and turrets, the soaring jagged skyline: Sleeping Beauty's palace, abandoned by the modern world.

The Warrington Hotel was the second to last, and the least loved, of the various establishments on a shabby crescent of large white stucco houses just off the Euston Road. A bucket filled with dirty water and an old mop stood on the top step. The 'a' was missing and it gave the sign frontage across the first-floor railings a curiously blank appearance. As I stood beside the bucket and looked up I had a last-minute urge to turn around and go back home, to let myself in and throw myself on Mum's bed, hug her tight, tell her I wouldn't have anything to do with this new past I'd been presented with, make her sit up and smile. But I knew I couldn't. The genie was out of the bottle now; it couldn't be pushed back in.

Mounting the steps, I pulled open the stiff door with some difficulty and presented myself at the front desk. A blonde, perky lady, not much older than me, was tapping furiously at a desk, but she looked up.

'Good morning, there!' she said, in a sing-song Eastern European accent.

'Hi,' I said. 'I'm here to see my—' I stopped. 'I'm here to see George Parr.'

She looked blank. 'Let me check. I am not sure we have anyone of that . . .' More furious typing. 'No! I'm afraid there's no one here of that name!'

I stared at her. 'There must be.'

But she was shrugging again. 'No! Only four rooms occupied, none of them by a George Parr.' A bright, brisk smile. 'How else may I help you?'

I felt almost dizzy with disappointment: what new nonsense was this? 'I don't understand. He said—' I took out my phone, and checked the address. Then I saw it – the P.S. at the end of the email.

P.S. Ask for Adonis Blue at the hotel.

'Oh,' I said uncertainly. 'I'm supposed to ask for Adonis Blue, apparently. Is that . . .?' I trailed off. It sounded ridiculous.

The words had a magical effect. The lady jumped up, and smiled. 'Oh, right! Mr Blue, you're here to see? He is very funny man. Has me laughing. I said to him, you're not called Adonis . . .' She pronounced it *Add-on-iss*. '. . . and he's promised me he is. Is it true?'

'No,' I said, trying not to show my irritation. 'His name's George.'

'OK,' she said, looking at me curiously. 'Well, he's in Room 4. First floor, along the corridor. Shall I let him know you're on your way?'

'Don't worry,' I said. 'I'll surprise him.'

'Nina?' my father said, flinging open the door a minute later. 'Yes, it is you! Marvellous. Well, come in. Bit strange, entertaining you here.'

I simply stared, drinking in the sight of him. Those dark brown, restless eyes that didn't quite go with the tanned face, the blue polo shirt, the chinos.

He didn't try to kiss me again, but patted my shoulder. 'Thank you so much for coming.'

I went in, hands in my pockets, trying to seem nonchalant. The room was tiny, stuffed with far-too-large furniture: a heavily lacquered four-poster bed, a desk festooned with foil-wrapped biscuits, tea bags and a kettle. And two large armchairs and a glass table.

George Parr pointed at the chairs and table. 'They always have this table-and-chair arrangement in hotel rooms.' He smiled at me in a friendly way. 'And it's so strange. Who actually ever uses their hotel room as a lounge? You don't ever think, "I'll have a cup of tea and a nice sit down in my hotel room." Do you?'

'I don't really stay in hotels much,' I said.

There was a pause. 'Aha.' He gestured to one of the chairs. 'Well, let's sit down and test their usability. May I get you a coffee?'

I shook my head.

'Or tea, or something . . .?' He looked at his watch. 'Bit early for something stronger, but this is rather momentous, isn't it? Wouldn't blame you if you wanted a whisky.'

'No, thanks.'

He tugged neatly at his trousers, just above his knees. Malc always did the same, and I felt the first stab of disloyalty, then shook it away. He sat down opposite me, and again I tried not to stare at him too much. My father. This is my *father*.

I licked my dry lips. 'So, why did you want to see me?'

The easy smile remained fixed on his face. 'I thought it'd be good to spend some time together. Just you and me.'

'But you didn't come back because of that, did you?' I said, my hands still in my pockets. 'The other night you said you want a divorce. That's why you're here, isn't it?'

'Partly. A little of this, a little of that. I wanted the chance to explain it all properly to you. Just the two of us.' When he smiled, the wrinkled skin around his eyes almost swallowed them up into nothing. 'Re the divorce, as I mentioned on Friday, I met someone several years ago now – a wonderful girl called Merilyn. She is very keen – as is her family, to whom I've become very close – that we marry. They're a prominent family in Ohio. I live in Ohio, did you . . .?'

I shook my head.

'No, of course you wouldn't. Anyway, you see . . . Merilyn . . . she's—'

'Not well, you said.'

'Yes. She's had thyroid cancer. Oh, it's perfectly treatable. She's doing awfully well. But the poor girl's been through a rough patch, and after all she's done for me it's the least I can do, don't you think?' He beamed at me.

'Yes. That's – that's . . .' I didn't know how to respond. 'I hope she makes a full recovery.'

'Thank you, Nina. Thank you.'

'So . . .' I was trying to get his motivation straight, trying to work out exactly why he was here. 'It's just, the other day, you said you were also back because of something to do with your mother's ashes. That's right, yes?'

'I'm killing two birds with one stone, as it were, yes. But, Nina, listen, I . . . I wanted to see you, too! You must understand that!' he exclaimed. 'Honestly, my dear, it was a very hard thing, leaving.'

'I'm sure,' I said, dryly.

'Yes. Well, I expect your mother hasn't provided the most flattering picture of me over the years.'

I flared up at that. 'That's not fair. Mum made out you were a hero. She used to talk about you all the time. Tell me stories, show me photos. I was so proud of you, growing up. She did everything she could to make sure I knew you, knew how happy we all were . . . you two were . . . before you died. Died—' I shook my head. 'Hah.'

He tapped at his eye, as though trying to shield himself against the light from the window. 'I apologise. I assumed otherwise. Never make assumptions without evidence. It wasn't quite like that, you see – the way I remember it – but then, I suppose my opinion's not worth much, is it? I'm the one who buggered off.' He smiled. 'Do you know how nice it is to be able to say that phrase? In the States they think you're about to sexually assault them.'

'Do they?'

'Look, Nina. You've no reason to believe me or even listen to me. It's bloody decent of you to come. I know your mother doesn't want you here. I only wanted to meet you properly. Explain myself. Tell you a bit more about my side of the family. I don't know what you know about it. About my mother, about Keepsake.' He cleared his throat. 'Listen, let me just get this straight. You haven't been there, have you? To Keepsake, I mean.'

'Of course not. I didn't really know about it till you turned up yesterday.' But I couldn't resist asking, 'It's . . . it's lovely, then, is it?'

'Ah . . .' He closed his eyes, and a curious smile spread across his face. 'It's extraordinary, Nina. Magical. Like a time warp. When you're there, it's hard to believe there are cities, or . . . or aeroplanes . . . or the rest of the modern world . . .' He trailed off. 'Mind you, it's a strange place to live. My house in Columbus was built in 2008. No ghosts, no paintings that stare at you – and personally, I like it better that way.' He glanced at the wall clock. 'Anyway, to business. First things first – would you mind giving these papers to your mother?' He handed me the bundle of papers on the desk.

'Oh . . .' I took them, weighing their heaviness. 'Yes, of course.'

'Explain she needs to telephone Charles Lambert at Murbles and Routledge to make an appointment. She can file for divorce if she wants – we've been living apart for over five years, and they expect it should be awfully simple if neither of us contests it. I imagine she'd like the whole thing sorted out as soon as I would. That chap,' he added, almost casually. 'Malcolm? He's her new fella, then?'

'No. They've been together for years,' I said. I didn't want to tell him anything more about Malc, I wasn't sure why.

His face cleared. 'Marvellous. So she's keen to get the business sorted out then, too. Tell her to give Murbles and Routledge a call. Chap called Charles Lambert, he's our guy.'

'Murbles and Routledge,' I said, repeating the words carefully. 'I've heard of them, I think.'

'Well, they're a pretty big City firm. Used to be in Truro then they set up shop in London. Been the family solicitors for decades.'

'OK.' I took the thick envelope he gave me and put it carefully in my bag. 'I'll pass it on to her.'

'Tell her it'd be good if—' he began, and then stopped. 'Excellent.'

'Look, I wouldn't worry,' I said callously. 'I'm pretty sure she doesn't want to be married to you any more, put it like that.'

He winced. 'Fair enough.' The kettle boiled and he stood up.

In the silence between us I began to feel the weight of it all, pressing down on my breastbone, my throat thickening. My father was fiddling around with tea bags, trying to sling one into a cup, the thread tangling around his fingers. It was the sight of these normal things, the little details of life, that kept me short-circuiting at the enormity of it all. Did he drink tea, or prefer coffee? Did he like thrillers or non-fiction? Had he watched *The Wire* or was he more into *Mad Men*? He was so posh: his voice was properly, plummily upper class. Had he always spoken like that? Did he still have his half of the Vashti Bunyan album somewhere? And did he have my toes? Mum had long, slender feet, and always told me my curled-up, ugly toes were beautiful. That they weren't just a result of wearing ill-fitting shoes for so much of my childhood but because 'you have your father's feet'. It used to confuse me terribly, when I was four or so: I didn't want a dead man's feet.

'Can I ask you something?'

'Of course, of course,' he said at once. 'Anything.'

'What were you doing all this time?' I said. 'Twenty-five years. Where have you been?'

'Oh . . .' He handed me a cup of tea but I pushed it away, not trusting myself to speak. 'I can't even begin to sort of . . . um . . . draft an apology, you know. Nothing quite does it. Look. I . . . I had to go. I'll be honest right now and say I'd have been an awful father, I'm sure of it.' He fixed his gaze on the floor. 'I suppose you don't even know what I do now.'

I shook my head.

'I'm the Professor of Entomology at Ohio State. And I'm a visiting professor at Iowa State. I publish under the name George Klausner – you might not have found me if you were googling me, you see.'

'I didn't ever google you,' I said in a whisper. 'I . . . I thought you were dead.'

'Of course.' He glanced up, and rubbed his forehead, almost angrily. 'Oh God. Let me try to explain what happened on the expedition. It was damned horrific, actually. George Wilson had a heart attack on the tiny plane we took out to the jungle. Poor old George. Very hot. There was a thunderstorm – you know what these little planes are like, made out of sticking plaster. The museum

179

got the wrong end of the stick when we finally got a phone line back to England. They thought Peter – that's the chap leading the expedition – said George Parr. Maybe he did, in the confusion of the moment . . .'

He ruffled his head, fidgeting. I noticed he fidgeted all the time – those long, fine fingers constantly plucking at something or rearranging something else.

'Chap called Simon went back in the plane with the body and the rest of us went on with the trip, further into the jungle. Did some wonderful work on the Glasswinged butterfly. It's quite tricky, finding them, they're fiendishly difficult to spot. That's the point of them, avoiding predators, you see? Anyway, we were there for a couple of weeks, incommunicado, and then we returned to the camp and the chap there told us there'd been this mix-up, that it had been reported wrongly – oh, what a mess! I had this moment, there, in the cabin. I put my net on, and I realised, it was as though *I* was invisible, for the first time in my life.

'Reuters would correct it, but it'd take days before it'd appear in the papers. And in the meantime, I was dead, to the rest of the world – and if people looked me up on the microfiche of some library they'd see I was dead. You understand?' His voice was hoarse. 'I was free. For the first time. I could go anywhere, be anything, not be George Parr any more. My father's name was Klausner – I was registered as Klausner on my birth certificate because of some cock-up in Truro when I was born. My mother was furious about it, but she never got it changed. Perhaps because she didn't want me to be a Parr – I always thought that was the case. So I'm not saying I wanted to go because of you, Nina. It wasn't that . . .'

He was far away, as he was telling me this, not here in this cramped room, his shoulders sloping, his face white under the biscuit tan.

'. . . it was that everything at home was wrong. I'd made all these mistakes. And I knew, the way things were with your mother, it was best I didn't go back. She knew it, I knew it. You saw what it was like the other night. I decided to leave the camp that day. I caught a bus to Caracas. Stayed with a chap I knew from the old expedition days.'

I rubbed my throat. 'But I don't understand. What did the others think when you didn't reappear?'

He gazed at me with those unreadable dark eyes. 'Oh . . . I don't know. I told Peter I thought it was time I jumped ship, too. Think I told them I had to leave early . . . see a man about a dog.'

'But, didn't Mum . . .? Didn't anyone tell her?'

'I don't think she looked that hard for me,' he said, simply.

'Well, you're the one who did a runner.' I cleared my throat, swallowing hard.

'Absolutely. Look, I've no excuse for it. I told you, didn't I? I'm a pretty damned terrible person, Nina, and I don't blame your mother for not being able to stand the sight of me.'

I didn't want to understand him, to feel sympathy for him. It was much easier if he was an out-and-out villain. I said, with difficulty, 'What did you do next?'

'Oh, I stayed in Caracas with Alphonse for a few weeks, doing some work for free at the Ciencias Naturales, then I flew to the States. I knew if I could get there I'd be OK. Fresh start. I'd been promised a grant at Ohio State if I was interested. I was working on a revolutionary theory about Batesian mimicry – now, let me try and explain—'

'I know what it is,' I said, softly.

He looked startled. 'You know about Batesian mimicry? This is extraordinary.'

'I read up on it when I was a teenager.'

'Why on earth did you do that?' he said, taking a sip of his tea, amused.

'I wanted to know more about you,' I said. I hated how sad it made me sound. I wanted him to think of me as a self-sufficient, successful person, someone utterly unaffected by his absence.

'Oh.' He was taken aback.

'I didn't really know anything about you. I mean Mum used to tell me things, but then it sort of petered out. So I thought if I found out about this, then I'd know what you were like a bit . . .' I trailed off, swallowing again. I couldn't bear it if I cried. He'd think it was for him and it wasn't; it was for six-, eight-, thirteen-year-old me who'd wished her dad was alive. 'I know about Glasswinged butterflies, too. Their wings have a nanoscale structure. That's why they don't reflect.'

My father put the tea down. 'This is wonderful.' He took one of my hands in his and then looked down, as if surprised. 'Nina. Really? Are you interested in them? That makes me very happy.'

'That was when I was younger,' I said, dully, taking my hand away. 'I don't remember any of it. I'm afraid I don't really like them much now.'

'Don't like butterflies? Why on earth not?' He looked astounded.

'Um . . .' I pulled at my sleeve, wanting to chew it but restraining myself. 'They remind me of you. And they made Mum really sad.'

He drew breath with a whistling sound. 'Ah. I'd love you to understand how beautiful they are. How important. They're a bell-wether for everything on the planet. If they're flourishing, we're flourishing. I wish people would see that. They're not just decoration. If you saw them at Keepsake, saw what we'd done to make the place welcoming for them . . .'

He trailed off, eyes slightly closed, head swaying minutely. As though he were in a trance, and then he opened his eyes wide for a second. 'Yes. Yes, you should. Damn it, of course you should. Why not?'

'Should what?'

He gritted his teeth. 'I wish you'd come with me to Keepsake. Just once. Even if just to see them. What we've got there.'

'Are there lots of butterflies, then?'

He laughed. 'You could say that. I say – really, seriously – would you come with me? It's yours, after all.'

'But I don't know the first thing about it. You say it's mine, but no one's ever been in touch with me, to inform me I've inherited a crumbling house on a creek in . . . where is it, exactly? I've only got your word for it.'

He was silent for a moment. 'I know. I don't know why they've never looked you up, old Murbles and Routledge. I mean, they've been the family's solicitors since old Murbles was a one-man-band outfit in Truro, aeons ago. They know more than I do, I bet you.

All I know is, the house is yours.' He slapped his knees. 'It'd be typical of her, to shut you out of your own inheritance for some strange reason. Perhaps because you're my daughter. Some last act of spite.' He gave a quick, expressive heave of the shoulders, then rubbed one slim finger down the bridge of his nose. 'Forgive me. Old ghosts. Suppose it's on my mind, rather – what with having to go back there. I don't think about that life much these days. Try not to.'

This seemed rather at odds with the rhapsodic way he'd described it earlier. 'Why?' I asked.

He exhaled. 'Let me explain about Keepsake.' Again, the narrowed eyes, as though he was sizing me up. 'Men can't inherit, not unless there's no other female heir in sight. Charles II, old Charlie boy, he's in a tight spot, you see? Hides out at Keepsake and there's our ancestor – that's the first Nina, and a beauty into the bargain – well, him being him, he gets her into trouble. She's hanging up there in the hall. Looks just like you. I swear it.'

I blushed, uncomfortable at his compliments.

'Nina writes off to Charles complaining he's left her with the upkeep of this vast house, no parents or much of an inheritance, and a baby to boot. We've got the letters, you'll see them. I can—' But he stopped. 'Anyway, Charles writes back. Gives her this decree. Sort of a pension every year for helping him, and some promise that Keepsake is hers and their daughter's. Sends her a socking great diamond brooch too, only she bloody sold that—'

'Who? Teddy?'

'Yes. Long story. Just before the war.' He scratched his nose again. 'When I read that bit, I have to say, I did slightly scream on your behalf, Nina.'

'Read what bit? Where?'

He gave me that blank look again. 'Oh, she wrote – er, well, she wrote to me, explaining it all, before she died. Listen . . . so, that's what I know of the situation. Probably rather rusty. Not much call for English hereditary law in Ohio, you understand.'

He sounded so affable. I thought then of Sue and Becky at work, of their *Downton* obsession. They'd love my father, his cut-glass accent, his flyaway blond hair: a TV drama version of an Englishman.

'My mother, Theodora Parr, was the ninth woman to inherit. There were a couple of men along the way, when there weren't any women. Frederick, he was a great collector, of first editions, doll's houses, oh, all sorts. Very interesting man. He was my great-great-great-grandfather. And, of course, Rupert the Vandal. Demolished the back of the house. They say he strangled a housemaid when she wouldn't . . . ah, well. Stories. He was a lunatic. Nasty piece of work. One comes to know them all, when one grows up there, rather like housemates . . . it's strange. Yes, Rupert was a bad lot.

'Now, to me and to most of us, the interesting one has always been his granddaughter, Mad Nina. She's the one who smuggled in the butterflies from Turkey. She's down there, too – of course she is . . .' He trailed off, and shook his head. 'She planted a mulberry tree that she brought back from Turkey. It's still there, two hundred years later. At least, I presume it's still there – oh, never mind all that. Old stories, as I say. I've grown up with them.'

'I know a bit of it all already,' I told him. 'The first Nina Parr, anyway. That book of yours, the one you left me.' I saw him start, just a little. '*Nina and the Butterflies*.'

'Gosh. I haven't thought about that book for . . . half a century. Haven't seen it since I was a boy.'

'But I have your copy,' I said, smiling at him.

'Don't think so. I didn't have a copy of my own, it was my mother's. Isn't it funny, how it's all locked away somewhere in the dim recesses of one's mind? *Nina and the Butterflies*. Jolly good little book, weird story and all.' He blinked. 'Wasn't there a list of her favourite butterflies at the back?'

'Yes,' I said, pleased he remembered. 'Eight or so. The Small Copper, and . . .' I trailed off. 'It's at home, though, I've always had it. You must have taken it with you to Noel Road.'

'Perhaps I did,' he said, vaguely. 'Can't think why. I hated thinking about the place, after I'd left, you see. Could you bring it with you, if . . . if we go?'

'Oh,' I said. 'Of course . . .' I hesitated.

'Your mother got it. She wasn't close to her parents, either. I never told her the full story, but I'd talk to her a bit about my family. She was almost the first person to understand, really.'

'Understand what?'

He said, with a gaiety that irritated me, 'Oh, that she was probably making a mistake, taking me on. All my problems.'

'What problems?'

'Growing up in a place like that . . . with a mother like that.'

'I still—' I stopped, and began again. 'I still don't understand what you mean about her.'

'I mean that on the subject of my mother I don't have a good word to say. Isn't that terrible?' Pink spots of colour appeared in his cheeks. 'I can't really explain it – I've had years to think it over, you know, but I can't seem to make sense of it, still. My new life is so very far away from it all, that's how it gets to one, occasionally. I'll be at my desk on campus, writing some paper or talking to some student, and it's all so clean and shiny and new, you know, and I realise this building we're sitting in is younger than the student in front of me, and then I remember Keepsake. It was being built while Shakespeare was writing plays. My room had frogs in the casement and moss on the floor, I always saw my own breath inside, and at night I heard things.' He gave a tired smile. He looked frightened; why was he frightened? 'I was cold for eighteen years – there, and then at boarding school – till I went to Oxford. There was no one who loved me, not one person, you see, not until I met Delilah. She was—' He broke off. 'It's a magical place, but I was wretched there. Rather dread the idea of going back. I can absolutely picture it . . . the river, the steps, the path up to the house . . . and it's all so real. Gosh, the unicorn.' He was blinking. 'Merilyn's been very helpful. She believes in total transparency. You see, I don't think my mother ever loved me at all.'

'I'm sure that's not true.'

'She always said everything changed with the war. It sucked life out of the living, and she was one of them. If you ask me, that was just a get-out clause.' He took a gulp of tea. 'Some people are meant to have children. Some aren't.'

I thought of Mrs Poll again. How some people who aren't your parents are better than parents. Of Malc, his hand on mine on Friday, how he'd seen right through my father. 'I don't know that that's true.'

'Well, it was in my case.' He put the empty cup on the bed, and said, suddenly, 'I'm painting far too gloomy a picture. Nina, what do you think? Will you come with me? Come and see Keepsake?'

'I don't think I can, no,' I heard myself say, like he'd just asked me to go for a sandwich down the road. 'Sorry.'

My father swallowed, and twitched his trousers at the knee again. 'May I ask why?'

I pulled at the skin at the side of a fingernail. 'I don't know you. And like I said – I've never heard the house is mine, or anything about it, other than in that book, and because I don't know you, and – well, I don't want to hurt my mum.' I picked my bag up. 'And . . .' I really didn't know how to say it. 'I'm just not sure I believe you. I'm sorry.'

'You – you don't *believe* me? What part of this don't you believe?'

'Not sure. I am sorry,' I said again, weakly. I felt rather desperate, like this was not how the reunion I'd been dreaming of should end.

'Nina, look. Come with me to Keepsake, just once. I won't ask anything else of you, you know.'

I watched him carefully. His eyes were dull, pleading. 'Don't you want to see if I'm lying? Put me to the test? Don't you want to at least see the house, so you can say later, when you're older, and you wonder where you came from, that you knew it, you stood in the place where your grandmother stood?'

I shifted uneasily under his gaze. 'But I never knew her. I don't have any—'

He hurried on before I could speak. 'I know *we* don't know each other, I certainly know you don't owe me a damn thing. But when all's said and done, I'm your father. Would you please—? Hah . . .' He bent his head, and to my astonishment a half-sob escaped from his throat. 'Please, do this, for the rest of us at least. That's all I ask of you.'

I stared at him, at his face, at the gesturing hands, the polished brogues.

'OK,' I said, eventually. 'I'll come with you.'

He nodded, head bobbing for slightly too long. 'Fantastic. Fantastic.'

'When?'

'I was thinking Wednesday. That suit? I've booked a hire car. Going to drive down.'

'Fine,' I said, wondering how I'd explain this – to Bryan and work, to Mum. 'What'll you do till then?'

'Oh – you know. See a man about a dog, and all that. I'm so bloody glad you'll come with me, Nina. I can't wait to tell Merilyn.'

'Can we get there in a day?'

He stood up. 'You'd better say you'll be away for a night. It's a long drive.'

I nodded. 'I'll have to find some excuse. And when it's over—'

'That's it. I completely understand,' he said, his wrinkly brow clearing straight away.

I stood up, wanting to get out of there now.

My father reached forward and squeezed my shoulder, awkwardly. 'I think you'll be glad you went.'

We stood facing each other, staring uncertainly at one another and I found myself wishing I'd said no. And yet, to finally be there . . . To test the theory of this fantasy world which kept intruding into my drab, grey existence. I'd agreed to go now, and I had to see it through. In the next room a door slammed, and heavy footsteps thudded past our silent room. My father started.

'I'd better be off,' I said, and I slung my bag over my shoulder. 'G-goodbye, then.'

He handed me the papers. 'Don't forget these. Bye, Nina.' He kissed my cheek, awkwardly. 'I am awfully glad you came.'

I didn't know how to answer him. I simply nodded, gave a half, helpless sort of shrug, and shut the door quietly behind me.

Chapter Fourteen

I tramped back up Pentonville Road in a brief but piercing cold June shower. Rotting, brown blossom leaves mingled with rubbish along the roads and as I walked through the slim, spine-shaped gardens of Colebrooke Row, watching the toddlers out with parents, dog owners chatting together in the one respite of green amidst the urban terraces, I kept thinking about my father. There was, I realised now, so much I'd forgotten to ask him. What was Merilyn like, where had he met her? What did he do all day? Why had he come back on my fourteenth birthday? Why – so many whys.

But I'd see him again. We'd have hours in which to do nothing but ask and answer questions, on the way to Keepsake, wherever it was. And once again I wondered how I'd explain this journey to Mum.

When I arrived back home, shivering in my thin cardigan, Mum was still in bed. When I went out that evening, to go to my old flatmate Elizabeth's for dinner, she was snoring – I could hear her as I came downstairs. She was still in bed the next morning, as Malc and I ate breakfast together in awkward silence.

On Monday afternoon, when I hadn't heard from him again, I emailed my father. He replied immediately.

Come to the Warrington, first thing Weds morning. The earlier we start, the better. Is 6.00 OK?

Hope you don't mind if I say that I was terrifically proud to have met you and seen what a remarkable young woman you are.

Enough of this! See you on Wednesday.

Your father

George

I rather admired the way my father, in defiance of all modern speech, used words like 'terrifically'.

That night I had strange dreams about driving down long roads, giants lumbering towards us, in a tiny two-seater. I kept hearing that rhyme again; I didn't know that I'd remembered it.

Nina Parr, locked herself in, Charlotte the Bastard,
    daughter of a king . . .
And then comes me, little old Teddy, the last girl you see.

But I felt as though I had a purpose now. I can't explain it other than that I was waking up. That something in my life was happening and I was part of it. Because my father had come back – anything was possible.

Sebastian kept texting me.

When did you last see your father? (too soon?) Call me x

Is your mother out of bed? My mother thinks he's after your money. Mind you, so is she now she thinks you might be a landowner. She's being very nice about you, I have to tell you. x

Do you want a drink tonight? x

Though the sight of his name flashing up on my screen made my heart leap alarmingly, though it made me blush, glancing over my shoulder to see if anyone nearby had noticed my reaction, though I couldn't think about him without closing my eyes and smiling, I managed to ignored these messages like little flags, waving cheerily down at me from the Heath. I knew I'd have to see him properly at some point. But not yet. I had to work this out first.

On Tuesday morning I came down to breakfast. Malc had gone for a run. I emptied the dishwasher, made some coffee, packed my bag for work, had a banana and a slice of toast. I put out the recycling and fed the goldfish (which Mum had bought when I'd got married and which now lurked, unloved, in a corner of the kitchen). I put some washing on and then got a tray and, climbing the stairs, kicked the piles of old *National Geographic*s and Penguins out of the way. I knocked on Mum's door and, without waiting for an answer, I went in.

She was sitting up in bed, holding a cup of tea, reading.

'Hi,' I said, putting down the tray. 'I brought you some breakfast.'

Mum said nothing, though her eyes stopped moving across the pages of her book.

'I'm off to work now,' I said. 'I came to give you something, since I haven't seen you for two days. I met up with Dad on Saturday, and he asked me to give you these divorce papers.' I dropped the thick envelope on to the bed, and she looked at it. 'It seems very straightforward. There's no financial settlement, he waives all right to any royalties from your books, and the solicitors are waiting to hear from you to set up a meeting so you can go in with the papers. I've emailed Bryan – he says he can act for you if you want, as you should definitely have your own solicitor, even though it should all be pretty simple. Bryan Robson,' I said, because she was still silent. 'My boss at Gorings.'

I looked down at the crumpled old duvet. It was from Habitat on Tottenham Court Road and she and I had bought it one Sunday in the sales, giddy with the excitement of purchase. It had red, pink, blue and green asymmetric patterns all over it and had been the most exotically new and trendy item in our house for years. I hadn't noticed – I was rarely in my parents' bedroom, obviously – how it was worn, the red faded to salmon, one corner frayed and torn.

'Mum?' I said, trying not to sound desperate.

She sort of gave a half-shrug, as though she didn't want to totally ignore me and put her tea down next to the bed. But she carried on reading her book.

I put my hands on my hips, and bit my lip. 'Mum? Are you listening to me? *Mum?*'

Still she didn't react and suddenly something snapped inside me, like an elastic band. I tore the book out of her grasp, and threw it on the floor. 'Look at me!' I grabbed her face in my hands, fingers pinching her soft pink-and-white skin, and I stared at her, teeth bared, breathing hard, nostrils flared. She met my gaze, her green eyes hollow – no expression in them at all. I was crouched over her and I tightened my grip on her, her head jerking up and away from the bed.

I was horrified as I was doing it, one part of me flattened against the wall, watching this scene at a distance. But I couldn't stop myself, this other part of me that had said nothing for years, not asked questions, tried to be good, to pretend everything was always OK, smiled when she was sad.

'I asked you a question, Mum.' My breath was hot, heavy on her face. 'I asked you a bloody question.'

We were frozen together, me over her like some kind of beast, she in her pyjamas, her head twisted towards me. She didn't even seem to react.

I thought I might hit her. Or strangle her. I have never felt rage like it; I hope I never do again. She reached up, then, and put her hand on mine, the one gripping her neck, and instantly my hold loosened.

Then, quite quietly, she said, 'I heard you. Now, could you leave me alone?' She picked up her cup of tea, took a sip, and stared into space.

Already shaking, I climbed off the bed, picked up her book and gave it to her.

'Mum . . .' I blinked, then wiped my face. It's impossible to know how to behave, how to react, when someone simply blocks you at every turn. So I said, 'I . . . I don't know what to say to you. There's so much I want to ask you about.'

But she just opened *The Talented Mr Ripley* as though I wasn't there.

'I'm going away with Dad tomorrow,' I said, staring at her. 'I'll be gone for the night, maybe two. I'm telling you so you know where I am. When I get back I'm moving out of here. Elizabeth's sister is going away for two months and I can stay there till I find something else.' I turned back at the door, tears running down my cheeks now. 'OK, then. Bye.'

I heard the sheets rustle, something move as I closed the door, a light thud, but I was probably imagining it. On the way downstairs, I kicked the rest of the magazines out of the way in a fury, and slid on one, landing on the hall floor with a painful thud. Mum's messiness used to drive even the usually calm Mrs Poll sometimes to distraction. 'Delilah, dear, someone will break their bloody neck,' she'd exclaimed once, after skidding down the last three steps on a pile of *Private Eyes*.

I looked at myself in the hall mirror. My wet lashes had streaked mascara on to my brow-bone above my eyes, and my face was burning red. I put my hands to my hot cheeks, looking at myself. I wished I'd left already, that I was away from here, on the road with my father on our way to Keepsake.

Chapter Fifteen

I went to work and tried to concentrate on Bryan's latest case – a probate dispute involving a lonely old man who'd left everything to his home care helper and whose family were disputing the terms of the will – which was, by turns, mundane and horribly distressing. I went with Sue to the work kitchen for 'a private chat' when she asked, and said I'd help her plan Becky's upcoming baby shower. I listened to Sue's concerns about the non-light-blocking blinds her daughter Li had chosen for her new conservatory, and the fun they'd had picking out cushions. I even remembered Bryan's meeting at twelve thirty, and extracted him from a difficult phone call. This was what I needed – the total focus of doing something else that heartbreak gave you. My mum's face, my hands gripping her, my total, utter blazing fury with her for lying to me and absenting herself, then and now, plus the fact that – well, she didn't really seem to care.

At lunchtime I walked down to the London Library. I was climbing the back stairs of the Stacks towards the butterfly section, when I heard a voice.

'Nina?' someone hissed from the nearby shadows.

I turned, and there was my father.

The strange thing was that it was as though I'd almost expected to find him here. Still, I said, 'Well, my goodness!'

He kissed me, a broad grin on his face. 'What a lovely surprise – though, of course, why should it be! So you come here, do you?'

'Most lunchtimes.' I frowned at him, arms crossed, heart thumping at the sight of him, and suddenly I wanted to burst into tears, and I found myself wishing I could throw my arms around him, sob on his chest, tell him all of it. I swallowed, wrinkled the prickling feeling in my nose away. 'I like it here.'

'That's absolutely wonderful.' He looked so pleased, it was almost touching.

'Well, you gave it to me,' I said.

'Yes, yes . . .' He paused. 'What's that?'

'The membership. Life membership to the library.'

'Oh.' He looked rather vague. 'Did I?'

'Yes, you bought it for me before you left. On my sixteenth birthday they wrote to tell me I could start using it now, and it was thanks to you.' I smiled. 'Don't you *remember*?'

'Oh.' There was a strange look in his eye and then he said, 'Don't remember a lot of things. Of course, of course. It's a wonderful place. And here we are.' He collected up the pile of books he'd amassed and tucked them under his arm. 'Such a lovely day. Will you come and sit in the square with me? I've got some sandwiches. We could have a sort of picnic.'

'Absolutely,' I said, and I smiled happily at him.

Outside in St James's Square he spread out his newspaper, then his jacket, and gestured for me to sit down.

I protested. 'I'll be fine. You sit there. I don't want to ruin your jacket.'

'Nonsense!' he said. 'I'm used to sitting on grass. Most of my undergraduate years were spent on wet grass, debating something or smoking something else.' He gestured again.

This time I complied. 'Thank you.'

'My pleasure. It really was so lovely to see you on Sunday.'

I felt oddly shy. 'Well, I'm all ready for tomorrow.'

'Grand. Marvellous. Yes, I've been working up to it. Got a few extra books out to study in case we see anything out of the ordinary.' He patted the pile next to him and I glanced at the spines, curiously. *A Field Guide to the Butterflies of Turkey, Anatolian Skippers and Mutations, The Müllerian Myth, A Corner of Eden.*

'Just some light reading, then,' I quipped, and he smiled rather uncertainly. I took my shoes off, pressing my toes into the soft grass. 'I've told Mum it might be two nights, just in case.'

'Right. Well, I don't expect so, but yes, that could be a wise move.'

'OK. But, you know, if we're there for longer than we realise—' I sounded overeager.

'Sure.' He drew his knees up in front of him, hugging himself boyishly. 'Nina, I can't wait for you to see Keepsake. I wonder whether we can stay there or not. If not, there's a nice old pub down the way on the river. Well, there used to be.' He looked uncertain for the first time. 'Be interesting to see what state the house is in. The chaps at Murbles and Co. weren't sure. Mother was pretty eccentric towards the end but she was absolutely passionate about the house. It was the one thing she actually liked, you know. After Father and Tugie died.'

'Tugie?'

'Our dog. Stupid mutt. Some people thought he was intelligent. I never saw it myself. He bit me once.' A shadow crossed his face; he looked almost petulant.

'It'll be pretty strange for you, to go back there. After all this time away.'

He nodded. 'Yes. And again, you know, I don't think I've quite apologised enough for not being in touch. It's rotten of me. I'm so glad you're being so decent about the whole thing. To be honest, I'm awfully glad you're coming with me. I'd be rather apprehensive, going back there alone.' He must have seen my expression change. 'Oh, not because of anything sinister, you understand. There's no ghosts—' He stopped.

'You don't sound quite sure.' I tried to sound jokey, and waggled my toes.

'Ha! Course there aren't. Don't you worry about that.' He leaned across me and took a sandwich out of his jacket pocket. 'Beef and watercress, I hope that's OK. Share it with me, won't you? Merilyn doesn't eat meat, and since she does most of the cooking it's a real treat for me to have it.'

'So how did you meet her?' I said, accepting one half of the sandwich. I was ravenous.

'Oh, you know.' He waved his arm. 'She's from a fairly prominent Ohio family. They're major donors to the university, always have been. Her father gave us the new Entomology building three years ago. Very sadly – rather tragic, in fact – the old gentleman had a stroke last summer. So Merilyn and I met at the opening ceremony.

She'd been abroad, studying, so we hadn't met before. We both gave speeches. And that was that.'

'How old is she?'

He raised his eyebrows.

'If you don't mind me asking.'

'Why should I mind!' he cried. 'She's thirty. Next year.'

I took another bite of the sandwich. 'Great.'

'Yes. She's wonderful,' he said. 'I can't wait for you to meet her, Nina. She's very good for me. Pushes me on. Drives me to be better. Her father sold milk machines. Dairy's their biggest industry there, you know. The man's a multi-millionaire. Grew up in a one-room shack outside Toledo, done it all through sheer self-belief, and Merilyn's inherited that. The American dream.' He took a big bite of the sandwich, and chewed ruminatively.

'What does she do?'

'Merilyn?'

'Um . . . yes.'

'Oh, this and that. She's always busy! She's a fund-raiser. She's trying to persuade her father to settle some money on us—' He smiled. 'On the university, I mean. The Entomology department and our campus. We have to expand to remain competitive. There's a big drive at the moment to increase admissions – we're a little down – and also to increase the standard of admissions. We want to lead the field in exploratory theory, in the understanding of diurnal lepidoptera and conservation. We want the university to be really up there. The best.' He swallowed.

'What do you have to do to get to those standards? Find a new butterfly?'

He laughed, and started to choke a little, and I had to give him some water.

'Something like that,' he said, eventually.

We sat in companionable silence, as the trees above us swayed in the light breeze, as the office workers around us gossiped over their lunches, read papers, dozed. I stole a glance at him occasionally, hoping he didn't notice, but it was so nice. My father. My real, actual father. The hotel room seemed like a bad dream. If I'd ever idly imagined what I'd want my dad to be like, it had been something like this: sitting outside the London Library, eating sandwiches and chatting.

'Will you bring Merilyn over?' I asked him.

'Yes—' For the first time, he looked uncomfortable. He looked at me, as though weighing something up, then said, 'I'm afraid she's not all that keen on . . . um . . . coming here, until we're married, you see. It's been rather difficult to persuade her to let me come at all, until I realised I'd have to, to sort it all out.'

'But why, though?'

'Oh, I think she feels I'll . . . I don't know. Some rubbish about your mother. Dill is rather the bogeyman in her eyes. She's convinced we'll meet again after twenty-five years and instantly fall into each other's arms.'

Despite my anger with Mum I couldn't help laughing incredulously. 'Is she serious?'

'Oh, quite.'

'Well, you should tell her not to worry. I can't imagine who Mum loathes more than you. Boris Johnson, maybe.'

'Who's he?'

I stared at him, then shrugged: why would he know? 'He's Mayor. Of London.'

'Ah. Forgive me. It's been so long.'

There was an awkward pause.

I said abruptly, 'When did my grandmother die, by the way?'

He screwed up his face. 'Not sure. Fourteen, fifteen years ago?'

'Was it when . . .? Is that when we saw you?'

'When you saw me?'

'It was my birthday. Outside the house?'

'Ah. It was a few years before then. I'd come back to see – well, I wanted to see you, actually. Rather silly. Cowardly.'

'Did you have to come back for her funeral?'

'Oh, nothing like that. In fact, I should have taken the ashes back then. I just couldn't face it. She—' He pressed his hands to his face. 'I'm telling you all my secrets. No, I suppose it made me think of you – her dying, and all that. There was a conference I'd been invited to and normally I'd just have said no. I wasn't interested in coming back to England. But this time I told myself I'd pluck up the courage to try and see you.'

I picked furiously at the scrubby grass underneath us, not trusting myself to meet his gaze. 'I wish I'd known that.'

'I wish I'd been brave enough to do something about it. I'm afraid I walked past your house several times. Hoping to see you, and your mother—' He covered his eyes with one hand. 'Oh, it's pathetic – when I damn well deserve nothing, anyway. But I felt I had to try.'

Very quietly, I asked, 'Why didn't you just cross the road? Say hello?'

'It's the way she looked at me,' he said. 'Absolute loathing . . . and fear. I knew. I saw that chap with her. I made assumptions – rightly. I was going to, Nina.' He took my hand, folding it in his, suddenly, and shook his head, blinking hard at me. 'If you imagine I haven't spent every day thinking about you . . .' his voice thickened, 'you're damned well wrong. I have. So—' He dropped my hand suddenly, and I jumped. 'It's no excuse, my dear. I'm a chicken. That's the only excuse I have.'

'Mrs Poll always used to say weak people give multiple excuses. That if you just want to get out of something or explain something, give one reason only.'

The first time I hadn't wanted to go upstairs to see her – when Malc had let me watch *Four Weddings and a Funeral* on video after school as a treat for getting an A in my maths test, as I was terrible at maths (the trouble he got into with Mum afterwards for allowing me, aged eleven, to see a 15-rated film, we will pass over here) – I'd called up the stairs, instead. 'I can't have tea today, sorry, Mrs Poll. I've got a sore throat. And Jonas might come round. And I have to wait in for Mum. She's forgotten her key.'

She'd opened the door to the flat and stared down at me, the light from the afternoon sun framing her in the doorway. I couldn't make out her face.

'If you don't want to come up, just say so, Nina darling. I don't need three different excuses. See you tomorrow.'

That was the only time she ever made me feel small, or uncomfortable. Three months later, she was dead. I shook my head, willing the memories away.

'Mmm,' my father said, watching me carefully. 'Yes, quite right. Who is this Mrs Paul you keep mentioning?'

'Our upstairs neighbour. She used to look after me when I was young.' I added, 'Mrs *Poll*. She was wonderful. You'd have liked her.'

'Terrific.' He wasn't really listening. 'Oh, I say. Shouldn't you go, Nina?'

I looked down at my watch. 'You're right.' I scrambled to my feet. Bryan had a meeting at two thirty for the probate case; I was expected to show them up, fetch them coffee. 'I'd better run. Are you staying here?'

'For the moment. I have to meet someone later.'

'Oh.' Again the yawning gulf of ignorance between us loomed. I smiled, politely. 'Old friend?'

He stood up too. 'Something like that. Family business. One last thing to arrange. I'm not sure if it's the right—' and he stopped, and cleared his throat. 'I'll . . . well, I'll be able to explain it tomorrow, I hope.'

I didn't want him to feel awkward. 'Of course. I'll see you then. Bright and early. Yes?'

'Yes, very bright and early.' He leaned forward swiftly and grabbed my face between his hands, exactly as I had done with my mother, that morning. 'Goodbye, Nina.' He kissed my forehead. 'Look, let me say it properly. I'm jolly proud of you, you know.'

But you don't know anything about me, I thought, as I gave him a hug, wanting to nestle into his arms, knowing I had to leave. You don't know I was married, or that I have twelve copies of *The Secret Garden*, or that I had an imaginary friend, or that what I really want to do is be a teacher but that in fifteen minutes I have to fetch coffee for a man who didn't visit his own mother for a year but wants all her money.

I said, 'Bye, then.'

And he said, 'This has been wonderful. It's really made me . . . glad.'

'Glad?'

'Never mind,' he said, and he clapped me on the shoulder: my father / George / Dad. What should I call him? We'd discuss it tomorrow on the drive down to wherever it was, I said to myself as I walked out through the square. Devon? Gloucestershire? The Isle of Wight? It could be anywhere. So much we each didn't know. But we had to start somewhere.

As I turned up the street I took one last look at him. He was watching me go, waving and smiling.

Chapter Sixteen

Like the child who can't wait for holidays, I packed early when I got home from work that evening, humming to myself as the spring sunshine flooded my room with honeyed light. Sebastian messaged me again:

> Are you alive? Did I do something wrong? Am I sending the world's most needy messages? What's going on with you? Don't shut me out, Nina. Don't care how sad I sound, CALL ME. S

I folded T-shirts, jumpers, Converse and skirts into my overnight bag and wondered where my wellingtons were, and whether I'd need them – there was a river, wasn't there? Something about a boat? So it might be muddy? I wished I could think of an excuse to go into Mum's room. To apologise, or at least start talking. But the door was shut and I wasn't brave enough to venture back there.

And I wished, too, that I was the kind of person who knew how to just walk in and start talking; a person more like her, in fact. I wondered again about genes: I didn't really take after her at all, did I? The fact was I was half George Parr, half my mother. Not the child of Dill and Malc, which I'd been since I was eleven. 'Malc's your father now,' Mrs Poll had told me, as she left for the holiday from which she wouldn't come back. She'd kissed me hard on the cheek, stepping into the rumbling black cab, pulling her fine leather gloves on, bag swinging under her arm. 'Remember that.'

Jonas had come round for tea and to watch *Home and Away* and I was annoyed with Mum for pulling me away from him to say goodbye to Mrs Poll. I remembered my impatience at her saying that to me – it was embarrassing to talk about Malc like that in front of him – and my faint feeling of disgust as I wiped the wet kiss she'd left on my skin away. Her face in the rear window of her taxi, watching us, pale as the moon, Mum gripping my arm, forcing me to wave at the retreating cab.

'Don't be so rude, honey. She's not been well. She's going away for a month. You'll miss her.'

'I know. Can I go back in now?'

'Wait till she's round the corner.'

Then she was gone, and I didn't realise. Until it was too late, of course.

I finished packing, thinking about it all, then I went downstairs. I'd emailed my father – *Should I bring wellies?* – and was going to make myself something to eat, then head back upstairs for an early night.

I hadn't noticed before but now I saw that the kitchen was spotless – Mum must have been down here while I was out. I wondered if I should just take her up a cup of tea. I called up to her room. 'Mum? Mum, do you want a cup of tea?'

No reply.

I crept back up to her room, and stood outside. I knocked, very softly. 'Mum? I'm sorry about earlier. Do you want anything to eat?'

I heard the duvet rustling, and the sound of the TV coming on, and the volume, some quiz programme, getting louder and louder.

'Mum?' I said, this time almost shouting above the unbearable noise of it. 'Mum, are you in there?'

Then I heard her, voice hoarse, yelling above the reverberating voices, almost unbearably loud. 'If you *really* do go with him, don't come back here afterwards. You'd better pack your things now and stay with Elizabeth! You understand?'

'OK,' I shouted back. 'That's fine.' Pretending it was normal, that I was busy, occupied, I went back downstairs, heated up some soup, and turned on the TV too, slumping into the battered old sofa in the corner of the kitchen.

I sat there until it was almost dark, not really concentrating on anything, just stagey reality shows and feeble comedies. I couldn't find anything else to watch and couldn't make the effort to find something to take my mind off the noise from upstairs. I didn't want to, anyway. I was going tomorrow. I was out of here, literally. I was going west – it had to be west, didn't it? – with my dad. As I stood up to make a hot drink to take up to bed, Malc walked in, making me jump violently.

'Sorry I'm late,' he said. 'They found the body. In a suitcase. I've been in Hemel Hempstead.' He rubbed his eyes. 'It was . . . actually, it was absolutely horrific.'

'You like horrific bodies, Malc.'

'Maybe I'm going soft.' He shrugged, wearily.

'Oh, Malc,' I said, looking at him carefully. 'Have you eaten?'

He ignored the question. 'What's going on?' He gestured upstairs, where the noise from the TV was still dominating the house.

'Um . . . Mum. She's had it this loud for a couple of hours now.'

'Why?'

'I . . . I've upset her.' I didn't know how to start to explain. 'Sorry, Malc.'

Malc looked up. 'Don't apologise, love. None of this is your fault.' He looked around, as if spurring himself on to action. 'I'll have some tea, I think. Maybe with something stronger in it.' He pulled two mugs off the shelf. 'Sit down.' Malc, so gentle in so many things, likes his tea precisely brewed. Gratefully, I sat down on one of the kitchen stools.

'I don't know why she's being like this,' I said, after a few moments' silence. 'I . . . How can she just lie in bed, not wanting to explain any of it to you? To me? How can she do that?'

He didn't reply immediately. 'Nina, love,' he said eventually. 'I don't think one gets to grips with something as big as what's happened straight away . . . do you? You thought your dad was dead. You know now she knew he wasn't. I suppose the issue now is whether you accept your mother's explanation for lying to you.' He handed me a mug of tea. 'You see, I do.'

'You're OK with it?'

'You know . . . yes, I am,' he said. 'It was tough for her.'

'I know it was tough,' I said. 'I bloody know it was.'

'In ways you don't remember, Nins,' he said, gently. 'She had a lot to put up with.'

'Yes, but . . .' I trailed off.

'Not just coping,' he said. 'I mean coping with having prolonged the lie.'

'So you really didn't know?'

'Oh, I realised a while ago. Maybe when you were fourteen or fifteen. After the previous time on your birthday when she confined herself to bed. I realised then he couldn't be dead.' The tea was scalding, and I winced. 'Have some milk.'

'How did you work it out then?'

'She was always funny about him. Angry, you might say. There was an energy there, and you don't talk like that about dead people. So I started to wonder. And I decided there must have been a good reason for her to think he'd gone away for ever.'

'Why the hell didn't you just ask her?'

'I tried to, believe me. But she shut it down. She shut so much of herself down, Nina, it's amazing she's been able to function for all these years. I believed he was alive, and I knew if he was alive and she was concealing it from both you and me that there must be a reason for it. And that it must have cost her a great deal. I didn't want her to have anything else to carry. She's carried too much over the years, you know.'

'Oh.' I stared at him. 'You're a good man, Malc.'

Malc chuckled and reached for the biscuit tin. 'Och, no. Have a Jaffa Cake.'

'Maybe I should have guessed too then,' I said.

'No, Nins, no. She wouldn't have wanted you to know. I'm sure of that. I think she thought she was protecting you.'

I could feel my stomach churning, and I said, 'Did you know any of the rest of it? About the house, or my grandmother? Or why he came back?'

'Well, of course not. I don't think she would have done, either. But she never trusted him, so you have to wonder why he's back.' He shrugged. 'Look. It is big news, I know that. But it doesn't change some things. She's still your mum, and a wonderful mum, and I'm still . . . I'm still your only stepfather. And I don't want to make some big speech about it, so I'll just say, you're like a daughter to me and you were from the moment I first saw you with your tangled hair and your wee little face buried in some ballet book. And you always will be to me, and it's been my great privilege to have helped bring you up. Right?' He glanced up at me for a split second, then went back to staring into his tea.

'Right.' Tears stung my eyes. 'Oh, Malc.' I stood up and hugged him from behind, put my head on his back, and he carried on stirring his tea, but I could tell he was smiling. I knew I had to tell him. I said, 'I met him on Sunday. In a hotel. My father. And today. I saw him for lunch.'

'I see.' Malc slid the biscuit tin back towards me.

I was taken aback at his total lack of interest. 'He's my dad, Malc.'

'Of course. So what did he want?'

'He . . . he wants me to go back to Keepsake with him.'

Malc glanced at me. 'Why's he wanting to do that, Nins?'

'To see it. And, well, it's mine, Malc. So I do need to go there.'

'You know it's yours?'

The question tripped me a little. 'Course it's mine.'

'How do you know that?'

'Because he . . . he says it is.' I stared at him. 'I've said I'll go. Tomorrow. Just this once. He's not back from the States for long and he's said he'll take me.' I realised I sounded as though I wanted Malc's approval, when I knew what I was doing, I knew why I'd agreed. 'Look, I'm going – I have to go. Don't tell me I'm making a massive mistake.'

Malc put the mug down noiselessly on the marble counter.

'Malc?'

When he looked up again his mouth was set in a small, tight line. 'Don't go, Nins.'

'I know. I know he's weak and stupid and he did a really bad thing, and he's probably making it all up. But he's my father.'

'Yes.' Malc looked down, and said something, quietly. 'Of course he is, love. But that doesn't mean anything.'

'No one could have been a better dad than you, Malc,' I said, my throat thick with unsaid things. 'You know that. It's more that Mum has to understand he's—'

'Nins, you know what your mother told me on Friday night? After he'd gone?' He stopped, and the sound of characters shouting at each other on the television upstairs blared louder than ever. 'She tried to kill herself, seven months after he left. Did you know that? That's how bad a state he left her in.'

I stepped back a little, so that I was leaning on the kitchen counter. 'What?'

'She left you with Mrs Poll and took an overdose. She had to have her stomach pumped, did you know that?' Malc rubbed his head again.

I said, in a small voice, 'No. Course I didn't know that.' I pursed my lips, trying not to cry. Because if I was completely honest, it wasn't that great a surprise.

'Well, she did.'

'You never knew?'

'Well, after we'd got together, she told me she'd tried to once, a long time ago, but she didn't tell me why. The electricity had just been cut off and she couldn't wash your nappies, Nina. And she was so ashamed of relying on Mrs Poll, of asking for money when her giro hadn't come through, of having nothing. She was at rock bottom. Do you know what she said? She said she honestly thought you'd be better off with someone else. And she was convinced he wasn't dead by then, but she'd given up hope of hearing from him. She knew he had money, and she thought this might be the only way to get him back, get him to give you a better life.'

The idea that she thought anyone would be better than her. The idea that Mum could ever be replaced. 'Oh, Mum,' I said, my throat hard. 'Poor Mum.'

'I know she's not easy.' He gave a small smile. 'I know she's hysterical and unreliable and she's selfish – oh, goodness, she's so selfish – but . . .' He rubbed his nose. 'What he put her through, it changed her. I know it wasn't entirely his fault, but he was the cause—'

'*You* really think she's selfish?' In other circumstances it would be extraordinary that we were breaking our self-imposed rules, talking like this about her, that he was saying these things.

'Nins, I know she's not allergic to balloons. I know she lies to get out of seeing my friends when they come round. I know there's no new book, that she likes the way she's treated with kid gloves because she might be writing one and she's too terrified to actually finish it in case it's no good. I'm sure she drove your father up the wall, but—' He stopped. 'Actually, you know, I bet she didn't. He doesn't seem like the type. I think she blamed herself, when he's the one who'd have left no matter whom he was married to, you know.'

'He's really very nice, if you give him the—'

'When she told him she was pregnant,' Malc said, 'he said, "Oh, for God's sake, why did you have to go and do that?" I think that's pretty strange, for a scientist. Not knowing the basic rules of conception.'

'That's not true,' I said. 'Honestly, I think sometimes she—'

'Aren't you listening? I know she exaggerates, I know she's tricky. But she's become like this, more and more, over the years to hide how much she hates herself for lying to you, for trying to kill herself, for not being able to cope when he left, and so on. For not writing more books, for acting the way she sometimes does.' His eyes twinkled. 'She thinks if she behaves badly, or pushes us away, that we'll have reason to not love her, to leave. Don't you see? Don't you, of all people, see that?'

The sound of the theme music of some programme coming from Mum's room was so loud the speakers crackled with excess static. I wondered how she could stand it.

'But Malc, when I was little, I didn't care about any of that. I wanted someone who knew my shoe size or made me a proper tea. Not Mrs Poll, all the time.'

'But again, don't you think that's remarkable? That she let Mrs Poll in? That she let her basically bring you up like that? How damaging it was for your mother's self-esteem? You know, you called Mrs Poll "Mummy-Poll" for a while when you were young, and it made her so upset, but what could she do?' Malc spread his arms wide. 'Very little. I think she sort of backed herself into this life and found herself trapped, and the good things – you, the books, Mrs Poll – she found it harder and harder to know how to do right by them.'

'But—'

'Honestly, love. That's why I think, if you go, you'll . . . you'll be sending her a message.'

'The house. It's mine,' I said. 'Come on, Malc.'

'Let's find out more first. Do it with her. Not him. Go to these solicitors instead. Ask them. Ask Lise Travers. We can look it up. Just don't go with him.'

It was very still in the dark room. Bitter tears stung my eyes, hurting my throat, my nose.

I took a deep breath. 'Look,' I said, 'I'll be back by Thursday. I have to see the place, understand what made him like that. Why he . . . what it's all about.'

I reached for his hand but he moved back a little.

'It won't be anything,' he said, smiling, angrily. 'I tell you, it's a whole heap of rubbish and heartache for nothing, Nina, and it's ye and your mother who'll get hurt, not him, ach—' He shook his head.

'No.'

'But why?'

'Why? I've never done anything brave in my life. I'm not like her, even though you say I am.' I tried to stand straight and look at him. 'Marrying Sebastian was the only outlandish thing I've done, and it wasn't brave, it was stupid. I have to see it – to understand – I'm sorry, Malc.'

He turned away from me then. I pulled my bag over my shoulder, and went upstairs, without another word. What could I say? I covered my ears as I passed Mum's bedroom.

Standing on the staircase I heard Malc pick up his running things, and in a couple of minutes the front door closed. I went back down to the kitchen and made him a sandwich, just the way he likes it. Roast chicken with chicken jelly, Stilton, lettuce, Dijon mustard. I put it under a plate and stuck a note on top, which read:

I've never needed another Dad
apart from you.

(Sandwich under here)
↓
X X X

Back in my room, I closed the door and sat down on the single bed, covered with my mother's old quilt, all the way from New York. She used to talk about her childhood bedroom. It was huge and draughty, her parents lived in a big old apartment building where the heating frequently failed. There were icicles at the window and snow ploughs every year, and a man in the flat next door, around a corner, who played in a band and used to argue with his wife a lot. One day, when Mum was small, through her window which backed on to theirs, she saw him hit his wife and she didn't get up. Mum didn't tell anyone, as she was afraid of the man in the band; he had shouted at her once. She never saw the wife again. I hate to think of her there, small, sad, worried, sitting on her bed alone, waiting for things to get better.

The quilt was soft, the rose pattern worn away, and it seemed always to smell of something exotic, old. Not musty, just . . . different. It had always been on my bed. When I was a baby and she looked into my cot and thought about killing herself, when I was fourteen and I bled on it when I got my first period and wanted to hide away with shame, and now, aged twenty-five, still a child in this house, the child of my brave, scared mother. Mum who, after a girl pushed me over and then threw my packed lunch in the canal four days running, stormed into the playground at primary school one Friday lunchtime, grabbed Amy-who-looked-like-a-boy's ear, pulling her towards the tree by the canal, and hissed into that ear that if she ever laid a finger on me again she'd end up in the canal. Mum, who with one hour's notice assembled me a costume for 'Heroes Day' at school of a twinset, a greying blonde wig and some court shoes, and made me, aged eleven, go to school dressed as Shirley Williams. And you know what? I went. And it was kind of cool.

I lay back on the bed and I stared up at the ceiling. *I've never done anything brave in my life. I've always hidden from things.*

I must have fallen asleep then myself, because I woke up in the middle of the night, fully dressed and with hair wrapped around my face, mouth furry and stale, the curtains open and the room full of blue shadows.

Chapter Seventeen

The next morning, I was up and out of the house as dawn was breaking: Malc was an early riser and I couldn't bear to see him again. Morning dew glittered on a spider's web on our railings as I closed our front door very quietly behind me and walked up the road, shivering in the sharp, early summer morning chill. George had told me to meet him at 6 a.m. I was going to call in sick to work, say I had the flu. I'd been prepping the day before: coughing, occasionally sighing, eliciting sympathy from Becky and Sue.

When I reached the Warrington Hotel, all was in darkness. I climbed the steps and rang the night porter bell. Nothing happened.

I rang the bell again and then, gritting my teeth at the jangling rattle in the peace of dawn, again. And at last, somewhere inside the building, I could hear the noise of movement. I waited, and shivered. I had never understood the term 'a goose just walked over my grave' until that moment. Doubt assailed me. What if I'd missed him? What if he was waiting, and it was me, holding him up? What if—?

'What do you want?' came a rumbling Eastern European voice, and a beefy man appeared at the door, in a vastly oversized blue Aertex shirt with 'The Warrington' incongruously embroidered in teeny purple copperplate.

I peered over his shoulder. 'I'm waiting for someone,' I said. 'I'm supposed to meet him here.'

He glowered at me.

'Can I have a look? Is he in the lobby?' I tried to keep the desperation out of my voice.

'No.' The porter shrugged, and turned away, completely uninterested. 'I have to keep this door shut.'

I followed him in, pushing the door open. 'Sorry, but can I just ask? Has he checked out?'

He turned back in annoyance. 'How would I know this?'

I looked evenly at him. 'Could you have a look? Thank you. Adonis Blue. He's been here for five days.'

'Ad-Done?'

'Adonis Blue. That was the name he . . . he checked in under.'

It sounded so far-fetched. The name. The whole story, now that I thought of it.

There was no answer when we called his room.

'Could you call again? Just in case he was in the shower or . . . or asleep?'

The porter gave me a cold stare, the kind that means *Stupid bitch*. I didn't care any more.

I folded my arms. 'Well, can I check his room?'

'No. Look, I don't know what you want, but—'

'I'm his daughter.' I felt as though I was lying, to get what I wanted. 'He's supposed to be in there.'

'What if he's just gone without you?'

'He might,' I said, 'but I am almost a hundred per cent sure he wouldn't have done that. So either he's there and a bit deaf, in which case I'm sorry for bothering you, or he's not, in which case I'll need to phone the police and file a missing person report. He's my father. I think I know my father, wouldn't you say?' I smiled politely, hoping he couldn't hear the quavering in my voice.

As we walked along the carpeted corridor I started to fear the worst, images of suicide or murder or night-time attacks filling my head, and I had to shake myself. *This is real life. He hasn't been murdered. Calm down.* But I couldn't calm down, couldn't stop trembling, my heart racing, throat dry.

When the porter opened the room and there was no one in there, nothing at all, I was relieved to start with.

'You see this?' He thumped the wall gently. 'Nothing is here.'

There was virtually no sign of my father's occupancy. The bed, only slightly rumpled on one side. Towels neatly folded on the chair. A cheque on the desk, in his handwriting.

He'd gone.

As I sat on the steps of the hotel a few minutes later, staring at the brightening morning sky, my bag between my legs, I wondered if he'd ever meant to come with me. If anything he'd said was true. Malc had been right. Mum had been right – my bruised, fragile Mum had warned me. She'd tried to tell me, hadn't she? She'd taken to her bed, for God's sake, and still I hadn't listened . . . Oh, Nina.

A pair of heels clattered on the steps and I looked up to see the receptionist from my previous visit standing in front of me, looking more immaculate and perky than one has a right to at that hour of the day.

'Good morning. May I help you?' she said, politely.

'I was just going,' I said, trying not to sound rude. I picked up the bag.

'Thank you!' she said, stepping over me and opening the door. 'Have a good day!'

'Excuse me,' I said, calling her back. She turned on the threshold. 'Did my father – Adonis Blue, did he mention why he was leaving? Did you talk to him at all?'

She licked her moist, freshly pink lips and ran a strand of hair through two fingers. 'Oh, you're his visitor from before, yes?' she said, nodding at me. 'I don't know, did he go?'

'Yes,' I said. 'He's left you a cheque. He must have taken off in the middle of the night.'

'I wondered what was wrong.' She nodded, calmly; you got the feeling she'd seen it all before. 'He was very angry yesterday after-noon. Came back from day out, and said his business had not gone well. He asked many questions about security and phone calls. He wanted to know what details we release. What we tell if people want to reach our guests.'

'Why was he angry, do you know?'

213

She shrugged. 'I was dealing with another guest, I only overheard snatches of the conversation – we were busy. I'm sorry,' she said, smiling down, angelic, imperturbable, almost regal.

'Did he say anything to you? About where he was going? What he was doing?' I screwed up my face. 'Please, if you could tell me anything . . .'

She looked down at me. 'He was here on business, that's all I know.' She smiled, courteously. 'Excuse me. I must go into work now. I must relieve the night porter.'

'Yes . . . thank you,' I said.

She stopped and looked at me again, hands tightly clutching my overnight bag. 'He's your dad, right?'

'Yes.'

'Huh.' She pushed open the doors, and waved goodbye, carelessly, half politely.

I sank back down on to the steps as the door shut behind me. For the first time in years I wished I could speak to Matty; I saw then, as I hadn't ever before, how useful she had been. Someone to talk to, someone for me to organise, to feel in charge of. Someone who listened, even if she wasn't really there.

And as though she were behind me, whispering in my ear, I heard Mrs Poll say: *Get up, darling. Come on, then, you can't sit there all day.*

I shook my head.

There was the slightest, faintest breeze at my right shoulder; traffic purred in the near distance. Wind rustled the trees above me. I stood up.

You need some breakfast. Everything looks better after some toast. Off you go, Nina. Off you go back home.

'It's not my home,' I said aloud. 'I'm moving in with Elizabeth. Tomorrow.'

It is your home. It always has been.

I looked up, at the thick bower of frothy cream-and-green horse chestnut, and for a moment I wondered if maybe she was up there, calmly perched on the branch of a tree, it was that real to me: *Keepsake doesn't matter. Your father doesn't matter. What you have already matters.*

The wind was picking up and the June skies were darkening, in that sudden, swollen spring fashion. The hotel door banged again, sharply, and this time I jumped. I did what Mrs Poll said, and stood up. I would have time for breakfast, before work.

Still, as I walked briskly into town, I wondered where my father was. On his way to Keepsake now? Or just around the corner, lying low, because all of it was a lie? Though I knew it couldn't be. I knew that house. I had to find my own way there now.

The Butterfly Summer

(continued)

I have only had fleas once, and along with childbirth it is an experience I have no desire to repeat.

Two weeks after my arrival in London, unwashed, almost mad with hunger and wearing the same clothes in which I had left Cornwall, I stood at the foot of the steps of a grimy mansion block in Bloomsbury, trying to resist the urge to scratch. My skin was red-raw in parts, with patches of flaking, oily dead scales which seemed to fall away from my body whenever I looked: so I'd stopped looking. I rarely undressed, anyhow; I was too afraid of having items of my scant wardrobe stolen.

My foolhardiness in coming to London grew more apparent every day. For many reasons, not least the last stated above, I could not fail at this interview, otherwise all really would be lost. The remaining note and few coins I had left were clutched in my hand, which rested in my skirt.

It's strange, isn't it? The tiny, casual decisions one makes that will ripple out in ways one can have no idea about: I thought often now of my last morning at Keepsake. How I had got dressed, a fortnight ago, having no idea I'd be leaving for ever that evening. I had packed ridiculously: silk shirts and even a crêpe de Chine dress, all thrown hastily into the much-mocked Gladstone bag. But that was all to naught: it had been stolen from me at a Lyons Corner House, the day of my arrival.

Only by some fortunate last piece of luck, it happened that I had placed my notebook and my leather purse-book – with my money and my mother's butterfly brooch in it – momentarily upon the table. I had only the clothes I stood up in, as the song goes. These were: a tweed skirt, which was warm, but only up to a point. A shirt and cashmere jumper, thank God. My sensible brogues, and my new Aquascutum overcoat, a present on my eighteenth birthday. I had worn only these items for the last two weeks.

I had failed to take into consideration the difference in London prices too and, having disastrously under-provided for myself, my twelve pounds had dwindled now to ten shillings. I had no return ticket. I could not sell the diamond brooch – every jeweller I took it to refused to have anything to do with it. 'Crest's ancient. What's that written on the spine?'

'"*What's Loved Is Never Lost.*"' The words sounded ridiculous when I said them aloud.

'Hmm. It's a good piece,' one of them – an old man in a tiny shack off the Gray's Inn Road, with enormous tufts of white hair sticking from his long ears – had told me. 'Where'd someone like you get it, then?' he'd demanded.

'It's my family's,' I'd said, drawing myself up to my full height. 'But I have no need of it now. I want to sell it.'

'Don't believe a bleeding word of it, lovey,' he'd said with gusto, sliding it back across the wooden counter, and lowering his voice as he took in my dirty hair, my baggy stockings, my grimy shirt. 'You've stolen it. I don't handle stolen goods, you hear? Now clear off. This is a decent business.'

It was the same wherever I went – from backstreet places in the Dickensian alleyways behind Holborn, to the more salubrious jewellers in the West End – and as time wore on, my appearance, so crucial to this kind of transaction, worsened. Thanks to an advertisement on the board in the Marylebone Public Library I had managed to find for myself a Ladies' Hostel in Bloomsbury, full of actresses, waitresses and the like. It became clear soon afterwards that some of the ladies were perhaps not entirely respectable, but the place was clean, and quiet. The only drawback was that I had nowhere to wash, and no money for new clothes. I tried rinsing the tweed skirt out in the cracked old basin in the shared bathroom, but it really only made it much worse, carpet-like in appearance and smelling of horsehair and sweat. I slept in my woollen vest.

If I ate one meal a day, there was enough money for another week here. I had, you might gather, entirely miscalculated the situation. I do not know if you will recall earlier mention of my aunt, Gwen, but it amply illustrates the fleeting nature of the role she had up to now played in my life that two or three days had passed before I remembered that I could always call upon her for help, if the situation became dire. She was something of a stick-in-the-mud; she had never liked my beloved grandmother, probably because Gwen was terrified of anything that lay outside what she saw to be the normal way of the world, and my grandmother was blissfully unconcerned with the opinions of others. Trousers on women were Aunt Gwen's greatest fear and following my second trip to London, aged twelve, Mother and I often recalled with mutual enjoyment her horror on being approached by a saleswoman in Harrods who offered to show us some of the latest slacks.

'Let us leave *immediately*, Charlotte!' she had cried, pulling at my mother's velvet arm, and hurrying away from the proffered wares.

Gwen had married a Scottish landowner she'd met when she and my mother had their one Season in London, a summer my mother spoke of with loathing – she hated being away from Keepsake. But Gwen had flourished in London, met her prince, who obliged her by dying of diphtheria two years into their marriage and leaving her comfortably established in a tiny house off Brook Street. She never came back to Cornwall. I had never known why before – but, as with so much about Keepsake, I understood a little better now I was outside its ancient walls.

I knew I would remember Gwen's house if I walked over to Mayfair, but I was wholly unsure of the reception I would receive: I was, by then, beginning to itch somewhat and she would have been horrified. And initially, though I was rather up against it, it was still glorious to be independent for once. For, though I spent my days drawing out cups of tea in cafés, endlessly writing down ideas for jobs, or plots for novels I told myself I should attempt, or simply adding up columns of sums, trying not to listen to the gnawing pangs of hunger that racked me, I was free in this magical city. Free to wander into the National Portrait Gallery and stare all day at Charles II. Free to lie all day in the park, or walk up Charing Cross Road, staring into the huge, gaudy Amusement Arcade, at the joshing young men in sharp suits and trilbies drinking light ales in the doorways, free to stop and stare as long as I wanted at the golden lights of the theatres and the crowds surging inside, and the wonder of Leicester Square, the milk bars open twenty-four hours a day, the neon-lit Empire with its vast advertisements. When I arrived, *Jezebel* was showing, and there was a huge advertisement of Bette Davis's imperious, wicked face smiling down on the crowds queuing up to see her. I saw *Jezebel*. I fell in love with Bette Davis, and practised that sideways, arrogant glance in the mottled glass of public house signs and phone box windows.

I was down, but I wasn't out. I could not risk giving all that up and being packed off back to Keepsake, or taken in by my aunt, forced to live the life she'd like her niece to be living, that of a young aristocratic debutante. A Cornish girl I knew of was married from St George's, Hanover Square, as I was walking past one afternoon – orange blossom, a phalanx of bridesmaids in chiffon and silk, wire-and-silk floral coronets on their gleaming heads, the men clutching top hats in the playfully sharp wind. The groom, thin-faced, sloping shoulders, nervous; the bride, wrestling unsuccessfully with her lace veil in the breeze. The two of them, glancing sideways at each other in surprise. That could have been me, and I knew it, and knew how lucky I was to be avoiding that fate, even if only for the present.

My daily routine revolved around my visit to the Reading Room of the British Library, where I waited for my chance to scan *The Times* for the news but mostly to check whether Matty had sent me a message via the Personals column.

I had no idea what role those damned Personals columns would play during my time in London. At home, of course, I had the wireless, and my father's copy of *The Times* to glance at while he was out or dozing. Here, something catastrophic might happen and there was every chance I wouldn't hear about it – there was no wireless at the Ladies' Hostel, no newspapers. Hitler had invaded Austria, supposedly peacefully, in March and had said he would 'rescue' the Sudeten Germans living in Czechoslovakia, over the

German border. The situation was strange: everything outwardly so calm and yet every day one noticed little changes. The signs appearing on the streets: 'ARP Station'. The trenches being dug in Hyde Park. From a distance, they looked like nothing more than giant molehills – when I remember it all, that was my first perception that things weren't quite right.

The previous day I had been in the British Library's Reading Room, scanning *The Times*, trying to pretend I wasn't hungry, or desperate, or curiously aware now of the eyes of strangers upon me – *Why's that girl so dirty, so unfragrant, so odd? Why does she scratch? Why's she always in here?* – when, thankfully, my eye was drawn to one of the notices in the Personals column. And really, everything came from that advertisement.

THE ATHENA PRESS, 5 CARLYLE MANSIONS, HANDEL STREET, WC1, IS URGENTLY SEEKING a young person with minimal typing skills, excellent administrative abilities; quick-witted and literate; of good background; able to handle comical and yet obstreperous cats and dogs; able to read fast and organise an office of 2 persons; also some light domestic duties. Accommodation included. Write Box T345 *The Times,* 72 Regent Street, W1.

I wrote immediately and was asked to attend an interview at Carlyle Mansions the following day. Greatly daring, I had taken two scant pennies to the cleaners along the street from the hostel, to wash and press my skirt and remove the horsey smell. Thankfully I was also able to borrow a silk shirt from Marie, a nice shop girl at Heal's who occupied the room next door to me, though she was plumper than I was so the shirt slid open somewhat and had to be buttoned up to the top. Then, trying not to itch, I presented myself at Debenhams and asked if I might try some Yardley Complexion Milk and Complexion Powder. The bored shop assistant fell upon me with enthusiasm and I left twenty minutes later smelling like a bordello and resembling, when I caught sight of myself in a looking glass, a very, very over-made-up and unremarkable showgirl from the Palladium: pale caked-on face, ears, hands, neck red-raw from the rash over my body. I longed to itch, to step into a telephone booth and scratch all over. Only the greatest self-control, drilled in over the years, stopped me.

When I reached Carlyle Mansions I rang the bell and stepped back, as the itching overtook me again.

'Is this you?' a high voice called out from somewhere above me, in a thick accent.

I looked up, and around, not sure if I was hearing things. 'Oh – Theodara Parr. From . . . I have come about the advertisement you placed in *The Times*. Athena Publishers.'

'No. The Athena Press,' said the voice suddenly, buzzing through the intercom. 'It is wrong.'

'I'm sorry,' I said. 'Should I . . . is this the correct day?'

'Yes, I suppose it shall have to be. Come in, then.'

The door buzzed open. The hall was cool and dark, with black and white, square marble tiles on the floor, several cracked or missing. It was quiet, except for the sounds of someone singing, a rich bass. I realised I had no idea where in this large, cold building the voice had come from, so I kept climbing up the stairs, hoping someone would call out again.

When I reached the top floor I looked around, unsure as to what I should do next. My head was light with lack of food: I had fainted on a tram the day before – most embarrassing. I stood there, gripping the bannister, looking at the broken and missing balustrades, hoping I wouldn't fall through them, when the door opened, and a shadow, the perfect outline of a young man, fell over me from the doorway.

I won't be able to describe Al to you properly without making you look out of the window, if it is a sunny day. Look at the blue sky. Look at the brightness, the clarity of that blue, the way your eyes hurt afterwards because it's so dark everywhere else. That was what it was like, seeing Al for the first time.

'For whom are you looking?' The shadow was real: boyish, slim, high cheekbones, slightly slanting dark eyes. The youth stepped forward and, with a birdlike movement I would come to know so well, swift and assured and yet tentative all at once, touched me with one finger on the forearm. The eyes, so frank, so full of laughter, the slightly crooked smile, the faint flush on the cheeks, the slim, long hands, the variable accent – sometimes hard cockney, sometimes Googie Withers, sometimes low and serious – which was the only changeable thing about Al. I have changed myself utterly in the course of my long life – I have been so many different versions of myself. Al couldn't be anything other than this beautifully handsome, godlike being, full of cheer and humour and a dark, sweetly heady set of movements, like a cat, stretching after too much sunshine.

'I say, are you all right? You're pale as a sheet.'

'Rather faint. Long time since breakfast.' I blinked, aware of my strange appearance, the horsey tinge to the tweed skirt which I was aware had not been entirely got rid of, the pungent smell of the Yardley Complexion Milk and Lavender Water, my scaly, red-raw hands. 'I'm absolutely fine, thank you very much.'

'Ah.' There was an awkward silence. 'Well, I don't think you want me, do you? Unless this is my lucky day.'

I said, primly, 'I most certainly do not. I'm looking for Mr — for Athena . . . the Athena Press. I'm here for an interview.'

'That old crook? Well, I'm surprised.' Al had a wide smile, which I saw contained one chipped tooth, just very slightly, giving a rather piratical air, though otherwise – from the sleek, dark hair to the slim feet – everything else was perfection. I knew that then. Right away. It was so simple. I wanted to reach out, and I can still feel the urge of my hand, to feel that smooth, creamy skin under my fingers. The tiny splash of red-pink colour on the cheeks, like sticky jam in thick cream. The lips, slightly parted. The eyes that watched me carefully, curiously, trying to sniff me out, work out if I was who they wanted me to be.

'I don't see why you should be surprised, since we don't know each other.'

'I'm surprised at anyone who falls for his con tricks. He's an old crook.'

'How so?' I looked down, thinking I heard movement on one of the floors below.

'Oh, it's a vanity press,' Al said. 'Gets you to pay him to publish your work. They all think they're signing with Michael Joseph or Gollancz, and instead they're paying someone to publish *The Big Adventures of the Littlest Kitten* or *My Life in Buttons* or whatever bilge dear Sir or Madam has come up with. Then they're bloody furious not to have sold any copies and turn up here threatening recourse to the law, and he sometimes gives them a bit of money back, sometimes not.'

'How do you know that?'

'I sent him my memoirs. About my time as a medium in Torquay.'

'Stop being flippant,' I said, and we both smiled again, less shyly than before.

'Sorry. They come up here by mistake. Always do. I like old Michael. He's insane, you understand, but he's jolly entertaining. But he's an absolute snake. I've told him, time and time again, to put a sign up by the door to let people know it's the ground-floor flat but he doesn't.' Al shrugged. 'Afraid of identification, you see. So now I've taken to telling them the truth. What's your novel about, may I ask?'

'I haven't written a novel. I'm applying for a job there.'

Al's eyebrows raised high above that shock of black hair. Just then a voice below me said, 'Aha! We are here. You are up there?'

I looked down the curling staircase to the black-and-while hall, and there was a figure, hands on hips, glaring up at me.

'I wasn't sure where to go, I'm afraid. This . . . he was just redirecting me.'

'She's coming downstairs, Michael.'

Michael waved up. 'Al, my sweet. Good morning to you.'

'Morning.' Al turned to me. 'Jolly nice to meet you. I'm Al, like he says. Al Grayling.'

I looked surprised.

'It was my father's name. Don't ask me why I got it, it's been something of a burden.'

'I . . . your surname. That's the name of a butterfly.'

'A what? A butterfly? Oh. Didn't know that.'

I found this coincidence far more interesting than the Grayling family did, evidently. 'Yes. It's a beautiful butterfly – at least, the female is. The male's very dingy.' I blushed; I was still always trying to work out how one talked to people. 'They love the cliffs, chalk . . .' I trailed off, and looked down at Michael, waiting for me. 'Just coming. I am sorry . . .'

'Oh. That's very interesting,' said Al, politely. 'I'm afraid I'm as thick as cream when it comes to the outdoors. What's yours? Name, I mean?'

'Theodora – oh, it's Teddy. Parr.'

'Well, hello, Teddy Parr.' We shook hands, still looking at each other. 'I say, good luck. Be nice to have someone young round here. Come up one day if you get the job, and I'll give you lunch. Knock on the door. I'm always in.'

'Oh.' I started for the stairs, raising my hand to the impatient figure below. 'What work are you in?'

'I'm a writer. God's honest truth.' Al stood in the doorway, grinning, then pointed downstairs, giving me a Good Luck thumbs-up. I wished I was staying up there, but I turned back and walked downstairs, staring at my quarry.

In the summer I spent at the Athena with Michael Ashkenazy I only saw him wearing black. Once, he picked up a dark green jumper and toyed with it, caressing it softly and slipping it upon his head, but just as swiftly he removed it, muttered something, and Misha appeared to pick it up as it fell to the floor.

'Awful,' he said, with a shudder.

'I know,' she agreed fervently. As though he'd been about to slip into a vest of snakes.

He was now, of course, dressed head to toe in black, a thin, feminine man with a square head, dark deep-set eyes, lips permanently pursed, his default expression that of a slightly put-out goat.

(How strange, the luxury of allowing oneself to think, to write about him after all these years. He was a very dear man.)

'My apologies for the confusion,' I said, shaking his hand, when

I reached the bottom of the stairs. 'I wasn't quite sure where you were.'

'Do not concern yourself over it.' He stared curiously at me. Abruptly, he said, 'Are you a rich girl? This get-up. Is this a joke, that you come here today? A big sport, to tell your friends?'

I stared at him, as shocked as if he'd slapped me. The desire to itch my leg suddenly was extraordinary. But I knew I couldn't look down, or move. I had this sliver of a chance to stay here. I must keep staring at him, making him believe that I was a convincing and wholesome young person. 'I have left my family home.'

'Where is that?'

'A long way away.'

'Why did you leave?'

Keepsake, golden in the morning sun. The Helford, glistening in the spring breeze and fringed with new green. My mother's skeletal, arched body. The door under the stairs, the women who spoke to me at night . . .

'I had to,' I said quietly.

'That's not an answer.'

'I . . . I . . .' I took a deep breath. 'I want to be a writer, and live in London.'

'A writer?' His eyes flashed. 'A meek little thing like you?'

I looked over at the shut door, which presumably was his flat. 'I can write your letters, and answer the phone in a pleasing sort of way, I hope. I'm keen, and organised—' I racked my brains, trying to think what else I could tell him, realising then how woefully out of my depth I was, just as Michael Ashkenazy pointed at my arm.

'You have a companion.'

The flea was large, almost the size of a lentil. Michael reached forward and drove a thumbnail into my arm. Blood, my blood, burst forth from the black-red carapace, on to Marie's shirt. 'Apologies,' Michael murmured. 'I do not know—' He looked around. 'It must be our dog.'

I shook my head. 'Sir, please don't worry. I . . . it's . . .' *Me. I have fleas.* I swallowed. 'I don't mind fleas!'

'What an interesting girl you are.'

I held my palms out, and said frankly, 'I will be an excellent employee. I am literate. I am quick-witted. I am truly desperate for work. I am also very hungry. I have no money left. If you take me on, I promise you I'll give you the best of myself.'

'The best of yourself. Ach,' he said, nodding, still looking me over. 'My wife bought crumpets. We love crumpets. So funny. Well, young lady. Will you sit down and have some?'

'Absolutely.' I sounded more fervent than I'd have liked.

'What's your name? I have forgotten. Forgive me.'

I hesitated. 'Teddy. Parr. Teddy Parr.'

He looked at me with those bright, dark eyes, head cocked on one side. 'Is it now? Well, my name once again is Michael Ashkenazy, and you are most welcome to join us, Teddy Parr. Come inside. Come and meet Misha.'

He opened the door and, with no other choice but to do so, I followed him.

Many years after this, one rainy day walking past the window of a tiny, exclusive gallery in a little street in Kensington, I saw a painting that had been in the Ashkenazy's sitting room. A lady in a black dress, holding a child, her eyes playful, the child reaching for a brooch on her chest. It was by Berthe Morisot, and was priced at £50,000, even then. I stopped, buckling over, as though a fist had landed square in my gut. I'd looked at that picture every day. Why was it here, where had they found it? I went in and asked the gallery owner whether they knew who was selling it, where it had come from. An estate sale, was all they'd tell me, and they did it in a manner that suggested I was poking my nose in where it didn't belong.

The Ashkenazys' flat was absolutely crammed floor to ceiling with art and furniture. I have never been in a place like it, nor will I ever be again. Sagging armchairs in once-magnificent blue-and-gold silk brocade, far too big for their humble home, edged against vast, ornately carved bookcases, built for holding grand, thick, gold-tooled atlases and rare plates of birds and the like. The walls were covered with paintings, landscapes, group scenes in bars, men and women dancing, a whirl of brushstrokes, portraits, watercolours, hung floor to ceiling – those unfortunate enough to be at the bottom of the wall being frequently licked by the dogs. Something must have happened to all of this opulence, afterwards. To this day, I wonder who bought the sweet-faced mother and her laughing child. What kind of room it hangs in now.

I gazed about me while Michael fiddled with a lamp. 'You have so many beautiful things.'

'We have here the remains of our old life,' said Mr Ashkenazy, waving a hand around. A cat, asleep on one of the chairs, woke and caught sight of me, straightened his back in outrage, and shot behind a chest of drawers. 'All the treasures of our families, carried with us. Misha! Misha!' he shrieked. 'The girl is here. Bring some crumpets. Some tea.'

Misha appeared from what I presumed to be the kitchen, a book in hand, and looked at me angrily. 'This is her?'

'Yes,' said Michael.

Misha brought the book to her chin and looked over it at me, dark eyes raking me up and down. Her fingernails were painted a livid purple.

'She will do.'

Then she turned abruptly away and disappeared back into the kitchen.

That was the beginning of my time with the Ashkenazys, and the start of my summer. The crowded sitting room was the headquarters of the Athena Press, and somewhere amongst the clutter were two desks and a little armchair for prospective clients. There were two bedrooms: theirs was a grand affair off the other side of the hallway, looking out on to the quiet street, filled with as much furniture as the sitting room. The second bedroom, mine, was tucked away at the back of the building, and opened up into the garden. It was long but extremely narrow, room for only a single bed. Behind me were rickety French windows to the garden, and sometimes I would hear mice, scuttling in from the garden and under the bed. I was a country girl and this, along with the many daddy-long-legs jostling drunkenly by the windows, did not bother me. Neither did the other privations of the flat, such as noise, the permanent smell of cooking oil and the Gold Flake cigarettes that both Michael and Misha smoked incessantly. They thought nothing of walking through my room on the way to the garden, nor indeed of simply wandering in at any hour.

Misha and Michael were Russian, but had fled to Vienna during the Revolution. They were not Bolsheviks, or Communists, as such. I never heard them talk about politics, beyond the usual concerns that obsessed us all in those days. They had left Vienna to come to London, which was by then the capital of artistic expression, since

Berlin and Vienna were under the Nazis and Paris was looking anxiously over its shoulder. I soon came to know all about their early years, about Misha, who was the pampered daughter of a White Russian army captain – she had been to the Winter Palace in St Petersburg – and the scruffy young boy she had met skating, aged fourteen, and instantly fallen in love with: Michael, the son of Bohemian early Bolsheviks. I learned about how they were married in secret, and their life in St Petersburg before the Revolution. I never knew anything of their lives after Russia. They only talked about Russia, never Vienna. They had been in London for four years.

To me, used to order and echoing silence, their lives were extraordinary. I'd appear each morning to find Michael asleep at the large table, face down in a pile of cigarette stubs, with the gramophone soundlessly pivoting, and around him several guests sprawled over chairs, dead asleep: I never really knew where they came from, but they were all obviously unencumbered by jobs that required attendance in the mornings. Most of them were perfectly friendly, if unintelligible; often they spoke only Russian, or Greek, or Hindi (I would be informed, since I had no knowledge of these languages myself). I would make them coffee on the stove, and Michael would scream at me that there wasn't enough sugar in his cup. At night people crowded into the flat, drinking vodka and sherry, of which Misha was extremely fond. One of their friends, a rather unpleasant sculptor and professional drunk called Boris, had a mouth organ and played unexpectedly beautifully – and still, whenever I happen to hear that lilting, sharp-and-sweet sound, it instantly, painfully, recalls me to that summer, to the happy innocence of its beginnings.

After a week or two it was as though I'd always been there. There was something about beautiful Misha, her melancholy glamour mixed with total pragmatism, and charismatic Michael, with his fits of jumping rage and crazy plans, that drew you in and made you their slave. On the nights there were no visitors I had assumed I'd go out by myself in London, or go to bed, but it became clear the Ashkenazys liked company. And food. They really did need someone to cook for them; they were childlike in their need for an extra person around. I was shy at first but soon got used to those evenings with them, though I did sometimes find it strange that they always wanted people there, someone to listen to them rail against Stalin, as they sang old Russian songs from their childhood, which were hugely depressing, and talked about books they'd read, poets they liked, while drinking strong gin martinis, or gin and tonics. They were extremely keen on gin.

As the weather grew fine we sat out in the garden more and more: the Ashkenazys and the ashtray and the crystal tumblers filled high with gin; and me, my legs tucked underneath me, gingerly sipping my drink and laughing at their droll, passionate, funny conversation. They endlessly asked my opinion on things – on poets, novels, music – and asked questions (which I did not answer) about my childhood; they were fascinated by such scant details as I gave them about Keepsake. They were fascinated by so much of English society. The polite façade, the curious habits. The obsession with tea. The phrases used around town ('Mind your Ps and Qs', overheard by Michael on the 38 bus, fascinated them – and I couldn't explain it) and on the underground ('Please alight here'). 'Who in this world in this country uses the word "alight", Nina?' Misha would demand, twirling her hair behind her shoulders and folding her arms, staring at me. 'Do you ever say "alight"?'

'How will you ever fight Hitler?' they'd both say. 'You are all too polite.'

I found I rather enjoyed the 'light domestic duties' so vaguely referred to in the advertisement. The Ashkenazys fell, pathetically gratefully, on my suggestions: they were astonished that the gas lamps worked now, that there was bread all week round, that they had clean sheets. In fact, I worked more as a general housekeeper for them than as an office clerk, but I enjoyed it. I had never had responsibility like this at home. I knew about yields and crops and every inch of Keepsake and its history. But I'd never done my own laundry. I didn't know the simplest things, like scrambling eggs, or how to toast crumpets, the knack of flipping them over on the toasting fork at just the right time. I have never watched anyone like I watched Misha as she prepared stew with dumplings, crooning softly as she stirred the meat, sometimes flicking affectionately, chidingly, at my cheek with one blood-coloured nail. I'd never prepared a rice pudding, or stored milk and butter in a bowl of ice water covered with a wet cloth set outside in the coolest part of the garden, never made my own bed, much less the gallons of coffee I grew used to brewing every single day.

I had no concept of the possibility of making a home for myself, and it was the Ashkenazys who, in their haphazard, kindly way and primarily through omission, taught me. And that ability to shift for myself stayed with me, for the rest of my life. Towards the end of my life, it saved me, in fact.

Al had not been entirely right in calling Michael a crook. The Athena Press had been founded with the aim of publishing the work of comrades and dissidents who could find no other home. Short stories about women freezing to death in fields, poems about pogroms witnessed by the author as a child, furious ballads about Trotsky's murder: these had for a few years been Athena's stock-in-trade, until sales dwindled to the point where Michael had to find other authors. As I said, they were in it for profit by then, and he saw nothing wrong with the fact the authors paid him: he was wholly pragmatic about it. Perhaps what he did was a little disingenuous. An old retired Indian colonel would write, enclosing his memoirs of his time in India for our consideration. We would read them and then – even if it was the most stultifying prose imaginable – we would write to the author, setting out the terms upon which we would agree to finance the publication of the book. We covered printing and production and editorial costs, and the grateful author paid us a sum of between ten and twenty guineas.

But we made our authors happy, I'm sure of it. The aforementioned Indian colonel, the retired railwayman with a tale of moving to Hampstead Garden Suburb, the faded beauty fallen on hard times with her mysterious pseudonyms for gentlemen whose favours she had enjoyed at her flat in Drury Lane – all were welcome at Athena, and virtually all made us money, either by dint of their paying it to us, or because sometimes, astonishingly, the books were bought by the general public. Penguin had even asked to read the faded beauty's memoir, which we were very excited about for a few days, because it meant they might take it up for a paperback, but unsurprisingly they'd rejected it on the grounds of 'unsuitability'. We were rather flattered.

The only part of my job that was absolutely compulsory was to cut out the Personals column in *The Times* every day for them, placing it on their joint desk for them to see as they came in. The same Personals column I had spent all those hours scanning in the British Library; in those days, it was often the only way of communicating if one had to, and the Ashkenazys were rigid about this one task. Even Misha would stir herself when I called out that the column was on their desk. They would lean over Michael's table, scanning the close print, then stand up, he murmuring, 'All well,' and sometimes patting his wife's back. Then Misha would return to their room, free for the rest of the day now to write her own poems and lie in bed, talking to the two cats, Harpo and Gummo.

They were an unlikely couple but undoubtedly devoted to each other. He called her 'Mishki' and she called him 'Bug'. She could wrap her arms around his tiny waist so that he nestled in her bosom, and there they would stand for a minute or so, quietly breathing with each other.

It makes me extremely sad to recall it now. After the war was over I tried, many times, to discover their fate. It wasn't until a grey day in 1961, in a bookshop on the Charing Cross Road, that I'd find out the truth. For then, all I knew was that, like me, they had come to London to run away, and I respected their silence. We all held secrets.

During those first two weeks with the Ashkenazys, I saw very little of anyone else and when I was not absorbed by their company, I'd walk through London, hour after hour, looking around me, at the idling Daimlers outside fashion houses in Mayfair, the barefoot children running wild in Clerkenwell, the reed-thin women coming out of the Savoy, the sea of bowler hats around St Paul's. And the city at night, the random and disconcerting acts of violence or passion: a young pale woman spat at in the face by an older man in Soho, who then hissed at her, 'cunt' – I'd never heard the word before. The couple kissing passionately behind Sheekey's, in one of the dim courtyards of theatreland, her hands fumbling to ruck her stiff silk skirt up above her waist band, his teeth and tongue hungrily on her neck, splayed hand squeezing her blue-veined breast, which had fallen out of her brassiere – I stood and watched them for several seconds, agog, blood rushing through me, before I forced myself to turn away.

But rarely was I dissatisfied. I felt released, carefree. I had seen Al a few times since our first encounter, but briefly. Either one of us was coming, the other going, or we were on the street and never seemed inclined to stop and engage in conversation. Once, I saw Al arguing with a wronged girlfriend of some sort on the steps of our building, and I scurried in, embarrassed for them both. The girl was wearing an extremely unflattering bluish-purple lipstick and kept saying 'Alayne'.

'Alayne,' she moaned in a sort of broken way, as I fumbled with my own latchkey. 'Oh, Alayne, please don't be like this.'

'Look, I am sorry . . .' said 'Alayne', in a quiet voice, and I found my heart lurching at the sound of that low, kind voice. 'Hello, Teddy.'

'Hello, Alayne,' I said, and was given a small, cryptic smile in return.

One evening in mid-May I was sitting in the Ashkenazys' living room, wishing they'd pack up and go to bed so that I could creep back into my room and shut the garden door. It was a beautifully warm night and they and three guests were outside in the garden, and had been for a long while. Candles had burned down to bubbly medallions of wax, the great blue glass ashtray the size of a human head was almost filled to the brim with cigarette butts, and from my room the gramophone was playing Rachmaninov's Symphony No. 2: Michael always played Rachmaninov when he was feeling angry. The news had just come through about the football match between England and Germany the previous night in Berlin, where the English players had given the Nazi salute. The atmosphere was febrile, muttered talk of betrayal in the air.

Misha and Michael were entertaining one of their old friends from St Petersburg, a terribly sad woman named Katya. The previous week, Katya had received word that her husband, Stefan, who like Michael and Misha had originally left Russia and moved to Vienna, had been taken away by police who would not say why, or where he was. He was Jewish. Amongst the other guests were an angular, kind sculptor named Ginny and her husband, Boris (the hard-drinking Russian who played the mouth organ). Boris was intense and boorish, unlike the Ashkenazys' other friends. He was repre-sented by the Gremalts – who were well-known art dealers in Paris, as well as old friends of the Ashkenazys – and this gave Boris a licence he would not otherwise have had. In my first week, he had grabbed my breast as he passed by my bed on the way out, reached down and, thumbing my flesh painfully hard, had hissed, 'This cherry is nearly ripe, hmm?'

I pushed him away, turning over and murmuring that he should get out. I remembered thinking to myself then that being bohemian could be rather trying at times.

'Dieter says he is gone,' Katya was saying. 'He says the apartment had been ransacked, that none of our things remain. Stefan would never go away without sending me word. They have taken him.'

Misha's voice, tight and small, stuck with me for days afterwards, because I never heard her mention home, or why they'd left, never heard her refer to the international situation in anything but general terms. 'Michael. They are taking them already. *Michael.*'

And Michael's answering reassurance, his voice soft. 'There is time. They are busy building their empire. There is time, my love.'

Snatches of murmured conversation came through to me from the garden as the others comforted Katya and discussed what they could do. I didn't like the idea of Boris trooping past me as I pretended to sleep in my bed, so I stayed curled up in the armchair reading a thriller till about 1 a.m., when the talk was louder than ever and the assembled company seemed to show no signs of moving. My eyes started to droop. I pinched myself to stay awake, but it was no good. My head lolled and eventually I stood up, just as the door to my bedroom swung open and Boris appeared from the garden, carrying the empty cocktail mixer.

'Ah,' he said quietly. His eyes were glassy, staring at me. 'You're hiding here.'

I rubbed my eyes as he came closer. 'Do you need something?'

I didn't understand why the Ashkenazys were friends with Boris. I didn't like how he looked at me, or the way he kicked his legs out, not minding when he scuffed Ginny's calves, or the way he wiped his mouth on his sleeve and took all the gin. I sat up, and he said, 'Yes, little one. Little sweet cherry, ready to pop.'

It was so sudden I had no time to react. He shut the door from my bedroom towards the garden, and, coming over to the armchair, grasped my shoulders and began kissing my neck; I could feel his teeth, scraping against my skin, and I struggled out of the chair, wriggling my arms to try to shake him off. But he pinned my arms to my side, and pushed me against the wall with a hard force that made me cry out.

'Be quiet. Stand still,' he said, and banged my head against the wall so that I felt the bones in my neck crack. 'It will not take long.' His huge, hairy hands were tugging at my slacks. Not really even tugging: pulling so hard that the button tore off and the zip started to tear away. This was what was extraordinary about the whole episode: here was a man who was brooding and silent most of the time, if a little lewd, and now, suddenly, he was a raging animal. His strength was remarkable.

'No!' I said, trying to push him away. 'Leave me alone!' I wasn't scared, just angry. I was unused to this treatment and I am glad still that I reacted as I did.

But he shoved me against the wall again and held me there, one hand pushing on my breastbone, so hard that I couldn't breathe, and then he slapped me around the face, exactly as my father used to. 'I must do it.'

I must do it. All the time, you see, he was thrusting against my leg, his hardness pushing against me, and suddenly the pace increased, and something inside me broke the dam of my last reserve. Rage gave me furious strength. I would not be pushed around here as I had been by my father. I would not be forced into the shadows, made weak by this man – no, no, not when I had risked everything to leave that other life behind. I would not. Yet I knew he was stronger than me. I hated him with a black loathing, for trying to squash me, make me small, and so with every last piece of reason I told myself to be calm, use my brain. I understood I couldn't reason with him. That he was in a rut, quite literally.

So I smiled at him. 'Please, let me help you,' I said, and I reached for his trouser area, and held the hard thing in it.

He released me, and took his hand away. My breastbone was being crushed underneath his massive palm. With the one hand I touched his trousers and gave him a sickly grin, and just at the moment he relaxed, I gave his hard thing a mighty twist, *yank-yank*, and kicked him, as viciously as I could. He fell backwards with a huge screaming cry of pain.

I bared my teeth, with a sharp intake of breath. 'Next time, I will kill you,' I hissed. 'I promise you.' Spit flew from between my clenched teeth. 'If you touch me again, I will kill you.'

'Bitch!' He staggered towards me, and I kicked him again, then pushed him back, as hard as I could, with a roaring scream of almost primal rage. I heard a deadening thud as he hit the floor, but I didn't stop to look. I jumped over the arm of the chair and out of the door, into the hallway.

I knew what to do. I ran up the stairs, all the way to the top, and hammered furiously on Al's door.

'I'm sorry,' I said, breathing hard, as Al looked at me, curiously. 'I didn't know where else to go.'

Al put an arm around me and drew me into the flat. 'You poor thing. What's happened?'

I could feel the imprint of Boris's hand on my breastbone, and looked down, expecting to see some kind of brand there, only to be horrified to discover my pretty shirt torn, ribbons fluttering around the green enamel buttons. I had been so proud of that shirt with its printed floral crêpe de Chine and the little buttons. I had bought it at Jaeger, on Regent Street, with the first of my money from the Ashkenazys. I saw with alarm there was blood on the white of the black-and-white, flowery pattern. Mine, or his?

I covered myself with my hands. I had a camisole on but it was sadly torn, too, the shoulder strap ripped. And yet adrenaline pumped through me; I felt almost exultant.

'Do you have a shirt I could borrow?' I said. 'And a drink?'

'I'll lend you the shirt. And I'll give you the drink,' Al said, and clucked sympathetically. 'Goodness, someone's had a go at you. What happened to the other guy?'

I gave a near-hysterical giggle. 'I'm not sure.' I found I was shaking. 'I . . . I might have killed him.'

'We'll worry about him later. You need a whisky. Go and sit down. I'll fetch you something to wear first.'

Al turned away while I put new clothes on – Al was slim, and slight, so they fitted well. The soft cotton shirt was cool, soothing against my bruised bare skin. I sat on the threadbare sofa, juddering.

'I can't stop shaking,' I said. 'Sorry.'

'Now let me get you that drink.' Al disappeared into the kitchen. I drew my knees up under my chin, hugging myself, and looked around. The room was pale green with a big pair of French windows which opened on to a small balcony. The walls were decorated with cheap prints of paintings, portraits of various people, mostly by Hogarth. *The Shrimp Girl* hung above the sofa. It's my favourite painting to this day.

I was never happier than I was in that room. When I woke in the mornings, as I did for so many years, and felt that cold, cruel metal helmet sliding over my head so that I could see nothing but blackness, I'd try to force myself to go in my mind to Al's sitting room, to the biscuit-coloured parquet floor, the bright orange-green-and-yellow Omega-style rug on the floor, the worn black sofa, the prints I came to love, the battered piano with the metronome. Frequently, over the years, I could not bring myself to get there: sometimes I could not even glimpse it from afar. Now I am old, I find I am able to recall it all, every detail, and I find too that to do so brings me immense comfort.

Al reappeared from the kitchen carrying a sandwich on a plate, a glass of ale, a glass of whisky and some water, and sat down on the armchair opposite me. 'Drink the whisky first.'

The smoky, honeyed taste of the liquid burned and slid down my throat, and I closed my eyes. 'That's lovely.' I spilled some, and put the glass down. 'Sorry.'

Al handed me the sandwich, and our fingers touched. 'Have this. Good to eat after a shock. It's cheese and ham.'

The bread was a little stale, and the ham was cut into slightly chewy lumps, but it was the most delicious thing I had ever tasted. I ate it all, ravenous, then looked at Al. 'I say – thanks.'

'My pleasure, Teddy. You poor sod.' I laughed; later I'd learn that Al's East End accent came and went in times of stress. 'Had you eaten today?'

'Yes,' I said hastily – I didn't want to prolong the idea I was some kind of down and out. 'The Ashkenazys give me board. It's just—'

'They don't protect you from molestation.'

'Something like that.'

Al was examining those long, pale fingers. 'Do you like them?'

'Oh, yes. I really do. You're wrong about them, you know. They

242

have their . . . peculiarities.' We smiled at each other. 'But they've been wonderful to me. I don't want to speak ill of them.'

'I wonder how long this whole situation will last?' Al said. 'I say, drink more of your whisky.'

I was feeling much better, the whisky having already induced in me a woozy kind of comfort, and I took another large sip. 'They're all very gloomy tonight. The English footballers in Germany yesterday, did you hear they gave the Nazi salute? Even Stanley Matthews?'

'Yes. But they were told to, by our government. You can't blame them.'

'I don't blame them, but—' I shrugged. 'You're right, I suppose. I don't know why it sticks in my throat. I want peace, too, and I don't mind how we get it.'

Al's thin face had a neutral expression. 'You don't mind what he's up to?'

'What, Old Nasty? I agree with Mr Chamberlain,' I said, my British Library newspaper reading and incessant radio listening making me confident. 'He says the Sudeten Germans want to be part of Germany and not Czechoslovakia, and I believe him. Germany has suffered so much – and the Anschluss was peaceful, wasn't it? I think that's all Hitler wants. I'm not saying that he is a pleasant person to have as a neighbour, but nor is Stalin, and—'

'Don't you listen to the Ashkenazys?' Al said. 'Can't you see why they're so worried? They came from Austria.'

'I know that,' I said, stung.

'Well, do you know that already the Jews in Germany cannot work, cannot sit on certain benches in certain parks, cannot belong to clubs, much less operate their businesses and earn a living?' Al's cheeks each had a dot of burning red, the sign of passionate indignation that I would come to recognise as one of Al's central, perhaps the most central, characteristics. 'They want to wipe out the Jews. All those people in your flat, they will be killed. Already they are sending Jewish people to camps in Poland. Families. Young children, Teddy. And we appease Hitler because we're afraid of a war as bad as the last one. But this one is quite different, and it's worse: I tell you, no one here sees anything. I only hope eventually we'll get a shock big enough to make us sit up and realise we need to prepare. Otherwise it'll be too late. It probably already is.'

The whisky was all gone and my head spun slightly as I tried to take in what Al was saying. The image of Boris, falling backwards, his body now perhaps drained of blood, dead on the Ashkenazys' floor – had I done that?

'I don't think war will happen. No one wants it—'

'It's coming.' Al held up a hand. 'I'll bet you. What's your most precious possession?'

'My mother's brooch,' I said.

'Mine's my mother's wedding ring. I'll bet you her ring by the end of September we'll be at war. If we are, I get your brooch.'

I laughed. 'It's a bet.'

'And you,' Al raised a whisky glass at me, 'will have a great deal more to worry about than drunken attacks from crazy men.'

'I can't see what could be a great deal worse than that,' I pointed out, slightly stung and disliking the insinuation that Boris's attack was somehow of minimal importance. 'That's what war is, isn't it?'

Al shrugged, and drank again. 'They will bomb London. They can kill eighty thousand of us in the first couple of weeks.' Al's face was flaming red. 'Teddy, darling, they have poison gas. Did you know that, too? Did you know we have a scarcely functioning air force and depleted navy? That we are sleepwalking into this disaster because we want to give this man the benefit of the doubt? I tell you, by the end of September, we could be at war, and it will be like nothing before.'

'I hope you're wrong,' I said, trying not to sound as frightened as I felt. 'Is your family Jewish?'

Al unfurled those long legs from the chair and stood up, as I watched, and came and sat down next to me on the sofa. I turned around a little, so that we were facing. 'Oh, way back at some point. We're East End. Most nationalities pass through there at some point. My father worked down the docks. Unloading red lead. Like my grandfather, and great-grandfather. Well, he had Russian and Greek in him. Even a bit of Chinese, they say.' Al smiled with something like pride.

I thought of the generations of Parrs mouldering away at Keepsake; and this young, vital stripling in front of me, the antithesis of inbreeding. 'He doesn't work there any more?'

Al shrugged. 'He died last year. Accident.'

'I'm sorry.'

'I'm sorry, too. He was lovely.'

'Is your mother still there?'

'Oh, yes. Same old place. We've got a flat on Arnold Circus.' I looked blank – I'd never been east of the Lyons Corner House at the Angel – and Al said, 'I'll take you there one day. It's a nice place to grow up if you've no money.'

'Do you have any brothers or sisters?'

A pause. 'I had a brother. He's dead.'

'I'm so sorry,' I said. 'How awful. When did he die?'

I watched as Al's beautiful, heart-shaped face changed and the dark eyes filled with tears. 'I can't talk about it. I have to say the whole thing and I can't bear it. Another evening maybe. Sorry, Teddy.'

'Oh . . .' I watched Al, almost crossly scratching at an insect bite, my heart flooding with feeling. More and more I realised how ill-equipped my upbringing had left me in situations like this. 'No, I'm sorry.'

'It's fine. I took his place at the Bethnal Green Boys' Club, they let me run around with them. I had to train myself not to miss him.' A shrug of the slim shoulders: later I would learn that Al, for all that cool exterior, cared more deeply about things than anyone I have met. Strangers or intimate friends, the situation at home or abroad: there was compassionate love for everyone in Al's heart. 'And living round there, you're in and out of each other's houses all day. You know how it is.'

'Not really, no,' I gave a nervous cough and Al looked at me, curiously. 'I'm an only child. But my family's quite . . . um . . . there wasn't much running in and out of neighbours' houses.'

'I see. Didn't you know your neighbours? Or did you live abroad?'

I shook my head, wanting to laugh for the first time that evening, even though the conversation was serious. 'No, in the countryside. I'll explain it another evening, too, if you'll have me back.'

'A woman of mystery. How intriguing.'

'Not really.' I changed the subject. 'What kind of writing do you do?'

'I'm a cub reporter for the *Daily Sketch*. In fact, I've just been given a new position. I write about nature.'

'Nature?'

'The countryside. Hedgeways and . . . er . . . our noble land.'

'Hedgeways?'

Al thought for a minute. 'Hedgerows? Is that the right word?'

'Yes,' I said, laughing.

'Well, all of that. And farming. I'm not a countryside person. As you can tell. I wouldn't know a bird if it hit me. Which I sincerely hope it doesn't.'

'You'd never heard of a Grayling,' I said, remembering.

Al laughed. 'Still don't really remember what it was. A butterfly, that's it, isn't it?'

I nodded, smiling.

'Well, that's something. Anyway, I'm scared of butterflies. I wouldn't know what to do if I saw a cow, either. Saw one out of the window once, when we all went to Whitstable for the day and the train had to stop in a sidings. It came over and licked the window.' Al shuddered slightly. 'Oh, we all screamed our bloody heads off. Their tongues! Size of your head.'

'You townie.'

'Yes, and proud of it. Now I have to write winsome columns about Mother Nature. It's awful.'

I thought of the screams of the newborn lambs as the waiting crows swooped down and pecked out their eyes. The owls who nested in the disused stables, tearing apart one of their owlets to feed to the rest of their brood. The caterpillars that absorbed the poison of their food and somehow, miraculously, converted it into noxious secretions as butterflies, to ward off birds and other rivals. It seemed like another world, here in this safe, warm flat.

'Mother Nature isn't that winsome, honestly.'

'Really? I don't know. The old girl who writes the column at the moment is all about baby lambs gambolling in verdant pastures, and the gentle robin's trill.'

'Robins are pretty aggressive,' I said. 'I had one once that—' But I broke off. I didn't want to remember Keepsake.

There was a pause and Al took up the reins again. 'Anyway, it's a bind. I want to work on the news desk but I'm afraid that's a way off.'

'Really?'

'Many chaps, all better connected than I am.' Al's dark face was angry. 'That's why I was still awake, you see. Trying to finish this damned piece about cow parsley. I'm not even sure I know what it is. I want to be reporting on what's going on, what's happening now. It seems bloody ridiculous to write about nonsense like daffodils in fields when the world's about to end.'

I wanted to say, but was too shy, that the point of fighting was surely to save a world you wanted to live in, which was things like daffodils in fields. Instead I ventured, 'I'll help you, if you want. I'm a country girl.'

'Of course you are.' Al gave that big disarming, open smile. 'Do you know what birds are what, and wild flowers and . . . oh, all that?'

'I should say I do,' I said. 'We can help each other.'

'Good idea.'

Our eyes met again, and I felt that strange, unfurling ache inside me that I had had before, when we had first met.

'I'm glad you came up tonight, Teddy.'

'I'm glad, too,' I said.

'I say. You are awfully lovely.'

Then suddenly Al moved gently forward and stroked my hair, so that the knuckles pressed against my cheek, as the fingers worked through my scalp, towards my neck, and I jumped, and then was still, breathing heavily, swaying slightly as we stared at each other, on the sofa. I closed my eyes, astonished at the feeling it gave me, and when I opened them, Al's face was in front of mine, and then we were kissing – oh, that first kiss. That feeling of hands on my neck, the astonishing thrill, like a jolt of power—

I sprang back, after the briefest of moments, clutching my cheeks. 'What are you doing?'

Instantly, Al said, 'I'm sorry. I'm awfully, awfully sorry. Got confused for a moment.'

'It's fine.'

We watched each other, chests rising and falling. 'Really, Teddy, I shouldn't have. Don't be cross—'

'I'm not cross,' I said, seeing that Al looked really alarmed. 'Really. It was . . . it was lovely. But it's wrong. We shouldn't.' I shook my head, tired, confused, wanting to cry. 'I . . . I don't—'

'You've had a night of it, haven't you?' said Al, softly, and then put a hand on my shoulder. 'I really am sorry. After everything, too. Do you want to go downstairs? I'll come with you.'

It was fine. I knew it was, just as I knew I could trust Al, that this was no Boris, no brute.

'It's all forgotten, honest injun,' I said, setting my glass down on the table. 'But look, I don't want to go back there – not tonight, I mean. Might I stay here?'

'Of course,' said Al, with a quick movement of relief, dashing a hand across a pale forehead. 'Gosh, I'm glad I haven't upset you. I was going to suggest you stay, anyway – I'll sleep on the sofa. You take my bed.'

'I can't do that,' I said, embarrassed. 'No, really.'

'I insist.'

'Well, then, thank you. I accept. First, though, would you be very kind and—'

'Come with you and make sure he's alive?' Al stood up, put the glass on the side. 'I suppose we should make sure you aren't wanted for murder. Listen, I'm jolly glad you came up here.'

'Me, too,' I said.

And we looked at each other, both a little breathless, and I saw Al's chest rising and the little flush of colour on the high cheekbones, and wondered if I appeared the same, that if anyone saw us on the stairs they would know how wrong the thing I had almost done was, the shame that I was made this way, that I felt . . . I cannot explain yet how I felt. I am a coward.

Outside the pub where Al and I would occasionally drink, in a cobbled side-street opposite an old mews, the landlord had set out a blackboard upon which he had scribbled in chalk the legend:

Don't look so solem Percy
Nuffing's appened yet
Why worry about tomorrow
Taint ere yet

I was like that, that summer. Trying to pretend I wasn't worried. Al was still convinced war was coming, and would remind me about our bet. 'I'll have your mother's brooch come October, you know. You'd better let me see it now, so I can have it appraised.'

The only upshot of my encounter with Boris was that the Ashkenazys were, to my surprise, displeased with me over the whole affair. In fact, Misha was almost angry with me.

'You might have killed him. He is our friend. We need him,' was all she said, turning her head away in that haughty way she had that I'd always found charming before. I thought they were trying to suggest that it was probably my fault. Many little aspects of London behaviour confused me, not least this: after chewing it over, I eventually did put it down to my own wildness. I told myself I'd never been taught to curtsey or bat my eyelashes, I wasn't made to be a fawning, doe-eyed appeaser. So this had obviously acted as a red rag to Boris, and I was to blame.

I took to sleeping in Al's flat, on the sofa or sometimes in the bed – we'd take turns. I continued to stay on at the Ashkenazys when I knew they had no company that evening, though I was afraid Boris might turn up, or that they'd scold me. I knew little else – and besides, I really did love their company. I'd roast a chicken, Michael would mix cocktails and tell me about Russian winters, or the time he saw a brown bear killing a man after being baited in St Petersburg, or the afternoon he met Misha, skating on the frozen Neva river in winter. She would turn on the wireless, scanning it for jazz tunes, or read us her latest poem, and they'd ask me what I'd been up to with Al, what we'd seen. They'd ask me about home, about Keepsake. They were magpies, picking over everything to find the bright spots. Above all, we'd just chatter, chatter, chatter – it was always so easy with them. Sometimes Al would come downstairs and join us, and we'd sit up till all hours, arguing about everything, but often I'd go back up to Al's flat at the end of the night. I felt safe there.

We saw no more of Boris, not until the end of the summer. After several weeks of silence on the subject Misha mentioned, almost in passing, that the cut on his head where he'd fallen backwards was still giving him pain and that, in addition, Ginny, his wife, had left him. I felt glad for Ginny, who had soft grey eyes and a sweet, low voice and should not have been married to a man like him. I took this to be a form of acknowledgement and maybe even apology from Misha, although deep down I was certain it wasn't meant like that. Misha didn't ever admit she was wrong.

If I wasn't with the Ashkenazys I'd go upstairs and wait for Al, reading or trying to write the tortuous novel of my ancestor Nina and Charles II which I had begun in a fit of creative enthusiasm and which I was increasingly certain would amount to nothing. I had got no further with it since I came to London: real life was more interesting.

Then, the click in the lock, Al's low, happy voice:

'Teddy? Are you there?'

I'd jump up from the sofa or the bed, trying not to show how excited I was: there was something cool about Al, for all that boyish, enthusiastic charm. I was always myself, but I wanted to be the *best* version of myself for those evenings together. I knew Al liked toffee eclairs, could get through a whole bag in an evening. I liked mints, so we would buy each other paper bags of both from the old confectioner's around the corner. Al preferred cats, not dogs – cats were urban creatures, like Al. And babies, and families, and the seaside – holidays, family, sweets, even – all everyday things that were fascinating and wildly exciting to me, though from my birth I had wanted for nothing, had slept in an oak bed under silken eider-downs, with maids to wait on me and an estate that would one day be mine.

'I'm here,' I'd call.

'Come with me, Teddy,' Al would say. 'There's a woman over in Spitalfields Market who's selling Jack the Ripper artefacts for a shilling.' Or, 'I say, Teddy, get your hat. We're going sailing on the Serpentine.'

And the best part of the day would begin. We'd go walking down to Smithfield or to the river, or through Bloomsbury and past Gray's Inn and the Inns of Court, like medieval colleges, green lawns gleaming, warren-like buildings, serene and untouched by the scream of car brakes, the roar of the bus conductor, the shouts from the street vendors outside. Or, if we were feeling rich, and lazy, we could leave the flat and walk to the Dominion on Tottenham Court Road and within ten minutes be watching a Jessie Matthews picture or, even better, a Laurel and Hardy, they really did make both of us roar with laughter. I loved how quick to laugh Al was, the deep chuckle and the pulling of hair which stuck up in curious directions as its owner rocked back and forth. Some evenings we stayed in the flat, and either read – we both loved crime: Ngaio Marsh, Josephine Tey and Dorothy Sayers – or listened to the wireless. I coddled eggs, Al mixed drinks – and all the time, we talked.

Gradually I told Al everything – almost. About Keepsake, about the history and what awaited me back at home – but not all of it. I spoke about my wonderful grandmother, her love of the land and of the butterflies, but not the ancestral madness that got to her in the end, as it had to all the others. It seemed like a bad dream, our house and its secrets, when you examined it amidst the bustle and excitement of London. I talked about the butterflies themselves, about the killing jars, the hunt for new specimens, about my beautiful, sad mother and my stickler Aunt Gwen, whom we might see at any time in London, about Jessie and Pen, and about William Klausner whom I was supposed to marry.

And slowly, I learned more about Al. About Al's dad and how he could play the piano, and how his favourite song was 'My Old Man'. About Uncle Percy who lived with them, who had a weak chest and couldn't work, who sat in their flat in Arnold Circus, all day wrapped in mustard plaster, smoking and listening to the wireless. About Al's mother, who worked and always had done, the only mother in the Circus who did. Mrs Grayling was a seamstress at one of the grandest fashion houses, on Dover Street. She was the only married lady on the team and Al was awfully proud of her, you could tell. She made all their clothes. And Al's happiest memories: being on the train to Whitstable every summer. Going crabbing, skirts tucked up in knickers, Uncle Percy slicing and dicing up oysters, like he'd been taught by his mother, who'd worked as an oysterwoman there for years. Everyone stuffed full of strawberries and oysters, falling asleep on the charabanc home. Billy, Al's little brother, tried to eat a shell once, and was sick for days.

Then, about a month after Boris's attack, Al told me about Billy. We were walking through Primrose Hill, after a trip to the zoo – I'd last been there with Aunt Gwen, and it was strange to go again, to see the same animals still there, padding disconsolately around, looking up from deep pits and out from behind bars. We'd seen chimpanzees, and the poor, hot polar bears on their concrete hills. We'd seen a keeper with a peaked cap feeding penguins fish from a battered old bucket and the penguins waddling after him for more as he walked away. Al, who loved physical comedy like this, had laughed and laughed, and then was uncharacteristically quiet as we left and strolled up Primrose Hill.

'Everything all right?' I asked, once we were at the top, looking out over the spires of London, the black smoke belching from the warehouses to the east of the city, the rose-red sunset to our right smudging the blue sky overhead.

There was no answer. I looked over, and to my horror saw tears pouring down Al's cheeks.

'Al – Al, goodness, what's the matter?' I put my arm around the thin shoulders, wiped the tears away, almost frantic. Al who never lost control, was always happy, determined, full of guts, was shaking, slim shoulders hunched, hands pressed to face, choked words sputtering through tears.

'Billy . . . It's Bill. He loved them. The penguins. It was his birthday treat. We took him here when—'

It took me a few moments to understand. I stroked Al's back, softly, for ages. 'You don't have to tell me.' I pulled the sobbing head on to my shoulder and was silent, stroking the smooth black hair, until Al sat up, dashing the rest of the tears away, and noisily blew into my proffered handkerchief.

'You always have a handkerchief on you, Teddy, it's one of the things I love about you.'

'I'm glad. I'm so sorry you're upset, though—'

Al put one hand on my arm. 'No. I'm sorry. I didn't really think about it beforehand. I wanted you to enjoy the zoo again.'

'Me?' I was startled.

'Well, you said you'd been with your aunt, and it was miserable because she hated the smells and your mother fainted.'

'Yes . . .' I shook myself.

Only on my last trip to London with her, when she had come up to see the doctors, had I realised that my mother was not well. She had crumpled on to the muddy ground around the polar bear enclosure, and I dithered over whether to leave her like that, a collapsed welter of silk and hair on the dirty ground. In the end I had to run for a keeper, and then she had clutched my hand so hard it hurt, and then pretended it was all right afterwards, that she had merely tripped. I had believed her, or thought I believed her.

It was, of course, typical of Al to remember it, to try to make it better.

'But that's so kind of you and you shouldn't have – I wouldn't have, if I'd known it was going to make you sad—'

Al said vehemently, 'No, no. I sort of pretended not to think about it and then it was too late. He really did love the zoo, you see.'

Al's nose was pink at the very tip.

'He was a lucky boy to live fairly close to it,' I said, not knowing what to say.

'Oh, yes. It was his birthday treat to come here. Every year. He was only six when it happened, you see, he'd been fine up till then. He used to feed the penguins, that keeper we saw, he'd recognise him. "There's my friend," he'd say. "There's the fine fellow who always comes on his birthday!" And Billy would clap his hands, he was such a happy little sod!' Al's eyes were filmy, shining at the memory of him. 'He was a nice man, that keeper. I wanted to— He'd let him reach into the bucket and feed them. One of them half nipped off his finger, once. Mum was furious. Said we weren't going again, and Bill cried and cried . . . he wouldn't eat for two days. I wonder if that was why? I've always wondered.'

'What do you mean?'

'Well, he got ill afterwards and perhaps if he'd been eating properly . . .' Al gave a huge sniff. 'It's so quick. He was fine in the morning, full of beans, and then—'

'Oh, Al. What – what happened?' I asked, softly.

Al's face crumpled. 'Measles. He . . . he kept saying he didn't feel well. Then he got a fever. We thought he was just putting it on, he was like that. Mum said he could go in Uncle Percy's bed just in case, though—'

'Why not his bed?' I said.

Al looked at me. 'We didn't have beds, Teddy. He and I, we slept on the mattress on the floor. Anyway, he was like that for a day or two. I bought him a toy I borrowed from the Boys' Club, a train engine. He was ever so pleased with it. He wanted a peaked cap to be a proper engine driver. That evening, he looked at it, and he couldn't speak. He sort of couldn't make the words come out. He lost consciousness. His curls – he had these brown curls, and they were wet with sweat, plastered on his forehead. We got John from next door to run for the doctor. But he wouldn't come. *He wouldn't come.* I was holding him when he died. In my arms.'

Al's lips were tight, mouth pursed tightly. 'I stroked his hair. He was soaking wet.

'They wouldn't accept the engine back, them at the Boys' Club. They said I should keep it for Billy. We buried it with him. The coffin, Teddy, it was so small. Just this wide. The hole they dug, I could barely have fitted in it. I wanted to.'

I shook my head, tears dropping on to the grass.

'It killed my dad, eventually. It did for him. My poor dad. You know, on the day of the funeral he kept bowing, I always remember that, and I didn't understand why, till I realised it was the effort of not crying. He carried the coffin into the hearse for the funeral. Just him, this little coffin. We couldn't afford the funeral. But we had to do right by him. Every single person on Arnold Circus, they came out to see him off. Lined the streets, total silence, there was. The meals we got given, people bringing us things for months afterwards. And no one else from outside cared, no one came to ask why a little kid should die that way. We looked after ourselves. That's what you do when you have nothing.' Al's shoulders shook. 'And that's what makes me angry. Still makes me angry.'

We were quiet. I put my arm around Al, kissed the silky black hair.

'I'm so sorry,' I said. 'I wish I knew what to say.' I thought of Mama, of her frenzied death-grip, of her relief as she knew the end was near. 'You were the last thing he'd have known, Al, he'd have died knowing you loved him. Perhaps if the doctor came, they'd have taken him off, he'd have been in a ward without you . . . you were with him.' I shrugged. 'I don't know. I was glad I was with my mother when she died.'

Al turned. 'I didn't know that.'

'Yes.'

'Was she conscious? Could you talk to her?'

'Yes. And she was glad to be going. She was glad I didn't have to—' I stopped. 'She was glad she wasn't suffering any more.'

We sat there, as the pink sunset flooded the horizon. I moved my hand down and took Al's fingers in mine.

'I'm glad I've told you,' Al said, blinking and staring out at the city. 'I felt something wasn't right, you not knowing.'

The terrible irony was, as I learned later on, that this tragedy helped Al, in the long run. A reporter, covering poverty in the East End, had written about this tragic little funeral in the *Picture Post*, which ran a photograph of young Al, in Sunday best, walking behind Billy's coffin. The reporter, Thomas Fisher, had kept in touch with Al, doing the occasional story on this wide-eyed, bright creature, and eventually became a sort of mentor, when the time came, paying for a course at the Printers' College. When he died suddenly, two years previously, Al was found to be the heir to his estate. It was modest by some standards, but riches beyond the dreams of most; and there was a flat. A flat in Bloomsbury. A sum of money enough to pay for a doctor for Al's uncle. Al's mother said she couldn't stop work, though. What would she do without it? Sit around the house with Percy, missing her kids?

I never met Al's mother or uncle: one of the many regrets that dog me, in these endless last days. They must have been good people, for Al was. It was Al alone who showed me, that summer, how I might be a better person. No more killing jars, and hunting, and slyness. I had never been taught compassion. I was a cold, curious child. I had been made that way.

We stood up, arms chilly in the cool of the evening, and made our way back down to the bottom of the hill. 'Shall we go into Covent Garden, get fish and chips from Rock and Sole Plaice?' Al said. 'We can eat like the penguins.'

'That's a good idea,' I said. I turned and looked back at the park, the heavy trees green-black silhouettes outlined against the rose-and-blue sky. I could hear the birds in the zoo, calling out their evensong. I thought I heard a nightjar, and my heart sang, swooping dizzily for a moment, so powerfully that I stopped. A longing for home – for clear skies and sweet salt air, for the feeling of freedom and soft earth beneath one's feet – hit me.

'Teddy,' said Al, breaking into my thoughts. 'May I ask you something?'

'Yes,' I said, hurriedly dismissing the images in my head, the feeling of longing for my home. We turned into a row of shops.

'On a night like this, when the city's so beautiful, and everything – oh, hang it!'

I asked, my heart hammering in my chest, 'What do you mean?'

'I just wonder sometimes when you'll leave?' Al's arms were folded, eyes fixed on a post box some yards ahead. 'Go back to Keepsake. You must miss it.'

Sometimes I felt as though Al walked in and out of my mind as if through the open door of a flat. 'You mean, will I stay in London?'

'Yes, in London, what did you think I meant? I'm never sure, you're so reticent about the future, I don't know what you see yourself doing in a year's time.'

'I—' I was startled into clumsiness. 'Oh. Well, the war's coming . . . I want to stay, of course. Do you need me to find somewhere else to sleep?' I said, and there was a tense silence for a moment, as the *tap-tap-tap* of our shoes echoed on the darkening street.

'No, no,' Al said eventually, hesitantly. 'I was just wondering. I think you should stay, that's all. I mean, properly stay. For ever. You – we – could share my place together, if you liked. Or somewhere else, if you prefer. Think how much fun that'd be.'

To stay in London, to be with Al, to see the Ashkenazys every day – concerts, films, laughter, arguments, conversation – throbbing, exciting life in the heart of the city, as the noose of danger tightened around us. I pushed Keepsake from my mind.

'Yes,' I said, walking on, so Al wouldn't see the flush creeping up my breastbone and over my neck, the fear that must be kept in, 'perhaps I should stay.'

One kind, early summer's evening in June a week or so later, the Ashkenazys and I were leaving the Queen's Hall, standing in Langham Place wondering whether to take the omnibus or walk back to Handel Street. We had seen Jelly D'Arányi play the Tchaikovsky violin concerto and they were in raptures. Michael had studied violin as a child and Misha 'knew' about music. She said it was 'because I am Russian'.

We paused for a moment on the crowded street as Michael lit a cigarette. 'Still, perhaps she was not dynamic enough,' said Misha, demonstrating with her elbow.

'What?' Michael frowned. 'This is simply not true. Misha, you know nothing. Her phrasing was perfect. Perfect.'

'She should have tugged down, like *this*, in the final movement. It is *allegro energico*. Energetic!' Misha yanked her elbow sharply down and sang, 'Duh, duh-di-dah, dom duh, duh-di-dah, dom duh!' Her eyes were shining. 'Ah, but it's a fine piece of music, isn't it?' She tucked her arm through her husband's; he pulled it through his and gave me his other arm. People were staring at us, as they often did at the Ashkenazys. They were gorgeously exotic, and not just because they were so obviously Russian. There was something about them that said: *I don't care what you think.*

'Oh, but I loved it,' I said. 'I'm so glad to have seen her, she was—'

And then I froze. On the other side of Regent Street, immaculate in lace and a long bustle skirt, buttoned-up gloves and parasol, and standing stock-still like a Victorian doll, was my Aunt Gwen.

'Yes?' said Michael, curiously. 'Teddy, dear, what did you think?'

Then I knew how grave what I had done was, because Aunt Gwen – who never raised her voice in private, let alone on a busy thoroughfare – actually called loudly to me, across the street:

'Theodora! Come here at once! *Theodora!* Come *here!*' She looked the same, other than that her hair was now almost completely grey.

I stood perfectly still, scanning her face.

'Why, Teddy, that woman, she wants you,' said Misha, stopping and looking at her with interest.

'It's nothing,' I said, but I carried on looking at her, at the expression in her huge dark eyes. She was so like my mother.

'Theodora! Please!' I heard in her voice that thin impatience, that tone of command, and I stiffened with fear. 'You have to go back, don't you understand that? You're making things much worse for yourself. Don't turn away from me. Come here! *Theodora!*'

'We should hurry, the bus is approaching,' I called to the others, as a fresh crowd of passers-by surged past.

Misha stared at me. 'But she's calling you, Teddy! She calls you Theodora.'

'I don't want to speak to her,' I said, woodenly, and I turned away.

'Let us go,' said Michael, huddling further into his great black coat: Michael never wanted to involve himself in the affairs of others.

'Yes, let's go.' I tucked my arm through his, and Misha shrugged. Briskly, we turned towards Oxford Circus and were lost in the hot, seething sea of humanity, and I dared not look back again in case I saw her, and saw how very like my mother she was.

We were silent on the bus journey home. When we arrived back in Handel Street, we stood outside the entrance to the flat.

Misha, with the keys in her hand, said, 'I should ask, Teddy. You are not . . . Are you wanted by the police?'

I almost laughed with relief. 'No, no, I'm not. I ran away from home. I wasn't happy there. That was my . . . my aunt.'

Like a wave, hitting me, I was felled with grief, of missing my mother. Suddenly her face, thin and intense and beautiful, appeared before me, imploring me to leave: it was all I could do to bat away the image. I swallowed, a desperate longing for Keepsake overtaking me as it had done that evening at the zoo, like a primeval force, something I could not control. And I was scared, then. But, oh – to smell the sweet evening air, heavy with honeysuckle, in the garden, to watch the swallows and swifts, dancing and swooping above us. To be alone instead of here, jostled, hot, surrounded on all sides – to hide. 'I expect my family is looking for me.' I bowed my head, feeling miserable. 'But I don't . . . I don't want to go back.'

They accepted this immediately, though I wasn't sure it was true.

Michael put his hand on my arm. 'Ach. We are all runaways. We will ask you no more questions.'

'Just one more,' said Misha, glaring at him. 'One more, only. Who is Matty?'

I started. 'Matty? Why?'

'I have heard you call her name.'

'When?'

'In your sleep, Teddy. When you are sleeping here, I hear you. You talk in your sleep, did no one tell you that?'

'No . . .' I said. Who would have heard me? I'd slept alone in my small square room with its three-foot-thick walls at the end of the stairs since I was a child. 'Matty was a friend of mine. Back in Cornwall.'

'Cornwall?'

'Yes.' I didn't want to tell them any more, about how I dreamed of Matty most nights, how she came to me, mocking, whispering in my ear what she knew to be true about me, my deepest, most shameful fears, that she knew I was abnormal, flawed in the making. 'If that's all . . .'

'Yes, yes.' Michael waved me away, but Misha carried on looking at me, and I didn't like the expression on her soft, white face. 'Go upstairs to your young beau. And be early tomorrow. The printers are collecting the pages at midday.'

'Of course.'

'No "of course",' he said, pushing me up the stairs. 'You're getting later and later to your desk each morning. I hope whatever you two are doing, it's worth it.'

'Who was Matty, then?' Al said, after I relayed the evening's events.

I took a deep breath. 'She was my best friend. My only friend there. She helped me get away.'

Already the evening – with its drumming, dreamlike music, the vast carved hall, the sight of Aunt Gwen – seemed from another world, compared to the bliss of normality once again, of sitting in Al's armchair, gazing out of the French windows, listening to the gramophone.

'You and this mysterious house of yours. It's like something out of a fairy tale.' Al lay back on the sofa, and lit another cigarette.

'Wait until you see it,' I said, not really thinking.

'Me? Oh, no, Mistress. I'm too 'umble to cross the battlements of somewhere like that, Mistress,' Al said, in a terrible accent. 'Me just a poor child from the slums, you a proper lady and all.'

'It's not like that. I'd adore it if you came with me. But it's a long way away,' I said. It sounded weak.

Al kneeled up, eyes sparkling. 'Teddy, I do believe you're a snob. You, of all people.'

'I'm not. It's just – well, we can't go there without Father finding out I'm here.'

'I thought it was your place?' Al's tone had a little edge to it.

'It is, but—'

'But you don't want to show up with a cockney who doesn't know how to use a soup spoon. I understand.' Al picked up the newspaper, and shook the spine out.

'You use a soup spoon to eat soup. Don't be dense. Besides, we never go to Arnold Circus, and that's only a bus ride away,' I pointed out, snappishly.

'I don't *want* to go, Teddy. Just so you understand. I wasn't *angling* for an invitation to your made-up family steed.'

'Homestead,' I said. 'A steed's a horse—'

Al glared at me and said, angrily, 'You can be so – oh, *Teddy-ish* sometimes. Who the hell cares? You know damn well what I mean.'

I stood up and walked over, pushing the paper gently away, and I sat down on the sofa. 'I do. Don't be cross with me. I can't bear it. You're the last person in the world I'd want to hurt.'

'You're such a child,' said Al. 'Teddy, I don't think you know anything.'

'What do you mean?'

Al's voice was hoarse. 'Oh, nothing. You don't understand.'

But I did understand.

'I kissed Matty,' I said, quietly. 'On the night I left. We kissed. I'd never kissed anyone before.'

'Oh.' Al looked up, alert, watchful.

'I wanted to tell you that. In case you found it—' My heart was in my throat, thickening my speech, thumping hard as I tried to find the courage to say what I wanted to. I looked down at Al, inches away from me. I wished I knew the rules. 'In case you were disgusted by that. By . . . by me. If we are to live together.' I saw that Al was frightened too, and it made me strong.

'No. I'm not disgusted. I'm glad you told me.'

We had never spoken of our relationship. I knew why. We both knew we had to wait for a day to come when it would change, and suddenly I knew it was here. It was now.

Fleetingly I wondered if I would ruin everything if I took the next step, but I couldn't stop myself. I was not nervous, not with Al. Every part of us belonged to the other. We knew each other so well, already. I put my hand in the space between our legs, then leaned forward and kissed Al. I had to be the one who moved first, you see. My heart was beating in my throat, blood drumming in my ears.

'Don't be cross with me. Don't be sad. I couldn't bear it if I made you sad,' I said, and I bent down and we kissed again.

I shifted my body weight, twisting so that we were facing, and gently held Al's face. That dear familiar face. The creamy pale cheeks were cold from the sharp evening air outside.

Before we kissed I was scared, and full of shame. I felt as though I knew what I was doing was wrong.

But I knew I must do it. I knew I must give in, otherwise how would I know? And besides – oh, Al, you know that I wanted to kiss you. I wanted to so very much, my dear.

At first we were perfectly still, then I closed my eyes. Wanting to be still, to savour the moment and then – it was blissful – slowly, steadily, Al's tongue moved into my mouth, and at that my body leaped with a gush of longing I can still feel now, sitting at my desk, recalling this June evening with such clarity. Al's tongue was insistent and hot in my mouth, warm, firm hands on my waist, and I kneeled so that I was straddling, pushing Al back. The curtains fluttered in the breeze; together we opened our shirts, undoing the buttons one by one, silent the whole time. We kissed and touched each other for what seemed like hours. Perhaps it was: I was light-headed, unaware of our surroundings, uncaring of time, only of the present.

It was always going to happen. We had never thought otherwise.

My breasts, blue-veined and full, with their tiny shell-brown nipples. Our bodies, I remember how different our skin was. Al's white with a touch of pink, mine tanned, light caramel. Both young, and smooth – ah, youth. Smooth, cool, sweet flesh. I ground against that hard young body beneath me, as the supple, soft hands moved up to my breasts, warm kind mouth kissed the nipples, licking the tips and smiling, moaning as if they tasted delicious, and we were both breathing loudly, in rhythm, like wind sighing in the trees outside.

I am crying as I write this. I recall Al's touch so perfectly. The rough, black wool rug on my shins, my heels digging into me, the delicious feeling of air on my naked breasts, my unbuttoned blouse fluttering gently on my thighs.

'I say . . . it's . . . it's all right, isn't it?' Al said, as we fused together.

And I smiled. 'Yes, darling. It's all right.'

'You're like a butterfly,' Al said, breath on my skin. 'My own beautiful butterfly.'

We watched each other: I was trembling. I swallowed, trying to tell myself to forget the voices that shouted in my head, telling me what we were doing was wrong. Al misunderstood.

'Don't be afraid. This is good. It's wonderful,' said Al, with so much kindness and affection that I was undone. I could not help wanting it and so I stopped listening to the voices, for the moment.

'I don't know what to do next,' I said, shaking my head, helplessly. And Al kissed me again, taking my head in those warm, slim hands, and then stopped.

'I have to do this now,' Al said, and I shook, and felt the hardness inside me, the ring of muscle at my wet, tiny, slick entrance rippling, clenching Al tighter around me, and as we continued to touch and stroke each other and I closed my eyes, letting the humming questioning that rang inside me all day silence itself, as I breathed in and relaxed, I felt it coming. I knew that I was experiencing it at last. I cried out, afraid of its power, then with pleasure.

Lying back on the sofa, I lay on top, and we wrapped our arms around each other. I pushed Al's hair away from the forehead dewed with sweat.

'Have you . . . done that before?' I said, curiously.

'Not like that,' Al said. 'It was always rough, or not the way I wanted. I came, didn't you?'

'I don't know what that—' I began, then stopped as Al laughed, gently. 'Oh, yes. Yes, I did.'

I was still wearing my shirt – Al was, too. We took off all of our clothes, then lay again together on the sofa, naked, our flesh touching, wet and warm and pulsing gently, our hearts both beating, our fingers entwined.

It was nearly Midsummer's Eve, and not quite dark yet over the city. Outside, I could hear someone calling downstairs on the street. High up on the top floor of that beautiful red-brick building – now nothing more than memories, ghosts, ash and rubble – we lay together. We stayed that way until morning, when we did it all over again, and then again.

In the weeks that followed we were so happy. We woke and made love, we drank coffee and ate toast, we read aloud to each other – the same old thrillers, or poetry, or sometimes even a book on butterflies or birds in my ongoing quest to educate Al about the countryside.

The great beauty of Al was the honesty, the openness we had together. Al didn't care about whether I'd had other lovers, nor did I. We didn't bicker over the little jealousies that tormented other couples I'd see around town. I knew Al was more experienced than me: I was glad, I suppose, at first, because it was not always me leading the way.

I loved watching Al sleep, curled up like a hedgehog, back turned away from me, snuffling and twitching, the merry certainty of the day replaced by a sweet, boyish vulnerability. Now that we were together every night, and not separated by a wall, Al complained that, as Misha had said, I talked in my sleep. But thankfully, it seems I never talked about Matty now. Instead I would wake up to find Al holding my hand:

'Teddy. *Teddy*. Stop talking about butterflies.'

I didn't say I dreamed of them every night, that I'd jerk awake in the never-dark bedroom, at the sound of a hackney cab or some city noise, and I'd think, for the briefest second, that I was back at home. And then I'd realise I was here and panic would jab at me, sharply. I didn't say how, when I was alone, I thought about what we were doing and how wrong it was, that I thought of my father and how he would probably kill me if he ever knew. I didn't say I missed Keepsake and thought about it more with each passing day. There was no point in saying any of these things, not even to Al.

* * *

Al's first present to me was on the day of the advert in *The Times*, when I suppose you might say a cloud scudded on to the horizon, a little thing, barely noticeable, but it was the beginning of the end.

We were lying naked on the rug, at the end of June. A hot, heavy night. No breeze. I wanted Al again, already, but Al was distracted, a little, and I had learned to temper my desire sometimes, though I never wanted to. Sex ruled me, it was often all I could think of, sitting in Misha and Michael's hot, airless sitting room, praying for a breeze to move across my skin, moving slightly on the hard leather chair, feeling the twinge of desire slide inside me, and I'd look up, breathing hard, hoping they hadn't noticed. I thought everyone must see it in me: I was blooming, rude with wanting, with coming all night, thinking about Al all day. Sometimes, though, I would see a couple on the street, a girl with her arm around a young man, and I'd stop at them and wonder why it was so easy for them, and not for me. How I was made this way, with this affliction. How strange it was that I could love Al and know what we did was evil.

Sometimes I'd see Misha watching me. That day she'd been a little difficult again: as the summer wore on, she seemed more and more on edge. Today I had not fetched *The Times* early enough and she had practically torn the Personals column out of my hand.

'No, nothing. Nothing,' she'd said, staring fixedly at it for a few seconds, then letting it drop to the ground, floating on to the thick carpet. 'Why do you make me wait like this, Teddy? What is it about you?' Then she'd stalked into her bedroom, to stay there most of the day again – she seemed to hardly work these days, just sit in bed, not reading, not eating, surrounded by ashtrays and the cats.

'I say. What do you know about the Ashkenazys?' I asked Al now, propping myself up on the rug. 'I mean, where they came from.'

'They came from the Soviet Union originally. They moved to Vienna.'

'I know that. I mean, why did they leave Vienna?'

'Because they wanted to make money here. They saw the way things would go for the Jews and they were right. Their children live in Vienna with Misha's sister.'

I sat up. 'They have children?'

'Two, I think.'

'Michael and Misha? Are you *sure*?'

'Yes. I got their post once, just after they'd arrived. It was addressed to "Mama and Puppa". Written in a child's hand. Terrible writing, in fact – but perhaps they were used to writing Cyrillic. I slid it under their door, never mentioned it.'

'Why not?'

'You know them. You can't, somehow.' I nodded.

If only we had, though. If only we'd asked.

'I talked to Ginny about it once, when I used to go to theirs for drinking sessions, when everything was a bit jollier. Ginny said something about them.' Al's nose was wrinkled. 'Yes, I'm sure she did, although it was pretty late, vodka had been consumed – you can imagine. Misha's sister looks after them. She's in Vienna. Katya?'

'Katya we've met. She was here – her husband got taken away by the Nazis. I think you must have got your wires crossed. She's not Misha's sister.'

'Oh. How strange. Listen, are you hungry?'

I pulled Al's arm. 'Wait a minute. They told me they had no children when I joined. That it hadn't been possible. They said they left because they were being persecuted for founding a dissident magazine.'

'Same difference.'

'No,' I said, and I was surprised at how confused I felt at the idea they might have been lying to me. 'It's two totally different things. I just wonder sometimes with them—'

'What?' Al touched my chin with one finger. I looked back, at those dark eyes with the glint of wild humour, the black cropped hair that fell into place across the smooth forehead, the wide cheekbones, the heart-shaped face, the little mole on the neck, just above the clavicle. That's what you do when you're drunk with love. Try to remember every inch of the person.

I caught Al's finger, bit it slowly, tasting it. 'I don't know them. I like them so much but do you know what's strange?'

'What?' Al was listening now.

'We never talk about anything proper. We chatter, about silly things. About dresses and music and books and – oh, the authors and their odd books. And Michael recites poetry and we drink a lot. But I don't really know what they're up to. I feel as though I could come down one morning and they'd be gone with the wind.'

'I think we can agree they're a little eccentric. But I don't doubt they had to flee Russia for their lives.'

'I agree.' I chewed my lip. 'But look at this,' I said, leaning over, reaching for my book. I took out a piece of paper, folded inside. 'This was in *The Times* Personals column a few days ago. She and Michael, they absolutely stared at it and then just let it drop to the floor. I picked it up and then—' I cleared my throat. It was strange to read it aloud. '"*M&M: Be ready. The friend is ready to grant our wish. Wait to hear from us or Dubretskoy.*"' I was almost relieved when Al didn't react. Perhaps I'd got myself worked up over it, and it was nothing.

'Who's Dubretskoy?'

'I think it must be Boris,' I said, uncomfortably.

'Rapacious Boris? Gosh.'

'Boris Dubretskoy. He's a character in *War and Peace.*'

Al stared at me, impressed.

'My governess and I – we read it together.' Miss Browning, with her serious face, her concerts, and her deep, passionate love of Russian literature. I wondered, with a pang, what had happened to her, whether she had had enough to live on after leaving, whether she had had to sell her beloved books, if her mother was still alive. 'They're always going on about Tolstoy.' I stared unseeingly at the wall. 'They've been even more strange than usual, this week.'

'Teddy, I wouldn't worry. They've always been unpredictable. As has that Boris chap, though if he should come back and try anything again—'

I turned around and sat up, so we faced each other. 'Would you fight him for me, my brave knight?'

Al kissed me. 'I would die for you.' The voice was small, and serious. 'I would kill anyone who hurt you. I *would*. I would rip out his heart and eat it in front of him if he hurt you again.'

We stared at each other. I can still perfectly recall it. Al's eyes and the depth of love in them.

'I . . . I know,' I said, and I pulled away, stepping back a little, swallowing, blinking hard. I felt faint, sick.

Al's honest, open face registered surprise, and then resignation.

'I wish you'd believe me,' Al said after a moment.

'I do. I do . . .' I wanted to explain, say how hard I was finding it, this being in love, this committing a sin, when it was so utterly unlike who I'd been before in my rigid, confined little life. *Give me time*, I wanted to say. *Let me get used to it.* 'Al, I do, darling—'

Al squeezed my fingers, kissing them impulsively. 'Oh, sweetheart. Look, I might as well do it now. I bought you something. Let me fetch it.'

'What is it?'

'I don't want you to miss home.'

I was handed a package, wrapped in brown paper. I tore it open, and there was a small wooden case marked with age, a glass top and a catch lever. It fitted into my palm. Pinned to the centre of the spotted, ancient silk was a perfect small butterfly.

'Clifden Blue.' I clutched the case, my hands smearing the glass in excitement. 'I can't believe it. I have never seen one. I always wanted—' I looked up at Al, who was watching me in sweet, almost childish joy, and I couldn't get the words out. 'Al, you shouldn't have. I hope it hasn't wiped you out.'

'No, not at all. I had a friend who had a friend.' Al tapped the side of the nose. 'Someone in Brick Lane knows a chap who sells off butterflies. This is old. Forty years or so. You have to keep it that way up.'

The wings of the Clifden Blue are a more brilliant colour than anything you will ever see. A pure, brilliant turquoise. Trust me. You may think you see it on the wing, but you have probably seen a Common, or a Chalkhill Blue. The Clifden Blue is rich, powdery, jewel bright – and perfect. It is known as the Adonis Blue now – I have never been able to establish precisely why. But I will always know it as the Clifden.

In my mind's eye I saw the land above the house, saw the grasses, the purple knapweed, the haze of the sun, saw Matty and I creeping stealthily out of the gatehouse across the meadow, black cut-outs against the blue horizon. I saw the fire on the beach, smelled the charred mackerel, heard the lap of the velvet water on silken sands, the rush of wind in the thick, dark trees. I saw it all with a longing that left me breathless. I wondered if it had been this bad before: I thought not.

'I'll catch them all for you. We can have a whole room of butterflies, if you want. If you'll just stay here, with me.' Al's jaw was tight, dark eyes so serious, hands tightly clutching my fingers. 'Please, Teddy. Just say you won't go back there.'

I sat on my hands. I wanted to leave, and I couldn't. I wanted to stop the voices that called me back home, jabbing, piercing voices daring me, goading me. 'You know I . . . I don't want to go back there.'

'But that doesn't mean you won't.' Al smiled, and moved a lock of hair from my cheek, pushing it behind my ear, fingers trailing down across my skin.

I caught the hand and sucked the thumb, slowly, feeling the whorls, the nail, the joint, taking it as far into my mouth as I could.

'I love you, Teddy.' Al's cheeks were flushed, eyes dark with intensity.

I slid the thumb out of my mouth, kissed it gently. 'I . . . I love you.'

'Don't.' Al's voice was harsh. I looked at the spots of burning colour on the cheeks. 'Don't say it because you feel you have to.'

'I'm not,' I said.

'You're holding back from me Teddy. Don't be a coward.'

'Don't call me that.'

'I don't know whether you mean to do it, but sometimes you make me feel like a . . . a . . .' Al brought one fist down on to the side table. 'Dammit, Teddy. Like I'm a dirty secret. As though we . . . we are bad. Abnormal.'

There was an awful silence.

'Don't shout at me,' I said, shaking my head. 'Give me time. I love you. I do. I only want you. Always. It's only that I've been so – I need to get used to it. To being like this.'

271

'You've always been like this, darling.' Al gripped my hands. 'Darling, you're like this, and so am I. You belong here. Will you stay with me? Or are you going back to financing your father and putting up with him till he dies or hits you too hard one day, so you can marry that fish-eyed chap who's already dead from the neck up, to lie there while he grunts on top of you, flopping around, trying to possess you?'

I shook my hands away. 'Stop it.'

'He can't. They can't. You're mine. You'll always be mine. And I'm yours.' Al moved our hands to my heart. 'I can feel your heart beating. You know it, I know it. I know it's hard. But you have to decide at some point, Teddy. You can't just drift along from day to day.'

'It's not drifting, it's—' I began. 'You don't understand.'

'Darling, I know I want us to be together. Always. Don't you? It's the easiest thing in the world. Nothing else matters, does it?'

'But we're—'

'No.' Al's hands closed over me. 'None of it matters. Who we are, what we are, where we came from. I love you. I won't ever love anyone else. I love how there's nothing between us, nothing except truth and kindness and everything that's – oh, I don't know, *good*. Like the sun's always up. And it's the two of us together who make it like that, not you on your own, darling, because you're an awfully gloomy person, you'd be the first to admit.'

I laughed.

'But it's true, isn't it?' Al leaned forward, so we were an inch apart. 'I sort of round off that bit of you that needs it, and you do the same to me.'

I said, 'I do want to stay with you. For ever.' I looked over at the butterfly, pinned in its case, back at Al's kind face. My heart swelled with love. 'I will. I will stay. I won't leave.' I smiled, at the idea that what I'd said might be true. 'Yes. Oh, Al. Yes.'

I looked up and saw Al's eyes, glinting with tears, the mouth fixed, rigid with emotion, the heart-shaped face flushed creamy pink, and I knew there were no words to say. So we were both silent, staring at each other, our fingers laced together.

We lay back down on the rug, Al's head on my chest, breathing soft and hesitant. I felt powerful, strangely sad and, for the first time in my life, grown-up. It was then I knew with certainty that I would hurt Al. That I would cause harm in this place, one day, soon.

Oh, my dearest one. We come to the hardest part of my story now.

Part Three

Chapter Eighteen

London, 2011

Everyone has a stroke of luck at some point. Sometimes when it's useless, sometimes when you need it most. I never thought of myself as particularly lucky. Now I know I am.

Lise's block of flats was called the Pryors. It was Saturday morning, four days after my father's disappearance and I'd come back to the Heath because I didn't know what else to do. I'd been standing outside the Pryors looking up at the turrets and wondering where on earth I'd go next; I don't know that I was thinking I'd actively stand there until Lise appeared. But just as I was telling myself I should go now, I saw Abby and realised this was my best chance.

She was striding towards the flats with that same purposeful air, wearing the same kind of sporty clothes, and I knew it was her. I ran across the road that skirted the Heath, waving apologetically to the cars that screeched to make way for me, honking furiously as I skidded past them. And then, I halted at the edge of the scrubland, several metres from her, assailed by doubt. As she produced some keys, trying to juggle them with a large plastic bottle of milk, some biscuits and some pink gerberas in cellophane, I made my mind up and I stepped forward.

'Excuse me.' I cleared my throat, trying not to sound too weird. 'I'm sorry to bother you. Are you Abby? Do you look after Miss Travers?'

'Yes,' she said, barely turning around, her voice cautious. 'How can I help you?'

'Oh.' Now I had her attention I had no idea what to say. 'I'm . . . I need to talk to her. Is there any way I could come up with you? She wants to see me. I can't really explain it out here.'

'Right.' Abby had managed to wedge the milk bottle against the door, and with one finger hooking it she put it, along with the other items she was carrying, on the floor, then turned to face me. 'I'm sorry. Miss Travers isn't seeing anyone at the moment. She's not at all . . .' she hesitated, 'well.'

'Oh no. Is she in bed?'

'Sometimes. She likes going out on the Heath, still, when it's warm.' Abby shrugged her shoulders. 'It's not an illness like the flu. More that she's weaker and weaker. She's ninety-three, you know.'

'I understand . . .' I paused, torn between pushing my cause and letting it be, certain that Lise wanted to hear from me and shrinking from bothering a sick old woman. 'But, she knows me. I'm . . . She knows something. She has something to tell me.' I was aware of how extremely badly I was explaining this. 'We've met in the London Library, a couple of times, she and I. And I've seen you outside, dropping her off. I wrote a note asking you to contact me, you probably won't remember. She's given me some photos, of my grand-mother. My name's Nina Parr, Abby, has she ever mentioned me, or my grandmother?' Was it my imagination, or did something, some recognition, flicker briefly across her face?

Abby smoothed out her ponytail and said, frankly, 'Look, as you may know, Lise has dementia. She hasn't been well for a while, but in the last couple of weeks she's gone rapidly downhill. In fact, the library was the last time she went out.' Abby bent over and was picking up the food and flowers, putting them into a folded canvas bag she'd taken from her handbag. 'She ran into someone there a few days ago and when I picked her up she was very agitated. She's been bad ever since. Can't sleep, very upset. She keeps trying to leave. She wants to find someone. That's the thing with dementia – when they get an idea in their heads it's very hard to . . .' She passed a hand over her forehead. 'When she remembers, that is. Otherwise she's very quiet. Much more so than usual. When she was fine, before, you really could still talk to her. Now—' Abby picked up the bag and slung it over her shoulder. 'It's as if the lights have gone out.'

'Oh,' I said, softly. 'I'm sorry. That's awful.'

'It is, because I knew her at the beginning when she was still quite well and it's been very slow, until now. She was a remarkable woman. She knew everyone, went everywhere, and she'd had such an interesting life too, you know – so much sadness.'

'How so?'

'Oh, she lost her great love in the war – she nearly died herself, too, in fact. Her family was all killed, and her husband died when she was still very young. Yes, so much sadness, I wonder if it seeps into you. She's seen some awful things. I don't know—' I wondered if Abby was still talking to me or to herself. 'The acceleration in decline during the last couple of months has been pretty marked. Nightmares. She screams about people. She's very withdrawn.'

Though the day was warm I shivered. 'What kind of people?'

'It can be anything. I don't think she knows, any more.' Abby shifted on her feet. 'Look, Nina. I wish I could help you. But I can't. She shouldn't see anyone. Doctor's orders. Mine, too.'

'But I'm pretty sure she wants to see me.' I cleared my throat. 'Honestly, that sounds crazy but I think it's true.'

'She hasn't mentioned it to me. And I asked her about you, after your note,' said Abby, flatly. 'She didn't know your name, she had no idea who you were.'

'She does,' I said softly. 'I'm so sorry. But if I could just—' I took an envelope out of my bag. 'Is there any way you could give her this?' I'd taken copies of the photographs she'd sent me for myself, and somehow thought she should have the originals back.

But Abby shook her head. 'Thanks, Nina. I can't give that to her. I'm not giving her anything that's going to upset her. I have to go back up to her now, she's been on her own for nearly an hour. Sorry. I wish I could help.'

She didn't sound particularly sorry and with that, Abby turned and gently shut the front door.

I could feel the photos, banging against my leg in the pocket of my skirt, as I walked. When I reached Parliament Hill I stopped and sat down. The whole of London was spread out below, a sea of cranes and tower blocks and obvious wealth. It was a city increasingly alien to me, these days: a place so huge, so obsessed with size and homogeneous internationality, a city utterly unlike its own history.

I didn't know where to go next. Then the sense of being totally alone – one person in a sea of millions down there – hit me, as it kept doing these past few weeks. I had to go somewhere, see someone I loved, who knew me – and of course, then, I knew where I should go. Couldn't understand why I hadn't sooner. I watched the smog-like haze rising up below me, stretching out towards Kent, and then I stood up and began walking down the hill again, but this time with a purpose.

When Sebastian opened the door, I smiled nervously.

'Hello. I'm sorry it's been so long.'

'Nina.' He scratched his head; he was in a white T-shirt and tracksuit bottoms.

'How are you?' I said. I leaned forward to kiss him, but he didn't react.

'I'm fine.' He didn't look fine. There were dark hollows under his eyes, and he was pale.

I followed him, shutting the door behind me with a bang, which made me jump; I'd forgotten the banging door.

The front door of what had been our home opened straight on to the sitting room, a beautiful room with original floorboards and wooden shutters, but it was – and always had been – a mess of old saggy sofas, piles of books and, in pride of place, a red-and-azure-blue-and-green kilim rug. How we fought over that bloody rug! He'd bought it from the Turkish place down the road when we had barely enough money for food and bills, let alone unwanted floor coverings. It had been the symbol to me of my fear of poverty, which I remembered so vividly from childhood, versus Sebastian's being a bit short of cash and getting a bailout from the bank of David and Zinnia. Such a waste of money, but so jolly. It made the flat feel like a home. And I'd stood on it there, right *there*, with my backpack, and told him I was going back to Mum's, and he'd laughed to begin with, before we'd started shouting. As though he couldn't believe it, thought it was a joke.

Now, as I remembered it all, Sebastian put his hand on my arm. 'Do you want a drink?'

'A drink? What, alcohol?'

'No, Horlicks. Yes, alcohol.' He disappeared into the little galley kitchen and I followed him. The same old rickety fridge, the tiny walled garden with its cracked concrete surface. The geraniums I'd put outside in pots were, by some complete miracle, still alive. Sebastian drew out some wine from the fridge and poured two glasses.

'Um . . . just a small bit,' I protested. 'Honestly, Sebastian. I can't, I've got loads to do this afternoon—' Even I thought it sounded weak.

Sebastian looked up, fixing me with a blazing stare. 'For fuck's sake, Nina,' he said. 'Have a bloody drink. One drink. You can't just expect to waltz in here like nothing's happened.'

I took the glass. 'Look – I'm sorry I haven't been in touch.'

'Yes.'

'I don't know what to say.'

We looked at each other, tentatively, as silence settled in the tiny room where so much had happened. The spider that crawled into the Marmite. The couple upstairs and their annoying yappy dog. The noisy kids from down the road, the drug dealer three doors up, the drunk man who used to piss outside, up against our front window. The dinner party where a cookbook fell on to that very gas ring and nearly burned the place down; the time we rowed so badly I threw Sebastian's phone in the loo.

It was very *very* . . . everything was extreme, dramatic, heart-breaking – and it was so silly, all of it, really – but standing here again I experienced exactly, so sharply, the bittersweet memory of that time. Because for much of the marriage it was like when Dorothy opens the door after the cyclone: technicolour life after black and white, and it was wonderful.

Who the hell was that girl who lived here with him? Where is she now? I missed her. I wanted, just for an hour, to be her again. To be brave, to feel love, to know I could take on the world.

'It's—' I shrugged my shoulders. *Don't cry.* I felt light-headed:

Abby, the heat, nothing to eat since breakfast. 'Look. I *am* sorry. I came here to say sorry. And to talk.'

He looked surprised. 'About what?'

'Oh. About – well, you know. Us. What happened, that night . . . um, you know, my dad came back. And—'

'Oh, *that!*' Sebastian exclaimed, sarcastically. '*Right!* The thing when we went for that drink a couple of weeks ago and I told you I loved you! And texted you every day and called you and kept asking how you were and what was going on! And then heard absolutely nothing, *nothing at all,* back! Oh, *yeah!*' He clapped his hands. 'I wasn't sure what you were talking about. *That!!*'

He stopped, red in the face, eyes glittering with anger, then picked up a tea towel and started polishing the kitchen surfaces with it, which was lunacy because a) I'd never seen him do any housework before, and b) the tea towel was one I'd inherited from Mrs Poll's flat, in fact it was one of the only things left behind after she died and the clearance company had done their work. It had a Bette Davis quote on it: 'Old age is no place for sissies.'

'I love that tea towel,' I said, after a pause. 'It was Mrs Poll's. Can I have it back?'

'Nina, is this a bloody joke?'

'Sorry, no – no.' I held my head in my hands. 'You keep the tea towel.'

'*I don't care about the stupid fucking tea towel!*' The veins on Sebastian's neck were standing out. 'I want to know how you've been, what the hell's been going on. That's all. And you give me absolutely bloody *nothing!*'

'I know. I know. Only it's been crazy. My father . . . Mum—' I held my hands up. How to explain it all: my father's disappearance again, my mother's retreat from daily life, Malc's anger with me. 'It's a long story.'

'I want to know it. Stop pushing me away. You always do this.'

'It's not your problem any more,' I said, honestly. 'Sebastian, I wasn't sure how things were with us – and I didn't want to involve you.'

'But, Nina, wouldn't you want to help me, if I was having a tough time?' He put his head on one side, looking down at me, his thick, strong arms folded, and I had the most powerful, fleeting sensation of wishing he would simply curl me up into an embrace, that we could stand there together, holding each other, not thinking about any of it for a little while.

'I suppose so,' I said in a small voice. 'I don't think of it like that.'

'You're silly. I want to help you,' he said, coming forward.

I brushed his cheek with my hand. 'You are lovely,' I said. 'I'm lucky to know you.' He shrugged. 'But you can't help me. You can't tell me what to do.'

'I wouldn't ever do that.'

'I mean, I want someone to do that. I wish there was someone, someone who knows about it, who could help me. And no one does.'

'I'll tell you who wishes she does, and that's my mother,' said Sebastian, leaning against the kitchen counter.

'Your mother doesn't want anything to do with me, trust me.'

'Well, I know she doesn't like you much. But I mean, since she heard you've got some ancient family house and title business going on, she's all over you like a cheap suit.' Sebastian took a sip of his wine.

'That's not true,' I said, already feeling a little better, that warmth that always hung around Sebastian beginning to thaw me out as it always did.

'Not strictly, but I have noticed a distinct mellowing towards you in the last week or so, and it's all since I told her. It's a definite step up from the usual, which is that she has to pause in the midst of a conversation when I mention your name so she can gag quietly into a handkerchief.'

'Oh, lovely. Well, I knew one day I'd win her round,' I said. 'You know, supposedly only women can inherit this house, so . . .' I trailed off.

'Your dad's out of the picture, you mean? I see. So if we got married again, you'd be the chatelaine and I'd be the humble sidekick, servicing you and your needs,' said Sebastian. 'When do we move down there?'

I smiled at him, awkwardly. I couldn't see it, though. Any of it. You know we all love to try to visualise ourselves at the new school, the new job, with the new boyfriend. *It'd be like this . . .*

But I couldn't imagine myself at the Keepsake from those photos and from *Nina and the Butterflies*, much less with Sebastian at my side. It was silly. Me, in a great house, ordering servants around, tending the lavender – would I wear a quilted jacket, would I have dogs and listen to *Gardeners' Question Time*, or make mead and spin and dye my own wool? I'd read everything from *Noggin the Nog* to *I Capture the Castle* – I knew what the basics of living in an ancient castle were: moats, cold, stone steps, battlements, spit roasts, stables? Mottes? But when I tried to picture myself around any of them, it didn't ring true. And for the first time, I found myself wondering whether any of it *was* true. It would make sense, wouldn't it, if he'd just been lying?

'So your dad's left,' Sebastian said, breaking into my silence.

I nodded.

'I'm sorry.'

'Don't be,' I said.

'What was wrong with him?'

I shook my head. 'I didn't trust him. I wanted to like him . . . and he was rather amusing. He's not a very nice person, though – I mean, he can't be.'

'How come?'

'He ran out on Mum. Twice. Oh, and he lied about stuff. He's lying now, I'm pretty sure.' But I thought of his face, as he considered going back to Keepsake, as he begged me to come with him, to take his mother's ashes back there. 'I still don't know. I kind of feel sorry for him.' I shook myself. 'Sebastian, I do apologise that I didn't return your calls or anything. I just didn't know what to say.' I looked up at him. 'About any of it.'

'No, Nins.' His eyes bored into mine. 'Honestly, no, it's me who should apologise for hassling you. But it's been driving me mad, knowing you're having to put up with all of this business with your parents and not having anyone to talk to. You always do this.'

'What?'

'Go into a cocoon. Unresponsive. And at the very least, you could have—' He stopped. 'Forget it. I sound desperate. And whiny. And I don't want to be. Whiny, I mean. I love being desperate, on the other hand. I absolutely love it and—'

I put my hand on top of his drumming fingers on the counter and he stopped, immediately, and we looked at each other. I knew I had to say what I'd come to say now, before I chickened out altogether. I felt sick.

'We can't get back together,' I said softly. 'We can't.' I squeezed his hand. 'Oh, Sebastian, I'm sorry.'

The merry, smiling face was perfectly still. 'OK.'

'Look, I wish it wasn't like this. But it is.'

'Is it?'

We were both silent.

'Yes,' I said slowly.

'You really don't want to see what happens?' Sebastian said. He moved away so he was leaning against the fridge, arms still folded, looking at me. 'I mean, if we tried it again but in a different way.'

I loved him then, for his honesty. No macho posturing, just truthful. The thing about Sebastian is he had reason to be confident: it might have seemed like arrogance in some people but it wasn't with him, and it was what had always been so attractive about him.

'I can't, Sebastian,' I whispered. 'Please, don't.'

'Why?'

'If it went wrong . . .' I began. 'It nearly finished me last time. And you. Especially you. And I love you enough—' I broke off, confused. 'Look, your mother's right for once.'

He said, sharply, 'What do you mean, she's right?'

Crack.

A loud, crunching blow hit the sitting-room window, and seemed to glance away, but not before the windowpane had cracked into shards, four jagged pieces smacking on to the floor, and spare splinters of ice flying through the air. I pushed Sebastian back towards the kitchen. There was a muffled bang against the front door.

'Fuck off!' Sebastian shouted.

'Fuck you, man!' Laughter, murmured low conversation, thudding feet running away.

'What on earth—?' I ran towards the door, but he grabbed my arm.

'No. Leave it for a bit.'

'What the hell is that?'

'Three or four boys. They're kids, children. They do this all the time. The old lady down the way, they've broken in and stolen her stuff twice. Put her in hospital.' He shrugged. 'It's this lane, it's not on the road, it's right between the estate and the railway tracks, you don't get any passing traffic.'

'Call the police,' I said. 'For fuck's sake, they can't do that!'

'There's no point.' Sebastian was scratching his head, looking at the glass on the floor. 'Jesus. I'll have to call Gary out again.'

'How long's it been like this? We didn't use to have anything like that when I was here.'

He called out from the kitchen, 'They were scared of you.'

'Ha-ha.'

'Don't know. Things are tense, more than ever this year, don't know why. Perhaps it's summer in the city. People get antsy.'

I'd opened the door and was looking out down the lane. There was nothing unusual. No noise. But I knew they were probably somewhere nearby. 'Little fuckers,' I said, fear and anger mixing with the adrenaline already coursing through me. 'I'm going to have a look for them.'

'Nina, seriously, come back!' Sebastian yelled. 'Don't make it worse.'

'I'll be fine. Don't worry!'

'God!' he shouted, exasperated. 'You sound like your mother.'

I stared at him. 'Well, you sound like *your* mother.'

'Well,' he said mildly, 'sometimes she's right. Not all the time, but . . .'

I stared at him. 'When did you become so Zen?' I said, shutting the door.

'After you left,' he said, nudging me.

I opened the kitchen cupboard and took out some plastic bags and the brown tape that was still there. He swept up the rest of the glass and I taped over the window, and we talked as we did, calmly, and then—

You see, I think I knew it would happen, somehow, in the way that a shock makes you crave things. I made him a cup of tea, and he fixed some toast – peanut butter and loads of melted butter, my favourite – and we sat on the sofa.

I touched the kilim with my big toe. 'Be honest. Do you like that stupid rug?'

Sebastian looked around, bewildered, then down. 'Oh, that. Noooo. No. I just wanted to annoy you.'

I laughed, and found suddenly I couldn't stop laughing.

He watched me. 'Remember, you were – well, you weren't very good at compromise. Only Child Syndrome, I reckon.'

'That's rubbish for starters,' I said, wiping my eyes. 'Most only children I know are much more all-round sane than people from big families.' He laughed. 'It's true!' I said, trying not to sound defensive. 'You think, of the two of us, *I'm* the one who's not good at communal living? You, who locked the bathroom door and refused to come out when we had Leah and Elizabeth over because I wouldn't open your wine.'

'I'd bought it specially to go with the fish—'

'Sebastian,' I said patiently, 'we were twenty years old. We had no business serving fish with a matched wine at dinner parties.'

'One should always aspire to better oneself.'

'No, one should not be a pretentious wang.'

We grinned at each other, tentatively, and then someone banged on the front door and I almost jumped out of my seat. Some kids ran past, laughing.

'Jesus, it's them again!' I said angrily, leaping up.

'No, that's another lot,' said Sebastian. 'It's Saturday. They're bored. At least it's not a school day, that's worse.' He took my hand. 'Don't be jumpy.'

'I'm not,' I said, shaking my head. I felt very calm, actually. The kids, the flat, the tea towel, the memories. 'Look,' I said, suddenly. 'We can't go back, can we? You understand, don't you?' I searched his face.

He turned towards me, chewing the inside of his mouth. 'Yes, Nins. Maybe I do.'

I drew a quick breath. 'You need someone – oh, who's glamorous, and writes history books as well, and can hold her own with Zinnia, who knows everyone and has umpteen PhDs and wants to go on holiday to Isfahan and Micronesia.'

'But that's not who I want,' he said, and his smile was painful. 'I want you.'

'No. You want us to have worked out, my love, and we didn't.' I took his long fingers and held them in my hand. I looked at them, each knuckle, the jagged scar on his thumb from the boat accident when he was ten, the mole on the crease of his left palm. And that girl was me again, the one who did things, who knew the right course to take.

'I did love you, Sebastian,' I said. 'Honestly. It wasn't games. It was real.'

He stared at me. 'I know you did, sweetheart.'

The silence roared in my ears. We stared at each other. I could hear my heart, thumping fast in my chest.

'Fuck it,' he said, and he kissed me.

Our hands were still entwined. I moved against him, and he sighed, in his throat, then gripped my shoulders, his lips moving to my neck, and my cheek, and then we sat back, both of us breathing hard, and I gave a small, tentative smile and said:

'It's just—'

'Just what?'

'It's just your mother—' I began.

And he really laughed. 'Stop bringing up my mother. The two of you are as bad as each other. I'm telling you, if you mention her again I'll throw you out on to the street.'

I smiled and shook my head. 'Promise.' Then, 'This sofa, do you remember—'

He shook his head. 'No, Nins, don't do remembers. Yes?'

His eyes were huge, dark now in his strong face, his hands lifting me towards him, and I pressed myself against him, wanting to cry. Sharp, pricking tears, an ache in my muscles, in my throat, because I knew it would be the last time, and – yes, it was the right thing to do.

He carried me into the bedroom, just picked me up, the way he used to, and I clung on to him, feeling the reality of him, his hard shoulders, arms holding me tight, how wonderful it would be if – if – if – if.

But we knew things. That we were growing apart and friendship had to remain, but in a way this . . . us, struggling desperately out of our clothes, my skirt, leggings, bra on the floor, his jeans, the weight of him on me, the rolling, gorgeous feeling of our smooth naked skin against each other, how much I missed him . . .

I can't explain it, just that we both knew it was the last time.

He made me come before he entered me, like he always used to do, and I felt a single tear roll down my temple, into my hair, and we moved together, as the sound of the laughing, grunting, running chaos of kids in the street outside floated over to us in the small, white room at the back of the flat. Then we both slept, tangled up together, sprawling, exhausted, for hours, until I awoke and it was night-time, the sky light teal with a yellow half-moon peering in above the taped-over window, visible through the open door.

I had never slept deeply when I lived here, and it was the same now. I felt restless, itching for something. I kneeled, watching him curiously. He was heavily asleep, passed out face down, gently snuffling, and my eyes found themselves travelling up and down his body, like a map of memory. His big, stupid arms, the right one with the pinkish scar where he'd broken it falling off a swing in the garden. The thick, hairy calves. His tight, neat bum – I used to watch it admiringly, walking ahead of me to lectures, never knowing its owner would notice me, much less fall in love with me. His thick, funny hair, curly, straw-blond. The fine scroll of his ear, the tender, bow-shaped upper lip.

He woke up as I looked at him, as though I'd brought him to life: opened his eyes from the deepest sleep and took my hand.

'Hello, you're still here.' He raised his head. 'What time is it?'

'Three. It's very early. Go back to sleep.'

'No,' he said, pushing me gently back against the duvet, fully awake now, and we had sex again, this time slow, sleepy, strange at first, the moonlight shimmering across the shabby, messy room, and then urgent, fast, more intense than it had ever been, no words, just us, staring at each other, until we were only this one being, not two. He made me cry out this time, loud, urgent, and then he slid off the bed and, with one leg kicking out, knocked a stale cup of coffee on the bedside table on to himself, all over the floor, over my skirt and leggings.

We laughed about it, about how ridiculous sex is, but like the boot with the faulty zip that made my heel bleed and sent me up to the Stacks, or the hooting horn of the white van driver the first time I saw Abby, that final act of us together – him thrusting into me, the mess it made – changed everything. A tiny little action.

The next morning my clothes were covered in coffee, too stained and damp to wear and, hunting for something else, I found the dress I'd worn the day after our wedding, my going-away dress. I'd opened the door of the cupboard by chance, not really expecting to find anything there; it swung precariously on the wire hanger and as I reached for it, memory flooded back. It was bought from a stall on Camden Passage, I'd found it in amongst the musty Chinese silk jackets and sixties kaftans, incongruously stored, then and now.

It was from the thirties or forties, creamy-grey-and-blue-flowered silk, three-quarter-length sleeves, mid-calf length. I'd not tried it on, just held it up against me, Sebastian laughing, kissing my neck and telling me it was perfect. It was only ten pounds.

Thinking it was just a sweet, pretty floral dress I'd brought it with me and put it on in Claridge's the morning after our wedding, alone in our room. Sebastian was downstairs, having breakfast. We'd rowed already – about the wedding, about staying there, about our parents – and I was suddenly sorry and hurried downstairs, pausing to look at myself only briefly in the mirror.

I was totally wrong: it wasn't a sweet little dress, not at all. The silk was heavy, it fell over my hips, hung on my breasts; it was vampish, dramatic, the navy flowers eye-catching on the sheen of the light background. I didn't look like me: I remembered how exposed I felt, putting it on. It should have stayed in Matty's room.

I felt uncomfortably grown-up, like a little girl playing dress-up again, as Sebastian and I sat shivering in the sudden July gloom in the Fairleys' haphazard sitting room for a hastily convened Celebratory Lunch. There, still slightly incongruous in that setting, were Mum and Malc, sitting identically on one of the brocade sofas, legs apart, leaning forward, clutching champagne flutes and looking grim. There was Zinnia directing the patrician, handsome David to fill our glasses, Mark and Charlotte giggling in the corner, and Judy, wearing a dress: both of us for years afterwards agreed this might well be the oddest by-product of the whole affair, Judy in floral Laura Ashley.

Zinnia had raised her glass and said, 'Welcome to your new home, Nina. Welcome to our family.'

It felt all wrong, and for ages I thought it must be because of the dress. Over time it assumed a strange symbolism in my mind, whenever I opened the wardrobe door to see it hanging there. *Even the day after the wedding*, I'd think to myself, as I flung clothes in there or slammed doors, angry at Sebastian for something or other. *Even then I knew this marriage was a mistake.* So, two and a half years later, when I moved out, I couldn't bear to take it back to Mum's with me. It remained here in the flat, hanging alone on its spindly wire hanger in the old built-in cupboard at the back of the room as I idly flung open the door that morning, looking for something to wear.

Sebastian put it on me, smoothing it over my body. For the rest of the day I could feel the movement of his hands as they pressed on to the silk. 'You look like someone else,' he said. 'You're as beautiful as ever, but you don't look like you,' and his hand moved up between my legs.

I wish I had delayed leaving, had him once more, stared into his good, steady eyes, felt him inside me.

He handed me an apple as I left. 'You can't go and not take anything with you,' he told me.

I brushed a stray piece of broken glass from the previous night's drama towards me with my toe and picked it up, gave it to him. He wrapped it in a tissue, set it carefully on the hall table.

'When will I—' I began.

And he said, 'Not unless you want to. I don't want to see you unless you want to. Think it over, Nina.' He held up his hand. 'I love you. But this can't be a thing we do. It'll drive us both mad. You tell me what you want.'

'How long have I got?' I tried to sound jovial; I felt happy, for the first time in weeks, and it was because of him.

He wasn't smiling. 'Not long. I want us to be friends but I won't wait for ever. Stop living on pause, Nins. Press play.'

Chapter Nineteen

I walked in a tired, dreaming daze through the dusty streets, uncaring of how out of place in amongst Sunday-brunch-seeking hipsters and parents with young children I looked in my strange blue dress. I touched my bottom lip once and shook my head. It was so hot, the sky thick with dirty-yellow clouds. Smiling to myself and not really thinking, I crossed the road that led up to the Heath.

'Someone's cheerful today!' a black cab driver called, out of his window.

Yes! I wanted to shout. *Yes, I am! I slept with Sebastian! It was amazing!*

It had been ours, the Heath: we spent most of our free waking hours here, in summer and in winter. Whether walking up to his parents' via the eastern edge of the Heath or birthday picnics with plastic cups and sausage rolls, or winter walks when the cold stuck in your throat and the setting sun blazed low and red behind the tracery of bare, black twigs. Or simply strolling by ourselves, hand in hand, finding a spot on Parliament Hill to sit, drinking beers and sitting on that Bette Davis tea towel, me lying with my head on his stomach, reading some worthy OUP collection, him stroking my hair or just snoring (he slept better than anyone I have ever known) – I had blocked all of this out, simply redacted it, these last few years.

The Heath shimmered in the early morning light, and everything was still. I looked up: the clouds overhead were dark and it was too hot, too still. For the first time, I seriously asked the question. Could we try again? Could I be that girl again? No: not a girl. A woman, who stayed with him, had a career and a place in the world, saw out the long years ahead, had his children, made a home with him.

It was terrifying to think, because if it went wrong it'd be much worse. A waste of time. I felt suddenly dizzy; my head spun. I sat down on a bench. You have made things worse, not better, I told myself. But it didn't feel worse, it only felt wonderful.

I sat, drumming my sandals on the spiky, dry grass for a few moments, smiling, and then I stood up and carried on walking, and as I walked the clouds broke, and it rained. Hard, splattering rain that fell in sheets and obliterated the view ahead. At first I tried sheltering under a tree, but there weren't any big enough in the immediate vicinity and the one I ran to was soon waterlogged, dropping great cupfuls of water on to me. Soon I was wet through, the dress clinging to me, all former symbolic dust and sweat from its single previous wear rinsed out.

Still the rain didn't stop, so eventually I walked on, my hair matting nicely in plumply soggy rat-tails, until I reached Parliament Hill. I was the only person around. As I turned to go, from the corner of my eye I saw the half-finished spike of the Shard, struck by lightning, a great, zig-zagging golden crack as loud as the shattering window last night. I stood there and didn't move, enjoying the view: you reach a point when you can't get any wetter. A great black crow flew above me, buffeted by the wind and the rain and almost driven to the ground by the force of the storm, and I watched it try to rise again, with a thrill. It was like the end of the world.

My feet were filthy with the sand and dust made into mud, and the dress was heavy and stiff. I walked for five minutes, flapping out the skirt, humming to myself, enjoying the sound of pattering, heavy rain on the canopy above me, and as I reached the edge of the wood I stood still, considering how best to avoid more rain now that I had dried off a little. I picked up my pace, walking fast uphill through the slippery lanes. The best way was up through Hampstead to the tube, past the Pryors, Lise's flat, and briefly I wondered if I could just avoid it, leave via the winding villagey lanes in the Vale of Health, but I couldn't remember how to get there and it was raining harder than ever now. I gritted my teeth, but I was smiling, because it was ridiculous, the whole thing.

It was then I heard the sirens again, louder now, and realised with horror as I turned the corner that they were heading for the Pryors, that smoke was coming from one side of the building sheltered by trees, smoke that, even in this rain, still poured black and grey out into the swollen sky. And I ran, up towards the red-brick block, not caring now whether this was officially stalking or not, and as I rounded the corner a fireman, younger than me, appeared in the open doorway at the bottom.

'All out, boys!' he called. 'Let's get the turntable moving. The hydraulics can come back in.'

'Oh, it's under control,' a young woman next to me cried. 'Thank God.'

'What happened?' I panted, trying not to drip over her.

She looked me over somewhat strangely, as well she might. 'Oh, someone left a lit cigarette in one of the sheds adjoining the flats.' She was holding a cat in her arms; it wriggled, desperately. 'The shed caught alight and the fire had got into the building, too – it was making for the trees on the edge of the Heath before that deluge. If it hadn't been for the rain, it'd have gone up like tinder, wouldn't it? We were lucky.'

I nodded. 'I should say. Phew.' I loved the randomness of London, how big dramas flared up and then were tamped down, how the confluence of millions of people together created these sparks that either ignited or merely burned out into flecks of ash. And indeed, that evening, on the local news, there would be a breathlessly in-accurate report on the fire that wasn't: 'Millionaire block of flats in Hampstead ablaze'.

'Is everyone out, though?' I asked her.

'Yes,' she said, struggling to contain the furious cat. 'And now we're all absolutely soaked. So irritating.' She seemed more annoyed with the fire service for evacuating them than she did with the owner of the lit cigarette.

I thanked her and cut up through the grass that led on to the main road, so I didn't have to walk past the flats. I really didn't want Abby to think I was harassing them.

My hair swung, heavy with water, in front of my face, and I squeezed it out, turning to take one more look at the fire, and as I did I glanced to my left, at the vast oak tree by the beginning of the avenue.

And there I saw a figure, quite alone.

She raised her hand, as though she'd been watching me all along, simply waiting for me to come to her.

This is how I saw I was lucky. I wouldn't understand why for a long time yet, but this was the second piece of luck to befall me that day. I know Malc says there are no coincidences; maybe he's right. I only know now, writing this these years later, now that she is dead, and I have the full story, that I was supposed to meet her like that. The hot weather that made the fire ignite, the rain that put it out, my night with Sebastian, my conversation with Abby – all of it, all of it rushing back in time for weeks and maybe even months, all leading up to that point, that moment, so that I could see her there, as I did then. It was always meant to be like this, some old magic at work again.

Chapter Twenty

'Look at the flames,' she said.

'Yes, I know,' I said, carefully. I looked around for Abby.

'Quite disappointing, really. Just smoke. Is that all there is? To quote Peggy Lee.' She watched in silence and I went and stood next to her, under the spreading shelter of the tree.

'Are you on your own?' I said, looking around.

Lise looked up at me and I saw her eyes. They were terrible pools of blackness, empty of any expression.

'I'm waiting for someone,' she said, eventually.

'I'll wait with you,' I told her.

'I thought you'd come,' she said, suddenly. She fumbled in her pocket. 'Would you care for a mint?' She handed me a small stone.

'Thank you,' I said. My hand shook as I took it, and our fingers touched.

'Why are you here now, Teddy?' she said. 'How did you know I live here?'

'Miss Travers—'

'That's not my real name, you know,' she said, and she shook her head, smiling. 'Mark made me take it when we married. That dress, it's beautiful on you. I haven't seen it before. You used to have one like it. You wore it on the day you left.'

'Miss Travers, do you know where Abby went?'

'I've told you, Teddy, that's not my name.' She closed her eyes. 'I don't know why you'd call me that. You know my name.'

Sirens were still screaming, on the nearby streets, storm-related car crashes and pedestrian accidents and other calamities unknown to us, as I stood there with her in the sheltered peace of the tree, wishing I knew what to say.

'We're all clear to go back inside!' came a booming call from outside the flats. 'All clear!'

Lise started. 'What did they say?'

'We can go back in.' I put my arm through hers. 'I'll take you, if you want.'

'No.' Instantly her eyes darted around, over behind me, fingers scratching on my arm. 'Don't make me. I don't want to go back in there.'

'Why?' I said, softly.

'Just—' She looked up at me and I saw something in her eyes flickering. 'Teddy, don't. Don't make me.'

I put my arm round her, and she leaned into the crook of my elbow, and cried, heartbroken, almost like a child.

'But—' I said anxiously. 'You like Abby, don't you? She's kind to you, isn't she?'

'I don't want to live there without you. I miss you. I hate it.' She spoke in short, staccato phrases that seemed to catch in her throat. 'And I hate missing you. I forget all about you. I forget who I am. I do it all the time, lately. Why didn't you come back?'

'It's all right,' I said, and I stroked her back, as the rain thundered around us, and we were dry in the shelter of the tree. 'I can wait with you. Don't worry. I know who you are.'

'But I don't. I've stopped being myself.' She clung to me. 'You thought it was unnatural, didn't you, Teddy? Oh, you never said it but I knew. You thought what we were doing was wrong, and – oh, I don't want to go back there! They tell me I've got it wrong and I haven't, I *haven't*, I haven't got it wrong.'

'What did they tell you you'd got wrong?'

'You loved me, Teddy, and I loved you,' she said.

'You loved me . . . ' I paused, and then nodded. Teddy.

'I'm right, aren't I?' She seemed calmer. 'I've got it right for once. Haven't I?'

I didn't know what to do, so I just kept patting her shoulder and gently rubbing her back. 'Yes,' I said.

'I shouldn't have changed my name,' she said, and she bent over and wiped her face on her skirt, lifting the black T-shirt material up to her face utterly unselfconsciously. 'I liked being Alice Grayling. I liked being a Grayling. Billy was a Grayling. Now there's no one left. No one who remembers. You left me. They all died. When I found them—' She broke off, and rubbed her eyes. 'You know, I forget some things. But I haven't ever forgotten what they looked like when I found them. And I can't tell anyone but you.'

'Who?' I said, gently, but she pursed her lips.

'Mishki and Bug.' She clicked her tongue. 'They loved gin. Don't you remember? I remember that. I don't remember some things. They come and go. When the bomb came, the building was flattened. Whoosh.' She mimed it with her hand. 'I should have been there but I wasn't. I was at the pictures. *The Godfather? Gone with the Wind.* It was *Gone with the Wind.* I wrote that film, you see. And I came back and everything was gone. I should be dead, but I'm not. All the things that happened to us there . . . whoosh! Our flat, our lovely flat, none of it's left now. The money you gave me, all gone. I was poor again. You knew that, didn't you?'

'I didn't know any of it,' I said, truthfully.

'That's because you left, Teddy. You lied, you did a bad thing. You said you loved me and you left. I knew you found it too hard, a woman, a woman. But it wasn't wrong when we were alone, was it?' She clung to me, her eyes alight, and she was young, I swear it, it was extraordinary, young and vital and athletic, and I understood her, the half-woman I'd met before. As she smiled I noticed for the first time the tiny chip on her front tooth, and I thought how attractive she must have been when she was younger. 'Was it? Tell me. We loved each other, I'm not wrong about that, am I?'

'No.' Tears filled my eyes; I didn't know what to say. 'I'm sorry. I'm so sorry Miss Tr— Alice.'

She smiled again. 'Don't call me that. Mark insisted. He *insisted*.'

'Your husband's name was Travers?'

'I changed it for him. Mark didn't mind that I liked women. He was very smart, Mark. His family lived on Regent's Park. I knew if I married him, I'd go up a notch, that I'd never be poor again. Oh, I betrayed myself. Isn't it strange?'

'Yes,' I said, wondering, wondering.

'I used to want to change the world. I was going to, wasn't I,

Teddy? And instead I . . . I stayed safe. I wrote silly stories. About silly people. Made-up people.'

'But you've done so well,' I said, able now to tell her something about herself. 'All those awards . . . your films, so many people love your work. That matters, doesn't it?'

She rolled her eyes, childishly. 'No. That means nothing. Nothing at all.' Her hands flopped to her side. 'No more Al, no more Graylings . . . not any more. The Grayling butterfly never opens its wings when it's settled. You told me that once, do you remember? I always thought how apt it was. How sad.' She was calmer now. 'Would you like a mint?'

I shook my head, biting my lip and blinking hard. 'No. Thank you.'

'I liked toffees, you liked mints, Teddy. I kept mints for years, in case you came back. I slept with men. That's all right, isn't it? All the time, when I realised Mark didn't love me either. But I never liked them.' She lifted her skirt up again and wiped her nose, the last of her tears. 'Do you remember Jacky the Clown, stealing the newspapers?'

I nodded helplessly.

'I do, too. Sometimes I remember it all. I remember everything, and I think about it, and I think about you.' She blinked, slowly. 'I saw the lightning today. I watched it from my sitting room. I knew it meant something. A storm this bad – we used to get them all the time. Lately, the weather is fine. You remember what I said to you when I left? The weather is fine. When I came back you were gone. I remember that.' She held both my hands in hers. She was smiling. 'The weather is fine, Teddy.'

'There you are, Miss Travers,' said a red-trousered gentleman of a certain age, striding over towards us. 'Abby's looking everywhere for you!' He peered down and smiled, as I stared at her. 'Let's get you back to your flat, shall we? She says it's time for your rest.'

'Are you my husband?' Lise Travers said.

'Would I were so fortunate, Miss Travers! I'm Robin Parker,' said the red-trousered man, all blustering joviality. 'I'm your neighbour.'

'I've never seen you before in my life,' said Lise, not impolitely.

'Ha! Well, I own the wine shop.'

'How interesting,' she said.

Robin Parker said, 'You bought all that wine for your eightieth, do you remember? You had a party in the flat and the police were called.'

'Really?' said Lise, and I saw a small glimpse of humour in her eyes.

'Oh, it was quite a bash. You broke most of the glasses, you had that game based on a Greek wedding. You made me smash one myself.' He was peering closely at her, his loud voice blaring like a horn at her. She watched him, not saying anything. 'Come on, then, let's get you back.'

'Would you like a mint?' she said, and she took a stone out of her pocket and gave it to him, and he took her by the hand and led her gently away.

I watched them go and then she turned and called over to me, and I ran towards them.

'Aha!' Robin Parker said, not without relief. 'There's Abby! I see her now.'

Into my ear, Lise Travers hissed, 'When I made enough money myself, I bought another brooch just like the one you sold, you know. Only black – jet black – because you broke my heart. You went back there and got married and had a son and I saw him once, saw him give a lecture in Oxford, and I knew he was your son. And till you sent that book you never got in touch, Teddy.' Her black eyes filled with tears again. 'Why didn't you just write, or telephone?'

Robin Parker looked rather taken aback. Abby was getting closer, still a small figure in the distance, though.

Why? Why?

'I don't know why,' I said. 'I don't know why. I'm sorry.' I closed my eyes. *Walk towards it. Don't be frightened.* 'But I loved you. All of you. Always, I did. You know I did.'

'Yes . . .' she said, slowly, eyes fixed on me again. 'Yes . . . yes, you did, didn't you?'

We stared at each other, and I held my breath.

'Lise?' Abby was closer than ever, and she stopped to talk to Robin. 'Lise – Miss Travers' She looked over. 'Nina?' she called. 'Is that you? Nina?'

I glanced down at Lise Travers and I saw something, the drifting clouds part. She peered at me, leaning towards me, and we were inches apart. I bent over and she stared into my eyes.

'Oh,' she said, abruptly. 'You're Nina, aren't you?'

I nodded. 'Yes.'

'I know who you are. Yes. Yes, I do. Be quick. I gave you those photographs, didn't I?'

'Yes, Miss Travers, and—'

She shook her head, swallowing, clutching my hand again. 'Listen to me. Do you have the book? Do you have your grandmother's book? Answer me now. Quickly. Before it goes.'

'The one about the butterflies? *Nina and the Butterflies?*'

She shrugged, impatiently. 'She wrote it about me. She sent it to me, before she died. Our butterfly summer. The memoir . . . one for your father, one for me. She didn't want you to know any of it, but she's wrong . . . I read what she wrote, I know her and she's wrong.' My hand ached from the pressure of her grasp; she hissed: '*Do you have it?* I can't find it any more. I think I burned mine; I don't know why. I forget things, you see.'

The book? I nodded, bewildered. 'I think . . . yes, I've always had it. It's at home.'

'You do? But you don't sound so sure.' She was staring at me, disappointed. 'You know it all, then?'

'A children's book, about butterflies?' I said, and she laughed.

'No, no, no, not that, Nina. You haven't found it, have you? You have to find it. Go to Keepsake. Or find your father. He had the other copy. Just two copies.'

'But I don't know where Keepsake is,' I said.

'Someone must do. Someone who knew your father. I never went, you see. Who knew your father?'

'No one – my mother . . .' I began, and trailed off.

'Then the answer's at home.' She nodded, then held her hand up to Abby, who was waiting a little way beyond. 'I'm coming. I am coming. Good.' Then she blinked rapidly, and fumbled in her pocket. 'Would you like a mint?'

So I said, 'Yes, please, Lise . . . Alice,' I said. I looked up, and the sky was blue and white, the rain faint now. *The weather is fine,* she had said. 'And . . . thank you.'

'Al. You always used to called me Al.' She removed something, folded it into my hand and walked on, hesitantly, utterly unresponsive. I looked down and uncurled my fingers, blinking. And there, nestling in the crease of my palm, was a mint – snowy white and hard as a new-laid egg.

Chapter Twenty-One

I shut the front door quietly, and leaned against it for a moment. It was late afternoon. I felt dizzy; I hadn't really eaten since lunch the previous day.

Slowly, I took off my sandals, to go and get some food. I was tiptoeing quietly along the worn raffia towards the stairs when a voice at my elbow said:

'Nina? Thank God.'

I jumped violently and looked up. There, on the third or fourth step, was Mum, sitting so still I hadn't noticed her in amongst the coats and piles of books and magazines.

'God,' I said, holding my chest. 'You really scared me.' I cleared my throat. 'You're out of bed, then?'

'When my daughter doesn't come home for twenty-four hours, I get out of bed, yes,' said Mum, quietly. 'I thought something had happened to you.'

I laughed. 'Don't be ridiculous, Mum.'

'You could have called me.'

I was too tired to be polite and smooth things over. 'Why on earth would I have called you? You don't have a mobile and the landline's in the kitchen, so I knew there was no point.' I started to walk downstairs.

'I went to the solicitors this morning,' she called, through the bannisters.

'It's Sunday,' I said impatiently, and disappeared into the kitchen.

'I signed your father's papers and dropped them off with a security guard. Are you happy?'

'That's great, Mum,' I yelled up. 'Really great.'

Mum appeared at the top of the kitchen stairs. 'So – will you tell him, when you see him? When . . . when are you going to Keepsake?'

I said shortly, 'I'm not going.'

'What?'

'He took off. Again.'

She came down the stairs so we were standing together under the harsh spotlight at the foot of the staircase. Her hair was greasy, flat on her head, her skin waxy and pale with the lack of a week's sunlight, and there were huge circles under her eyes. She looked at me curiously, in my stiffly dried old dress and rat-tailed hair.

'Oh,' she said. 'Right, then.'

I turned away and switched on the kettle. 'I'm still off tomorrow,' I said. 'I'll take a bag to work and then move in with Elizabeth for a couple of weeks while I find somewhere else.'

'But you don't have to go.'

'What, because I didn't disobey your instructions in the end? Right.' I chewed some bread.

'No, because, I don't want you to go,' said Mum. 'I mean it. Please stay, honey.'

'I have to, Mum. This – this isn't working. It's best if I go. I want to be on good terms with you. At the moment I think if I carry on living here we might end up not actually having a relationship at all.'

I saw how surprised she looked, but I was tired, sweaty, grimy, and now I was surprised, that I simply couldn't play along. I didn't care.

'Nina, I know you think I'm a bad mother—' she began.

I shook my head, wearily. 'I don't, Mum. Look, can we just leave it? I'm really tired. Isn't it best we just have some time apart?'

'Oh, I'm sorry,' she said, her mouth wobbling, and as I watched her, I felt something surge through me, a rage that I hadn't known was quite so close to the surface.

'You're not, Mum, though,' I said. 'You're not sorry. And I'm sick of pussy-footing around you – me and Malc – till you decide you're better. I know you've had a tough time. But I let you off the hook all the time because you have to be told you're not a bad mother.' I held out my hands. 'You're not a bad mother. Hardly anyone is. I can't keep saying that to you.' I swallowed some more bread, trying to pretend I was in control of this. I raised my arms. 'But, yep, it's true, you weren't that great a lot of the time. Is that what you want to hear? I love you, but it's true.' My arms flopped to my sides. 'Let's just forget about it.' I took some more bread. 'I'm going to go and pack up some of my stuff.'

She took a deep breath. 'Well, if you feel that way, of course . . . b-but, Nina, I think some memories get warped with the passage of time, you know.'

'Christmas Day, 1999!' I shouted suddenly. 'You spent all day in bed because you didn't feel like coming downstairs. Seriously, you're going to try and pretend it didn't happen? You've done it all my life.'

'What?'

'Let me down when I most needed you.'

We stared at each other and I think we were both amazed I was saying these things but now I was like a child poking a stick into a wasps' nest, unable to stop. I put the heel of my palm to my forehead. 'My school play first night, when I was Helena, and I had a whole speech to myself, you didn't come because you had a reading in Bristol. Remember? And, Mum, it really wouldn't have mattered, I knew you had to work, only you cried and made such a huge drama that *I apologised to you* for having the first night of my play on the same day as your reading. You make everything about you!' I was shouting now. '*Every fucking thing!* My dad comes back, after twenty-five years, and you've been lying to me the whole time and you have me, *me* feeling guilty, *me* being told off by Malc, while you go to your room and sulk for days on end. And don't try and make out it was anything more than sulking. I needed you.' I felt drunk, high, adrenaline pumping through me. 'I know things have been unbearably tough, I'm sorry you took the overdose. I'm sorry I was a terrible baby who screamed all the time, and I'm sorry Dad left, and he was shit in the first place, I'm sorry for *everything*, but – Mum! *None of it's my fault!*' I yelled. 'None of it! So . . .' I paused for breath. 'Stop taking *all* of it out on me. I'm not doing this any more. I'm done. OK?'

Mum's head was buried in her hands.

'Sit up,' I said. 'Look at me, for God's sake.'

'Don't talk to me like that,' she said. 'Don't be rude. I don't have to look at you, not when you're—'

'You just don't get it!' I actually stamped my foot. 'You're not listening to me, Mum! *This isn't about you!* Just this once it really isn't!'

She looked up, and laughed, quietly.

'Why are you laughing?'

'It just seems funny, that's all. Honey, you tell me not to say I'm a bad mother, then you list the many ways in which I have, in fact, let you down. How there was no one to look after you. It's a miracle you turned out how you did.'

'I had Mrs Poll,' I said, and there was a tension-filled silence.

She nodded. 'Of course.'

'It's not a miracle. It's because of her,' I said, flatly. 'We both know she's the one who saved us both. Until Malc came along. It's them. It's not you.'

I saw Mum's face crumple, and I knew I'd gone too far then.

'I know,' she said. She wiped her eyes and mouth savagely with her knuckles. 'That woman – God, I loved her, but sometimes I think she was sent to show me up for the charlatan I really was.' She shook herself. 'Forget it. You're right. You're totally right.'

'Mum – I'm sorry. I went too far . . . I . . . I know Mrs Poll got all the good bits.'

'Oh, not necessarily. She did the difficult stuff, too. She's the one who told me when you had nits and when you were having nightmares.' She shrugged. 'I wish I'd been better at all of that. But I started to believe I'd screwed it up already so much it was a damn good thing she was around to make a better job of it. To save you. To love you.'

'That's crazy,' I said, my eyes stinging. 'Come on, Mum, she wasn't you, she was never you.'

'Ha.' Mum raised her eyebrows. 'You know, when I'd try to read to you, you'd squirm off my lap and shout, "Mummy Poll! I want Mummy Poll!"'

'That's awful,' I said, my cheeks flushing. I was aware of standing there in my ruined dress, my hair still damp at the back. 'Mum, it's only because—'

'She was much better at it. She was better at everything.' Mum grimaced. 'God bless her, but she really did make me feel crappy, sometimes. And then, leaving us the flat, and the money: it made her a saint. Like I'd never be able to pay her back. I know she didn't mean it like that. I'm so grateful to her . . .' She trailed off. 'Forget it.'

It was the first criticism of Mrs Poll we'd ever uttered in this house. 'She only wanted to help,' I said uneasily.

'I know.' Mum gave me another hug, patting my back, reassuringly. 'I know, honey. But the thing with her was—' She broke off. 'You know what? It's all in the past now. I can't change it.' She pushed all the rubbish off the kitchen counter and stretched out her hand. 'So I wasn't the mum who baked the cakes and plaited your hair. Can I be the mum who's great at other things?'

I took her hand. 'You were anyway, Mum, don't be silly. You nearly tore Amy's ear off when she was bullying me. You let me watch *Buffy* with you when I was way too young 'cause you knew I'd love it, and you were right. And you got me drunk before I went to UCL so I knew how awful it was and never wanted to do it again. And when I left Sebastian, and came here, you . . . you *never* said I told you so. You never slagged him off.' Tears were in my eyes now, and I swallowed, reaching for the kitchen roll. 'You just told me how nice he was and how it sucked that it didn't work out. You made me feel normal, for the first time in my life.'

She stared at me. 'But you are normal, honey.'

I laughed. 'But I don't feel normal.'

Our hands were still clasped together. I leaned across the counter and kissed her cheek, and she pushed a strand of hair out of my fringe.

'You're still my little girl,' she whispered, and I could hear the pent-up, pain-filled release of tension as she said it, like breathing after being underwater for too long. I swallowed again, and gave a small sob, and she smiled.

'Don't cry, honey. Don't cry because of me. It's fine, now, OK?'

Perhaps we spend our whole lives waiting to find out our parents aren't perfect. I loved Mum very much in that moment, because I knew she was trying. And I saw that she'd probably let me down again, and I could either let it eat away at me, or get on with it and be grateful she was here, that she'd chosen to stay. I pushed myself away from her, as gently as I could.

'Let's have some tea,' she said.

'Can we have a drink?'

'Good idea.' She took a bottle of wine out of the fridge, and opened it. The first sip was delicious: minerally and cool, rushing to my head. We clinked our glasses, not quite sure what we were toasting, smiling shyly at each other.

'This house,' I said, eventually. 'The whole business with my dad. I don't know what to do. I met someone today who said I should ask you. That you'd know.'

'Who was that?' Mum said, amused.

'It's a long story,' I said. 'I told her you didn't know anything about him, or the house. Neither of us did. And we don't, do we?'

Mum took another deep breath. 'It's funny, I was remembering something,' she said, pulling out one of the kitchen chairs. 'On our third date your father never showed up. That should have been a warning, huh? We were supposed to be hiring a punt and taking a picnic up the Cherwell and he'd got scared about the whole thing. Thought I was coming on too strong so he went off to a friend's house for the weekend. I waited there by the bridge with my stupid paste sandwiches for hours.' She shook her head. 'I always thought with him that I just didn't know something vital about him. I think we still don't.'

'Like there's a whole other story we don't understand?' I said, wondering again about Lise and about Teddy's book, about what we simply didn't know.

'It's frames within frames, isn't it? We're living in one frame, and there are other worlds in other frames. But you need to try to find him. And this house.'

'Do you really think so?' She nodded. 'So do I. But I've rung the solicitors,' I said. 'And emailed them. They took ages to reply.'

Mum said, 'Which is so weird, because they couldn't get back to me quickly enough about the divorce papers.'

'They did pick up eventually. They've made an appointment for me to go and see one of their junior partners in a fortnight's time,' I said. 'But even that was like blood out of a stone.'

'Would they tell you where the house *is*?'

'No! They don't reply to any of my questions. It's so strange. Like they don't want me to go there. Or like the whole thing's made up . . .'

'Hmm.' Mum gave a grim smile. 'Have you googled it? What's it called again?'

'Keepsake. Maybe it's marked on some Ordnance Survey map or something, but I don't know where it is. And if you read *Nina and the Butterflies*, Keepsake is hidden somewhere off a wide river.'

'That kooky book Mrs Poll and you were always reading?'

'It was Dad's book, he left it behind when he went.' She shrugged, vaguely. 'Mum, do you remember *anything* about him, his family? Anything at all?'

'He used to say he had this family situation that was very strange . . . but he didn't really ever talk about it. He liked his father well enough, I think, but he'd been dead for a while by then. He said he wasn't close to his mum . . . and he didn't go home that much.' She screwed up her eyes. 'Look, it was the seventies, you know. People were doing their own stuff. There was this one story about his mum, though, I remember.' She blinked. 'I'm trying to remember. My brain is addled with lack of activity. Forgive me.'

'It's fine – we can do this later—'

'No. Now. I – there's something there.' She narrowed her eyes to slits, staring at the knots and whorls on the table. Eventually she said, 'What did he say when you met him? Did he give you any details?'

'Not really. He said it was beautiful. And secluded. He really didn't say much. But there's a photo of my grandmother, one of the ones Lise Travers gave me – she's on a boat . . . in a, well, it could be a creek. A river . . .'

Mum's eyes were closed, but she opened them and looked at me. 'A creek. Yes. Of course. My God.'

'Mum?'

'It's in Cornwall,' she said, slowly. 'I've been there. He took me there.'

'Mum, are you serious?'

She pulled at her hair, eyes wide. 'How could I not have thought of it? Oh my God, was that it?' She whispered to herself. 'Is that what he meant?'

I gripped her arm. 'When? When did you go?'

'It was the end of the first year we spent together. Summer of seventy-nine.' She winced a little. 'Gosh, oh my gosh.'

'You don't have to—' I began, but she shook her head.

'We drove down from Oxford. Took hours. We stayed in this little village. Helston. Heldone . . . Helford. Beautiful place. And one day, we went—' Her hand closed over my wrist. 'Oh my goodness, Nins. We drove to this house. He said they were old friends of his family. That he'd read about the house and never visited. What a bullshitter!' She looked at me. 'Sorry, honey. But apparently we couldn't go in – you can't get to it by road unless you walk for miles. He said there wasn't a drive there any more, they'd bricked it up so you have to go there—'

'By boat, down the creek,' I finished for her, and we stared at each other again. 'Mum,' I said, very carefully. 'Did you go to the house?'

She said, slowly, 'Yes. We did. We hired a boat, and George rowed us down there, and I remember being so impressed, a little surprised you know? Because he was so kind of *inside*-ish, you know? I had no idea he could actually do stuff, like row. I teased him about it. He was rather cross.

'But there he was – steering this little boat down this river, along this offshoot, the creek. And it really was remote, you know, with these thick swathes of trees on the banks on either side. And we finally get a little further down the creek and he ties up the boat and he says, "We can just go up. The people who live here, they're like family to me." I thought he was being a little pompous about it actually, but he was like that, George – he came off as pompous and sometimes, oh . . .' the two lines between her brows creased into deep folds. 'Oh, you know, it was just awkwardness, shyness.

He was such a complicated boy. So cocky – he was so handsome, your daddy, but he was so unsure of himself . . .' She trailed off.

'Anyway, we climb up these stairs, cut into the rock. We get to the top, and there's a path, covered with ivy, and it's really dark and he's saying, "Careful, don't slip," and, "It gets really bad in winter," all of that, and it's really steep—'

She stopped.

'He'd been there before. He *knew* it. You understand? But I didn't see it then. We clambered along this path for ages, picking through trees and fences and all, and there's this – this house.' She swallowed. 'Oh, it was strange, peering through and seeing it like that.'

'Why? What was strange?'

She shrugged. 'I don't know. He wouldn't go any further. He suddenly turned back. Said someone was there and we'd be trespassing.' Mum's eyes were flashing, her cheeks flushed with colour now. 'We turned around, went back down, got into the boat, rowed back. We didn't mention it again. I kinda knew not to.'

I blinked; my head was spinning. 'Did you see the house, though?' I said. 'Did you see anyone there? What was it like?'

'There was a gate, a big stone gate, with a . . . was it a lion? A lion and a fox, butting at each other.' Mum spoke slowly. 'I remember that. There was a house through the gate, but – oh, honey, I couldn't really see much. It was so overgrown. But there was smoke, coming out one of the chimneys.'

'Someone was living there, then.'

'Uh-uh. Oh, and it had these battlements running along the top, and it was long and low. Really old. And there was this oriel window at the side. I remembered that because of being at Oriel College, you see. That's—'

'That's my house,' I said. We blinked at each other, smiling slightly, unable to keep the excitement out of our voices.

'I wonder why he wanted me to see it.'

'Because he was in love with you, he wanted to show it to you,' I said.

'But then to back out, to leave . . .'

'Mum. Do you think you can remember how to get there?'

'Get there? Honey. You mean by ourselves?' Mum took a big mouthful of wine.

'I'll go on my own, if you don't feel you can come. But it'd just be much better if you were there.'

I picked at the skin around my nails, not daring to look at her. I wanted her to come, but at the same time I was still always a little afraid she'd pull something, ruin the whole thing.

'Of course, of course I'll come,' she said.

'Are you sure?' I said. 'Cornwall's a long drive.'

Mum held my hands. 'Absolutely. One way or another, we'll find that house.' She stopped. 'If that's it. If that's the place. You know, I sort of don't believe it. I don't get why no one's telling you the truth about it. It just seems fishy to me, somehow.'

'And me. I'm not sure what we'll do when we get there,' I said, sobering up at the thought. 'Or what we'll find.'

'Never mind. We take action! We leave tomorrow!' said Mum, dramatically striking the kitchen table. 'I shall make food! I'll bring the pastrami and pickle sandwiches of my country!'

'OK,' I said. I knew she'd forget, and I'd make them in the morning. But that was OK. It was all OK.

Chapter Twenty-Two

We left before breakfast in Mum's beloved but battered Golf, after I'd cleared it of the usual detritus of food wrappers, tissues, contact-lens cases and newspaper articles of interest to her that she'd torn out, probably while driving. After we'd bounced up and down hard, which was the only way to get the ancient engine to start, we were off.

Malc stood in the doorway waving goodbye. I felt he probably thought the whole enterprise mad, but wouldn't say so – and I couldn't bear to ask him, in case he did. He went out to the café around the corner and bought us fresh croissants and coffee in paper cups. And even though my heart ached at the sight of him so very alone, his stocky form framed by the doorway like a little boy trying to be grown-up, we had to wave goodbye, and eventually we were off, driving down the deserted street.

I had emailed Bryan Robson the night before, to explain that urgent family business had called me out of London, and that I'd be away for two days. And, in a self-immolatory act of rashness, added:

I'm very sorry for the lack of notice, and for my lack of commit-ment to the job the last couple of months. I understand if you feel the need to terminate my position.

It was not yet seven thirty as we drove through Bloomsbury, and the roads were empty, filling up gradually as we headed west, through Piccadilly and Green Park, swerving to avoid the vast blacked-out Range Rovers that, even at this time of day, clogged up Knightsbridge. We passed Harrods, which had once been my favourite shop because of the Fossils, and which I hadn't visited for years now. It was still closed. A young, lounging, playboy-ish type sat outside the ornate windows in a bright yellow Maserati, apparently oblivious to his surroundings, blocking most of the road. We honked at him to move out of the way and, without even looking, he raised one finger and continued playing with his phone.

'Hey, you!' my mother yelled. '*You!*'

He turned around.

'This is a city, we all live here. Have some respect!'

'Fuck you!' he screamed, still not looking at us. 'You fucking cunt!'

'You're a massive dick!' Mum yelled out of the window at him. 'With a really, *really* small penis!'

'I don't think the Fossils would recognise that kind of language,' I said, as we sped on, towards the Victoria and Albert Museum.

'People always say, "Isn't it a shame how cities change?" And they mean litter and tower blocks, and I think that's horseshit. This is what's ruining our city,' said Mum, jerking her head back. 'These people. This money. I'm telling you, this isn't London. It's an Emirates First Class Lounge.'

'With the Olympics next year—'

'They keep saying the Olympics will change everything. That's horseshit, too. You'll see, in three years' time London'll be falling to pieces and we'll still be paying for it all.'

I loved Mum like this: fearless, in control. 'You're not nervous, are you?' I asked her, as we hit Richmond, and London receded, replaced by green suburbia, flashes of the Thames, hints of countryside.

'Nervous? I'm absolutely terrified,' she said, raising her hand to thank a motorist for letting her into the fast lane. 'I have no idea what we're getting into. I don't even know where we're going.'

'We'll work it out when we're closer,' I said. I sank down a little in the seat, gazing out at the road ahead. 'We'll get there.'

My phone ran out of battery somewhere the other side of the Tamar Bridge, and by the time we were past Truro I was relying on our ancient road atlas, which – as my phone-averse parent and her equally phone-averse daughter took great pleasure in pointing out to each other – was actually much more useful than navigating with a phone. There was something exhilarating about seeing the spread of our journey, the counties opening up to us. I never left London, and here we were, journeying west with the sun at our backs for most of the way.

We stopped once, at a service station in Hampshire, and there, sitting under the fluorescent strip-lighting surreptitiously eating my sandwiches and drinking metallic-tasting coffee, surrounded by either retired couples sipping tea in silence or desperate families wrangling over screaming toddlers, the whole enterprise suddenly seemed to me to be utterly foolish. Even if we did find the house, could we walk in, just like that? Was there someone else now living there, an aged retainer – the stuff of stories – or a distant relative, someone else to reckon with?

Was my father there?

But once again Mum surprised me, not least in the stamina she had for long drives, but also in the cheeriness of her attitude, of her excitement. I was tired, and jumpy, with that dull ache in your forehead from too much time spent in a car, as we passed Falmouth. We drove through another village and towards the river – I could see it, glinting in the distance, the sea beyond – and then we came to a sign which peremptorily warned us against driving our car any further between May and October.

'What shall we do?' I said, gazing ahead at the steep lane down which I could see a few roofs, and hearing the roar of the wind in the trees. It was quiet, no other traffic on the wide, empty road – the school holidays were a few weeks away yet. Mum drove the car into a siding, turned the engine off, and climbed out. I followed her, and stood there shaking out my cramped limbs and looking around me, while she scribbled a note and stuck it under the windscreen.

'There,' she said, tucking her arm through mine. And she smiled at me and I felt then that it was OK, it really was, if she was with me. 'Let's go.'

It wasn't until we were several paces down the road that I broke away from her, ran back and looked at the note. She'd written:

Looking for ancestral home of only child. This sounds unbelievable but is true. Hopefully they'll have parking. Move car when finished or found it, whichever sooner. Apologies / Thanks.

We walked down the road, which narrowed into a curving lane. Glimpses of wide river, blue-green and fringed with heavy trees, flashed in and out of sight as we wound our way down, surrounded by hedgerows flushed with sweet, musky elderflower blossom. At the bottom of the lane we could see the wide expanse of the Helford river. It was calm, occasional splashes of sunlight like glitter on the gently eddying waters, and in front of us was a tiny beach, a shingle-and-sand affair. There was a cluster of white cottages, a pub with tables outside, a booth selling ice creams, a jetty and, on the beach itself, a duo of little red-haired girls throwing stones into the water with sturdy determination.

'Let's ask in the pub,' said Mum, heading up the steps. 'They can—'

I grabbed her arm. 'Oh – hang on, Mum.'

She turned back to me. 'Why?'

'What – they won't know, will they? I mean, it's a bit strange to have someone just turning up asking weird questions about a house, isn't it? Let's wait a bit.'

Mum clasped my hand and smiled at me, the apples in her cheeks shining. 'Honey, we've been waiting twenty-five years. Let's not wait any longer.' And she turned and walked up the steps.

But inside the pub they hadn't heard of a house called Keepsake, or a family called the Parrs. Neither the landlord nor one of the regulars at the bar, a red-cheeked old man in faded blue chinos, drinking ale. They called over the nice dreadlocked barman and asked him, and he shook his hair regretfully.

'I wish I could remember the name of the creek,' Mum said, as I hung back. 'Is there even a creek here?'

'There are about thirty of them,' said the barman dryly.

'Oh.' She was unabashed. 'Jordan Creek? Canaan Creek?'

But they all shook their heads, and the regular at the bar looked blank. So many second homes around here, most people didn't know the land as well as they used to. He was only down a few weeks of every year – and that was to sail, not look at houses.

'It's definitely near Helford,' said Mum, to which the nice barman guy said did we know we were in Helford Passage, and not Helford the main village?

'Where's Helford?' I said, heart sinking.

He pointed across the river at the collection of houses and boats clinging dramatically to the other side of the water. 'That's Helford.'

'How long does it take to drive there?'

He shook his head. 'No point in driving. Take you forty minutes at least to get to the other side. There's a foot ferry outside. My brother runs it. He knows every creek and inlet on this river. If you want to go and ask around there, he'll take you where you need to go.'

It was late afternoon by now, and the boat was waiting by the jetty. The boatman smiled when we explained our mission. 'I can take you to Helford,' he said. 'And back, when you're ready.'

The sun was warm, but hazy, and it cast a golden shade on the clear aquamarine waters. It was so quiet, out there on the river, the only sound apart from the engine the *chink-chink* of boat masts in the breeze, and the trees rustling.

As we reached the middle of the river, we could see its expanse spreading out before us: the wooded inlets, the creeks and coves upstream, and downstream the wide, open horizon that led to the sea. I had never seen anything like it before: the water like something you'd expect in the Caribbean, not England; the glorious sense of space, and silence, and yet feeling enfolded by the land, by history. I watched it all, entranced as a child.

'Do you recognise any of this?' I said to Mum.

She was muttering to herself, biting her lip again. 'Kind of. And yet – it's so hard. Macao? Manna? Oh, gosh. Hey,' she said, to the boatman, 'do you know Manna – Manna something, a creek called Manna something?'

'I sure do.' The boatman smiled. 'That is, if you mean Manaccan Creek?'

Mum clapped her hands. 'Yes! That's it! Can you take us there?'

'Mum – he just takes us to the other side,' I said, my uptight London Britishness asserting itself. 'He's not a personal taxi.'

'Oh, I am if you hire me, and if there's no one else wanting to come back . . .' He pointed at the other side of the river. 'And if the tide's in our favour, which it is. I'll take you to Manaccan Creek.'

'What's your name?' Mum asked him, folding his hand in hers.

'Joshua,' he said, slightly shyly, crinkling his eyes up as he smiled into her face. 'What's yours?'

'Well, my name's Dill, and this is Nina, my daughter, and you're doing us a most enormous favour. Thank you.'

Joshua spoke into his walkie-talkie, to let the other boat know where he was, and then he switched course upstream. 'Take about five minutes. Just relax and enjoy the ride,' he said.

He pointed out the houses as we went: the famous scientist who'd retired to the house on the hill; the teacher who sailed to school every day along the river. He showed us the oyster beds below us producing millions of oysters a year, the buzzards overhead being attacked by the young crows, and the silvery lichen like yellow-grey hair clagging itself to the trees that hung over the river. The banks on either side were thick woodland, the odd house and mooring dotted here and there. Otherwise it was just the fresh green of early summer trees, the deep turquoise blue of the water, the bright powder blue of the afternoon sky, and us.

Soon there were no more houses, only us and the birds, heading into Manaccan Creek, wide as a river, fringed with trees.

'How far do you want to go up the creek?' Josh asked.

Mum and I looked at each other and laughed.

'Do you have a paddle?' said Mum. 'Not sure. Is there some place we can stop?'

He shook his head. 'Not many places I can put you down, not at high tide. If we go right up to the head of the creek, it kind of runs out, just becomes a thicket of trees and creepers and all sorts. You shout if there's a spot where you want to stop, and I'll see what I can do.' He carried on. 'Nothing really here, except the trees and the water.'

319

I wrinkled my nose, trying not to sound as confused as I felt. 'No . . . no entrance to a house, or anything?'

'A house?' Josh smiled. 'I shouldn't think so.'

'I think there was a house here, once,' I said.

He shrugged. He was a very calm man. 'I've been on the river all my life, and I've never seen a house along here.'

And that's when Mum suddenly shouted. 'There! There it is!' She was leaning over the boat.

Josh grabbed her shoulder. 'Stay back, please.' There was a note of anger in his voice – these stupid Londoners, messing around in my boat.

But she wouldn't move. 'Nina! Look. I can see it. Oh, I can see something, anyway – can't you?' She turned to me and gestured, wild hair spilling over her face. 'Look! Just look.'

Just look. And I did. I clambered over to her side of the tiny boat and turned to see where she was pointing.

Through the thick wooded sprawl, underneath a willow that had bent and twisted itself over the years so that it hung almost into the water, there was something protruding. A small stone platform, a set of three steps, water licking the dark slate. And when you looked back at the whole thing, tried to see through the trees, you could make out something else. An arch jutting out of the riverbank, wide enough for a person to pass through, nothing more, but so overgrown it was barely visible.

We turned back to Joshua. 'Well,' he said, scratching his head. 'I've never noticed that before. Suppose you wouldn't. Look, the tide's going out. We can't stay too long, otherwise I won't be able to get us out of here again.'

'Just a little while,' Mum said, and gave him her biggest, gap-toothed smile. 'We wouldn't ask if it wasn't important.'

'What exactly is it that you're looking for?' he said, politely, and I shrivelled inside, with fear at being unmasked as imposters.

'It's nothing—' I began, but I felt a cool hand on my arm, and my mother said:

'Josh, my daughter's father's family used to have a house here. We've come to find it. I think it's probably nothing, but we've waited twenty-five years. I understand you've no reason to help us—'

'What did you say the name was?'

Something caught in my throat. 'Parr. My name's Nina Parr.'

He smiled back at us, and I knew he was on our side. Then he nodded, quietly. 'I've heard them say there was a great house up over there, that a family lived there for centuries. I'd no idea you got to it this way.'

'Really?' Mum said quickly. 'You've heard of it, though?'

'Only rumours, half-stories.' He moved the tiller slightly to the right. 'So you're a Parr?'

I shrugged and nodded as he turned the boat, cresting towards the tiny jetty, trying not to show how his recognition of my name affected me.

'How come you've heard of the house and your brother hasn't?'

'He only comes to the Helford for work. I'm on the river all day most of the year. There aren't many people who've lived here for generation after generation. They're all gone. It's holidays now, mostly.' He smiled. 'But there's a few who used to tell me things. Old folks, most of them dead by now. There's people who remember the Parrs. But I always heard they weren't here any more. That she vanished one day, and—' His face took on a closed look. 'Who knows? I couldn't say.'

'What's up there, then?' Mum said, squeezing my shoulder.

Josh smiled. 'Again, I simply couldn't say. Let's see how close we can get, shall we?'

Already, my heart was thumping in my chest, in my throat, blood drumming in my ears. We moored up. 'There's hooks here, look,' said Joshua, his voice changing. 'Someone used this place. Room for a big boat, if it wasn't so overgrown, I'd say. Right, I'll wait here, if that's OK.'

I nodded. 'How long have we got?' I clambered on to the short jetty, holding on to the willow branch, and extended my hand to help Mum to the shore.

'Thirty, forty minutes? That do you?'

It would have to. For now. In any case, what else could we do?

We didn't know where we were, and the car was on the other side of the river, another lifetime away. 'Of course,' I said, and turned towards the bank.

The water lapped at our feet as we climbed up the stone steps and then through the arch, which was so clogged with ivy we could barely squeeze through. Birds sang, high up in the trees. The faintest ripple of wind scudded the water behind us, and I tried not to imagine I was stepping into another world.

'Are you ready?' Mum said.

'Not sure,' I smiled, nervously. But I was. I was ready.

Up some winding steps cut out of the stone we climbed, blanketed by a ceiling of willow and ivy so that we were in the dark and had to bust our way out at the top. There was a metal handrail. Someone at some time had taken care over it. When we emerged, panting, we were on a tiny footpath that skirted the edge of the woods and looked down on to the river. We could see Joshua, several metres below us, on the water.

'This is it,' Mum whispered.

I shivered, and we walked on. Here and there were signs of humanity – a wooden post with an acorn sign denoting the path, a fallen tree trunk that someone had carved into a short bench for the weary traveller. But other than that, just the trees, rising up away from us.

'Now, where next?' Mum looked around. 'Oh, golly, Nins. I really can't remember what we did when we came here. It wasn't like this. It wasn't so . . . thick. Maybe I've got it wrong.'

'It has to be here, Mum. Has to.' I kept my voice light as we scanned the choked woodland, looking for a sign, a path, anything, but there was nothing. I tried to hide my disappointment and it wasn't until my eyes lost focus that, through a haze, I began to see something. Not a path, nothing as obvious as that. But something that had been there, once: a track, a slight gap in the vegetation. I pointed. 'Look.'

Mum said, 'Someone's walked along this track, quite recently. The path is clearer in some places.'

'Are you sure?' I said, trying not to sound afraid.

'Yes. Look at the grasses, and the way the moss has been trampled.' I'd always thought of her as a city girl, like me, but here she was in her element, the Delilah Griffiths who'd spent summers in upstate New York, who could spot a tick, shoot a raccoon.

The track wound higher and higher as the land rose above the water. The air was rich with wild garlic, flowering everywhere in the wooded gloom. It ran rampant over just-dead bluebells, nettles and ferns.

'How on earth did they cope with this path?' Mum said. 'Hauling food up, and all sorts.'

'I don't think it's always been like this,' I said, but just then she grabbed my arm, and I stopped.

Behind a heavy thicket of tangled bushes was a wall and a gate, painted green at one stage, many years before. I turned around: the creek was hidden now, only the fainted flash of blue-green through the trees. I put my hand on the old, rusted handle. The hinges were orange with rust, and half falling off: I did not expect the door to open, and yet it did, quite easily.

'It was that door, I'm sure of it,' said Mum. 'This is the boundary of the estate, Nins, it must be – oh!'

On the other side of the door the air was tropical, more humid. A palm tree, honeysuckle, more wild garlic, and the smell of something, I couldn't quite tell what. Something flew past us, and I screamed.

'It's only a butterfly,' said Mum, smiling. 'Darling, don't you remember?'

'I don't like it here,' I said, regretting the words as soon as they were out of my mouth.

There was a stone pillar on its side, and then ahead I saw a clearing, something light – the top of the hill, it must be – and I pushed ahead of Mum, because I wasn't sure what was there but I wanted to protect her from it if I had to.

And there – there it was.

Another wall of crumbling golden brick, and an archway. Ivy, creeping tendrils shooting up like spreading fingers. Some kind of stone animal lay on its side underneath the arch, blocking our way.

We stepped over it, and it was only then that I looked up and saw Keepsake for the first time.

'Oh, no,' Mum whispered, behind me. She clutched my shoulder. 'Oh, Nina. I'm so sorry.'

Chapter Twenty-Three

There was a house there – you could say that much about it. It had walls, windows, doors. But as I gazed across the patchy gravel court-yard, where dandelions and nettles sprang up like a hazy low wall of weeds, I felt cold. An outline of something magnificent stood before us, set behind a circular driveway: a frontage of golden stone, studded with windows, battlement-style roof running straight across the top and what had once been a straight portico of pillars below, behind which was a vast door that led to a courtyard.

But most of the windows had no glass, and of the portico only two pillars remained from what should have been six. A bird's nest poked out of the corner of one windowsill, and one side of the house, at the left, listed, even to the naked eye. I walked forward, feet crunching on gravel, up the crumbling steps and under the portico to the great oak door, bleached grey-white with age.

'Careful—' Mum said, as I touched it gingerly.

It opened and we peered into the empty courtyard. Nature had won the battle within the walls, too: ivy ruled here. It seemed to be tugging the bricks and stones back into the earth, tendrils reaching up to level the ground again. As we stood in the centre of the courtyard, looking around us, it was as though we were the only people alive in the world. That everything had gone. A sense of desolation hung in the air.

'Mum, stay here a minute,' I said, turning back. 'I'm going to look inside. I don't think it's safe.' Safe from what? Falling masonry – or evil spirits?

But most of all I felt something, as though they were watching me. As though someone was waiting for me, bursting to tell me something.

'Don't be silly, I'm coming with you,' Mum said. She took my hand and together we walked across the courtyard.

A mouse, disturbed by our entrance, scuttled along one side of the wall and disappeared inside. At the back of the courtyard there was a door, old and brittle, but it still stood there. *Perhaps they don't live at the front*, I told myself. *Perhaps everything's at the back.*

For a moment after I'd opened this door it seemed I might be right. There was, of all things, a coat rack beside the staircase and one wellington boot, which was now some kind of nest. Padded jackets and waterproofs hung there. I touched one – it was cracked, and stiff with mould. A teacup stood on the side table. Beyond the hallway was a long room running the length of the west side of the house.

'What a room,' Mum said.

I looked up around me. I supposed this must have been some kind of great hall, a big space with no upper floor save a gallery reaching around the back, by which means you could pass from one side of the first floor to the other. But the wood was decaying, and the great oak staircase, carved with leaves and helmets and shields, was rotten too, steps missing, cracked along one side, listing slightly from the wall: ivy and bindweed were pulling each stair apart from its neighbour. I put my foot on the first step – it bowed, alarmingly.

'But—' I rubbed my eyes. 'Oh Mum. What does it all mean?'

Because, as we gazed around us, it became apparent this had been someone's house. And the more you looked you saw that it was as though someone had merely got up and left one day, and never come back. As my eyes got used to the scale and haphazardness of it all, I started to notice things. A Ngaio Marsh mystery on a small drum table. Mildewed piles of magazines, *Radio Times* and *Country Life*, almost mulch now. A pair of half-moon spectacles, caked in dust, open and resting on the arm of a sofa. On the vast mantelpiece where the rain had got in were photograph frames, smashed and rotten with water. Armchairs covered in rich damask, chewed open by mice, pecked by birds – and whatever else – for nests. There were a couple of old torn paintings, listing on the walls, long-forgotten faces peering through the damage they had endured. And the silence inside the house was deafening.

'It doesn't make sense,' Mum said as she picked up a candlestick, rusted away to almost nothing. 'How's it been allowed to . . . how's this happened?'

'There's really no one here, is there?' I said, after a while. 'She's dead, isn't she?'

'I think so.' She slipped an arm through mine. 'No one's been here for years. Decades, Nina.'

'I still don't understand how they let it get like this,' I said, trying not to let my voice crack, to show how stupid I felt. My secret dream, that we'd stroll up the drive and a lovely old woman would be there, waiting to receive us. The grandmother I'd always wanted, full of fascinating histories and the truth about where I'd come from. I'd spent my childhood playing games with Mrs Poll that involved my father returning from the dead – and then he had. I think I'd told a little part of myself, since he came back, since this all began, that perhaps the same might be true here.

'This country is full of crumbling houses, my love,' said my mother. 'We're also in one of the most inaccessible places in England.'

'But it's Cornwall!' My voice rose. 'Come on. This is tourist central.'

She shrugged. 'You don't see this place from the road. There are no gates. This is a poor county, for all the wealthy second-homers. A lot of people aren't here all year round, isn't that what the guys said?'

'But I still don't believe a place like this could have just . . . crumbled. Didn't anyone care?'

'There's hardly anyone left who works on the land the way they used to. And those that do – well, time passes, and people can know something's there and not do anything about it. I'm sure there are locals who knew it was here and didn't think anything of it. An Englishman's home is his castle, I guess,' Mum said, a note of something bitter in her voice.

'But it's *my* home,' I said. I looked up, at the floor above, wondering if I should risk the staircase, half wanting to go up there and half terrified of what I might find. I could see that one room, with a door hanging off one hinge and listing on the ground, had a huge chest in it, a bedraggled tapestry hanging from the wall. My eye roamed along the galleried floor above us . . . and then I saw a face, and I gave a sharp cry.

I know now what it was, of course – and it was easily explained then – but I know she was watching me. I know she was.

'What?' Mum said, sharply. 'What did you see?'

I pointed upwards. It was a portrait, it was obvious now. It was old, very old – a woman in rose-coloured silk, holding an oak leaf, her dark eyes pools of black even in that gloomy place.

'Who's that, I wonder?' said Mum.

I knew. I could hear my father, for the first time since he'd vanished. *Nina Parr. She's hanging up there in the hall. Looks just like you.* But something made me not want to say it. To keep secrets.

'You'd be able to see the river from those rooms upstairs,' I said, instead. 'If only—' I looked at the staircase. 'Do you think we should try the stairs?'

'I wouldn't.' Mum shook her head. 'Jesus, what's this?' She pointed to the blackened, crumbling, wood-and-ironwork door under the stairs, almost invisible. Ubiquitous ivy pulled at it, damp oozed from it. There was a drip of water from within, now audible in the silence.

'Well, we can see the main problem here,' said Mum. 'Look at that.' There was a vast crack, zig-zagging out from the door, through the staircase and up past the great window.

'I wonder what's behind the door,' I said.

'My guess is it's been swollen shut for decades. Water's got in somehow.' She walked back, into the hall, stuck her head out of one of the empty window frames. 'There's a kind of bulge at the back of the house. Look. Windows, pointed windows. It's probably a little chapel of some sort. Water, and ivy. That's where the rot set in.'

I stared at her in amazement. 'When did you become the expert in house construction?'

Mum said, with grim satisfaction, 'When we moved to the flat. I'm the expert in dry rot and damp, I tell you. Ivy, too. It gets in the cracks and the holes, you see. It wants to smother whatever it fixes on. I had an aunt up in Rhinebeck who let the ivy get every-where without cutting it back. Pulled down the whole house in a couple of years. It must have had a good few centuries to work away at this place, honey. And clearly no one's done anything about the damp for decades.' She gave a small laugh. 'It's kinda funny. If this is where he grew up, it explains why your father had absolutely no idea about dealing with damp.'

Yes, my dad had grown up here. I looked around. Was that his set of encyclopaedias, faded and chewed, over there on the great windowsill? Had he ever been happy here, ever had days when it felt like his home? It didn't feel like that now. I couldn't summon up the imagination to see how anyone would have been comfortable or content here.

'Let's go upstairs,' I said, looking up at the picture of Nina Parr again, at the glimpses of other mysteries above us.

But Mum squeezed my shoulder. 'Honey, Joshua's waiting for us. We said half an hour, remember?'

'Let him go,' I said, staring around me, the magic of this place clutching at my heart. 'I need to stay a bit longer. See if I can work out what happened—'

Mum came and stood in front of me. 'Nina, we have to leave. The tide won't be with us much longer, that's what he said. We have no idea how to get back to the other side of the river. We don't have a map, or the faintest clue where we're headed. What happens when we try and leave on foot? How do we get to the main road?'

'I'll find it,' I said. I folded my arms. 'Mum, you go. It's fine.' She looked at me and I said, softly, 'I'm serious.'

'You can't stay here on your own,' she said, looking around her.

I nodded. 'But I can't leave yet. Not now we're here.'

'We can come back tomorrow.'

'I know.' I didn't want to say I didn't believe we'd find it again tomorrow, that it already felt like a magical place that we wouldn't be able to conjure up twice. 'You go and find Josh. I'll meet you later.'

'Darling—'

'Mum.' I reached out and clasped her hands. 'It's OK for me to stay. I know it is.'

'How can you say that? This place gives me the creeps.'

'Give me twenty minutes or so. Please.'

'Tell you what,' she said. 'I was looking at Joshua's map. You can walk along the coastal path to Helford village. That one we crossed to get to the house, the acorn signs. The path skirts along the river, I saw it from the boat. Why don't we meet you in Helford? I can get Joshua to take me there, that's his usual ferry route, and then he can pick you up, bring us back. There's that pub just along from where the ferry docks. The Shipwright Arms, I think it's called.'

'Oh, that's a great idea.'

'In an hour or so? If not, we'll come back to get you. By hook or by crook. Etcetera.' She gave me a hug and looked into my face. 'I don't want to leave you, honey. Why don't I just run back and tell Josh to go without both of us?'

'I need to be here alone for a bit,' I said, and I didn't know why I said it.

She nodded. 'Sure. Only – take care, honey. Please. There's something odd here.'

I knew exactly what she meant. But I found now that I liked this strange, wild feeling, that someone was watching us, that the ancient stones knew more than we did. I liked how calm I felt here, miles away from rows of streets and men in yellow sports cars, London rage, Lise's eyes, Sebastian's face . . . I felt OK here.

After she'd gone, I walked back into the central hall of the house. 'Bye, Mum!' I shouted. There was no reply: my voice echoed, heavily.

I was here on my own.

'You're mine.' I said it aloud, softly at first, then in a normal voice. 'Mine.'

There in the courtyard, at the centre of the house, I looked around me, then closed my eyes. In the silence, a slit into the past seemed to yawn open and for one tiny moment it was as though the place leaped alive: I could hear the call of servants, clanking barrels, the sounds from the kitchen, women folding linen in that walled garden behind me. The crackle of spitting meat, turning on the fire. The whinny of horses pawing at the ground. The yelp of children playing, as I moved back into the courtyard and stared out of the great front door. Smells of meat and manure, fresh laundry, bread and sweet ale. Smoke came from the tall chimneys; a dog ran past me. The old, rotting walnut tree in the courtyard was now thick with green fibrous nuts, the staircase polished and glowing warm in the late-afternoon light. The fox and the unicorn on the entrance arch proudly scrapped with each other.

And I stood in the doorway, hands outstretched, smoothing down my skirts, readying myself to welcome whomever might be approaching as Nina Parr, over three hundred and fifty years ago, had stood there waiting for the men who came from the river, tired, bedraggled, seeking shelter in the most secluded house in the kingdom.

I called out again, 'I'm here!' But nothing moved, as I hoped perhaps it might, from its enforced slumber. As I walked around the side of the house towards the walled garden I had seen through the window, I looked up and jumped. In a recess high up above the first floor stood a headless statue of a man in doublet and hose, one hand on hip. Who? The builder? The King? Was he my relative? There was no inscription, but he was covered in lichen, as was so much of the house. Idly, I tried the door of the chapel at the back of the house, but it would not give. I went back to the edge of the wall, where there was a low gate. I could see a path leading down a hill. I pushed the gate to one side: it fell on the earth with a crack, and I walked through the inner walls, and into a garden.

I knew immediately that this was no overgrown woodland. This was, or had once been, paradise. The high, secluded walls wrapped themselves around it; trees banked in the distance, and it was several degrees warmer here than in Helford Passage or on the boat. Late-afternoon sun beat down into this square suntrap. Thick scent hung in the air: a midsummer perfume of roses and honeysuckle, tangled along the old walls of the garden.

Then, I barely knew their names. Now I do. Palm trees, fig trees, bougainvillea, all here. Yellow, pink and white jasmine, running riot, its sweetly rotting scent filling the air. Chrysanthemums, not the gaudy blue and raspberry of retirees' bungalows but splashes of mellow cream and faintest pink, along with purple and red verbena and grey-violet lavenders of all different kinds. And down the middle of the garden – a tangle of green, sand and grey with splashes of colour – purple, blue and pink Granny's Bonnets, and the wild flowers again, poppies, daisies, delicate vetch, navy and white speed-well, rich purple campions, pinpricks of colours in the dancing, swaying strands of grasses, every colour of the rainbow there. Now it was simply a wilderness, and in that wilderness a miracle was happening. For there were butterflies there.

Clouds of butterflies. Dancing, flitting, their patterns individual, irregular. One flash of bright green, another flare of deepest purple, some swooping, some zig-zagging, some spinning high into the cloudless sky. Whites and yolk-orange Brimstones, blue butterflies of the deepest hue, Red Admirals and bright-eyed Peacocks, and yellow-and-black Speckled Woods, darting, fairy-like. Resting on the flowers, skidding through the sweet evening air, hundreds, probably thousands of them, soundlessly filling the sheltered, guarded garden with a beauty so unexpected my eyes filled with tears. I walked into the garden, in amongst them. I remembered the second photograph Lise had sent me, the formal tea, the little girl who was my grand-mother, her scratchy-looking dress. She had sat here, with her own grandmother, and I was here now.

I have read the diaries of my great-great-grandmother, Alexandra Parr. I have studied the butterflies. I have had to make it my job. I know them now, but nothing, nothing will ever compare to that first sight of the mystery of Keepsake spreading out away from my eyes: the sloping, vast garden that had entranced my ancestors, over the years, until it became the thing that obsessed them. I know about Nina the Painter, and her fruitless attempts to draw them, pin their beauty down on paper, about Rupert the Vandal, who demolished a wing of the house to give the butterflies more freedom and space, and indirectly destabilised the house so greatly that he set off its slow decline. And I know about Alexandra, and her endless hunting and cataloguing, her relentless killing, her drawers and drawers filled with dead butterflies, their brilliant colour preserved for ever. Lastly, I know about Mad Nina, Alexandra's great-grandmother. I know what she brought back to the house, and whether it still exists.

Then, I knew none of it. I didn't know about the pineapple pits, just beyond the meadows, installed by Frederick Parr, the first in the country. Or the Victorian greenhouses, smashed windows and rotting wood, bursting with geraniums and camellias for the house. Or the vegetable garden behind us, long colonised by the butterflies, which had provided food for a household of thirty at one time.

I simply stood there, in that rainbow paradise, watching those butterflies fly around me. And in that moment everything – the book, Lise's photographs, my father's reappearance, my mother's secrets, the night before with Sebastian, even the thunderstorm – none of it was coincidence. I was meant to come here, and I belonged here, I knew that then.

At the side of the walled garden there was an old stone outbuilding, rounded like an ancient hut, with a thick, varnished wooden door: an old ice house. I peered in through the small window, but it was thick with the grime of centuries and I could see nothing of the inside. I went up to it, and tried the handle. My hand tingled on the unexpectedly cold metal; I opened the door carefully.

It was empty. I stepped in, taking care to wedge the door open with a stone placed for that use. It was dry and warm inside, flooded with dark amber light from the dirtied window. And it was spotless. A stone shelf ran around the middle of the circular building. There was nothing else – then I saw the box, at the edge.

A fine wooden box. Later I would discover it was made from laurel wood, polished and smooth. No dust – there was nothing in that place to create, or cause, dust. It was a killing box, and the aroma of laurel – strong and bitter, like almonds, smoke, earth – rose up as I lifted the lid.

Inside was:

A butterfly in a case: blue, blue as the brightest summer sky. He was only an inch and a half wide, but the scales on his wings shimmered in the gloom.

An old bundle of papers, dully cold in my warm hand, and a

thin pamphlet: *English Butterflies, a Countrywoman's Guide* by Alexandra Parr.

A diary in bound leather, stamped with a butterfly in gold.

And lastly, I thought, a large Manila envelope, inside which was a manuscript, tied up in string. On top, the front page – thick, watermarked paper, damp to the touch.

The Butterfly Summer, it said, then underneath: *Theodora Parr.*

But the last item in the box was a small metallic container, and when I opened it up I saw it had a fine, grainy powder in it. I took a step back, foolishly frightened.

It was a funeral urn, and the powder was someone's ashes. Wrapped around them with a thin elastic band was a scribbled note in tiny, erratic handwriting on Murbles and Routledge headed paper. I'd utterly forgotten. I suppose I hadn't at all considered that he might actually come here alone, you see.

Mother

I write this scribbling in the cold & damp Butterfly House, I have only this paper, I can't really see.

I had no idea until I got here I'd want to leave something behind too. Here we are then.

I have finally done what you asked. Have brought yr ashes back here. 15 years after you made the request, but you're even more deluded than I remember if you think I'd have dropped everything to fulfill yr last wishes the moment you died. You could have asked anyone to bring them here – why me? 1 last joke on me I suppose.

I'm leaving the Butterfly Summer here too. Or BS as I like to think of it, as we say in the States. Why you think I'd want to read this story about what you got up to with some tomboy in the war escapes me but yr motherly instincts, even from beyond the grave, absolutely fucking suck which is something else Americans say. No –

No. No.

This is not how I wanted this note to be. I'm not sure what I want to say. This is the only sheet of paper I have with me. Let me start again:

I really wanted to say I've come back to leave the ashes as you wanted.

I have read The Butterfly Summer & will leave that too, it belongs here. I understand you better now. But I still don't understand you at all. This is my last visit back to England I think. I knew I had to come back, just once, just to see, just to lay it all to rest – I don't know if it was a mistake or not

You made me so unhappy, for so much of my life. My earliest memory is of running towards you on this damn terrace right outside where I'm writing this & you backing away, a look of fear on yr face. I was 3 or 4 I suppose. I wanted to show you the butterfly I'd caught.

You always made me feel as though I shouldn't be there. The idea that without me you'd have been happy. I couldn't wait to get away from here, go to school, get to Oxford. I can't forgive you. You were no mother to me. That's a terrible thing to write.

The damage you did, it affects all of us, Mother. You ruined lives more than just mine. I've read your story. You killed the Ashkenazys, sure as sticking cyanide sticks in their porridge. You ruined lives.

I loved Nina's mother, more than I can say. She was sunshine, & everything – everything you had with Al that summer I had with Delilah. My beautiful, curly-haired, golden girl. But you'd bent me out of shape so badly by then I couldn't do it. I tried to pretend I could: calling the child Nina, pretending, always pretending to be OK. I couldn't do it. I loathe & despise myself now, again thanks to you. I had to make them hate me & they do. You did that to me. You did.

I came back to explain things to Delilah and to file for divorce, complete all the paperwork.

Actually I'm lying: I came back because I wanted to see her & my daughter once more. Not sure if that was a mistake or not & something else I screwed up.

You'd be pleased if you knew Nina. She's exactly like you. I particularly resented what you wrote about letting Keepsake gradually crumble away without her knowing about it. Well, I told Nina. I think she should know. You don't get to play God & keep all your secrets you know.

I'll admit I bottled bringing her down here. Sort of couldn't face being the one who exposes her to this unholy mess, not in the end. As for her mother, it is the same as it ever was. I won't ever be the man who can live with her. But I also know I won't ever stop loving her. Her hair is short & she's aged but she's more beautiful than ever; life / pain is etched on her face, that's my fault. I consider that I don't deserve her, or this daughter of mine. They're far better off with me on the other side of the world.

Goodbye, Mother. I hope this brings you peace. I'm getting married next month: she's young, she's rich, doesn't want children. I will never come here again. Perhaps at the end I agree with you: May this cursed house sink back into nothing. In the end that's what I can do for Nina, get as far away as possible. What's loved is lost you see, it can vanish, you lose it for ever. I have lost things I loved & it is my own fault. You're wrong about that too. Gives me no pleasure that you are, strangely.

I'll shut the door on the BH and get in the car & I will be the last person who was here I hope. You & the ghosts can have it.

Yr son

George

I stood motionless for a while after I'd deciphered the cramped writing, trying to see what else I could take from this letter, when that was all he'd left, and it hadn't even been meant for me. Then I picked up the manuscript, the papers, flicking through them. And though I was there at last, I was terribly afraid now of what I'd discover, what would be in them.

I read the first page.

In the gallery at Keepsake, looking out towards the sea, there is a portrait of my ancestor Nina Parr.

I realised after a while that tears were creeping down my cheeks. It's hard to explain, but for so much of my life I had had this feeling, as though I was in a tiny room surrounded by doors – and that only one, or two, of the doors were ever open at the same time. There was so much I never understood: about my father, about my mother. About love, and truth, and marriage, being part of a family. I'd always known, I saw now, that something was missing. Here it was. This story, in my hands. I didn't feel like a stranger here, in this odd, silent, still place, someone who didn't belong. I felt natural. I was no longer an outsider – this was a place for outsiders.

Somewhere in the distance the crows began their evening call and it was that which eventually brought me to my senses. I stared down at the wooden box, the manuscript, the letter.

'I'm sorry, I have to take them,' I said aloud. 'I can't not take them.'

It was late. I set the ashes and the butterfly in its case on the windowsill, by the light, and gently closed the door of the ice house. Then, with the box in my arms, I walked back through the garden into the house again, picking my way over rubble where the falling timbers of the roof had dislodged bricks. I glanced up at Nina and her relatives in the gallery above, the faces torn, some portraits simply missing. She gazed blankly down at me again.

I looked over the vast entrance, wondering how I should leave it: the cracked, splintered hulk of wood still clinging to the door. Should I pull it to, like leaving the door on the latch? Was there a key? It was absurd, searching for a keyhole, and yet I wanted to lock it up, to close the door, to protect it.

Clutching the wooden box, I walked towards the gate again, looking up as I passed under the arch. I glanced back to look at Keepsake, glowing in the late sun. Then I strode away from the house around the front and off to the eastern side, climbing higher and higher until I was walking along by a wide, open meadow, where yet more butterflies danced, along with the bees and early moths, where the grasses and flowers ran rampant. I kept on walking, enjoying the pull in the muscles of my legs, the dry mud that flickered over my trainers.

At the end of the track, but inside the wall, was a tiny old house I guessed must have been some kind of gatehouse once, deserted, a sprawling cover of lemon roses frothing with abandon across its frontage. Next to it was an archway, a wide door painted in peeling, dark green paint, which opened, after a brief struggle. I emerged on to a quiet lane and closed the door behind me. Ahead was a brown sign indicating the route of the footpath and that Helford was three-quarters of a mile away.

I turned back to look at the door, covered in ivy, almost invisible from the road. You would, as so many had over the centuries, pass it by. I was the last person to linger there. The last girl, you see.

Three years have passed now and, to date, I am still the last person to have set foot inside Keepsake. I should say living person. The house continues to die quietly, although in other respects it breeds life. So much has changed in those years, and I have changed, too. I have come to understand exactly what a life at Keepsake might cost you.

The Butterfly Summer

(continued)

A rainy day, a warm bookshop, a story from many years ago.

For years I did not know what had happened to you, or Michael and Misha, and as I sank further into the house I managed to push them, and you, out of my mind. But at the beginning, in those years after the war, I looked for you – I did, Al – and I looked for them. I did not return to London for a number of years. I wrote to the Red Cross, to the Russian and the Austrian embassy – what there was of Austria, after the war. I wrote letter after letter to Carlyle Mansions, to you, to them, but none was answered. I even wrote to your mother in Arnold Circus, but heard nothing. And then I came back.

One dull November day in 1961, twenty-one years later, I found myself staring at the new concrete block being erected over the blackened hole of what had been Carlyle Mansions, and saw how futile my letters and cards had been. That you, and the Ashkenazys, were both long gone – alive, or killed in the Blitz, I had no idea.

Perhaps I should have left then, caught the train back to Cornwall. But my doctor had told me to have time away from my child, that it would help me with the nervous complaint that had left me so unlike my former self. Since I left you, Al, it is as though I am missing a layer of skin, one that kept me from bruising myself. For so many years everything hurt, every memory, every mistake, every curious glance. I had come to London to have a change of scenery. I suppose I enjoyed it, as much as I enjoyed anything in those days. Which is to say, very little. I seemed to have lost the ability.

My final morning was one of those rainy London days where the streets are running with water, one's umbrella has packed up, and a warmly lit shop beckons you in. So much of London had changed that I remembered the place only after I'd dashed inside: it was one of the bookshops in Charing Cross Road that Misha frequented. She'd come in to buy poetry, expansively discussing the merits and demerits of every offering presented to her. I was thinking sadly of this when I saw a figure, peering apprehensively over at me, and I had to rack my brains before I realised it was Ginny, Boris's ex-wife, clearly unsure whether to say hello.

I greeted her with pleasure, glad to see a friendly face after days alone. We fell into a slightly awkward conversation and while I was glad when she told me that Boris had left the country during the war and she had never heard from him again, it made me uneasy. It still does. I would rather know a man like that was in the ground.

'They were operating illegally,' she said, a little stiffly, when I asked why the Ashkenazy business had been dissolved, why I could find no trace of it. 'They were registered as aliens for only two years, you see. Their permission to remain had long expired.'

'Yet they stayed.'

'They could not return to Austria. They needed to make more money and they were waiting. Waiting to hear what to do next and, of course—' And then she broke off.

'Who were they waiting to hear from?' I said, curiously.

Ginny shook her head. 'You never knew, then?'

'Knew what, Ginny? What happened to them? What happened to Al?'

She pressed my hands, her thin face painfully alight. 'I thought it must be so. Of course. Ah, I hoped you never knew. I knew you could not be so selfish.'

A rainy day, a warm bookshop, a story from many years ago. And she began talking.

When I had heard it all, I walked through London in the rain back to my hotel and sank on to the sagging bed, but I could not cry. Afterwards, I returned to Keepsake, and the blackness of depression which held me captive for two decades set in. And I stopped trying to find you, Al. I stopped trying anything at all.

I've been lying as I wrote this story. Who am I writing it for? For you, Al, and for George, you too. But for . . . someone else, an audience? And so I am lying about that as well. I've been lying, all along, and I think you must have deciphered it by now. I find I can't write like this any more, and as we enter the final part of my tale it is impossible for me to carry on lying.

She was Alice Grayling.

She was Alice Grayling but I called her Al, because it made it easier, easier to have a man's name in my mouth as I loved her. And she was used to how she was made, but I was not. I found it – oh, the wasted moments – I found it upsetting. I could not reconcile myself to being a woman who loves another woman, even though I wanted it, more than anything. I wanted her.

You see she had put up with the catcalls, the men who jeered at her short, slicked-back hair and boyish clothing. She didn't care; she'd been raised to be tough. She'd had girlfriends, girls wise in the ways of London and being lovers, girls who knew clubs to go to, places to meet, how to express themselves, how to let another girl know they were available. She'd taken me to just such a place once, a bar off Heddon Street, but I'd had to leave: I'd run out, in fact.

'How can you go somewhere like that?' I'd shouted, when she followed me outside. 'All those girls together – that woman fondling that girl under her – in full view! The drinks – with those names, Al! What if we were caught, what if someone came in?'

'But we weren't,' said Al, stubbing out her cigarette. She held my head in her hands, trying to cajole me into acceptance. 'Darling Teddy, we're not doing anything wrong. I love you. It's simple.'

'It's illegal,' I hissed, looking about me, down the narrow passageway. 'It's – we'll be sent to prison. We'll be told we're mad.'

'That's men,' said Al. 'Not women. They tried to make it illegal, ten years ago or so.' Now she took my hands in hers. 'The House of Lords wouldn't pass the bill, you understand? Those old boys couldn't believe women are really committed to it.' She gave a short, hard laugh. 'Trust me, darling. They don't understand. None of them does. I could kiss you like this, now.' She touched her nose to mine, and smiled into my flushed face. 'There.' She kissed me passionately, hips against hips, firm bodies pressed together, and then she held my bottom, squeezing it so I rocked against her, and she tongued my mouth, smiling at me as I let her, helpless, almost unable to breathe with wanting her.

A man in a top hat and evening cloak hurried past, not looking at us. I watched him, not caring then. She had that effect on me, and always had done.

When he'd gone she whispered bitterly, 'They just think it's girls and their japes. Men can't seem to grasp the idea we might want each other and not them, the fools.'

I pulled away, trying to regain lost ground, wishing she didn't have this power over me. 'It's fine in the flat. Not here, darling.' I pressed my hand to hers. 'Don't do it again. You're playing with fire.'

She just said, 'We all are, darling. None of it's going to matter soon.'

That last morning, before the advert appeared, did I know? Did I stretch out and smile, and did you roll over towards me in bed, pulling me closer? Did we have each other once more, warm and achingly heavy with sleep, your soft white limbs clamped around mine, both stretching deliciously into each other? Did I, one last time, lean up on my elbows, stroking your hair out of your smiling face? Was I on top when we made love, because we both liked it when I was, when I was assertive and believed I could? Was it one of those sweet times like that, or did you take charge, whispering in my ear, dragging me down into wild abandon with you?

The lawn quilt – blue-and-green speedwell – torn at the corner, wadding fossilised with age.

The overglazed green-and-black vase on the windowsill, an ugly thing, the present from the ex-girlfriend who broke your heart.

The Shrimp Girl on the wall. The looking glass, circular, framed in ebony, the gift from your benefactor, and it gave a perfect view out of your room, through the corridor and of the balcony, the trees to the south, the green of Coram Fields.

I am old now, and I sit here writing this, waiting for her to come to me, so that I don't have to think about you any more. Because it still upsets me, and it's the one thing I can't make right. I remember it all, you see, from the pale coral shoes you wore on high days and holidays to your beaded pearlescent evening bag with the rusting clasp. Your lovely hats – the one with the feather in it, the teal-coloured beret that made your eyes flash, your hair – how it was thick and dark and fell in certain ways, no matter how you combed it. Your chipped tooth. I remember these details, but I can't remember what we said, what we did the morning before the message came, before everything changed, darling. Can you?

It was late August. I know that we had two authors coming in, a clash of appointments for which I was responsible and for which I was paying dearly in cruel remarks (Misha) and irritable muttering (Michael). I was in love, and I made mistakes, I told myself. I ignored the warning voices in my head that shrieked that I had played long enough, that I would never be able to stay. And lately, I feared the Ashkenazys a little and their nervous sideswiping, faces always at the window, eyes darting at any sudden sound. Yet with every passing day I grew a little more used to who I was, accustomed to the idea that I must accept I loved this woman, wanted to be with her, could imagine no other life than one with her. So yes, that morning I put the Personals column on the Ashkenazys' desk, then glanced at it again – I think I had cut it out in a daze – and then, of course, then I gave a cry. For in the middle, in between appeals for hospices and requests for furnished flats in Mayfair, was this, and the words leaped out at me:

THEODORA. ALL YOUR BUTTERFLIES ARE DEAD. IMPLORE YOU WRITE URGENTLY WITH YOUR ADDRESS. PO BOX 435. MATTY.

I looked up and around, as if someone were watching me. Silence roared in my ears. I took the piece of paper in my hand again, staring at it, trying to leech meaning from the black, blank ink.

The truth was that lately Matty was in my thoughts, all the time. All summer I had wondered about her, even as I lay naked with Al. I had known with the terror of certainty what I was that night Matty and I kissed. She represented the life at home I loved, the wildness of my existence there, the elemental part of me that longed to be outside and never be caught. There was so much I wanted to ask her. Had Turl revarnished the *Red Admiral* that year? Had Matty taken her out yet, up towards the sea, free, drunk with exhilaration, wind whipping her hair? That hair – was her honey-coloured hair still long and wavy, had she had it bobbed as she had sworn to? Had she agreed to marry David Challis? The butterflies . . . what did she mean?

My fingers smudged the newsprint as I clutched the page, rereading the brief notice. 'Implore you write urgently with your address.'

The fields would be heavy with golden-grey corn, the scarecrows busy, the farmers preparing for harvest. I was perfectly still for a moment. I saw the butterflies, I saw the honeysuckle sprawling along the ancient walls, the whole place alive, thick, rich, heady with scent. And I couldn't stand it, that I wasn't there, that something might have . . . that somehow they had—

What had happened? I stared into nothing, chewing my little finger, and then I stood up. I scribbled a note in reply, picked up my jacket, and ran to the door.

Misha was in the hallway with her pet dog, Hermia, staring down at the black and white tiles.

'Oh! Where are you off to in such a rush?' she asked, blinking and looking around her, as if not sure quite where she was.

'I have to run to *The Times* office,' I said. 'Would it be all right if I dashed out? I'll be back for lunch.'

'*The Times* . . .?' Misha's eyes widened. 'May I ask . . .? No. I hope that everything is well. With you.' She swallowed, and I could see fear ravaging her face.

I crammed my hat on to my head. 'No, it's a family matter.' Now I had decided to reply, I didn't want to stop to think too much, but as I glanced at her face again I saw she was trembling. 'I'm sorry. I . . . I know *The Times* concerns you . . . I . . . it is none of my business, but I know you're looking for something there—'

Like a light flicking off, Misha closed her eyes. She drew the dog's lead around her slim wrist, wrapping the leather cord tighter and tighter, her mouth set. I thought she wouldn't reply.

But as my hand was on the door, she suddenly hissed, 'Do not bother yourselves with *us*. Do not consider *us*. We do not need you to stick your perfect little English nose into our lives.'

I swallowed. 'I . . . I don't. Other than . . . you . . . it's my job—'

'You do.' Misha came nearer, dragging Hermia along so she whimpered unhappily at her feet. 'You sidle around, insinuate your way into Michael's affections. He thinks because you tell these stories about your house and life that you are someone important. That you can help us, that you will be on our side, and I know it is not true.' She laughed, wildly. 'You play at real life, you play with us, you play at love, with Al, you pretend with that poor girl, who is in love with you. But you don't mean it.'

'I . . . I do mean it. Misha, don't – please don't.'

Misha jabbed at the torn-out Personals column I held clutched between my fingers, suddenly, spitefully. She leered towards me, and I caught the acidic whiff of cigarettes and coffee on her breath. 'I wish that you could know what it is like to be like us. To be looking over your shoulder, *all the time*. To make friends, put down your roots, yet to know that at any moment someone will wipe it all out. You have your home, little Theodora.' She was pale with anger, her thin body vibrating like a metronome. 'We are Jewish. We have nowhere we can go. They are taking us away already. They are dragging us out of our houses at night, they are separating the mothers and their children, they are killing the men, they are killing us all. They want to eradicate us, do you know that? And we don't

347

even know . . . No—' She crammed her hand over her mouth. 'No!'

She pushed past me, flinging open the door. I put my arm out to stop her.

'Misha,' I said, grabbing her arm, horrified at how I had obviously upset her. 'Please, I'm so sorry if I have said something wrong. Misha—'

'No!' She was halfway down the steps.

'Is it your children?' I asked quietly.

'We have no children,' she said, blankly.

My voice shook. 'I heard you do.'

'Who told you that? They are liars.'

'Boris told Al that you had two—'

'Boris?' She was at the bottom of the steps now. 'We must all listen to Boris, mustn't we? We must all wait for him and listen to him . . .' and then she seemed to gather herself. 'I have said too much, Teddy. I apologise.'

'Please, if I have done anything—'

'I think perhaps you should leave here, my dear.' She looked up at me with a haunted, ghastly smile. Her large eyes were vast in her face. She was so thin lately, I realised. 'Go back to where you belong, because that is not here.' She banged the door open and ran down the front steps, towards the graveyard.

I caught the bus to Regent Street, hands twisting in my lap, scenarios flying through my head. At *The Times* Personals office, I took out an advert with the following reply:

MATILDA: DESPERATELY SAD ABOUT BUTTERFLIES. ALL WELL WITH ME. WRITE TO PO BOX 312 TO VERIFY IDENTITY. THEODORA.

The clerk behind the worn, mahogany counter at *The Times* desk looked at me as I handed over the form. My hands shook: the pull of Keepsake was stronger than ever though I tried to ignore it. He read it back to me in a monotonous tone and I wondered what he made of it: this was innocuous, compared with some of their advertisements. The one in the newspaper that had stuck with me most was: *Mother lost her baby girl. Please can the clown she met at the fair return her safely.* Bolshevik spies? Or domestic tragedy?

I walked home, wondering how I could make it right with Misha. The streets were quiet in the stifling heat, the crisp-dry leaves motionless. There was no breeze.

It was as though, in those dog days of August, the Ashkenazys moved further away than ever from us. Once, Al and I accompanied them to the Proms – Rachmaninov's 'Rhapsody on a Theme of Paganini', Michael's favourite. Al and I held hands surreptitiously throughout – I greatly daring, taking pleasure in the secrecy for once, in the love and pride in Al's eyes as our warm hands lay clamped together between our legs – and I saw the look Michael gave us, one of sad, almost fatherly, concern. I knew the evening gave them no pleasure. The atmosphere had changed. They were somewhere else, by then.

War was constantly talked of, in whispers, in sidelong glances. It became normal, these extraordinary things one saw every day: the trenches in parks almost complete now, sandbags piled up outside shops and institutions: the Café Royal, the gentlemen's clubs in St James's. Factories advertised for more labourers to produce enough gas masks for every woman, man and child in the country. People stopped joking about Old Nasty and his silly moustache.

And now both the Ashkenazys and I, along with hundreds, perhaps thousands, of people up and down the country, waited every day for the Personals and a message hidden there for us. One morning, Al and I woke late and I almost missed the first edition – and it had to be the first edition, as the Ashkenazys were always reminding me – so I ran to the newsagent's and had to beg him not to give away the last copy to the hotel around the corner. He only gave up the paper after I kissed him on the cheek, which I thought was an absolutely disgusting thing to have to do. But I did it, anyway. And I was right to. Sure enough, the Personals column that day carried the following advert:

MI&MI: THE PAPERS ARE ALMOST READY. YOUR PACKAGE
WILL BE DELIVERED TO PARIS. WAIT FOR A WORD FROM
DUBRETSKOY.

I cut the column out and put it on the desk, as usual. I said
nothing – what was I to say? And I watched, as Michael read it,
hand slowly curling into a tight, white fist. As he called Misha over,
I busied myself with a box of newly delivered books, making a great
show of thumping them on to my desk, piling them noisily high
and cutting brown paper and string up to make parcels. I caught
the crescent-moon shape of Misha's cheek and profile, the huge
dark eyes, suddenly hollow with terror.

'The Gremalts will not let us down,' I heard Misha murmur,
though I tried not to listen. Josef Gremalt had sold some of Boris's
work. I'd seen a photograph of the Gremalts' atelier in Paris, hung
with sensational paintings, in the *Picture Post*.

'They are our friends, Mishki. Dubretskoy will let us know,' he
said quietly to her. 'Almost ready, Josef says. We will wait to hear
from Dubretskoy.'

And then, Misha's voice, soft and sad in Russian, and I did not
understand her.

When I told Al about it, that evening, over a cup of cocoa, before
bed, I tried to make it sound amusing. Because I was afraid of what
it really meant, and I didn't understand.

'It's like a spy novel.'

'That's the thing about the Ashkenazys, though,' said Al. 'You
don't know if they're in a film or not. Sometimes I think a director
will appear and start telling them what to do next.'

We had tried having a paper delivered for a week or so but had
to discontinue it: if I didn't pick the newspaper up within a few
minutes of it being deposited on our front step, Jacky the Clown
would have swiped it. He was an elderly and harmless, but nonetheless still rather alarming, vagrant who pounced on anything left
outside with the alacrity of a monkey spotting a nut.

'The thing is,' I said, 'the more nervous I am around them, the more it slips my mind. This tiny little task, every morning, and I keep almost forgetting.'

'It's a mental block,' said Al. 'I had to write an article about it today.'

'How impressive,' I said. 'What about the country diary, isn't that what you do on Fridays?'

'Didn't I tell you?' she said casually, rolling on to her front. 'I managed to get moved off it on to the news desk. They want a plucky girl reporter out in the field, and Daphne got married last week so she's been chucked off the paper. It's all rubbish and I'm sure it'll be confined to reporting on fêtes and visits by Queen Mary to schools but—'

I threw my arms around her shoulders, lying on top of her and kissing her hard, all over her head, till she pleaded for mercy. 'You marvellous girl! Why didn't you say anything? You're on the news desk? Al, darling, that's wonderful.' I stared at her, once again in awe of her, how she made everything look so easy and yet worked, as I knew, so very hard. Her razor-sharp mind was able to dissect everything from films to books to news reports, and I never grew tired of asking her opinion.

Indeed, to this day I still set great store by things she'd say – even though they are no more use to me in this world. She never lit the fire before the clocks went back or after they went forwards, despite my pleading. She drank spirits, and never wine, because she said it didn't give you a hangover. She disliked the Kardomah and preferred Lyons Corner Houses, because there was a waitress who was kind to inverts like us and set aside tables for us at the Lyons in Piccadilly Circus: the 'Lily Pond', we called it. She was an excellent, economic housekeeper, knew the cheapest cuts of meat, the best ways to make food go further. She knew the best coal merchant was not the man on Judd Street, whom the Ashkenazys and the ladies in the flat below below used, but a little further on, off Lincoln's Inn. I came to believe she knew everything, that she could always make it right.

'Oh, it's not worth making too big a fuss about,' she said. 'I'm sure the moment things get sticky I'll be pushed off to let the big boys play.'

'If things get sticky the big boys will be off fighting and only the women will be left, Al,' I said, and we looked at each other in surprise, having never before considered the possibility of war, however much it was to be avoided, being something that might help us. 'Let me make you some more celebratory cocoa.' I got off the bed. 'You marvellous girl.'

'Stop saying marvellous.' Al disliked compliments as much as she disliked cheap shoes (a waste of money) and trams (death traps – far better to catch a bus). She followed me into the little kitchen, and changed the subject. 'About the Ashkenazys, Teddy. You just have to keep reminding yourself to do the column every morning. The trouble is, your mind is shutting it out because it's angry with them, for being so off-hand about Boris going at you, and latterly since they started being so cool towards you. And me.'

'But honestly, Al, I'm . . . sometimes I'm afraid of Misha, these days. She's changed. So's Michael, but it's deeper with her. She's terrifically on edge. If I forget again . . .' I trailed off, shaking the cocoa into the pan. 'I can't lose this job.'

'You can, now I've this new position, we've got—'

I put my arm gently on hers. 'Al, I can't live off you.'

'I didn't mean it like that,' she said, stiffly. 'It's only money. You'll get another job.'

'I came here to be independent. It's not saying much if—' I put down the pan.

'You'd be mortified if anyone you knew realised you were the mistress of an East End dyke. That's what you mean, isn't it?'

'No, no, no,' I said, shaking my head violently. The walls of the tiny kitchen seemed closer than ever, and I pushed away from her. 'Stop making it about that. I find it hard to accept – this, me, me loving you.' I shook my head, angry at how drearily selfish I was, being this person. 'You know I do. I am getting used to it, honestly. That doesn't mean I don't love you, that I don't want to be with you, that I wouldn't give up everything for you—'

'Everything?' Al's eyes were shining, her face red with emotion.

'Of course! Everything. You know I don't ever want to leave.' I leaned heavily on the stove, knocking the pan handle and spilling the milk. 'I don't. This damn— Ow!' I caught my finger in the gas flame and winced. 'Ow.'

'No use crying, it's only milk,' said Al and we stopped and both laughed. 'I'm sorry, darling. I'm really sorry.'

'No. You mustn't be.' I caught her hand, reaching for the cloth. 'I don't want to leave, Al. That's all.' And I kissed her slim shoulder, gently.

We mopped up the milk together and made the cocoa, smiling shyly at each other, because it was as if something had changed, and we knew it then, that we were bound together, a trial by fire on the gas stove.

As we were sipping from our mugs, Al said, 'Here, I've an idea. The business with the column – if you *do* forget again, why don't you simply substitute *The Times* you have from April, the one you held on to?'

I started: she was right, of course. I still had the copy of *The Times* from my train journey to London in my suitcase. It had been brought in to me on a silver tray, along with breakfast, and I had kept it. It symbolised, somehow, the break with home: my own copy at last, not my father's.

'You mean cut it out and leave it there and not tell them it's the wrong day?'

'Yes.'

'But it's lying to them,' I said. Secretly, I was also thinking: *What if Matty has written to me again?*

'You can always go out that afternoon and check the copy of *The Times* in the library to make sure there's no message for them. I know they insist on the first edition, but that's bunkum.'

'Yes,' I said, more happily. 'Oh, thank you, you are so clever.'

Al looked at me, curiously. 'They are very fond of you, you know.'

'I'm not so sure. I don't really feel as though I know them any more, Al.'

'I'll admit they are rather unreal.'

I pulled my too-small cardigan around me, more tightly, under my breasts. 'They are perfectly real to me.'

'But you know no one else in London,' Al pointed out.

'Marie from Heal's – though I've no idea what's happened to her. The Ashkenazys. Aunt Gwen. And you.'

'You and me,' Al said. 'Just you and me. We don't need anyone else.' She put her hands on my waist. 'Do we?'

I gripped her shoulders, and we stared at each other. 'No. No, we don't.'

The next day, I still do not quite know why, I wrote to Matty. I have the letter. It was returned to me when it was all over.

> *Dear Matty*
>
> *I am very well here in London. I have a job working for a funny old publishing company run by two Russians. I am quite sophisticated, quite the London girl about town, as you can see!*
>
> *I miss you. Will you come to London, to see me, and meet my friend Al? I think the two of you would get on. London's a marvellous place, Matty. I'm sure you could find work here. The war won't come for a while yet, we are sure.*
>
> *Love,*
> *Teddy*
> *5 Carlyle Mansions*
> *Handel Street WC1*
> *Telephone LAN 526*

That did it.

On the glorious blue day in September when Chamberlain flew to Munich for the first time, Al was one of thousands who flocked to Downing Street to see him off. We talked of little else in the days before, no one did. The Nuremberg Rally, whether Hitler would invade Czechoslovakia, how ready were we, and was Duff Cooper right? We could be at war in a week's time.

I would say it was a normal morning, but it wasn't – nothing felt normal, in those last days.

'Help, I'll be awfully late,' Al said, cramming a beret on and flying towards the coat stand, retrieving some coins from a bag. 'Look, I'll see you later, will I?'

'Absolutely. Listen, good luck, darling. Cheer him on for me.'

'Will do. Do you think I need a coat?'

'No,' I said. 'Lately the weather is fine.'

'You country girl. The weather is fine. I love you, Teddy.'

'I love you.'

And she was gone.

I had another slice of toast and marmalade, thinking about us. About what we could do next, what I should do, whether we should leave London, live together as spinsters like dreary Dora Meluish and her friend Ivy two floors below us, who took great pains to assure everyone they were companions. Is that what life held for us, smoke and mirrors, always looking over our shoulder, afraid we might be suspected? I thought of my darling Al. Did she believe what I'd told her on the evening of the spilt milk, that I would give up everything for her, that I knew our lives were together? My eye fell on the sideboard and the soft red pouch that held my diamond butterfly brooch. I virtually ignored it these days, and as I looked at it properly again and heard the eerie silence outside, something shifted within me. We needed money: Al's bursary ran out soon, and who knew if we'd be able to stay in London after the bombing started? If I could give a quantity of cash to Al that night, it would show I was serious, that I had truly cast off Keepsake, the past that held all my family in thrall. We did not have Gainsboroughs, or Fabergé eggs, or Grinling Gibbons staircases, or other treasures at Keepsake. But we had this: the King's brooch. His symbol of love.

I held the tiny thing in the palm of my hand, and the diamond-and-sapphire wings glinted, and the rose-gold thorax glowed, almost as though it really were alive and could fly away now. It was tiny, really, but every time I looked at it, its exquisiteness surprised me. *What's Loved Is Never Lost.* I wiped my hands and pulled on my jacket, and bent over to disentangle my handbag from amongst the welter of our clothes on the floor. We were, I'm afraid to say, mucky young pups. As I did, my eye caught sight of Michael, pacing about outside on the pavement, cigarette in hand, and I froze.

I had forgotten to go and fetch the paper again.

At the sight of him, furiously pacing, that little note of impatience that had sounded within me over the Ashkenazys these last few weeks rang out again, buzzing in my head. These rituals, the waiting for the paper, the cutting out, the strange ceremony of it. Why couldn't they go and get their own blasted paper, why couldn't they check the newspaper themselves and get some fresh air into the bargain?

So that morning – already jittery, anyway – my insides felt like liquid as I considered my latest error. I told myself defensively it was perfectly excusable that it had slipped my mind today of all days: cuttings on a desk seemed irrelevant compared to the half a million who had turned out for Hitler's latest Nuremberg Rally. Gas Mask Sunday, the previous day, had seen us all – society girls and queenly matrons, old men who'd fought before and young men spoiling for a fight – queuing quietly for hours outside Finsbury Town Hall to be given our gas masks.

I rubbed my face with my hands, wondering what they'd say, and then with fumbling fingers I pulled the Victorian loaf-shaped bag out from under our bed. It was dusty. It had been five months now.

I opened it up and took out *The Times*. Carefully, I cut out the column from the April edition, checking there wasn't anything in it to give it away – but no: it was the usual stuff. Stamps wanted. The annual meeting of the British Sailors' Society. And, more and more, notices from people, running away: 'Notice is given that Oskar Bukowitz of NW London is applying for naturalisation.'

Clutching the carefully cut-out section in my hand, I ran downstairs and flung open the Ashkenazys' door. 'Paper's here!' I called out to Michael, keeping my voice level. I slipped the Personals column on to the desk, praying he didn't ask to see the rest of it – but they never did.

'Sorry I'm a little late. I took the paper upstairs. Al was leaving for Downing Street, you know, Chamberlain's off today, and she wanted to check the route—'

One lie. It starts slowly, gathering speed and heft, and then it's rolling so fast it's too late to stop it. And why did I tell the lie? What would have happened had I told the truth? Would it still have been too late?

Michael appeared in the doorway.

'I'm stepping out again for a little while, I won't be long,' I said. 'I hope that's all right.'

Michael brushed past wordlessly; he murmured in Russian to Misha in the bedroom. I let myself out. I did feel a pang, as I looked into the flat from the street. They were there, framed in the window, both in black, curved over the desk almost in silhouette. Then Michael rubbed Misha's back, and I saw her look up at him, and give him the most devastating smile: terror, beauty, love mixed into it. I will never forget how she looked at him, when they both thought no one else was watching.

I went to the jewellers on Tavistock Place, swinging the door open, the bell jangling loudly, and walked confidently to the counter, a very different girl from the last time I'd been there. Today I was in a new, navy-and-cream crêpe de Chine dress with sweet forget-me-not-blue shoes. Then I had been itchy, famished, grubby and utterly unsure of my place in this city, let

357

alone the woman I was meant to be, loved by and loving another woman.

'Good morning.' I smiled politely at the lady entering numbers into her ledger, and removed the brooch from its soft pouch. 'I wonder if you would be so kind as to give me a price for this?' And I slid Nina Parr's diamond brooch, the gift of a king, out on to the gleaming mahogany counter, and watched with pride and misgiving as her eyes widened at the delicate, glittering little prize in front of her.

'Oh,' she said. 'This is a lovely piece.' Then she looked at me nervously, because she had betrayed herself.

I could not look directly at the brooch. I did not want to change my mind. I am sure that I accepted an inferior price for it, but I didn't think about it then. How bitterly I came to regret it later is another matter – how I could have survived for longer, how useful it might have been to me as a means of escape – but it was too late. I caught the soft glow of the pink-gold thorax, the glittering wings and, as the woman carefully replaced it in its bag, it disappeared out of my sight, for ever.

In the years since I have wondered who owns that brooch now, who knows that Nina Parr, mistress of the King and of her own castle, wore it as she starved to death, three hundred and fifty years ago. Does anyone love it? Is it still one piece, or broken up into three or four diamond-and-sapphire rings? Or, as I suspect, is it somewhere underground, lost in the rubble of the shop, which was bombed into splinters during the Blitz?

Like many parts of this story, I will never know the full truth. War destroys lives, it throws everything up in the air, buries it again in a different place. But if you should see a girl in the park, or a mother rocking a child or a young woman out at a restaurant one day, and at her breast or on her coat is a butterfly brooch, wrought so delicately it appears to be moving, and if you ask her and she tells you that upon the back is a tiny inscription in barely discernible lettering: *What's Loved Is Never Lost*, then you will know the history of it better than her. Perhaps you shouldn't tell her. Perhaps she should live on in ignorance.

I wandered around Bloomsbury in the sunshine for a while, delaying my return until I knew Michael and Misha would have left: they were meeting a prospective author that morning at the Russell Hotel. Then I walked back down Judd Street, smiling at the butcher's boy, who gave me a cheeky grin, and I went into the grocer's and bought a bunch of watercress, which reminded me of home, where watercress was everywhere that time of year. I felt like a bride, walking towards Handel Street carrying my green bouquet and I smiled at how pleased Al would be, how gratifying it was to be able to put the money on the table – five hundred pounds, a vast sum – to prove that we were doing this together.

When I arrived back at Carlyle Mansions all was silence. I thought I would dash upstairs and plunge the cress into water. But as I turned I saw the Ashkenazys' door was ajar. I had left it on the latch – they were always forgetting their keys, and Michael had once strained his groin quite badly, trying to climb over the railings and break into his own flat via the front window.

I glanced in and saw a shadow, falling on the carpeted floor. I tried to walk upstairs, to pretend I hadn't seen him, but he came out into the hallway. It was Boris.

'What are you doing here?' I asked, angrily.

'Where are they?' Boris said. He led me by my arm back into their flat, and shut the door. 'You're all alone?' He looked me up and down.

'They are in their bedroom,' I said, lying again. As I say, one lie loosens your tongue; after one you find you are able to just make up anything. And so I did.

'Tell them I want to see them.' Boris reached forward, and grasped my hand.

I pulled away from him, but his grip was – as it had been before – white-hot tight. I looked at him. *He is drunk*, I thought, or in the grip of some madness. He hadn't shaved for days, and thick brown hairs sprouted in unlikely places – on his cheekbones, at his clavicle. His already yellow eyes were bloodshot and he was shabby, his clothes worn and ripped in places, as though he'd been sleeping rough.

'They don't want to see you,' I said. I was terrified, but I knew that, as the last time, I mustn't show it – and somehow, even more than last time, I couldn't let him rape me. I wouldn't.

He reached for my neck, pulling me towards him. His large, pink hands pinched my bones together, pushing the breath out of me. I dangled in front of him, arms flailing. A crystal vase, perched on the crowded mantelpiece, smashed – Misha's cousin's, she had always said. She was looking after it and it was very valuable, worth thousands of pounds.

'I need to see them,' Boris hissed, into my face. 'Tell me where they are.' I flinched at his hot, meaty breath. 'Ginny said she'd help. She's gone, and—'

He broke into a stream of Russian, as the world swam before my eyes. I thought I would lose consciousness, and might have done for a brief moment, but with my hands free again I reached forward and kicked him in his groin, shooting myself back, so that I tumbled to the ground and he fell against the side table, and on to the floor. I felt something sharp as I landed, and I winced, but stood up, and faced him, as Boris scrambled to his feet. Then I realised I had badly misjudged my move. His face was frozen with a glazed expression, and he fumbled with his belt, walking towards me, as I backed away towards the sofa. This was it.

I kicked him once again, the pain in my foot sharpening, and said, 'OK, I'll tell you. They've gone. They left this morning.'

He paused. 'They saw the paper this morning? The message from Dubretskoy?'

If only I had asked him, would that have saved them?

But, 'Yes,' I said. One more lie. He'd go. One more lie. 'Yes, it was fine. They left immediately.'

'They did?' Boris grunted. 'Good.' With a pincer movement, he pinched me underneath the jaw, either side of my neck, and I felt dizzy again. 'You are sure? They have gone to Paris? I have extra money, they don't need the money?'

I blinked, trying to stay conscious, and I knew then I couldn't go back on what I'd said. He would kill me. 'I don't know. But they've left.'

'That is good, then.'

I rubbed my face with my hands, as he turned for the door and called over his shoulder, 'I'll come back for you soon, little one. I'll teach you a good lesson.' He smiled at the door. 'No complaining next time, eh?'

I said nothing, and he crunched over the shattered glass on the floor and banged the door behind him. It thudded loudly, bouncing back in the frame. My hands were shaking, my neck sore. It wasn't until I stood up that I realised my foot was bleeding, and when I took off my shoe I saw that a shard of glass from the smashed vase had become wedged inside my right shoe and dug into the arch. It stuck out, bloody, glinting slightly.

I wished Al were there. Not to take the glass out of my foot, in some fairy-tale manner. No, because I knew that already I had made a mistake, had told a lie too far – and this was not like the lies I told myself, or the ones I kept from Al. She would know what to do, she always did, and she would act calmly, make everything all right. If I couldn't go to the library, or somehow find a copy of the paper, Al would. I had to, now. I had to see what message was in today's paper for them.

Remaining as calm as I could, I slipped my shoe off and bent my head, placing both thumbs on the smooth arch of my foot, either side of the hole, trying to push the matchstick-head of glass out.

It was hard, because I kept thinking I was going to faint. I could see exactly the point of entry; there is something unreal about a foreign object sticking out of your skin. But my mind kept jolting, collapsing in on itself, overloaded with questions, and my hands were slippery with sweat as I attempted to manipulate the glass. I could feel it embedding itself further into the thin flesh of my arch, moving around under the skin.

Bile rose in my throat. My hand slipped, and at that moment there was a knock at the door. It was loud – furious, almost. I tried to stand up, and realised I couldn't, quite.

'Al? Is that you?'

The door hammered louder. I thought, *it can't be him, not again.*

Fear, hope, made me honest. Then, of course, I realised it must be Misha or Michael, without their keys.

'Push it!' I called. 'It's on the latch!'

I was glad, you see. I'd tell them: I'd explain it all. They'd go and find the advert now, and I'd be in trouble, possibly grave trouble, but all could be put right again. With a small click the door was pushed open, and I looked up at the figure in the doorway, hat in one hand, midday light rushing in behind him.

'You're here, then,' he said. 'Stand up when I talk to you.'

It was my father.

This is how it happened.

The Ashkenazys had two children, Valentina and Tomas. They were respectively twelve and fifteen years old and they had been left with Misha's sister, Anna, in Vienna four years before when their parents travelled to England to make a better life for them all.

Initially Vienna, that cosmopolitan, liberal city, was a safe place to leave their children. In the last year, with the Anschluss and the worsening situation, it was anything but. Tens of thousands of Jews were fleeing the country that autumn. Kristallnacht, the terrible night when hundreds of Jewish shops were smashed and thousands brutally taken from their homes to Dachau and the other camps, was still two months away, but already the situation was dire: September 1938 was the last chance for any Jew wanting to get out of Vienna.

If Michael and Misha had seen the advert, or if they had spoken to Boris, they'd have known the visas were ready for collection and that all that was required was the greased palm to release them: three visas that would take the two children and their aunt to Paris. But they would also have known that the situation was now dire: that Anna's apartment had been ransacked, their possessions stolen, Anna's husband one of thousands taken away to death camps. That Anna and their children were now in hiding in the basement of an old friend's house: sixteen people, in a dark cellar under the earth, with no light. If the Ashkenazys had acted immediately, they could have left for Paris that day.

But they did not know, and so there was a delay of four days.

The Gremalts were the ones who had organised it all. As well-known art dealers in Vienna, they enjoyed good relations with Nazi officers, supplying them with misappropriated paintings, but at the same time covertly helping countless Jews out of Germany, Austria, Poland, Czechoslovakia, using their influence and good standing until good will ran out or they, too, were arrested, whichever came first. The Gremalts were old friends of the Ashkenazys from the motherland, fellow refugees in Vienna: Michael had pulled Josef Gremalt back on to the train leaving St Petersburg when he fell off, and the Gremalts ever since had said they owed them a great debt, one that must be repaid.

So it was they who had arranged the visas. The Nazi officer, to whom they had promised some painting in exchange, wanted money, too, and that the Ashkenazys would provide. Josef and Yvette Gremalt did not have cash; they had paintings. So Michael and Misha were to come to Paris immediately, the moment they saw the final advert. They would hand over money to the fixer there, who would wire it to the officer in Vienna. He would release the visas, and all Michael and Misha had to do then was to wait for their children and Anna to arrive in Paris, then bring them back to London. It was, as desperate plans go, quite simple.

Unbeknownst to the Nazis, the Gremalts were themselves planning to leave for America. They had double-crossed too many people; the Germans were becoming suspicious. The Gremalts could not wait long for their friends to arrive. Accordingly, the notice in *The Times* that morning had said:

It is now. Find Dubretskoy. Go to Paris. Do not delay.

So the links in the chain had to work, had to hold strong. Anna, Valentina and Tomas could not remain in hiding for long; the Nazis could come and take them away at any moment.

But Michael and Misha never got the message, the first link in the chain, because of me. And when Boris, fulfilling his role, came to call, I sent him away – the second link in the chain that might have hauled them to safety, all of them.

I never saw them again. And of their whereabouts I heard nothing, for years, until that day in the bookshop on the Charing Cross Road.

A rainy day, a warm bookshop, a story from many years ago.

* * *

364

At first, we talked of them a little. 'They were waiting, you see. All that summer, waiting for the message. The code. I knew something of it, before . . . before I left Boris.'

I remembered Al and me, our joke about them being the worst kind of music-hall Bolshevik agents, so obvious to all except themselves. I said something about how they were always so mysterious, we'd wondered if they were spies or criminals. There was silence and Ginny frowned, but then her face cleared.

'You never knew, then. Of course, you were not to blame, but I wondered whether it was you who had said something. They were very upset with you. They thought you betrayed them.'

'No! Never. My father—' I blinked. 'I had to go back with him. P-please, Ginny – tell me. What happened to them?'

She blinked. 'I'm sorry to have to tell you this, then,' she said, into the silence. And a tattoo beat started in my head, drumming through my skull. 'They had a son and a daughter, did you know that?'

I shook my head. 'I . . . I was never really sure.'

She cleared her throat before continuing. I remember Ginny's hands, delicate, twisting together. I made her repeat the story, when she'd finished. I wanted to memorise it, what had happened, what I had done.

After she had finished we were both silent. I felt blackness, wrapping itself around my shoulders. It was only the two of us, in the yellow light of the cramped shop.

'For some reason you'd given them an out-of-date paper that morning.' She smiled, apologetically, as I felt my legs, arms, stomach turning to water, its heaviness sluicing over me. 'So they went out and weren't there when Boris came to ascertain, to double-check. Eventually I called round to see them, a couple of days later, as Boris had come back to our house to collect some of his work. He mentioned it to me, you see, said his debt to Gremalt had been paid, and he resented being the messenger boy, and he would do nothing more for them. He said they'd left, gone to Paris, that you had told him so.' She touched her cheek. 'But I knew they hadn't. I'd seen Misha, only the day before. I knew then something had gone wrong.

I ran to their flat, most of the way from Chelsea. I told them – told them Boris had tried to see them, that you'd sent him away. We ran to the British Library, and looked at the newspaper – from three, four days previously. We saw the message the Gremalts had placed.' She turned away from me then, looked down the shelves.

'It was too late. The officer had grown sick of waiting for his money, and had turned on the Gremalts. They had cleared out overnight, fled, first to Switzerland, then to America. The visas were not released of course because the officer hadn't had his money and no one in Paris could help them contact him. He denied all knowledge of having ever associated with them. Of course. So Michael and Misha tried to get to Austria, begged to be allowed to travel there, when thousands were leaving every day. They travelled on to Holland, but they were forced to turn back; I think by then they knew it was too late, but they still had to try. There were smugglers helping people across the border from Germany and Austria. They tried to go the other way – into Germany, towards certain death – to find their children. The smugglers laughed. I remember Michael telling me. "You are fools," one of them said to him. "You are free. You cross this border, they will take you to a camp."

'The day after the children and Anna should have left Vienna, the house was raided. Anna had been out to the railway station, to ask about the visas: she was desperate for news, and they followed her back to the house. If she'd left already—' Ginny stared at her feet. 'Sixteen people were there – the children – a baby. They took all the men away. Including Tomas. They were taken to Mauthausen. That's where they took most of the . . . the intellectuals. They rounded Anna and Valentina up, plus the other women, and the children too small to go to the camp. They put them on an island in the middle of the Danube, further upstream. A hundred others or so, all Jewish. They let them starve to death.'

I will always hear, buzzing close to any thought I have, the relentless monotone of those soft words, dripping into the cosy warmth of the bookshop, with the creak of floorboards, the distant voices in the street, and the soporific rain falling heavily outside.

'I had stayed in Vienna with Anna, in happier times. I had met Valentina. Tomas was on a climbing trip with some other boys. Valentina was ten or so then. A sweet girl. Very studious. Very shy. Given to writing in her journal. She showed me some of her sketches. She had drawn her parents from memory – she had not seen them for two years by then, but yes, it was the image of them. Extraordinary like-nesses. I . . . I try to remember her, you see, to remember them all.' She bowed her head.

'Tell me, please, Ginny, please, go on.'

'Berthe, the owner of the house, she was not taken. She was blonde, Aryan, not Jewish. She was able to write to Michael and Misha, to let them know what had happened; I wonder sometimes if she should not have told them.

'The Nazi officers would drive their families to the banks of the river, show them these people, for entertainment, so they could hear them screaming, calling for food, or simply standing at the edge of the island, staring at nothing. A few of them tried to drown them-selves – tied stones to what was left of their clothes and jumped into the river. It was winter by then. It was so cold, that winter. Berthe did not see Anna. She is fairly sure she saw Valentina . . . she was . . .' Ginny stared at me. 'She was lying on the ground by then. I hope it was soon after that. She was twelve, Teddy. Dear God.'

We were both silent. I put my hand on a shelf to steady myself. I had no right to faint, to want to close my eyes, to buckle as she told the story. I gritted my teeth. 'What . . . what happened to Michael and Misha?'

She said, very quietly, 'Al found them.'

'What do you mean?'

'Six months afterwards.' Ginny put her hand on mine. 'Oh, dear Teddy.' Her cheeks were wet with tears. 'After they had the letters about the island, after they knew there was nothing left. Yes, poor Alice found them. They had hanged themselves.' She heard them, when she came back from work. Weeping – Michael louder than ever. But it was usual by then, and they would not let her visit them, because of her association with . . .' Ginny hesitated.

'With me.'

She did not answer. 'They were angry with Alice and had turned away from her. She wished she'd gone in, but she didn't. And then she had this feeling, I can remember her saying it. A terrible feeling. So she ran downstairs – they always left the door on the latch, you see—'

'I know.' I stifled a sob. 'I know.'

'They were hanging from those ceiling-high bookcases, both of them. They had drilled holes in the wood. I often think they could have stopped, put their feet on a shelf at any time.' She shook her head. 'They must have wanted to go so very badly. Yes, I often think of that. I don't know – I don't know whether it's good they died. Sometimes I can understand why they would have wanted to.'

Ginny took my hand again, but I flinched, as though I was unclean, soiled, and she let hers drop. She was the last person to touch me with affection for many years.

'I . . . I didn't know,' I said.

'How could you have known, Teddy?'

'I should have done. And Al – Al found them, too. I didn't know that.'

I stared at a lurid noir novelette, with a shadow of a man in a fedora creeping around a wall. *Sixteen people . . . children, adults . . . a baby. Michael and Misha, too.* Ten or so people involved in this carefully crafted plan, working through fear and terror to free two children and their aunt, and I had undone it all.

'I killed them,' I said.

'No,' Ginny said, shaking her head so the hair flew around it, like a bright flame. 'You mustn't see it like that, Teddy.' She smiled. 'I can't think of them as dead, do you agree? It seems so very unlike them.'

I nodded. But I didn't know what to say. I had not just the deaths of one family I knew on my hands, but the lives of twelve or so others, people I'd never met.

'What happened to Al?' I said. 'Did she – do you know . . .?'

Ginny hugged herself. 'I'm not sure,' she said. 'You know that Carlyle Mansions was bombed? No survivors.' And, as I stared at her, she said, 'I don't know if she was still there – I mean – I don't know, dear Teddy. I lost touch with her. The war . . .' She passed her hand over her face. 'Poor girl. She went through so much. Losing her brother, and her father, losing you, finding Michael and Misha like that. She didn't deserve to die in that flat. She really didn't deserve it.'

As I say, when she had finished, I asked her to tell me again, so I remembered, knew what I had done. But after that I recall very little. I don't know whether I said goodbye to Ginny. In fact, I remember nothing else about the encounter but the story itself, the feathery rain outside, the cosy warmth inside as her sweet, hesitant voice told me these dreadful, inhumane pieces of information that lodged like shards of glass, only impossible to remove.

I walked from there to Carlyle Mansions, taking off my coat on the way, discarding my hat, dropping them on the ground. I thought I was burning; I didn't realise until later that I was drenched, soaking wet. I don't remember the journey back to Cornwall, nor the period of convalescence. In fact, I caught pneumonia, which kept me in bed for weeks afterwards, and when I was better I became ill again, with the disease that took over my mind, kept me imprisoned in my own torment for decades. It is a punishment I felt I deserved, too.

Yet I have lied again. I do remember one more thing from that day. I knew as I raised my hand to Ginny and walked away from the shop that I would never be able to find a way to atone for what I'd done. And from that day forward I had no peace, not for thirty years.

A few days after I had left London, on 30 September 1938, back at Keepsake, I heard Neville Chamberlain on the wireless addressing the nation, after crowds twenty, thirty deep lined the roads from Heston Aerodrome into London, waving and screaming thanks to him, thanks for peace. The words he said from which we drew most comfort were: 'We thank you from the bottom of our hearts. Now I recommend you all go home and sleep quietly in your beds.'

Everyone believed him, for a time. Keepsake had not changed in the five months since I had left. A few butterflies were still on the wing. A couple of sweet little Coppers, Cabbage Whites, the usual hardy Commas and Peacocks, but little else. One morning, I saw a majestic Silver-Washed Fritillary, like a dark tiger, brown-red and black, flying straight towards me, pursued by a lighter male, swooping and circling around her, attempting to mate. I turned away from this rare, extraordinary sight and went back inside.

The garden, thick and abundant with fading colours, the nearly-dead heads of flowers, was warm as ever, and I spent many hours in a deckchair, not looking for butterflies, just staring ahead of me, thinking. I was tired, and I could not stop sleeping.

It was not Matty who put the notices in *The Times*, of course. It was my father. I never saw Matty again: she and her mother had been evicted from the gatehouse by the time I was brought home in disgrace. I never discovered what happened to her. Her mother had very little and they had lived on the charity of the Keepsake estates, she taking in some sewing. David Challis, the vicar's son, was by now courting a respectable teacher's daughter over in Mawnan Smith and professed to know nothing of her, the lily-livered coward. When I'd sail up the river to Helford, or Helford Passage, or even up to Falmouth, I'd ask. I never found her or her mother, poor and female, driven from their home at the start of the war. Her brother had left for America, some years before. I like to think Matty and her mother went to join him there, leaving the gatehouse as it was when they left. I like to think of Matty, a grand lady in Manhattan, swinging along Fifth Avenue in high-heeled boots, catching sight of herself in glass shopfronts, and smiling.

Jessie, in whom I used to confide, was too terrified to talk to me now, having suffered greatly at my father's hands in my absence. Turl joined the navy when war broke out a year later and was killed in the Battle of Crete. I was, apart from the water and the wind and the house, alone with my father, a man who cared nothing for me save as the facilitator of his annual stipend. I have no doubt about this: if it had been easier for him to kill me, I would have been dead within the month. But I had to live to twenty-six, of course. '*To be inherited by her female heirs upon attaining their twenty-sixth birthday also, as long as she hath been once or more within the boundaries of Keepseke on that day.*'

As Keepsake slumbered into winter and I sank back into its rhythm, I stopped struggling, or trying to think, too much. When you are unloved and unseen it is easy to do. I married William Klausner, the lichen enthusiast, after the war ended. He served throughout the war, he was at D-Day, on Utah beach. He lost a leg, and for the rest of his life had blinding headaches, which confined him to his bed much of the time. He was a weak man, mentally and physically, and I never loved him, but I was fond of him. He needed me. We both needed each other.

Like my mother, I suffered much in attempting to give Keepsake an heir, a girl. I lost many pregnancies – four or five – and I found it very upsetting, every time. The blood, the pain, the secrecy, the shame. I found William understood, in his way. He had suffered, too.

My father died after a long illness, in 1947, and by then the damage was done. I had been there long enough to have the fight crushed out of me: I've seen it in terrified dogs who are beaten for years by their masters. My father would slap me when I showed dissent and this continued when I returned, now upon the slightest provocation. The same action: a wide, open-handed slap, his great hand on the side of my head, so that my bones crunched, my neck flew to the side, my eyes rolled back in my head. I'd back away, but the corridors echo and he'd always find me: it was easier to take the violence than run. I hated the sound of my own crying. I grew sick of it. He broke my spirit, as he had done with my mother years before.

I knew nothing of his early life until after he died. He had grown up in the North-West Frontier Province, in what is now the lawless tribal area of Pakistan. He had seen his father murdered by Pashtuns, and his mother taken away and killed. He had shot three men by the time he was thirteen, and was sent home to live with relatives in Yorkshire – I found the correspondence about preparations for his journey home to England between the kindly lady in Simla who took him on and his father's cousin when I went through his papers. He'd kept it, for all these years, and never said a word to me about it. It is one of many other stories we never really knew, the story of my own father's early life, what made him the way he was.

We buried him in the private chapel in Manaccan church – 'George Farrars, 1880–1947' was all that was carved on the gravestone. We did not bury him next to my mother; I thought she would not want that. William, Jessie and I were the only attendees. The war had moved people around. The Parrs were seen as local oddities – my father was not liked, and by now many families had emigrated. The new locals were often painters, sculptors, itinerants, holidaymakers. William and I were left to our own devices, in relative peace.

We had our son in 1959. George. A couple of years later, I came to London and met Ginny, and found out the truth about the Ashkenazys. I didn't really come back to London after that, but nor did I do a good job by staying at home, either. You would not recognise my offspring as mine, Al – he who is reading this, as well as you.

You see, I disregarded everything I learned from you. I was angry and spiteful with my small son. He knows this. I had no patience with him. I was terrified of him, of what he needed, that he had been given me as his mother. He horrified me, his small, wriggling hands, stretching out towards me from the old carved crib. The sturdy legs, toddling towards me, his anxious smile. His questions, when he could talk. Why is this our house? Why are there so many butterflies in the garden? Who is that statue with no head? Why do we live here? Meeting Ginny that day merely confirmed what I knew: that I was bad. That I could never be a good person, let alone a fit person to raise a child. That this house was rotten to its core. So I tried to make my son hate me. I made him like this. I warped his small mind with coldness and criticism. I sent him away to school as soon as I could. He was my living reproach, because I made him, and I felt I should never have had him. I should never have continued the line.

Every few weeks I would circuit the house, take note of the cracks, the ivy, the damp. I said nothing. But the day slowly came when I began to believe I had to kill this house, break the cycle and let it sink back into nothing; yet by my doing so my son was the one who suffered, and I am sorry for it.

Oh George. I am so very sorry. I did a good job with you. I took my time. I made perfectly, precisely sure you hated me, and the house you grew up in, and the life you had. You had dreadful nightmares, you were lonely and uncertain. It is on account of me, the person who should have looked after you, that you were confused, and sad, and miserable for so much of your childhood – until I sent you away to school, I imagine. I think I was glad to see you go, because I knew I had to cut you loose. To make you leave, run away and keep running. I trained you so very, very well, didn't I?

Oh, my dear one. I wish you happiness.

I saw your face as I was being pulled into the waiting taxi cab, my father's vice-like grip on my arm, yanking me like a little girl yanks her doll along the pavement. I saw you, Al. Walking towards me, hands in pockets, slim legs leaping up the five steps to the front door of Carlyle Mansions. Five steps, the second chipped, and you took them at a leap, either two evens one odd, or odd-even-even: we used to take it in turns. I could hear that familiar low, sweet whistling as you shut the door, while I was held in the cab, with my father's hand over my mouth.

The driver, blind to everything, in the worldwide conspiracy of men to keep us down, simply said, in a bland tone, 'Paddington Station you're wanting, then, sir?'

You would be staring at the open door of the Ashkenazys' flat now, peering at the chaos inside. Scratching your head, intelligent eyes peering around, stepping over the glass (you wouldn't step *on* it – you saw everything). As the car drew off from the kerb, my father released his grip on my arm. We sat in silence as we headed south, towards the centre of town, away from the eerily quiet streets of Bloomsbury.

Eventually he said, 'I have two things to say, and then we will never speak of this again. Firstly, you will write to this person again – not just a note this time – with whom you have been living in this disgusting, unnatural way, and you will confirm for them that all contact between the two of you is to be over.'

'No,' I said, and I tried to rattle the handle of the door, and the cab bounced alarmingly on my side. 'No, I won't. Let me out. You can't do this. You don't have the right. Father—' I pushed frantically at the door. 'Let me *out*!'

He laughed then, and I'll always remember the laugh. It was genuinely amused. Almost jolly. I'd never heard him so happy before. As though, finally, he had an adversary willing to take him on.

'Yes, you're a woman,' he said. 'And you're my daughter, and I have the right to explain to you that unless you do what I want, you will suffer for it. I have written to the trustees who oversee that flat and allowance. I've informed them of the predatory behaviour which has enticed you into this illegal relationship. They have agreed that the trust established for Alice Grayling by Thomas Fisher and the lease on the Carlyle Mansions flat shall instantly be at an end in light of this behaviour.'

I squeezed my hands together, one clamping over the bones of the other so that the bones clicked. 'You may not do that.'

'I may and I have, but please let me finish. Unless you agree instantly to drop any attempt to see each other again.' In a slightly different tone, he went on, 'You would always have had to go back to Keepsake, Theodora. When you are twenty-six, the estate is yours, and if you are not in Cornwall then we lose everything.'

'Why do you . . . why do you care?' I said, through clenched teeth. 'You hated Mother's family. You hate everything we stand for. Why on earth do you care if I'm there or not?'

He slapped me the traditional way, hard and square across the face, so that my neck clicked with the force of the blow, and I briefly saw sparkling stars in a black sky.

'Don't talk like a shop girl. I care, as you put it, because I spent twenty-five years managing the estate and ploughed my own time and money into it. If you lose it all, I have nothing.' He laughed. 'You silly bitch. I couldn't care less about the Parrs and their history. I care about having a roof over my head under which to die. Your fool mother left no provision for me in her will . . .' He trailed off, head shaking. 'We will discuss it no more. You would always have had to return to Keepsake. It is unrealistic to have supposed otherwise. And the manner of your leaving caused us a great deal of anxiety. You must learn your responsibilities.'

I said nothing, but stared out at the wide, calm roads of Marylebone and Regent's Park. A housemaid stood at a gate flirting with a telegram boy. I could hear her high laughter floating out to me.

Al would be in the flat now, would have seen the bloody shoe, the basket, and the watercress in the basin, the watercress I'd bought for supper. Perhaps she'd have seen the note I left her by then.

'Which is not to say that perhaps in a few years' time, after you've married, you might not come back to London, stay with Aunt Gwen, do some shopping as your mother used to. But until you are twenty-six, and you are true mistress of Keepsake, you are my daughter, and subject to my household.'

Al always put her hat on the hatstand, before anything else. Soft, the softest navy felt, edged with a grosgrain ribbon, trimmed with the prettiest small feather, red-green-orange-turquoise-cream it was, a bright thing, like a butterfly sitting on a person's head. I'm not describing it well, but with her glinting eyes and shining dark hair it was entrancing. She was beautiful; she hated to be told it, but she was.

I could picture Al now, and I knew it was happening at that very moment. That she was taking off her hat, seeing my note.

'One can say,' my father continued, as we rattled along the final stretch of the road taking us to Paddington, 'that a summer in London might have done you some good. Certainly Aunt Gwen said that you had been at a concert when she first saw you. But in future, you'll understand why I have to be so strict.'

Still then, as we came to the vast side door of the station, and I was escorted out, I might have run for it. I almost did. I was handed out of the cab by the driver, who avoided my gaze, and I was within a second of flinging him against my father and sprinting away towards Hyde Park.

I didn't leave much of a note: one line only. I wanted Al to hate me, you see, to think I'd run out. I won't even tell you what it said, because I fear your judgement on me, and already as I tell this story I realise how weak I was to go. How I should have fought, scratched his eyes out. Hang my bleeding foot! I should have raced back to you, to Carlyle Mansions, with both feet bloodied and raw, rather than condemning myself to years of misery, of black depression, of the very loss of myself. It was like another burial while still alive, only this time it was my turn to go in. I should have tried harder, I should have fought for you, my darling Al. I was weak.

But what would I have done? These little jagged facts kept leaping into my mind's eye. Al would have lost the flat, the job that had been so hard won, the chance to be the one in the family who broke out of the grinding poverty that had killed old Alan Grayling, and his father, and his father before him. We would have found somewhere to live, perhaps, or perhaps we would have gone to Al's mother. But would she have taken me in, too – Al's girlfriend? I do not think that she would. And what could I do? How would I stay with Al, believing, as I did, that what we were doing by loving each other was so wrong?

As we walked towards the train station, and my father took my ungainly brown case from me, I knew with dreary certainty I had to go back. Like Nina, I would wall myself up and try to forget what it had been like, this summer – to be free and to love – and I told myself that perhaps it was for the best, to forget.

We were shown to our carriage, and the porter took our bags. My father pulled down the shutter of the compartment. We were alone, and I sank into the upholstered seat. He hit me again, a thudding blow that made no noise.

'That's to remind you what trouble you've caused, you understand?'

But I felt nothing this time. Not outside. Inside, the pain was unbelievably black. And then I understood it. Only true love could hurt like this.

When I began writing, it was to explain, but the writing has been harder than I thought – and the secrets I hoped to keep, almost all of them, have come out. You see, I am dying. I don't have a great deal of time. I am almost at the end of my story – the end I chose, at any rate.

I returned to Keepsake in September 1938 and for almost thirty years I was barely alive. I have blocked out so many things: I don't remember when my son went away to school, or how I used to collect him for the holidays; I remember one wintry day when we went crabbing together, and had a fire on the beach, but now I don't know, I cannot be sure if I invented it, a pleasant memory, a lie to make me feel better. I don't remember any of the vicars at the church, though I saw one who had retired young and, I thought, disappeared from my life walking down the street the other day, and he called out my name – *Theodora! Mrs Parr! It's Adam Drysdale! Vicar of Manaccan church?* And I had to hide until he'd gone. I don't go to that area any more. I can't risk him finding me out.

For almost fifty years I ran the house, I received my modest pension from a long-dead king, I tended the gardens. Jessie died and my father and husband died. My son went to university and never came back, and helpers of various sorts, they came and went – chimney sweeps, cleaners, gardeners, builders – all itinerant, no one close. After George left for school I had dogs, three of them in total: Charlotte, Rupert, Tugie. I'd walk them, down by the creek, up on the meadow, out in the lanes. You have to leave the house, when you have a dog.

Gradually, very gradually, with time I found that the blackness loosened its grip, just a little so that I could contemplate a trip further afield than Falmouth or Truro. I went to Exeter on the train.

I went to the cinema and saw *The Godfather*. I bought a television, and laughed at *Poldark*. I even voted in the 1979 election. I had the *Red Admiral II* fixed up in Gweek and began to sail again, further than I had for years. I was no longer a timid, motherless girl, but a doughty, solidly built widow. I found myself rather ridiculous. I liked it. One day, caught out in the rain on the Helford, with Charlotte shivering miserably alongside me, I weighed anchor and walked up to the pub, the Shipwright Arms. I ordered a drink – a port wine – and I sat by the fire, Charlotte drying out at my feet. No one looked at me, another middle-aged, weather-worn country lady in a county full of them. I sailed home, under a weak sunshine, and as I walked around the back of the house I noticed the buddleia, growing in the cracks in the walls. I think I was happy, that day.

Every week I felt a little better. I grew stronger, as the house began to sink around me. I took my strength from its demise. I grew strong enough to know I could walk away from it. Perhaps it had to have been like that.

And with the years that became decades, and the times and seasons, I no longer felt disgust for loving you. I should have been honest in the telling of our story: but merely retelling it has reminded me of the girl I used to be. The girl who thought she was wicked, and unnatural, because she loved women. The girl who loved you.

I was never sure whether you were dead or not. And then, in 1972 – was it then? – I was glancing through the *Radio Times* and I saw an interview with you. Lise Travers, you were. I knew it was you, though. A writer, a screenwriter, the first woman nominated for a BAFTA for television writing. Just a photo and a paragraph, but it was you. Your smile just the same, the scroll of your ear, the expression in your eyes. You had a white shirt on, and tiny jet earrings. You were as elegant and boyish as ever. I cut the photograph out, and every night I'd stare at it, until it lost all meaning. I didn't know you any more.

It didn't make any difference. I couldn't contact you; you had married a man, you had changed, you who I thought would never marry. But I knew you were alive. Perhaps it is that fact of your existence – so uncertain for years – which, while I understood you must have turned your back on me, still gave me something, some kind of hope.

Many years later, I saw you. On the street. I was with someone, and I could not explain myself to either of you. I can't explain it here either; this is my final secret. You did not see me. You were the same: bright-eyed, your black hair a silvery bob, darting purposefully along the street. Know that my love for you never ended, that I hope some of it kept you warm when you were cold, or sad, or frightened. Know this now. Thank you, darling. I ended my life happy because of you.

Otherwise, let me say it again. I love you. I always will, my beautiful girl. The past is only the past to the living. When we are dead it becomes our own again. I will be with you again one day, of that I am sure. What's loved is never lost.

Theodora Parr
1996

Part Four

Chapter Twenty-Four

July, 2011

'But I don't want to live there,' I said. 'And fixing it—' I let my hands fall to my lap with a hollow laugh, and the young man opposite watched me, impassively. 'Fixing it'd cost millions of pounds. I don't have *a* pound.'

'Nevertheless, you are the rightful heir,' said Charles Lambert. He drummed a pen on his desk, and looked out through the glass windows that stretched, floor to ceiling, over the city. 'It is an interesting legal conundrum. Your grandmother's aim was that you know nothing about Keepsake until your twenty-sixth birthday, at which point we could provide you with the pension but leave you clear of the obligation. Your father was very wrong to have put the idea of going to Keepsake in your head. We told him explicitly of your grandmother's instructions that the house be left as it is. But you've been there, and in declaring yourself to us to be Theodora Parr's sole heir you are now by default in possession of it and have an obligation to the estate. What we need to establish, while acting according to your grandmother's wishes as well, is the *nature* of that obligation.'

'Well, I'm happy to be the heir,' I said, sounding more definite about it than I felt.

He nodded. 'Of course.'

I narrowed my eyes. 'But, Mr Lambert—'

'Charles, please,' he interrupted, smoothly.

'Charles. Look, the thing is, I don't want to go back there, does that sound mad?'

'It's not for me to comment,' Charles Lambert said. 'But of course, we will act in accordance with your wishes, Miss Parr.'

I stared at him, at his wispy blond hair, utterly correct posture, polite professionalism: couldn't he see that what I wanted was someone who'd tell me exactly what to do? This was my second meeting here. In the fifteen years since my grandmother's death what had once been a discreet family law firm with offices in Mayfair was now an international conglomerate with offices in Shanghai and São Paulo and, of course, the tax haven of Barbados. Charles Lambert had told me, in a rare piece of personal information disclosure, that he and his wife had recently returned from working in Barbados for two years, 'As we wanted to have our children in Britain, *obviously*.'

Obviously. The notebook I used to write in at the London Library, filling it with ideas and half-sentences about things, was now my Keepsake notebook, filled with furious, scribbled notes. I looked again at what I'd written down; I now knew the following:

1. THE INHERITANCE
Due to a quirk of the settlement, my own father's pension was fairly considerable (£20,000 a year) whereas I derived income only from the house and lands. At one time this would have provided me with an extensive income; not now. The Parr mines, from which a large proportion of the family's wealth had originated, had been out of action for almost a hundred years. Also, the arable and other extensive farming land around us had been sold off, piece by piece, by George Farrars, Teddy's father, to aid his gambling addiction. Both of these facts meant I was in possession of a piece of real estate that was, essentially, worthless. The land was worth a great deal, but you'd never get permission to build houses on it, much less pull down Keepsake; and I didn't want to do any of those things. The house couldn't be repaired – but even if it could, I wasn't sure I'd want to do that, either.

2. THE HOUSE
If there were items of value to be found at Keepsake, Charles Lambert had said, we could auction them. But I baulked at that, somehow: the publicity of a house sale, and going through items I had never known or handled, to make some cash. And

as my grandmother had said herself, there wasn't much of value in there. No Chippendales or tiaras. I was trying to get used to being this person, a girl who had meetings with lawyers, who had a ready-made family myth she slotted right into, who came from a line of women who'd variously influenced history. I couldn't sit in an auction room and watch a stranger flog off what was left of it.

Because Keepsake had never been listed, or examined by English Heritage, we were not under any obligation to repair it or maintain it. The fact is, however, it would have been, had it been discovered. But Charles Lambert, with excited lips pursed, had told me that was not a legal requirement of ours 'at this time'.

3. MY GRANDMOTHER'S INTENTIONS
The most important fact of all: I'd read my grandmother's memoir. I understood what Lise was trying to tell me all along, and yet I shouldn't ever have read it: Teddy hadn't wanted me to know, or go to the house. She'd wanted Keepsake to crumble away to nothing, to be lost in the mists of time. But both my father and Lise Travers, in their own ways unreliable witnesses, hadn't agreed with her. I looked down at the smudged hand-writing, the paper torn in places with the imprint of my biro, words written and crossed out again and again. I didn't know what to write about my grandmother. I knew her, and yet didn't know her at all. She had put all these plans in place, and here I was, barging in, all her fine work ruined, unpicking those plans.

'So my advice to you would be as follows,' Charles Lambert said, recalling me to my senses. He put his fingers together, in a roof shape, and looked thoughtful. 'I would leave the house as is. We will contact your father, care of Ohio State University. We will explain to him that you are cancelling his pension. You are entitled to that income upon your twenty-sixth birthday. The pension is merely within your gift and it's highly debatable whether he should have been claiming it for all these years. An oversight on our behalf, perhaps. And we will send someone to the house to obtain a list of assets of the property and the land. We have one already from your grandmother's time – she was most punctilious about everything – but it would be sensible to update it. Is there anything in particular you think may be of value?'

I shook my head, thinking of the diamond brooch. 'I just don't know. And good luck to whomever you send down there, I'll give you detailed directions. It's impossible to find.'

'We'll find it, don't worry, Miss Parr,' said Charles Lambert, slightly patronisingly, I thought. 'Other matters, just briefly: we will take care of the insurance and we will ensure that there is no need for you to return, unless it becomes of immediate importance. And until you decide what to do with the place.'

'Until then,' I said.

'Very good.' He scribbled for a moment in silence. I looked out of the windows at the heat shimmering over the city. Suddenly he said, rather curiously, 'It does look rather amazing.'

I nodded. I found that for all I wanted to stay away from there I longed to talk about it with people who'd understand. 'It must have been, at one time. When you're there . . . it's like being in another world. There's all these – little details about it.'

He put down his pen. 'Like what?'

'It's *alive*. Gargoyles above doors staring down at you, and portraits following you around the room, and plants shooting through cracks.'

'Jolly exciting. How extraordinary.' He looked like a small boy. 'Weren't you scared, though? It sounds like a pretty spooky place.'

'It could have been daunting, but it wasn't . . .' I faltered, trying to explain. 'I can't describe it. I felt – it was good to be there. That I belonged there. That's what I felt.' I shivered, chilly in the air-conditioned office.

'May I ask: so you really don't think you could live there?' Charles Lambert took up his pen again, and adjusted his glasses.

I hesitated. 'I just don't think so, no. I can't – I can't imagine it.' I bit the tip of my finger, trying not to feel faint. Since I had come back from Keepsake I'd hardly slept. I was so determined to be in control of this thing, to not hide from it, that I had started keeping all these notes, reading long into the night to get it all straight in my mind. I kept feeling woozy, like I'd fall over at any time. Mum said it was because I wasn't breathing properly, I was getting myself wound up, but I knew what it was: that day, the day I had stood there and thought I heard the house when it was alive again, had seen a crack in time, a part of Keepsake had entered into me. Really, I can't explain it without sounding crazy. Someone had flown inside me – one of those women, or a caterpillar, hatching butterflies, and that was what gave me that jabbing, fluttering feeling of possibility, of fear, of excitement and indecision that seemed to fly around inside me, all day.

Sounds a bit mad, I know.

But something about the house and the weight of all that history sent them all a little mad. I'd reread Teddy's memoir several times, draining it of all meaning, and besides that there were diaries and letters aplenty in that box: I'd read about Teddy's clever, beautiful grandmother, Alexandra, the true butterfly collector, about Rupert the Vandal, who'd pulled down half of Keepsake, thus beginning its long demise, about Lonely Anne, Alexandra's mother, who wouldn't leave the house and refused to see visitors after she'd been into the chapel and seen her ancestors' bones there . . . about Mad Nina, living in the Butterfly House, talking only to the butterflies who knew about her time in Turkey, the years spent as a slave in a harem . . . I knew them all, I knew the rhyme Lise was singing that day in the library, I'd learned it well now.

But I couldn't tell Charles Lambert any of this. I couldn't say: *most of them locked themselves into the chapel and starved themselves to death. There's rooms that haven't been touched for two centuries. You could open the place up to visitors and be the biggest attraction west of the London Dungeons! Yup!*

A plane flew past outside, glinting in the sun, flashing into my eyes. I blinked, and Charles stood up and shook my hand.

'We'll contact you when the pension is transferred to your name and when we have sent our assessor in to ascertain the house has no specific items of interest which need to be insured or removed. And we'll make contact with your father.'

'Half the pension,' I said, suddenly. 'Half. I don't want to take it all away from him.'

'Are you sure?'

'Absolutely.' I nodded. 'Not now.'

He stepped back and made a note on his pad, without comment. 'My apologies, one more thing. I'm afraid I don't remember your line of employment. For the paperwork.'

'I was an assistant at a solicitor's,' I said.

He gave a thin smile. 'So this is a busman's holiday for you, then.'

'Sort of. Actually—' I swallowed. At some point I had to tell someone what I'd done yesterday. 'I've handed in my notice. I'm . . . well . . .' I could feel myself blushing. 'I've been accepted for teacher training college. In September. I applied for the following year but they've had two drop-outs, so there are spaces, and . . . I had an interview yesterday and even though I hadn't prepared much . . . I mean, I'd read the material and the National Curriculum syllabus and, of course, brushed up on the texts, because I—' *He doesn't care, Nina, stop talking.* I gave an excited, small grin. 'I'm going to be an English teacher!'

He gave a tepid smile. 'Teaching. You're brave!'

'Oh. Well, it's what I always wanted to do,' I said.

'Gosh. Have to say, I wouldn't do it for all the tea in China. Good for you!'

'Thanks,' I said, not sure if he was paying me a compliment or telling me I was an idiot who should have become a hedge fund manager instead. I stood up to go before we misunderstood each other any more, hugging the Keepsake papers I'd brought with me. 'I'll look forward to hearing from you, then.'

Walking through the City, past the upmarket bars, stationers, outfitters, vintners, in my black biker boots and my black-and-grey, floral short dress, my black leather jacket, my long hair, tousled in the breeze, I caught sight of myself in a mirror and almost laughed, because I'd made a real effort that morning to look smart and businesslike, and yet here, in the City, I still looked akin to a dangerous revolutionary or a hobo. Everyone alongside me was in grey or black, too – but neat, not a hair out of place, immaculate. Every pavement spotless, glass sheets glinting, no flower boxes, or black-boards with funny signs, no beards, no birds. People walked fast, heads down.

All of it less than a mile from home, or rather Mum's. I walked back slowly, through Bunhill Row, and stopped at William Blake's headstone. I bought a coffee and a roll at the food market on Whitecross Street, then meandered up past St Luke's Church and the new estates with centuries-old names hurriedly built after the war, badly designed then, unloved today. And suddenly I heard something.

'Help! Help me!'

A voice, calling above me: I craned my neck upwards, at one of the highest tower blocks. It was a woman's voice.

'Help me out!'

I went to the bottom of the tower. In front of it there was a very young-looking mum, pushing a buggy listlessly around a dried-out grass rectangle.

'There's a lady up there, calling for help . . .' I felt a bit stupid, suddenly. 'Can I go up there, have a look?'

'Don't worry about it,' she said. 'She's been up there for two days.'

'What?'

'The lifts are broken. She can't get downstairs. She can't use her legs so she can't walk, can she? She's on the eighteenth floor. They keep saying they're on their way to mend it, then they don't fucking come, do they?'

'That's awful.'

'She's fine. Her daughter's bringing her stuff.' The girl shrugged, and twisted her hair around her hand.

'Is there anyone else—'

She cut me off. 'She's lived round here for years, since she was a girl, everyone knows her, she's got friends.'

'But still, she . . . does she need someone to go up, see if she's OK?'

The girl looked at me, then her baby gave a gentle, protesting cry. 'I think she's all right, thanks,' she said, politely.

389

There were two boys, standing aimlessly by the gate, as I went out and back on to Hall Street. 'Bye,' one of them said, tonelessly.

'Bye,' I replied. I looked up at the old lady, trapped eighteen floors up, like Rapunzel. I could just see her, in a lavender cardigan, waving. 'Help! Help me!'

I called the Council on my way home anyway. The woman on the phone was polite, but firm. 'It's private contractors. We've told them three times to get out there, and they just don't turn up.'

'But that's awful,' I said. The idea of her, up there, completely unable to get down – it made me itchy with panic. 'Can't someone carry her down? Can't you do something?'

'It's logged, and it's a priority, Miss Parr,' said the woman on the phone. 'It really is. Thank you very much for calling us.'

It was all wrong, somehow, and the heat of the day, the sleekness of the lifts at Murbles and Routledge, the old lady's hoarse, bellowing voice in the quiet of the estate – it made me all angry. More and more, I realised, I didn't like what London was becoming. How the things that seemed to be important in the city these days – money, making more money, protecting billionaires who wanted to make more money here – weren't important in real life, didn't help people in real life. 'I—' I began, and realised I was even more dizzy than usual.

'Is there anything else I can help you with today?' said the woman on the phone. 'Hello? Is there anything else, miss?'

I could hear her voice, tinny and faint, as the phone fell out of my hand and that whooshing, swooping feeling of light-headedness struck me again. I stopped, blinking, and sank to the ground.

Chapter Twenty-Five

The riots that summer – the riots of 2011, which began the following week – seemed to come completely out of the blue. No one was expecting them and, while they were happening, no one knew how to explain them, nor for a long time afterwards. For me it didn't come as a great surprise; I've lived in the centre of the city all my life, and I'm used to its history and beauty alongside casual cruelty and unexpected and terrifying outbursts of sudden violence. I'd felt something was different, these last few weeks, something unsettling in the air. But all over the country people were outraged: they had to be outraged about something, so they were outraged alternately by the actual shooting of Mark Duggan, the loss of control, the wanton destruction, the senseless violence, the youth's committing the wanton destruction, the police who didn't understand them, the politicians who were out of touch with everyone, the racism inherent in the system, the lack of structure in society that led to this.

Some of the people who caused damage were angry. Some just needed to shout, make some noise, some of them were in it for the smashed shopfronts and the chaos that comes with any disturbance, and some of them were bad people. But only some of them.

I met Sebastian on the Wednesday afternoon, the third day after the trouble began, in the midst of this strange situation of wondering how dangerous it would be that night. It was all anyone wanted to talk about, and the news was full of shops and houses burning to the ground all over London, someone dead in Ealing, in Croydon, Birmingham and Clapham, police out in force in East London and Tottenham and Liverpool. Three hundred people had caused havoc in Hackney the previous night and everyone was wondering if it would get to Islington, where there had been some disturbances already. All over London shops were boarding up early.

August is a curious month. The nights start drawing in and it's chilly in the evening but by day it still feels like summer. That day it was hot – too hot. Something strange was in the air, you could almost taste it. Summer madness. The day before I had gone into Gorings, to collect the last of my things. Bryan Robson had been wonderful: he'd paid me my month's notice salary and said I could leave a week later. He got a temp in, instead. She was called Cherry, she was from Hanwell, she had two children, and by lunchtime she'd sorted out the stationery cupboard and she and Sue had worked out their kids had gone to the same school.

Becky was on maternity leave from the following week so we shared an awkward little farewell tea together, she and I and Sue, Cherry and the partners: cakes and cups of tea around the reception desk. They gave Becky a baby monitor wrapped in a large cellophane ribbon, and some bath oil; I got a very handsome leather satchel, to keep my stuff in. I was really touched.

Bryan spoke about Becky, about how much they'd miss her smiling good humour and how she'd have to hurry back as otherwise who'd organise the Grand National and Eurovision sweepstakes?

'And finally, I'd like to say goodbye, and good luck, to Nina,' Bryan said, raising his mug to me. 'Nina is leaving us, after two happy years, to train to be a teacher. Isn't that wonderful?' He looked around the small, underwhelmed group. 'We always said she was destined for great things, didn't we? Well, there we are. Good luck, Nina, and keep in touch with us.'

I looked up and nodded, trying not to blush, mortified at the attention. I wondered what they all thought of me, these men and women shuffling back to their desks. Becky loved it, receiving kisses and compliments on her bump like a pro. But Becky had a photo of her wedding day on her desk. And when we'd had to have our new security pass photos taken, she'd loved it, smiling and striking a pose as Sue wielded the camera; she understood, of course, that at certain periods of one's life you have to be the centre of attention. Not for long, and hopefully for good reasons, but it's a fact: we can't always avoid the spotlight. Perhaps sometimes you just stand there and smile, and get on with it. So I grinned self-consciously and said thank you, then gobbled up a bit of cake, though I was feeling too nervous to eat much of it, then I went over to Bryan, and kissed his cheek.

'Thank you so much for everything,' I said. 'You've been really kind to me. I didn't deserve it.'

His eyes twinkled. 'Sometimes you didn't, no, but I always thought you were worth it. I said to myself on the day I took you on, "Bryan, this might be a terrible mistake, but you'll learn something from her."'

'What did you learn?' I asked, amused, as behind us Sue, who was fixing the photocopier, laughed.

'To stand up straight,' he said. 'You hunch your shoulders. You frown. You don't even realise you're doing it – there! Right there.' I laughed, and he patted me on the back. 'You're going to be a wonderful teacher, young lady. I think you'll love it. I can see you now, out of town in some lovely village, on your bicycle, cycling to school. Oh, yes.' He closed his eyes, and gently hummed. 'Oh, yes, Nina. You'll have a dog. I see it.'

I snorted. 'Me? I hate the countryside!'

'Who likes London any more?' demanded Bryan, angrily, as Sue nodded, eyes wide. 'This week, what's happening out there, people going mad, all sorts every night. You're better off out of London, young lady. You're not a child any more. You're growing up. Things change. You think you love the city, then one day: bam!' He pushed his fists together then apart, in an explosive gesture. 'You wake up and realise you haven't seen what's under your nose.'

'I'm more likely to sprout wings and fly,' I said, but as I said it it sounded defensive. And shortly afterwards, as I left the office for the last time, walking down Regent Street in the full flow of summer tourism with my new satchel, I stopped in the street, blinking fast, wondering if I was going to faint again like last week. If I'd always feel this way, if something was actually wrong with me. I wondered what would happen that night, how close to breaking point the city was.

And then the thought, the realisation that would alter my life for ever, came to me, a little red balloon floating into my eyeline. I stood still, outside the Apple store, looking at the giant photos of families on beaches and different, primary-coloured apps that would make your life beautiful. Calendar. Contacts. Photos. Calendar. Photos. Calendar.

How could I not have realised it before?

Palms sweating slightly, shaking, I crossed the road, suddenly sure of where I had to go next, what I had to do before I saw him. I passed the *Evening Standard* kiosk by Oxford Circus: 'London's Second Night of Riots?' I barely took it in, though: *Oh God. What if I'm right?*

So the following evening, I popped into the kitchen to fetch an apple – I'd realised an apple helped me feel less dizzy – before I went out to meet Sebastian, and to my surprise saw Mum sitting on a kitchen stool having a cup of tea. She'd been away the previous two days in Oxford, visiting a school and some libraries.

'Hello!' she said, with pleasure. 'I'm sorry. I didn't hear you come in.'

'I didn't know you were back. How was Oxford?' I said, kissing her, and throwing another apple from the fruit bowl into my bag.

'It was wonderful. I met another Nina.'

'Really?'

'Yes, she was five, and she had a brother called Alfie. She was adorable. She was very pleased I had a daughter called Nina.'

'That's great,' I said. I bit into the apple.

'Are you OK?'

'Just tired. Was it nice being back there?'

'Oh.' She pressed her hands on to the kitchen counter. 'You know, it was wonderful. I went to Oriel College and the Bodleian. I even went to Brasenose again. I told the porter it was my husband's college and he let me have a look around the quad.' She stopped and smiled. 'I'd forgotten you can see the Bodleian from there. And the sky – his room was at the top, and we used to look out at the stars.' She fiddled with her necklace. 'I remembered something, when we were there. Something he told me.'

'What's that?'

'He said he was always cold at home. And he was warm at Oxford. He couldn't ever see the sun, where he grew up. Because his room backed on to the trees and the house was always damp.' Her eyes were filling with tears. 'And that's why he loved being in that room. Sky. And since we went to Keepsake, oh, it's almost two months ago now, but I keep thinking about it. And reading your grandmother's memoir: "his anxious smile" – that's what she said about her own son, Nina, his anxious smile, and I can't stop hearing that phrase, how sad it is, how she screwed him up so badly he didn't really have a chance. Do you remember that bit?'

'Yes.' I'd read *The Butterfly Summer* so many times by then, I remembered all of it. 'I don't know, though. Poor Teddy. I think she meant well.'

'No, she didn't!' Mum said, with a half-laugh. 'I think she must have been a really bad person, Nina. I'm sorry. To have done that to him – and I keep thinking about how sort of undefined he was when we first met. How kind. He had this public-school charm about him, but it was as if he'd learned it like an impressionist learns to do a voice, or when a child copies another child at school.'

I shrugged. 'I think he'd have always turned out like that, though.'

'Like what?'

'Well – a little weak,' I said carefully, 'bit of a liar. A bit too used to relying on his charm and his posh accent.'

She shook her head. 'I don't believe he was always like that.' She smiled, and I caught that something in her eye, the look she had when she thought of him – the look he had, too.

I'd never told her about his letter, how he'd written that he'd always be in love with her. I know it was the right decision. The divorce came through and I expect they'll never meet again, but unlikely as it sounds I believe they still love each other, even after everything. I don't suppose I'll ever really understand them – you don't understand other relationships, do you? Much less your own parents. Who can make sense of my relationship with Sebastian, except the two of us?

'I'm cutting your dad some slack,' Mum was saying. 'He took

the ashes and the memoir back down to Keepsake. He followed your grandmother's last wishes. In the end, he tried to do the right thing.'

But I said nothing. We had still heard nothing else from him, other than via the solicitors, on the matter of the divorce. I accept this about my father, the invisible George Parr: I won't see him again, in all probability. And that, at least, is a strange piece of mental readjustment: the father who was dead but alive in my imagination is now alive and well, yet dead to me, in my mind at least. I don't know how I feel about it. Perhaps one day, a couple of years from now, I might just jump on a plane and go to Ohio, try to get to know him, meet Merilyn the millionaire's daughter. Perhaps that's all a lie, too. Perhaps he's someone else entirely. It's not neat, but families aren't. I spent all my life wanting a bigger family, and now I have one I realise that doesn't make you normal. Far from it.

'I'm glad you went back to Oxford,' I said.

'I'm glad, too,' said Mum. She got up and kissed me, fingers smearing away her lipgloss from my cheek. 'I'm glad I remembered that, about him, about your father. I want you to remember it, too, Nina. Whatever came afterwards, that summer he loved me and I loved him. The day we were married we were so happy. I want you to understand, Nina, that's where you came from.'

'Mum—' I began, and then stopped.

'What?'

'Nothing.' I looked at my watch. 'I have to go. I'll be late.'

'Be careful out there,' she said, as I went up the stairs.

I laughed. 'Come on, Mum. I'm a big girl.'

'I meant Sebastian,' she called. 'Go easy on him.'

Walking to meet Sebastian that evening along the canal, two boys on bikes cycled towards me, hollering exuberantly. One was the boy with the harelip I'd see around.

'Out of my way, bitch!' he screamed, almost crack-voiced with hysteria.

I backed up against the wall, terrified out of proportion, and then they were gone and the hazy serenity of the canal returned, lone moorhen cackling amidst the plastic bags and bobbing beer bottles, the muggy smell of coal smoke in the dead air.

How would I explain it to him? How could I make him understand? I quickened my pace, up towards the street.

Chapter Twenty-Six

Though I was at the nice hideaway pub on Camden Passage early, Sebastian was there already – he was always early, though he never minded if I was late. I took his hands in mine and stared at him, wondering how we'd get through the next hour or so.

'You all right?' he said, as I kissed him on the cheek. 'You seem a bit—'

'What?'

'Wild-eyed, I suppose.'

'I've been feeling quite mad of late,' I said. 'It's better now. Sorted some things out.' Suddenly I almost couldn't bear to look at him properly.

'Come and sit down,' he said, still looking at me rather curiously. 'I got us a table. Do you want a drink?'

'I want something to eat. I'm starving. Look—'

Someone ran, screaming loudly, past the window, and everyone in the pub jerked upright, faux-casually. But it was a laughing girl with a cloth bag running for something – a bus, a date, a film.

'Bit tense tonight,' Sebastian said. 'Isn't it crazy?' That was what everyone kept saying: *Isn't it crazy? Isn't it weird?* Looking at every person we passed in the street, suspicious, confused at the idea this latent violence was there amongst so many of us.

'Long time coming, I think,' I said shortly. 'Look, Sebastian—'

'Let me order a drink first. Let's celebrate. You and your exciting news. Will you have a glass of champagne?' His kind, brown eyes were hesitant. 'Will you, Nins?'

I had to say yes. 'Of course.' I took his hand. When the glasses arrived, I took a tiny sip, and clinked mine with his. 'To you. To—' I put my glass down. 'I'm sorry. I don't know what we're toasting.'

'Oh, you. The teaching course.' He looked surprised. 'And finding

Keepsake. And – it being a lovely night. Why shouldn't we have a glass of champagne?'

'Sure,' I said. 'I don't think the house is much to celebrate, though.'

'You, always looking on the negative side.'

'You haven't been there,' I said. 'You'll see.'

'I'm waiting for my invitation,' he said. 'Remember, I'm going to move down there with you and be your lord of the manor, servicing you and your . . .' He trailed off, looking at me. 'It was just a joke.'

'Sorry.' I wished I wasn't being so odd, that I could just power on through and tell him what I wanted to. 'Weird day. Listen, Sebastian—'

'I've been thinking,' he said. 'Being serious for a moment.'

The waitress appeared with our menus, and we both jerked back to receive them, in identical movements, and smiled at each other as she retreated, giving us a curious look.

'She thinks we're playing mechanical robots in a panto together somewhere,' I said.

'You don't get mechanical robots in pantos, you sad, deprived child.'

I gave a guffaw of laughter, and smiled at him, helplessly.

And then he said, hurriedly, 'You were right, Nina.'

'About what?'

'Getting back together.'

'How was I right?' I asked, carefully.

'Well, that we shouldn't do it, that it'd be a mistake. Isn't that what you think? I've been waiting for an answer, all this time since we slept together, and you were right in the first place. About us. Calling time on it. I wasn't seeing straight. I was thinking about old us, and we've changed, haven't we? We're not those people any more.'

'Oh – no, we're not,' I said, and then I took a gulp of champagne.

'I'm glad we . . . I'm glad we had that night together. It was incredible.' He reached out for my hand, and I could feel my face burning. 'Aren't you?'

I nodded. 'Absolutely.'

'Good. Because it was sort of like a goodbye, wasn't it? And you with the teaching, and me off to America for a couple of months –

did I mention that?' I nodded. 'You know, it'd have been a mistake, anyway – not just for those reasons, but because we're getting on with our lives.'

I pushed the champagne away. 'Sebastian—'

'No, let me finish. Please.' He bit his lip. 'I need to say it. I . . . I will always love you in a way, Nins, does that sound odd?'

I shook my head, dumbly. He seemed like a wholly different person then, far removed from me, from our old lives. I looked into my glass, wondering if I would be able to tell him or not. 'No. No, it doesn't seem odd.'

'I'm so glad.' And he kissed my hand.

'I'm glad, too,' I said, and I *was* glad. I loved him and I wanted him to be happy, and I saw it then, of course – we couldn't be together, despite everything. I saw only his goodness then.

He leaned back in his chair. 'I'm really hungry. Shall we order? We won't be attacked by an angry mob, will we?'

'Hardly.' I handed him the menu, wondering if I could face it.

'Did you hear about that restaurant in Notting Hill? They just ran in and started robbing people right there as they ate. Yesterday.'

'Oh, they were all millionaires,' I said. 'They can afford to lose a tenner or two.'

'You old Commie. You'd have been a great highwayman, back in the day, stealing off Charles II's mistresses and pocketing their jewels. Oops. I shouldn't speak ill of the family, should I? So, Lady Nina, the house. Tell me what's happening.'

I put my napkin down, woozy with adrenaline. 'The house . . .'

His brow creased. 'Hey. Are you really all right? You're awfully pale, Nins.'

I nodded. 'Fine. What house?'

'Keepsake. What's happening with—'

But I couldn't do it any longer. I'd thought I'd tell him a little later, when we were more relaxed, when he might be more comfortable with the idea. I stared at him, lips parted, throat dry. 'Sebastian. I have to tell you something.'

'What?' He leaned towards me. 'I'm going to get you a glass of water. You're white as a sheet—'

I put my hand on his, watching the last moments before I told him, and stared into his deep, kind eyes. 'No. It's not that. I'm pregnant.'

His fingers clenched under my hand. 'What?'

'I'm pregnant.' I closed my eyes. 'I . . . it's yours, obviously.'

'Obviously?'

My heart thumping wildly, I said sharply, 'Yes, obviously. There hasn't been anyone else, you know. It's over two months ago. It's that afternoon.'

'But we used a condom.'

'Sort of. Once. The time afterwards, it fell off – don't you remember?' I was blushing. Someone at the next table looked around at the word 'condom'.

'I didn't . . . we were—' He swallowed. 'OK. How long have you known?'

'I found out yesterday. So this is all kind of freaky to me, too!' I smiled at him; I sounded idiotic. 'I haven't been eating much, and I kept feeling strange, and I fainted a couple of weeks ago. I thought I was just stressed, all this business with the house. Anyway, it's probably got three heads and it'll come out as a ball of hair.'

'So you're keeping it?'

We looked at each other.

'Sebastian, I'm not asking you to be involved,' I said. 'But I think I want to. It sort of makes sense.' I rubbed my eyes. 'Well, no, it doesn't make any sense, because the PGCE starts next month and I'll probably miss most of the summer term, but they say I can make up the extra credits after April – if it's all OK, if I have the baby – you know, I'm still only nine weeks—'

'Of course.'

'The thing is, I kind of like the idea of me and Mum having this baby. Mum's really excited. She's going to be the new Mrs Poll, she says.' I was talking too fast, hoping he wouldn't remember how badly I lied. I had to make him think it was OK, that he didn't need to offer, that he wasn't tied to me, or me to him. He had to be free, if he wanted. I thought of Mum, and Dad, how they didn't work – and yet they still loved each other.

Someone behind me was handed a lamb burger with chips, and began eating it, loudly.

I said, hurriedly, 'Malc is over the moon. He says he's going to come to the NCT classes with me, but I've said a firm no to that – how weird would that be? So I think I'll stay with them for a while, and maybe if we ever move to Keepsake, which we probably won't, I can take it – the, the baby – down there, or get a job there, or something – I'm not sure.'

'Move to Keepsake?'

'That's another story,' I said. 'God. A lot's happened. Let's—' I looked out of the window, trying to ignore the burger-eater, astonished at my body's own reaction. 'Can we get out of here? I need some fresh air.'

Sebastian nodded, still slightly dazed. 'Sure. You OK?'

'Sitting down near all this food is making me a bit nauseous. Sorry.' I saw him looking down as I stood up, at my stomach. 'Nothing to see yet,' I said, and I gave him a smile, shyly.

'You're having – Jesus, you are having our baby.' He said it, slowly. 'Wow, Nina.'

We put some money on the table and left. It was a humid, cloudy night, very quiet on the passageway. We walked slowly up the Essex Road, and I told him about Keepsake, and everything that had happened there. About the letter I'd had from Charles Lambert that day: something about a charity called Butterfly Conservation being called in to identify some butterflies, and being excited about something. About the land being protected.

'I called him, but he wasn't there. It was eight thirty in the evening, though; I'm glad even Charles Lambert doesn't work that late.'

'Who?'

I shook my head. 'My solicitor. And it doesn't matter.'

'Did you see butterflies when you were there? Any of them look particularly exciting?'

'There were hundreds. Probably thousands. But it's hard for me to tell. I used to know about them, but it's been years. It was extraordinary. It's so wild and overgrown and warm and lush there, it's almost a mini rainforest, and the flora and fauna—' I stopped, and laughed. 'Well, it's a long story.'

Sebastian was nodding politely but he wasn't listening properly, I knew. He had his head low down, but at the sound of something like fireworks in the distance we both stopped, jerking our heads up. Because round there, the sound of fireworks rarely turned out to be actual fireworks.

'It's a bit strange to be out, maybe,' I said, thinking of the hysterical texts and emails we'd had from neighbours warning everyone not to step outdoors that night, wondering if they were right. 'Look, I might go back, anyway. I've been really, really tired the last couple of days. I can hardly stay awake past eight thirty. And I think you need some time to think about it all. When you tell your family – if you do – whatever.'

'Of course I'm telling them.' Sebastian's face was set. 'Let's not think about that now.' He gazed at me. 'I'm walking you back home first.'

I grabbed his hand. 'No. Don't. Really don't. I'm walking down St Peter's Street, it'll be fine. This is all blown up out of proportion, it'll be over tonight. Look, shall we meet tomorrow, or Friday? Afternoon?'

He shook his head, slowly. 'No.'

'No?'

'What if I said I wanted to be with you? Start over again, Nins? What would you say? Is there any point in . . .' He trailed off. 'Just tell me.'

'I don't know.' We stood there on the street, backs of our hands touching, all my former resolution gone. Suddenly I wanted him to stay with me, to always be there, so badly that it caught in my heart. 'I don't know,' I repeated, in a broken, small voice.

He pushed a piece of my hair behind my shoulder. 'Like I . . . I . . . *know* you, Nins. I just do. Even though we're so different. If we're having a baby – a baby,' he whispered, a smile breaking over his face, 'shouldn't we try?'

His child, my child, our child, and we had been married and we were still the only ones for each other, in so many ways. Ready tears dropped from my eyes on to the floor.

He looked aghast. 'Oh. Oh, Nina, darling, don't cry. I'm sorry—'

'I'm crying all the time,' I said. 'It's like the wooziness and the nausea. I thought there was something wrong with me before I found out what it was. I cried four times at the news this morning.'

'Look,' he said, 'why don't we sleep on it, both of us? I'll come and see you tomorrow, because this changes everything – it does. Maybe we shouldn't try, but you know what? Maybe we should.'

He kissed me on the lips. I still feel it as I write this now, three years later. I know what Teddy meant when she wrote that she recalled it all perfectly. I remember this moment, in exact, crystal-clear detail. Then he walked away, and he turned back and smiled happily at me, the way he'd done that very first day I saw him, by the UCL noticeboard, and then he was out of sight.

Life depends on tiny things that force our choices – the zip on a boot, a thunderstorm on the Heath, and the direction we take at a fork in the road. If he'd gone the other way, up Upper Street, would it have happened?

A freak thing – an accident – like coincidences, though, there are no real accidents, are there? I was always meant to meet Lise in the library that day. She was always meant to find me. And why was Sebastian there, too, on the day it all started, when we saw each other again for the first time in months? I know it's because he went there looking for me. It wasn't a coincidence. That's why I believe we were always supposed to have this child and . . . and perhaps Sebastian had to leave this way, though that, *that* I will never believe.

Up where the sound of the fireworks had come from, a group of boys, emboldened by the riots and the chaos, had smashed some shop windows, and had taken a box of fireworks from a supermarket. They were setting them off on the lonely, final stretch of the Canonbury Road up towards Highbury and Islington station. One firework hit a bus, another a jogger out for a run. Sebastian ran towards them, told them to stop. The police said he was running almost as fast as they were driving in their car: Sebastian, who knew when to leave well alone and when to step up.

Another firework, and the boys dispersed, terrified. And as Sebastian reached them, two more fireworks shot out, both together, and hit the building site behind the Union Chapel. The architect's sign – covered in loads of jargon about Considerate Builders, I saw it all at the inquest – was dislodged, and high, high above him, some brick and the metal signage cracked away from the wall, flying down fast, hitting him on the back of the head and knocking him to the ground, where he fell backwards, landing hard on the back of his head again. His skull was badly fractured in several places. He suffered intercranial bleeding, and then a haemorrhage.

After a week, Zinnia – magnificent in a crisis, calm, unbearably thoughtful and kind – asked for his life support to be switched off. He died a couple of days later in UCH, where our daughter was born seven months after, opposite the very place her parents first met. She is called Alice Fairley Parr, and she will always know who her father was. I talk to her about him every single day. She has a photograph of him and me in her room.

In life, we couldn't find a way to be together. But then he died, and left me with his daughter. So he is always in my heart, with me, every day. Isn't it strange.

Chapter Twenty-Seven

August, 2014

Summer comes early to Cornwall. The swallows and swifts are on the wing from April, and by May the trees are in leaf and, of course, there are butterflies in the heavy, sweet air, waiting for the rest of the country – and the light, for it is still often dark in the morning – to catch up.

I have spent a fair amount of time there, these last couple of years, since Alice was born. Not at the house – that would be impossible. There is a gatehouse, further down at the edge of the woods, by the entrance to the road that leads to Manaccan, where the real Matty lived before she and her mother were evicted by my great-grandfather. It had been in a state of disrepair and is still fairly inhospitable in winter, when the track leading to the front door becomes impassable, blocked with mud, ice and leaves. In summer, it is still dark, with no radio reception, shaded by trees, the only sound the nightjars and the owls. But now it is warm and welcoming. It has two cosy bedrooms and I have had the chimney swept so that we can light a fire. There's running water in the kitchen, and I heat up water for the bath on the fire. This is mine, too, part of my estate: the dowry left to me by the women who came before. I am happy to have it like this. One wouldn't want to stay there for more than a week or two but when it's warm and cosy and tidy it is magical. Alice loves it here.

It is where my mother and Malc chose to spend their honeymoon, and it means a great deal to me that they did. By August, Cornwall has been warm for months, and even in the shade of the trees the cottage is hot. We drove down early and joined them today, crossing paths at lunch. Malc grilled sardines and herby, crumbling local sausages and we ate like kings. Ally ate more than anyone else. She has a huge appetite: she can polish off two large bowls of pasta in minutes. She's very like her father.

After lunch, Malc pushed his sun hat a little further over his head and folded his arms. 'I'm done here,' he said. 'It's my turn for a rest before we go. Are you gals off to do the thing?'

Mum looked over at me.

'I might just go on my own,' I said, 'if that's OK, Mum?'

She nodded. 'Sure, sure!' she said, her voice a little tight, a little anxious, for she alone knew why I was going up there. 'I mean, I'd walk with you if you wanted, but not if you don't, honey.'

I hesitated. I'd wanted to go back there with only Alice. To lay this to rest with my daughter for company: I had in mind that it would be a symbolic moment, the last two Parr women, but then I realised I couldn't go without Mum.

Genes, families, ancestry, they're funny things, aren't they? I was convinced I didn't like *The Birds Are Mooing* when I was younger. Then when Alice was born I realised what a wonderful book it is. I just couldn't see it before, it was too close to our eccentric little life together. I read it to my own daughter now, it's her favourite book of all time just as *Nina and the Butterflies* was mine, and I think she already understands her grandmother wrote it, and I love that, I love it so much. My wonderful Mum.

I spent my life until the age of twenty-five wishing I knew more about a man whom I believed had died soon after I was born. Now, if anything, I know too much about him and his family. It's my mother's side I feel sorry for now – those under-appreciated East Coast Americans, academic, dry, sandy-haired. Mum's father died last year, and she went over for the funeral but I couldn't make it, so she and I have a plan to go back together sometime next year, if my holidays will allow for it. I will leave Ally with Zinnia, her other granny (never a more doting grandmother than Zinnia lived, none more convinced of their grandchild's perfection – but she's allowed to think that, I believe). We will go to Manhattan and pay homage to Mum's early life, then travel out to California to visit her aunt and cousins, whom I've never met and she hasn't seen for decades. Perhaps that'll be the only time we meet, perhaps not. I realise now you can tie yourself up in knots trying to make family work. Sometimes you can leave them alone, too.

That's what I'm going to do today. I'm going to leave someone alone.

Everything that began with Lise coming up to me that day in the library, everything that unravelled after that, came because of a strange idea of family. I'm nervous, because I haven't really told Mum exactly what I'm going to do, nor am I one hundred per cent sure I'm right, but I can't not do it. I have to lock Keepsake up and leave it behind, leave it for the butterflies and for nature to finish the job it is doing of reclaiming it, taking it back to the earth.

Alice's short, stumpy legs judder as we cut a slow, well-worn path up from the lodge across the meadow, but she doesn't complain. She insists on walking everywhere, despite the fact I have a backpack-cum-sling. She laughs and points at bees, buzzing above her, at the bright yellow ragwort like little sunflowers, and she cries when she pricks her smooth pink fingers on a thistle. She has never seen one before and doesn't understand it. But she isn't scared. She is quite unlike me, she has no fear. She looks like her daddy. She has his golden curls and his wide eyes, and sometimes watching her breaks my heart.

The afternoon is still, and a hazy golden glow has settled on the fields. In the distance – so far it is almost out of earshot – I can hear someone, down on the river. I wonder if those passing by ever look up to the trees, curious about what lies above them. Would they ever guess that the ruins of a house are here, that it was once one of the greatest houses in the land?

Mum holds Ally's hands, heaving her over a patch of mud. It has rained here recently, last week, giving the land a plumper, lusher feel than before. We are on the chalk-and-gravel path that winds down towards Keepsake, the meadows where my father hunted butterflies and my great-great-grandmother, Alexandra, taught Teddy everything she knew.

Alice says, 'Need water.'

Both of us, Mum and I, instantly fumble like cowboys at a shootout to be the first to hand her our own water bottle, and I reflect, as Mum helps Alice drink from hers, on how lucky this tow-headed determined child of mine is. I think of my father, playing up here alone, ignored by his mother and father, searching for butterflies, terrified of night-time, of being alone. Of Teddy, running away with Matty to Truro station at dead of night, boarding the train that'd take her to London, away from the pull of the house. I think of Mad Nina fleeing on horseback by moonlight, escaping for Persia, only to return a broken woman. Of the butterflies she smuggled back home as larvae in boxes for her children to breed, how my grandmother, and her mother, and her mother before that, did the same, tried to show their love in a similar way. I think about my father, and the letters I've sent him, the photos of his granddaughter that go unacknowledged, how stupid it is that it hurts me, and I think about Teddy. I wonder what she would make of all of this. Of where she went, of how she ended her days, of whether she was happy. Of whether Mum is right – whether it was too late for her to be happy, or not.

I think about this as we walk through the last of the glorious sunshine, our shoulders warm, my little girl's hand tight in mine, her humming and her chattering.

Mum says, 'You don't have to do it, you know.'

'I want to,' I say. 'It's for me to do.'

It's for me to lay this family to rest, so that we can get on with our lives to come. I won't have Alice feel what I felt, that one side of her is missing. She will know the truth about her father. She has the original tiger grandmother, too, of course – Zinnia cannot hate me now, because I gave her the only memorial to Sebastian that could ever help her through the agony of losing him. And I can tell Alice how much I loved her father. It was the wrong time for us – everything was out of kilter, before she was born, and she has righted it, in strange, small, often heartbreaking ways. I know that I loved him, and will never really be able to fill the gap in my heart that was taken up with loving him. I had a lot of time to think when I was pregnant. You do, don't you?

I completed my teacher training course after Alice was six months old; I have a new job in London, at a primary school in Hackney. My second year starts in September. Last year, I was involved with Book Trust, to make sure every child in my classroom had someone reading to them every night. I still go round to the homes of two children, once a week, to read to them before bed, because their parents don't read English. I'm living with Mum and Malc, but these days it's a blessing to share a house with them, for Alice to know them both so well and to have their help. We have the top two floors, she and I. Mrs Poll's old flat is back again, and her old kitchen is our kitchen again, converted with my pension money. I wonder what Mrs Poll would think of it all? I think she'd smile her calm smile and say, 'Aren't you marvellous, darling?'

So we are going back to the house today because of two things that I have not quite dealt with, yet. The last of my tasks, and then I can feel I've done the job I was supposed to do.

Three months after Sebastian's death, when the fog of everything had still not lifted, I received a call from Charles Lambert. I barely remembered who he was: it was hard, some days, to keep track of everything.

'Look, Miss Parr, I had to ring you,' Charles said. 'Forgive me. But you didn't reply to the message, or the email – it's about the butterflies at the house. You remember, we had someone from Butterfly Conservation Cornwall round to look over the place? The chap we sent in originally to do the valuation was something of an amateur expert. He saw the garden – is there some sort of wild garden there?'

I remember so clearly where I was for this conversation. Sitting in the kitchen, my tired feet up on a chair. 'You could say that, yes.'

'Interesting. Do you know of any reason why there would be species of butterfly there not previously known to be on the wing in Great Britain?'

'Um,' I said dully, looking out at the old guys fishing at the canal's edge. 'No, I've no idea, sorry.'

'I'm reading from the report the chap did. "Further sightings are needed as final confirmation that this is the only breeding ground of the Two-Tailed Pasha in Western Europe, and a major advance in entomology and taxonomy. It indicates the extraordinary, one might say entirely unique, conditions of the garden at Keepsake. Years of neglect, the sloping valley which traps the sun, the mineral-rich soil and the lush, wet climate have conspired to create a near-tropical environment which has allowed the rare Two-Tailed Pasha, not seen outside the Mediterranean and Africa, to breed here. It is not known how it arrived. It—" I'm sorry, what did you want to say?'

'I know,' I said. I was sitting up. 'I know how they got there.'

'Ah. Well, it will be an exhaustive process to ascertain the provenance of the butterflies, and I'm sure—'

'No,' I said, laughing. 'I really do know how they got there. My ancestor . . .' Then I tailed off. 'Actually, it's a long story. Go on.'

'This is good news, Miss Parr. They want to apply for a special protection order to forbid public access. They will need to carefully safeguard the site and continue to monitor the butterfly populations there. He says it's not just butterflies. The place is thick with kingfishers, owls, nightjars, you name it. It's quite extraordinary.'

'Yes,' I said. 'It would be.'

'Now, what makes it interesting is how this works for you. I think – and I am speculating wildly here – I think the National Trust might want to buy the land off you.'

'I won't sell it,' I said. 'I'll lease it to them, and they can manage it. I don't want them tidying anything up at Keepsake, you see. She left it like that for a reason. I still don't fully see why she did – but she did.'

'She?'

'My grandmother.'

'Oh – of course.'

'Charles,' I said. 'Do you know anything about her? About where she ended up? What happened to her?'

'I can't divulge that information to you. I wish I could, I'm sorry.' I remember thinking he didn't sound particularly sorry. 'Our first duty is to our client.'

'I'm your client.'

'Yes, but not in this instance. And—' He stopped.

'What?'

'Well, I don't know, either. I mean, it was handled many years ago. All of this business. So even if it wasn't illegal for me to tell you, I'd have to look it up myself, too.'

I'd been wrapped up in being alternately in shock at my pregnancy and in mourning for Sebastian. It had changed when I'd had my first scan, had seen the child I would hopefully give birth to one day. I knew, as of the week before, I was having a girl. I was an adult, with a history and a legacy attached to me, and I was going to be a mother. I could handle these things. I could do it.

'I understand. Look, talking of which, I'll probably need to make a will. Um . . . it'll have to have some quite odd stuff in it. I mean, I'm not planning on dying, but everything to do with the house—' I stopped. 'Do you ever have cases as strange as this?'

'Miss Parr, some of the cases we deal with make you and your grandmother's stories look pretty mild. I can draw up a will for you to look over, absolutely. Right,' he said, and I could hear the clicking of a keyboard, the drumming of the pen he liked, and I could picture him in his grey-box office, the boyish excitement perhaps alive in his face again. 'May I instruct them to send in a team from the National Trust, and may they contact you at the first opportunity? As you can imagine, they're all absolutely straining at the bit on this one. It's caused a hell of a lot of excitement—'

I cut him off, a wave of nausea flooding over me. 'Send them in. Of course. Tell me what they need.' I sank back into my chair: in truth, on that day, it all seemed so silly, fluttering insects and grown men clambering over rocks, when Sebastian was fresh in the ground and his child wouldn't have a father. I didn't see it then.

And then there was Lise. When Alice was six months old and I had begun to try to be a separate person from her – I'd gone to the shops twice on my own to buy some milk, and had a coffee with Elizabeth – I received a strange request. Mum had offered to give Alice a bath one evening and when I returned to Noel Road, having been for a rare stroll by myself, I found Malc standing in the kitchen, rather perplexed.

'What's up?' I said, trying to mask the terror one feels at leaving one's baby and returning to that sort of expression on someone's face. 'All OK, Malc?'

'Absolutely. Listen, Nins. Someone called Abby called your mobile,' he said, scratching his head. 'I answered it. She . . . she said you should come over. Right now. I said – I said it was rubbish, you couldn't just drop everything and run. But she said you'd understand, that I was to tell you and she needs to see you.'

He handed me my phone. Abby had texted me.

Hi Nina. Sorry to bother you. Lise is on her way out. She doesn't have much longer. If you get this and are able could you come tonight? Thx. A

I was already halfway back up the stairs, running towards the bathroom, where Mum was cooing brightly at Alice, who was lying in the shallow bath, bashing her legs furiously in the air and screaming with delight.

'Look at the rolls of chub on this little one,' Mum was saying, almost drunk with joy. 'Look at the smoochy face! Look at you!'

'Mum,' I said. 'I have to go. It's Lise. Alice Grayling. She's dying – h-her nurse wants me to go and see her. Can you put Ally to bed?'

'Oh.' Mum stood up. 'Oh. Of course—'

'Give her a bottle – there's one in the freezer. And make sure the room temperature is OK – it was boiling up there last night. And Mum, the zip on her Gro-bag is very—'

'God, I'll be fine,' said Mum, rolling her eyes. 'I had a baby, you know – you survived, didn't you?'

'Well—' I began.

'Don't be rude. And if you're about to bring Mrs Poll into this, I'll say no.'

413

I kissed her, and ran back downstairs, leaving Alice oblivious, blowing bubbles and looking with surprise at her hand, which she was pressing on to her face.

Chapter Twenty-Eight

In Lise's bedroom, an hour later, the curtains were still open. Late-summer-evening light from the Heath flooded in through the windows. Trees shook outside in the evening breeze. It was calm, serene, certain: unlike any deathbed scene I'd imagined. The room was beautiful, with floor-to-ceiling bookshelves, paintings, awards, photographs on every available inch of wall or shelf.

Her bed faced out over the Heath. *The Shrimp Girl* hung above the mantelpiece: she was faded, but still smiling. On the mantelpiece itself was a picture of Al and Teddy, arms linked. I had never seen them together, and I stared at it. Outwardly similar – short black hair, slim, young – but yet entirely different, from the eyes to the expression: Teddy's shy and adoring, Al's cheeky and provocative. And the clothes: Al elegant and modish, boyish in her slacks, Teddy demure and slightly more staid in a gathered, dark-and-white patterned shirt dress. They were beaming ahead, but you knew their smiles were for each other. They were such lovely girls.

'Why isn't she . . . should she be in hospital?' I whispered, at the first sight of Lise, breathing stentoriously, tiny in her too-large brushed-cotton nightdress, barely aware of us both as we huddled at the back of the large, light bedroom.

'I'm a nurse,' Abby said briskly. 'We have two other nurses on call in rotation. She planned it all very carefully, you know. She's very organised.'

'Yes, she was. Is,' I corrected myself.

'She's not responding now, not in the last couple of hours. But she talked about you often, when she was lucid. I was never quite sure whether she understood or not that she'd met you, and then other times she was so glad she had. That she'd made you understand about her and your grandmother. You see, you were her link to Teddy, but she couldn't quite grasp it. Even the first time she met you, she was so pleased, but she couldn't remember why almost immediately afterwards. If only you'd met each other a year before. Never mind.' And she went towards her, tenderly, pulled the duvet over her charge, smoothed back her hair.

The sky was flecked with apricot and rose and I was aware of time, that I could not – should not – stay too long or be in the way.

'Why did you ask me to come now?' I said.

'Well—' Abby bit her lip. 'I had to look in her purse today. I haven't been through it for so long – she hasn't used any of her bank or credit cards for years now. But there was one missing credit card that I've been trying to cancel before she— Before. So I checked again in her purse and found this.'

She slid her hand into her pocket and retrieved a thin, cream square of paper, a note, folded and refolded. Abby pressed the square into my hand. 'She burned the rest of it, you see. She told me.'

'Burned what?'

'The book, your grandmother's book – it was your grandmother, wasn't it?'

I nodded.

'She kept it for years, and when the dementia diagnosis came she put it on the fire, the whole manuscript. We did it together, actually. In the fireplace in the sitting room. She said she never wanted to come across it when she got worse and not to know what it was. To have other people read it, for it to be a curiosity. She said it was better locked away in her memory, to be slowly forgotten. But she must have kept this.'

I unfolded the letter and then stopped. 'May I read it?'

'Read it when you get home,' said Abby. 'Not here . . .' She paused. 'I think seeing you made things worse, you know. It hastened the decline.'

I pressed my fingers to my lips. 'Oh.'

'No, it's good.' Abby pushed her hand over her forehead. 'She wanted to go. She wanted it to be quick, as quick as possible, and it's taken so long.' Her eyes filled with tears: cool, practical Abby. 'It's a cruel, cruel disease, Nina. I think seeing you finally broke her

416

mind down, the last stage. You know, she'd been through so much. Being gay back then and trying to hide it when she wasn't ever the kind of person to hide anything. Losing Teddy. Losing her brother, her father . . . finding those people who hanged themselves in the flat. I mean, that wasn't nice, was it?'

I shook my head, wanting to laugh, wanting to cry. 'None of it was nice.'

'But I think it was all there, and you brought it back for a few weeks. You looked so like Teddy when she was young, and when she could grasp it all it was wonderful. But I think her mind was too far gone by then.' Abby sniffed. 'Anyway . . . I . . . I felt guilty. I thought it was doing her harm.'

'You were doing it for the right reasons, I'm sure,' I said.

'Yes, but it's not for me to play God. God's cruel.'

'"*God's cruel; He let us get flawed in the making,*"' I whispered.

'What's that?'

'*The Well of Loneliness,*' I said. 'We did it at university. I always remembered that line.' But Abby looked blank, so I hurried on. 'My grandmother believed she was flawed. She didn't ever even dream of a world where you could love who you wanted, live with whoever you wanted to. But Al, she knew it was right to love Teddy. She understood that's what we're here for.'

'We're all flawed, aren't we anyway? I don't think that quote's right,' said Abby.

'Exactly,' I said. We were both silent.

'Look, I don't think she'll know you're here, but you might want to go and say goodbye to her. Just in case.'

I walked slowly over to the bed, and stood beside it. There was an eiderdown covering the duvet; powder-blue silk, old and rather fine. I stroked it, and looked down at her. Her eyes were open, tiny hands clutching at the silk, fingers methodically opening and shutting, again and again. I thought of my own Alice, gurgling in her bath, blinking at her fingers, confused but determined. I stared for the last time into those black, beautiful eyes.

'I understand now,' I told her. 'Everything. I'm sorry I didn't before. I'll make sure you're with her, you know. That you're together.'

Gently, I bent down and kissed her soft forehead, and I too stroked her hair. The jet butterfly brooch was at the side of the bed, dull in the evening light. For a second, I thought she reacted, or smiled at me, a very, very small movement of the mouth, but I don't believe it. Real life doesn't happen like that, it's not really that neat.

When I left, I walked across the Heath, one last time. I allowed myself to think about when we scattered Sebastian's ashes up on Parliament Hill, Charlotte flying rainbow-striped streamers into the wind as we did it, Judy nodding, arms folded, Zinnia stiff as a poker. I thought of him and I, lying on the grass, murmuring silly things into each other's ears. And her, I thought of Lise, all those years on her own in that light, book-lined room overlooking the Heath, with only her memories. And then not even those.

I sat down to read the letter. At first I did not understand it, and then I realised it was the note my grandmother had written when she sent Lise *The Butterfly Summer*. It had been kept close by, read and reread, refolded so many times in places it was falling apart. It hung, delicately, across my fingers, like a web.

Al:

I imagine you opened this parcel with some trepidation. Who has sent this poorly typed manuscript to me, and what does she want?

What follows is an account of my life. I wrote it for you, my darling, and for my son, George. It is to explain (or attempt to explain). I enclose a photograph of my son. He's like me, isn't he? I wanted you to see him. I wanted him to have been seen by you. Read this, and think of him, and please, if you hate me, try not to. You see—

I am dying, and will not see you again. I have missed you in that time: I laugh at people who say, 'I thought of you every day.' Once a day! Every day without you has felt like an age to me. I thought of you every hour, and most minutes within that hour. The weight of being without you is something physical. A net filled with rocks that I drag behind me everywhere I go. Being without you is slow and steady torture.

And yet, I am not sad. When death comes, I will remember the good you did, and the good I did because of you.

Darling Al. What's loved is never really lost. I think we will not meet again now, but I will always love you. I will always be grateful to you. You infected me, that summer. You planted a seed within me, the idea of goodness. It took me a lifetime, but I die knowing I made it right, in the end, that I did some good.

I loved you, I still love you, and after I am gone I will love you.

Yours always

Teddy

Chapter Twenty-Nine

As we descend towards Keepsake on that final journey my heart is beating rapidly. I have walked across the meadow and into the garden many times since, but no one strays beyond the walls into the house. They don't seem to want to.

I am writing the story of our family, and this is it. One day maybe I'll publish it. But I'll probably leave it in the remains of the Butterfly House, to moulder away into nothing. When Alice grows up I'll tell her she is descended from a king, that if we lived in a different world she and I would be queens of this country. There's so much I can tell her when she's older. She will know where she's from.

Mum and Alice stay outside in the meadow as I unlock the gate and step into the grounds. The volunteers are not here today, they come once a week. The butterflies are everywhere, as are the flowers: purple buddleia, sweet pink-red roses and rambling honeysuckle. I know enough by now to recognise the bright blue Chalkhills and Common Blues, and I see Cabbage Whites and Tortoiseshells and Brimstones – whites, orange-black-purple, and sherbet-lemon yellow – as I walk past the lichen-sprinkled Butterfly House. The shadows are lengthening, just a little. Some butterflies like the early morning, some thrive in the evening. I am gradually learning again which ones. I want to know – they have wormed their way into my heart. That's my inheritance, too.

There is a rustle of something as I swing open the side door. A mouse, or a fox, or a daytime creature disturbed – or maybe someone from another time who lived in this place. But I feel someone watching me, and that old feeling again, the certainty that this house is alive in other worlds just out of reach. That were I to visit at the right moment and walk through the right door, I'd be able to step back in time and be there, hear the clink of the boat below bringing goods and visitors, the coo of the doves in the dovecote, the swish of my lady's skirts as she, whichever lady she was, walks the passages here. I know, know it now, that they are all alive somewhere, in their own time. And maybe they are all mad, and maybe it infects me, but in that moment I understand why they would so willingly walk into the chamber, and die.

My hand trembles as I lift the key to the rusting lock of the chamber under the stairs. But it will not open, despite my pulling and tugging. Perhaps the rain has swollen it permanently shut; in any case, I realise I cannot leave her there. My dream of laying Teddy and Alice to rest in that chamber with her ancestors, it's not to be.

Then I see it wouldn't be the right thing anyway. She and Lise should be outside, not here, not in this place of death. They should be free.

I go outside, into the butterfly garden, where the high walls surround me, and I feel safe, enclosed. From my bag I remove Teddy and Lise's ashes, mixed together.

I walk around the garden, scattering them on to the flowers, disturbing butterflies as I go. Pollen and ash and bright fluttering creatures rise up into the amber air as Theodora Parr and Alice Grayling are laid to rest in the butterfly garden, the two of them together at last. Then I leave the garden. I shut the outer door and go back into the house via the side entrance. Again, the rustling, the feeling of being watched. I touch the ancient wood of the staircase, look around and above me, through the smashed-in roof up at the sky.

'You can come out,' I call, loudly. 'All of you. I'm leaving now and we won't disturb you. You can live here again.'

I walk out, through the front entrance hall, across the grassy court-yard, under the crumbling arch, and as my shoes crunch on the stones I am sure I hear them all, running, flying back into the house. Up, up – back to the wide-open fresh air, where Mum and Alice stand, waiting for me. We will sail over to the beach and get an ice cream and throw pebbles into the river, then go back to the little cottage for Alice's tea.

We will not step inside that house again. We will leave them there. We walk away together, towards the sun.

Epilogue

123 Noel Road (Top Floor)
London
April, 1996

Dear Mr Routledge,

I must set this down; I must write it to someone, and you are the only person who knows the entire truth.

I always told myself I had to know when it was time to go. She's ten now. Ten years old, and a little dark-haired beanpole. She loves her stories, the ones I read her, the ones she makes up. Oh, she's my lovely girl.

Yesterday, I made her a special tea, her favourite. Lemonade, bangers, potato waffles, fried egg. She's always hungry: she's grown two inches in ten months, we've the markings on the wall to prove it.

We were celebrating because she got full marks on a geography test, which I know she hates. But she tries hard, isn't that marvellous? She's like her mother in that regard. She didn't get it from my side of the family.

I always told myself I had to know when it was time to go.

And it came yesterday, a little moment, but I saw it, and I understood right away. So my late career as Mary Poppins is coming to an end. I have to fly away, soon. Out of the window, up towards the clear blue sky. Then – where?

It's the little things that have filled my heart with joy, these ten or so years. Just sitting at the table, where we've sat day after day, when her feet were too small to touch the ground, till today, this point now, where I see a glimpse of the woman she will become. Those afternoons, her skittering tread on the stairs, my heart beating at the thought of her arrival, happiness filling up the flat. There's happiness all the time now, you see. I wake up in the mornings and I smile. Haven't done that since the Butterfly Summer.

'Malc's moved some stuff in,' she said, and when I turned to look at her she was eating the doughnut I'd bought at Raab's

425

that she'd managed to snaffle out of its paper bag without me noticing.

'Oh, Nina. How exciting.'

'He brought lots of cool books and some clothes and loads of tapes. Mrs Poll, he's got a compact disc player. It's fab. *And* he's got a coffee machine. It makes frothy milk. It whistles. He let me help him yesterday – it sends steam into the milk. It's amazing. Isn't that amazing, Mrs Poll?'

She went back to the doughnut, as if this was enough information. But I saw the shy, darting look she gave me, which she did whenever she wasn't sure of my reaction.

I didn't respond again immediately. I savoured the last few moments of normality. Moving round my little brown-and-orange kitchen, plopping my teacup into the bowl of water in the sink, squirting washing-up liquid in: isn't foam *satisfying?* We had nothing like that at Keepsake, not for years. I had a quick glance out of the window. The red barge, chugging towards the tunnel. Beautiful thing, Brunel's tunnel. Grandmother Alexandra met him once. A dinner at Lord Curzon's house. Who knows who Brunel is, or cares about poor old Curzon, these days? Or Alexandra Parr, that extraordinary woman – who knows apart from me about her, her books, her notes? In fifty years' time, she will have been forgotten, utterly left behind by history.

I am struck by the thought that when I go, there will be no record at all. Of Al and me, and what we had – how much I loved her, how sweet she was to me. She has no idea what she did. How she saved me. She has no idea whether I lived or died. I wonder where she is now? I saw her once, two years ago. She looked the same, even though she's a year or so older than me. Same hair– though it was bobbed, not cropped – same darting eyes, thin, restless movements, same lovely smile. She was walking towards us, and I thought she stared at me.

But I was with Nina – I couldn't go over, not without risking everything. I couldn't.

So I watched her, for a few seconds, and I thought again of

426

how love radiates out, how it can change everything. How to see her there, still so pretty, so happy, so much herself, was enough.

I feel panic, suddenly, as I watch Nina, munching happily on her food.

Am I right, to have done it this way?

Am I right, to have deprived Nina of the house, of her history? To have left her with nothing more than *Nina and the Butterflies*, which I brought here myself and pretended must have been her father's, abandoned in a bookshelf by him? My one piece of deception – no, that's simply not true. I have lied to them non-stop – my stories of my Russian husband (Misha's maiden name), my East End childhood (Al's), my training as a nurse (invented on the spot). I know Dill wonders where that book came from. I know she doesn't remember seeing it before I arrived. That's the one great risk I took. I wanted Nina to know the story, even though I don't want her to have to live the life. Oh – have I done the right thing?

The other risk is the London Library membership I've bought her, which she'll have when she's sixteen. It will appear to be a present from her father and so she will love the memory of him that her mother has diligently instilled in his child even more, though her mother (and I, unbeknownst to both of them) know it to be false.

It is all false.

Now I begin to doubt myself; my mind starts racing as I think. I must write everything down. I must go home, one more time, to collect the cyanide sticks, so I can die when and where I choose to. Then I'll go to the coast, to Lyme. I've always wanted to go to Lyme.

And my little Nina, she is still chattering about Malc as these thoughts flit like flimsy clouds across the sunny blue sky she has given me. 'Mrs Poll, we had a meeting about it. Mum and me. About him moving in. We voted. I mean, maybe you should have voted, too, but—'

I laughed. 'Poppet, it's none of my business. But how lovely, darling.'

Her face cleared. 'Oh, do you think so? I was worried you'd . . .' She trailed off. 'Doesn't matter.'

'Of course I do!' And I leaned forward, hugged her skinny little frame to me, felt the point of her shoulder in my chest, smelled that sweet, almond scent of her head, her hair.

My darling girl, my granddaughter, my Nina.

She was seven months old when I came here. Have you seen a seven-month-old baby lately, do you know how irresistible they are? How chubby, how smiley? They can sit up, though they still fall over regularly. They love their toes, their cheeks are flushed after they've slept, they have little soft curls at the base of their head, they look at you and they laugh for no reason. Nina did, at least. She was a perfect baby, a beautiful, perfect girl. I, who for decades thought my life was only blackness, can end it now, knowing I have been more fortunate than I could ever have deserved. So I must *never* doubt what I did. I must stay my course.

The first time I knocked on Dill's door, and she opened it, tear stains marking her tired, grey face, I said, 'Hello again. I was only coming to see if this letter was for you.'

She was holding her blue-eyed, dark-haired baby girl covered in mushed-up carrot, firm fingers clutching a spoon, tongue firmly outstretched, gurgling with joy, and I knew I had been right. That my third and final act would be worth it. That I could live here for a while, and that I could help until I was no longer needed, then fly away, away. I knew I'd have to leave, at some point. I knew it would be agony to leave them, but that was the deal I made with myself.

I am ill, you see. Funny tastes in my mouth, spasms and back pain all the time, losing weight, and rather yellow. Two weeks ago, they told me. I have seven months, eight at best. 'Maybe you'll see Christmas, but I don't like hanging on to hope with dates. Let's just see.'

She's a nice, if brisk woman, the doctor. My kind of girl. Sensible hair, tweed skirt, just gets on with things. She did it well. It's hard, telling someone they have cancer of the pancreas, no less. I know what that means.

So now is the right time for me to go: as I say, I always told myself I'd know.

Now, wiping my hands on the tea towel, I stood up and turned around. I squeezed her shoulders again, dropped a brisk kiss on her head.

She looked up at me, and smiled. Uncurling a leg she said, 'Malc makes Mum so happy. She sings around the house now. She sings these awful songs.'

'Bob Dylan. I know.'

'Mrs Poll? Can I still come up? Visit you? And . . . Matty?'

'Of course you can. Matty's always here when you need her.'

'You won't tell Mum . . . or Malc . . . you won't tell them about Matty? Or us reading the book, or any of it?'

'Of course I won't. It's our secret, birdie.'

'I don't really need her any more,' she said, her face clearing.

'I know you don't. But if you do, she's here.'

'Nothing's going to change,' Nina said, her little face over-hung with a frown. 'Promise.'

'It will change,' I said. 'Things have to change, my love. Now, you can get down and put your plate in the sink.'

She got up, came over to me and wrapped her arms around me in a great big hug and said something I couldn't hear, something muffled. And as I stroked her treacly soft, black hair I had to bite my lip to stop myself letting out a little sob. Yes, for the first time in many years now, my façade slipped a little. I couldn't think what Mrs Poll would quite say, not at that moment. She'd been a nice person to be, these last precious years. I'd borrowed facts from Al, or Misha, to be her, and it made me feel closer to them, having Misha's maiden name, talking about Al's family, extending their stories. I liked Mrs Poll. But in these last moments, I struggled with the role, even as I knew it was over.

No. I'd made reparation. I'd changed our family's story. I

429

am old, and I am dying, and it's time for me to go. You may ask how I came to be there at all.

It happened like this.

The letter from my son was quite out of the blue. It told me I had a granddaughter – Nina – that he had left her and the mother, that he was moving to the United States of America. To take up a position somewhere in the middle of the country – I forget where – it is a large place.

I knew George had married. He had written to tell me. Beyond that, we had no communication. He didn't care to come to Keepsake, you see. He couldn't bear the place – apart from the butterflies. Yet he never managed to spot the real treasure out there in the garden, Mad Nina's Two-Tailed Pashas, which have bred there for nearly two hundred years now, and nowhere else in England. Our secret. He always wanted money. Always wanted an easier life than the one he had. He's lazy, my son. Can't blame him for many things, but for that I can. He's lazy.

His letter arrived at a time when, having been gradually feeling better for a while, I was stuck in what one would call reverse forward – my progress slow, my mind shutting down, blank again. Some days, I didn't leave my room.

I had my routine. Radio, tea to start the day. Walk the dog in the morning, a light piece of lunch – sandwich or something – walk again, tea, spot of gardening, solitary dinner, lights out by nine. Tugie had died two years before, and I won't pretend I didn't miss him. I do. It just helps, having a dog to keep one company. Gets one out of the house. I became afraid, more shut in. Memories of Michael and Misha tormented me: I saw them, in silhouette, bent over the desk looking at the Personals, all the time. I'd wonder how they'd looked when Al found them, how they had hanged themselves, who had helped whom . . . what it was like for her . . . sometimes, it was all I could think about. *I couldn't block it out of my mind.* I saw Ginny, strawberry-gold hair in the soft lamplight of the bookshop, pouring the consequences of my actions into my ears.

I saw the ivy, creeping up the walls, the bodies of my ancestors below the house and I wondered if one day perhaps I would, in fact, cut back the ivy, lock myself in, snap the cyanide stick in half and eat it. Sit there with the bones in the dark, waiting for death to take me. An agonising death, but briefer than starvation. Some days it seemed the only sensible course to take.

But you see, he left her. He left that poor woman and her child. He ran away; couldn't cope. I knew why. I knew it was because having Nina had brought up for him what it had done for me: one's role in life, one's relationship with one's parents. I had hurt him, sent him out into the world a broken toy and now, because of me, he was doing the same, would do this to this child of his, and the mother. As I read his letter, full of self-justification, of pride at his achievements, with a request for money tacked on abruptly at the end, I knew I was to blame.

The day the letter arrived I threw it away. Walked down to the creek, crumpled the paper up and chucked it out towards the water. But it got caught on one of the bare, twisting trees and it was just there, stuck like a white ball on a branch, and I couldn't leave it there, for anyone to find:

> . . . I think she's quite mad, by the way. The upstairs flat is vacant and she swears the tenants haven't really left, that it's all a trick. She's been posting notes under the door. She's lost it since Nina came along. Yes, we called her Nina. God knows why. Some hangover of a previous life. I regret it rather now, but I can't explain to her why.

I scrambled down the bank on to the green, mossy, slimy mud – I wasn't crook then, like I am now, and I had my stick, with a new ferrule I'd bought in Falmouth, and it had a damn good grip.

The upstairs flat is vacant. I poked at the branch and the letter bounced down on to my head, and like an apple, like I was Newton, I saw it all clearly then.

We can redeem ourselves, if we really want to. We can change things. But we have to genuinely want to help others. We do it all the time, here in the countryside, don't we? The hours I spent helping the butterflies, pruning the ivy, weeding the honeysuckle, planting the vetch and the buddleia. The times I've moved a nest of starlings' eggs out of the reach of a cat into a higher hedgerow, moved a tired bumblebee from the lane and given it sugar water, the hours spent with Tugie as he was old and frail and incontinent – I did it for no reward from them.

It's easy to help animals, harder to help people. People are messy and complicated, and they don't thank you back. But I saw then that I could help, that I could be the mother I should have been, that I could pick up this bird's nest, place it out of harm's way – but I knew I could only do it if they didn't know.

The other realisation I had down on the bank was: I could leave Keepsake. I could leave it to crumble and be reclaimed by the land. I knew the terms of the covenant. I knew if she didn't go there before her twenty-sixth birthday, Nina would have no obligation to the house. The house was rotten. I knew it. I had given it my life, I had lost Al to it, I had lost my ability to love, to care, to see things as they should have been seen. I didn't want this granddaughter of mine to grow up like that. I wanted her to know only that she was loved.

And finally, I'd been mouldering here for most of my seventy-seven years. I wanted to go back to London. I wanted an adventure.

Dear Mr Routledge, thank you for reading this far. Thank you again for everything. I'm sure you must have thought I had entirely lost my mind, inveigling you into helping with the purchase of the top-floor flat, but you never questioned me, or said it was impractical. Thank you for helping me to become her.

I moved in in May, and by the end of that first, magical

summer I think Mrs Poll had saved Delilah, several times over. Not because of any special gifts I had, but because I know, when I had my own child, that blackness that came over me took a long time to lift, and I had a nanny, and money, and it was still gruesome. I found her when she took the second overdose. I stayed with her at the hospital, holding Delilah's thin, bony hand in mine, watching her try to smile as I jiggled her daughter for her. I made her soup, I got her to leave the house, put the odd pound coin in her purse when she wasn't looking – just now and then. I pushed her to write, I bothered her parents by letter and telephone into taking an interest in her. I looked after Nina, made sure she had enough to eat. I took her out for walks in the day, spreading the moth-eaten blanket I'd brought up from Keepsake on the grass of the little park behind St Mary's Church, seeing her delight at being able to sit up, the dark curls clustered around her perfectly round head. Just watching her, smiling at her gleaming, gummy grin, made me happier than I could remember since the war.

The hardest part was not letting Delilah know how much I was doing. I think I got that right. Only once did she say, when I bought her a bag of clothes from the charity shop, 'This is too much, I think Nina and I need some time alone.'

Oh, I retreated, I scuttled away. I didn't bother them for a fortnight. I saw my nice friends at the church hall (I told them I was a non-observant Jew) and my new pal, Rose, down the road whom I'd have tea with now and again, and I busied myself, walking about town, visiting the old haunts I'd loved with Al, taking in a film, or an exhibition or two. And a week later, as I was sitting there, reading and wondering what I'd do next, I heard her tread on the stairs and a tentative knock. And when I opened the door, Nina screamed with delight when she saw me and, throwing herself out of her mother's arms, launched herself into mine, snuggling her firm little body against me.

The happiest moment of my life, that was.

Delilah said she'd come to apologise, but I wouldn't hear of it.

'Oh, I should stop getting so worried about everything,' she said, laughing rather helplessly and pushing her wild hair out of her face in that sweet, worried way she had. 'It's only that you do so much for us and it makes me feel totally crappy, sometimes, Mrs P dear.'

So I told her the truth. I said, 'I've been very lonely.' I held her gaze. *I understand*, that's what I was trying to tell her. 'I've been very sad, at times. I've got no one except you two. You're doing *me* a favour, do you see? It helps me as much as it helps you, you know, darling.'

From that moment we were fine. We are all fragile from time to time.

Ridiculous to be crying at this stage in the game. Buck up, Thea! They don't need me any more. They've got nice Mr Malcolm, and he will take care of them, but more than that, they can take care of themselves. Both of them.

And she's getting older now. She's almost eleven, my dark-eyed granddaughter. She doesn't need me to smooth back her hair while I read her *Nina and the Butterflies* or *Ballet Shoes* or – of course – *The Secret Garden*. If only I had one more night with her, one more evening of playing Scrabble and making cheese on toast . . .

No.

She wants to be with her mother, and her friends, not the old lady upstairs. She doesn't need me to sit by her bed watching her fall asleep while her mother works, or feed her chicken soup when she's sad after school, or take her, with waddling gait and plump little hands pointing joyously at everything, to the canal to look at the boats, the ducks, the flowers, the water. She needs me less and less . . . and one day, she won't need me at all.

So I can go. I'm in pain most of the time. It aches, like a wretched screw turning within me, burrowing inside me, deeper every day. I'll go to Keepsake, see the old place one more time, pick up the cyanide sticks. Then I'll take myself to Lyme and I will write. I will write my story down, for Al, for George, for myself.

Dear Mr Routledge, keep this document separate. Burn it, if you must. Please remind yourself of my instructions. That the funeral be private. That the terms of the will bequeathing the property and £50,000 to Delilah Parr and Nina Parr are adhered to; they will not worry about money again. That my granddaughter never knows where she came from.

Perhaps I should tell her. Perhaps she should know I am her grandmother, that I have loved her all these years. But I see now that to reveal it would ruin everything. I have gone too far, and I have missed my chance. What would it serve to tell her when she is older? At some point we must leave our childhoods behind. We must strike forward, with optimism. Was it right? I think it was.

T.P.

Goodbye, sweet Nina. Perhaps I wish for you that you go there one day, just once. A holidaymaker, wandering down a shaded path. You won't know that it might have been yours. If you ever go, my darling girl, you'll hear me then, in the wind. You might glance around and not see anything, and wonder why you feel someone, nearby. Gaze into the river, out to sea, and you might see me. Not me now, old and eaten away by life, but Teddy Parr, the little girl I was before it all changed. Look out for me, dark fringe, happy eyes, crouched in the boat looking out for my mother and grandmother, looking out for you. I'll always be there, you see. Sailing towards the rising sun on a golden early summer's morning, the breeze in my hair, my hand, the hand that stroked your hair all those years, on the tiller, free at last.

Thanks to:

Jo Roberts-Miller, as is traditional, and for risking arrest and crawling through undergrowth with me to find Keepsake. Katie Cousins and Leila D'Souza for being excellent museum-visiting companions. To my mum for reading an earlier draft and not disowning me. To Nick Canty at UCL for showing me around.

Everyone at Curtis Brown, especially Jonathan Lloyd, Lucia Rae and Melissa Pimentel. Kim Witherspoon and David Forrer at Inkwell, and Karen Kosztolnyik, Becky Prager, Louise Burke, Jen Bergstrom and Jean Anne Rose at Gallery.

During the research period of this book I became obsessed with butterflies and it has been a wonderful thing. So thanks to Chris and Cora for bearing with me while I leap unexpectedly back down a country lane when I see a Speckled Wood or comb through nettles looking for Peacock eggs, muttering like a crazy person. If anyone wants a great beginner's book might I recommend Jeremy Thomas's masterly *Philip's Guide to Butterflies*.

Finally to everyone at Headline Books for what has been such a happy two years. Frankie Edwards, for absolutely everything, Elizabeth Masters, Viviane Basset and Barbara Ronan, Yeti Lambregts, Frances Doyle, Jane and George and everyone else. Finally my biggest thanks goes to amazing, incisive, kind and brilliant Mari and for the only time in my life I find I can't really write down how much I owe her, because it can't be put into words. Big love and eternal thanks, namesake.